Presented to Purchase College
by
Gary Waller, PhD Cambridge

State University of New York
Distinguished Professor

Professor
of Literature & Cultural
Studies, and Theatre &
Performance, 1995-2019
Provost 1995-2004

# A  RENAISSANCE
# STORYBOOK

# A RENAISSANCE STORYBOOK

❦ *Selected and Edited by Morris Bishop*

*Drawings by Alison Mason Kingsbury*

*Cornell University Press* / ITHACA & LONDON

*First published 1971*

International Standard Book Number 0–8014–0592–0
Library of Congress Catalog Card Number 79–129332
Printed in the United States of America by Kingsport Press, Inc.

# ❦ Preface

HERE IS a collection of stories from the Renaissance, a time when storytellers were honored and encouraged, when knowledgeable listeners abounded.

And what do we take the Renaissance to be? Most conveniently to our purpose, it is a historical period in western Europe's past. It attained self-consciousness in Italy in the mid-fifteenth century; it migrated to France and Spain and then to Germany and England, where it flowered in the great dramatic and poetic literature of the Elizabethan age. By the middle of the seventeenth century the Renaissance spirit was transformed into something else, which need not concern us here.

The Renaissance spirit is also a state of mind—progressive, impatient of the past, adventurous, experimental. It is marked by a new respect for man and his capacities, by an unashamed delight in life, by a cult of beauty, and by distrust of imposed orthodoxies, whether social or religious. One recognizes in its literature a reaching for new values. (Compare, for instance, the cynicism of Little Jehan de Saintré with the simple ardor of medieval romances; or Cervantes' brutal *Marriage à la Mode* with the love-idylls of previous times.)

Some of the examples here presented are famous; such are the histories of Romeo and Juliet, the Moor of Venice, and Dr. Faustus. Others will, it is hoped, be new even to those who know the Renaissance well.

The editor has made his choices chiefly because they seemed to him good stories, not because they illustrate Renaissance life and doctrine—although inevitably they do, often in subtle ways. Himself hostile to boredom, he has imposed no consecrated bores on his readers. Read then for pleasure, and if you gain instruction by the way, let it be not only in Renaissance life and thought, but in the delightful diversities of human behavior.

Unless it is otherwise specified in the headnotes, all the translations are by the editor.

It is customary in such forewords as this to render thanks to the editor's friends and helpers. They are hereby thanked; but chiefly he would thank the purchasers of the book.

MORRIS BISHOP

*Ithaca, New York*
*November 1970*

# ❧ Contents

# I

## ITALY

*Sister Savina*

# ❧ Sister Savina and Brother Girolamo

## by GENTILE SERMINI

Of Gentile Sermini we know almost nothing, beyond that he lived in Siena in the first half of the fifteenth century. He tells us that he fled the city during an epidemic in 1424, took refuge in the country, and beguiled his boredom by writing a number of merry tales, *Novelle* (first printed in 1474, in Livorno). They follow the formula set by Boccaccio, nearly a century earlier. They are more medieval than Renaissance in substance and mood, except perhaps in their freedom from moral restraint and their cynicism toward the church's ideals and practice. This story is Novella 2.

IN THE magnificent city of Florence lived a citizen named Lapo Macinghi. He had a daughter aged about ten. As the time drew near when he must think of marrying her, he was stirred by avarice to plan putting her in a nunnery. As the girl would have none of it, he made up a party of ladies, under pretext of attending a festival, and took her to a convent, the name of which I suppress out of regard for the reputation of the other nuns. Arriving there, she was admitted, and according to his orders she was forcibly detained by the nuns. Subjected to the rule, she regarded herself as gulled by her father, reproached him violently, and remained rebellious. The soothing words of the nuns were of no avail, nor did they keep her from cursing her father many times a day, as well as any accomplice of his. Her mother, broken-hearted, dwelt in great affliction of spirit; and, being pregnant, she was so grief-stricken that she died in childbirth. Lapo remained very well off, having enriched himself mostly by usury; and as he cared much more for property than for honor he consoled himself readily.

The girl, Savina, was now fifteen. She learned one day that her father was very sick; but this did not distress her much. Lapo's state worsened, and he died. Sister Savina became legally his heir, since he had no other children. She received the sum of four thousand florins, which were much dearer to her than the life of her cruel father. She was sensible enough to put them to good use in the service of her own comfort.

Thus she attained the age of nineteen. And one day Master Nicolao, prior of the Preaching Friars, came to visit the convent. He brought along Brother Girolamo of Fiesole, a very handsome youth of about twenty-five, who had all the look of a sanctified monk. He had made a special study of confession, and directed a great swarm of ladies in Florence; happy was she who could come to him to confess! So great was his reputation in this field that Sister Savina, seeing him in church, asked him to confess her. He consented out of holy humility; they betook themselves to a confessional with an iron grating, through which each could plainly see the other. And after Sister Savina had confessed to him various faults, she said: "Brother Girolamo, since I hear you are a man of saintly life, I will confide in you totally. The fact is that my cruel father put me in here out of avarice and against my will; and fate has decreed that in spite of him I have become his heir. So I find myself, thanks be to God, well supplied with this world's goods. But I am not happy; I don't want to stay here. So for God's sake give me your counsel."

"Why?" said he.

"Because I am not gaining any merit at all; rather I am sinning more and more every day. To tell you the truth, I haven't the temperament to be here. I am so lusty and hot that I can't live here. In summer it seems to me that the heat burns me up; and now that it's winter, the cold doesn't seem to cure me at all, and if I should stand all day in the snow I wouldn't be cured. So that for God's sake I beg you to give me some good counsel to save my soul and to give me some remedy for my present life."

Frate Girolamo, seeing how she was made, that she burned like the sun itself, and considering her malady and her words, was moved to pity by her waste of time. He replied: "Sister, I feel great compassion for you. But fear not; be of good cheer. I will provide a remedy for your affliction, if you do what I tell you. I see that you are naturally of a warm constitution; I will give you an appropriate medicine, which will mitigate your ailment."

She thanked him and begged him to provide the remedy quickly. And he, no less impatient of delay than she, replied: "If you want to get well, you must take the medicine repeatedly, as I shall prescribe. If you feel that you have the strength to accept it I will restore your health very quickly. The medicine has been thoroughly tested."

Then said Sister Savina, in her eagerness to get well: "Father, I will do whatever you advise me, if only I may be cured of this disease."

Said he: "Fear not; of all those who have tried it, not one has failed of a cure."

Having thus won over the physician, she replied bravely: "Any delay is injurious to me. I have so much confidence in you that I have decided to put myself entirely in your hands."

Said he: "If you have the courage to permit me to enter the convent secretly some night, and if I could be with you in private, to preserve both your honor and mine, I will offer to visit you. And I promise that before daybreak your infirmity will have been so mitigated that you won't be able to wait to repeat the treatment, in order to obtain a complete cure. For the remedy is not nasty or unpleasant to take; rather it is very agreeable. Therefore the patient who wishes to cure that serious malady must on the first night take the medicine every two hours all night until dawn; and therefore the physician must necessarily be continually at her side. And though it may seem improper that a cleric like me should visit you, or even lie down beside you, yet I would gladly do much more to bring you back to health. You are a sensible girl; choose whatever course you will."

Sister Savina, seeing that Frate Girolamo accorded with her own wishes for cure of her ailment, replied: "Father, tell me just what I have to do, and I will do it."

The friar, recognizing her pure and holy intention, asked: "Have you ever taken the medicine?"

"No."

"O unhappy girl!" said he. "How have you survived? What nun was your instructress?"

"Sister Lisabetta."

"May God pardon her! How could she have been so cruel as not to have put you in the way of curing your affliction? If you were dead or even deathly sick it would be her fault. Didn't your mother ever give you any good advice?"

"My mother died of grief because my cruel father put me here by force, so that she couldn't give me any good advice, and I never had any advice or help from anyone, and I never had the medication."

The Brother was amazed, and said: "My poor unfortunate, how can you be alive? But in the circumstances I will absolve you. If you had known the facts, I wouldn't absolve you without a license from the Pope, since if you had been instructed you would have been guilty of suicide. But I consider you excused, through your ignorance and your purity. And that evil-minded old Sister Lisabetta deserves a good whipping because she never instructed you. Don't worry; I will arrange with our Director General to have her properly punished. And don't say a word to her, for she is just waiting for you to die so that she will inherit your property. If you have any sense you will pay her back in her own coin, and follow my instructions. Tell me, Sister, how soon do you want to begin the treatment?"

"As soon as I can. Do you have the medicine available?" When he so affirmed, she said: "As for getting in, I will tell you how. Our gardener comes early every morning to work in our walled garden. He enters from the other garden which he rents from us; he has set up a ladder at the wall so that he can get in, as I told you. So come in to his garden this evening, and there you will find the ladder leaning against our wall. Climb up it and enter our garden. My cell is beside the little door opening into the garden, where we go every day for a breath of fresh air. I will open the door for you, and you can stay as long as you like."

"Since that is the situation, I will come, in your service, at about ten, or a little earlier, if you prefer."

Said she: "Father, don't wait so long. Come as soon as the great bell has stopped ringing. I know it will be all right. You will have some supper and will stay with me all night in holy companionship."

"Don't provide any supper. I have a fine roast capon, which a pious lady of my acquaintance sent me. I will bring that." But, wanting to honor him in every way, she replied: "Don't bring anything. Just come, as I have told you."

Said he: "Now above all make sure that you don't confide in anyone, if you wish me to come. I wouldn't set foot in the place if I thought that anyone knew of it, for these are matters that have to take place in secret. I want you to know the whole procedure. You must know, my dear simpleton, that in order that we clerics may pray with you to save all our souls, and to prevent our merely stimulating the disease, our sages and holy men of past times have ruled that you must be locked in and separated from all other people, and that, for the cooling process, we friars must visit and confess you and instruct you in what you need for holy living. Now we are commanded, especially in the case of young girls, that when we know truly and in conscience that you and your like need something, through the high temperature of youth, it is only proper that we should succor you with medicines appropriate to your illness. Indeed we are obliged to do so by our vow of obedience. And if ever I saw anyone who suffered that need, in fact that necessity, you are the person. So I will come punctually, as you have instructed me, and I will bring with me all that is needful for your cure."

Having made this pact and adjured her to secrecy, he laid his hands on her head and absolved her from all sin, imposing a rather heavy penance on her because she had run the risk of suicide through concealing her infirmity; and he ordered her to be wiser in the future than in the past. She accepted penance obediently, and promised observance. Thereupon Frate Girolamo departed cheerily, as did she, through her desire to recover from her illness. He returned to his monastery, more concerned with his project than with complines and the other sacred offices. And after the evening bell, as agreed, he set forth toward the convent garden with his gown tucked up and his capon in a basket. Entering, he found the gardener's ladder, climbed it, and descended in the walled garden. Sister Savina, on the watch, softly opened the door for him and received him in her cell. At her welcome, he said: "I am glad to see you, daughter. Have you waited for me long?" "No," she replied. After certain spiritual caresses they sat down to a table laid out with many various dainties. The friar's capon was added thereto, superfluous though it was; and both supped very devoutly and at their ease.

Then to make the medication more tolerable, Sister Savina said: "Since I am so ignorant, tell me what I have to do." Brother Girolamo replied: "Go and lie down on your bed and undress completely, and I will come at the proper time." Inspired by holy obedience, she did so. When she was in bed Frate Girolamo said: "Have you crossed yourself?" She so affirmed; and he stripped and lay down beside her, saying: "Dear Sister, to administer the medicine without chance of error, I must examine the composition of your character, in order to find out what I must do. So lie close to me." She did so; and he examined her attentively from head to foot. And holding her close, he said: "Don't be afraid, dear Sister. If you do exactly what I tell you, you will infallibly be cured." Obedient and disposed to follow the doctor's orders, she paid close attention. Then said the friar: "Dear Sister, I wish to cleanse you completely of your malady. And now that I have discovered the center of infection, you must take this medicine." Having disposed her properly to receive the draught, he indicated where the infection lay. She, in her eagerness for a cure, would have endured even torture, and consented without even a grimace as the friar applied the remedy. She accepted the draught complete. She required no orange or honey flavoring to make it acceptable; it did not seem bitter to her, but sweet and tasty. At the first dose the friar emptied the vessel; he said, as the two lay devoutly embraced: "Did it seem disagreeable to you?"

"No, Father; and if this is due to cure me, give me as much as you wish. And if you find that my constitution is strong enough to receive it every hour, you need not wait for two-hour intervals. But do what seems best to you."

Frate Girolamo, seeing that she had taken the first dose without distress, and that it had sat well on her stomach, was delighted, hoping to do her great good. So every two hours he prepared the vessel and gave her a draught, so that by morning she had taken six physics. Toward dawn, he asked her how she felt. She replied: "God must have sent you here. I think this medicine will do me much good." Said the friar: "Be comforted; you will be cured soon." She inquired about the regimen to be followed, professing herself ready for anything. The friar said: "Dear Sister, this medicine is of such a sort that to take it too often, or every night, would be excessive. It should be taken every third night, exactly as it was tonight." She replied that she put herself entirely in his hands and that she would do as he ordered. They agreed that he would return every third night, and every month review the symptoms in order to provide the needful supplies for the future.

Both of them being much comforted, he left her, and went out through the garden as he had come in, and so to his monastery. It seemed to her a thousand years till the third night should come for the treatment, such was her longing for a cure. And to the physician the deferment of medication seemed no less long than to her.

Three days later, as was agreed, the Brother returned, and was festively welcomed. After their supper he gave her the second treatment, which was received as eagerly as was the first. And as she had the will to be cured, and he desired the credit therefor, he treated her for a whole month, that is, every third night. Then she felt her excessive heat much reduced, while he was pleased with her progress. The following conversation took place between them:

"My dear Sister," said Frate Girolamo, "I see that you are already cured. Now I have to go on a pilgrimage to the Holy Sepulcher, and I must leave you. Pray God for me, and I will pray for you."

At this she almost fainted. She said: "O Father, my master, you who have brought me from death to life, would you abandon me? You promised to cure me; and now that I am on the way would you leave me? O my lord, in whom lies all my comfort and hope of health, who can do me good or harm as you please, would you be so cruel? Let me tell you this—I will follow you, or I will kill myself with my own hands."

Frate Girolamo, moved by compassion, said: "Sister, if you don't want me to leave you—and I am obliged to go away—we may come to an understanding, to your satisfaction and to mine."

"You decide," said she.

"There is one way by which we can go, under God's care, and live all our lives together. To bring this about, and to preserve the reputation of both of us, do this: begin to make yourself troublesome to the other sisters. While in the past you have been friendly and peaceful, take the contrary course and never stop bickering. Abuse them, quarrel with them, especially with Sister Lisabetta your supervisor. If you do this they will complain of you to me and to the other clergy. Just let them talk; and I will arrange with our Father General, who is coming soon, that you will be confined in our convent in Naples. And you and I will fix it so that we will go honorably wherever we please. And I will never abandon you."

Sister Savina, hearing this proposal, rejoiced, saying: "Father, order whatever you wish, and I shall be satisfied, if only I can be with you. I tell you this, because, thanks to God and to the property my greedy father accumulated, I can support the pair of us all our lives long. So don't be afraid of anything."

The friar was by no means displeased with this; and the two, in happy concord, made their plans down to the last detail. Sister Savina began to rebel against the nuns, opposing them, jostling them, treading on one or another, screaming at them from morning to night; and since she was a big, sturdy girl, she matched her fists to her words, striking them indiscriminately, but especially her directress Sister Lisabetta. As this way of life continued, the abbess and all the nuns complained bitterly of her. She was unmanageable, they said; she had changed in a few days from a good girl into a demon out of hell. They thought she had some evil spirit in her. They complained bitterly to Frate Girolamo. Said he: "Since I began to confess her I have always noted a bad disposition in her. May God grant her aid; she needs it. I can't tell you the trouble I have had in bringing her to the way of salvation; so that I am really ready to despair. I have been thinking that, now that our General is about to visit us, you should lay a complaint against her, asking that this scandal be ended. And on my part, since His Benignity is very kindly and affectionate toward me—not from any merit of mine, for I am a poor sinner— I shall ask his grace upon you, that he may relieve you of this scandal."

By these words the abbess and all the other nuns were deeply comforted; they begged him to do as he had proposed. That very evening, according to their routine, the friar was with Sister Savina. He reported the day's doings, to their common great pleasure and solace. Not neglecting the medicine, which was as delectable as ever, he set forth the procedure with the nuns and the Father General and her own procedure as well; and at dawn he left her.

Thus some days passed. The General of the Order came to Florence, and immediately received the laments of the nuns, complaining bitterly of Sister Savina. The learned General added thereto the testimony of Frate Girolamo, in whom he put great confidence. And considering the whole monastery's reclamation, after interviewing Frate Girolamo, he wanted to hear Sister Savina. Repeating the lessons of Frate Girolamo, she made an apparent effort to justify herself, but the more she talked the more she accused herself of sin. The General assembled the evidence, under the subtle influence of Frate Girolamo, and formally decreed that Sister Savina should be confined in Naples. After a fitting interval, with time for arrangements with the Naples convent, she left Florence on the first day of March, and, as was arranged, she waited for Frate Girolamo in Livorno. He left four days after her, with the announced purpose of going to the Holy Sepulcher.

The two met in Livorno; and after many caresses they cast off their clerical garments and disguised themselves. Under the names of Troilo Guinigi and his wife Pulissena, with a manservant and a lady's maid, they boarded a ship bound for Venice. After a fair journey they took lodgings there, giving out that their home was Lucca. Thus for five years Troilo da Lucca and his wife Pulissena lived there honorably.

But as Troilo was a very handsome young man, a young Venetian lady named Marchigiana fell desperately in love with him. By means of a go-between she arranged that Troilo should embark with her on a yacht on St. Mark's Day. They sailed in celebration to the music of harp and lute. And by her order they put out to the high sea, so that when night fell, Troilo was taken below to a cabin, at her command, with the understanding that he should repose there to avoid seasickness. When he was thus installed, Marchigiana came in to say: "My good sir, you are evidently not used to sailing, and so I am very sorry for you. But don't be afraid; I know good treatments and medicines for those subject to seasickness. So tell me if you need anything."

Troilo, who felt no qualms at all, looked at her beautiful face; and consulting his wishes, he made a play for her, saying: "I am not used to the sea. I have come here by chance, without consulting my wife and relatives. Your offer is a great consolation to me. I must confess that my head is spinning, and that I am frightened to death of drowning in the sea." Said the gallant lady: "Lie down, and I will promise not to abandon you." He lay down, and she beside him, saying: "Hold close to me, and don't be afraid of falling into the water." He followed her good counsel; the two were enclasped in such a close embrace that one could not have drowned without the other. Thus with great solace they assured themselves against submersion in the sea; and all that night they remained so closely bound that each fell in love with the other, and they could not bear the thought of separation. When morning came and they had to get up, much to their regret, they agreed to elope. Troilo found fresh provender preferable to stale, and likewise it seemed better and more satisfying to Marchigiana to live with Troilo than with her husband Marchetto. Thus Troilo abandoned Pulissena, as Marchigiana did Marchetto. They shaped their course to the high seas, and were borne to Barbary. This was the just vengeance of Venus for Troilo's betrayal of Pulissena, as for Marchigiana's of her true husband Marchetto.

Pulissena, finding herself deserted by Troilo, whom she loved so dearly, for several months waited in great woe for his return. Finally news came through that the two lovers were held as slaves in Tunis. Finding no other recourse, she came, despairing, to a decision. A Misser Morello di Capo d'Istria loved her dearly; she determined to escape from her embarrassments by yielding to him. By the agency of her faithful maidservant she spoke to Misser Morello, offering herself freely to him, but with the secret intention that, if he did not come up to scratch, she would find someone else who would. But Misser Morello was delighted. As he was wifeless, he brought her to his house with great festivities. And the inexorable forces of nature so operated that after a few months with her he died of exhaustion. Pulissena, who was now rich with her inheritance and with the property of poor Morello, decided to live free for the rest of her life. She put this program in effect, leading a splendid and ample existence, enjoying every dainty, cooked and raw, whether in bed or on board. Through frequent change of fare she completely forgot Troilo, and thus lived happily all the days of her life.

# ❧ The Amorous Booklover

## by GENTILE SERMINI

This story, like the preceding one, is from Sermini's *Novelle*.
It is Novella 13 in the 1874 edition, printed in Livorno.

MISSER MICHELE RAFFACANTI, mayor of Prato, was a very rich man. (His father had lent at usury.) He was chiefly concerned with display, since he was very pompous by nature. His household consisted of his wife, Mona Chiara, and a handsome fifteen-year-old daughter by a first wife, hence step-daughter of Mona Chiara. Her name was Baldina. Misser Michele, showing off in public but economizing in private, provided one bed for the two ladies, while he slept apart in a humble room. His secretary, a handsome young man named Ugolino, had a separate room. Mona Chiara did not like this arrangement at all. One day she said to Ugolino: "Cavaliere, you are a beautiful writer. I can read but not write. I wonder if you would teach me how to write."

"I should be delighted, Madonna," said he.

"Well, every evening my husband goes to bed at about nine. And when he's asleep, you could teach me for an hour or two. No one will know it. There is no better place than your bed-room."

"Madonna, I am at your service," said Ser Ugolino.

They arranged to begin the lessons that very evening. And when the time came and the mayor was in bed, the cavaliere was joined by Madonna Chiara in his bedroom. Not to be overheard, they locked the door. They sat down with their backs to the fire, and put the writing materials on the table. To begin, Ser Ugolino placed the well-sharpened pen in her hand and showed her how to hold it. Then taking the pen and disposing the inkwell, she began doing simple exercises. Soon she was writing better and better, showing a natural disposition for the work. She applied herself, and in a short time became an accomplished writer. She took much pleasure in writing, and kept the cavaliere with her most of the nights, so great was her determination to learn. She talked to him very freely, having the utmost trust in him, and knowing that he would have no less consideration for her than would her husband, Misser Michele himself. Therefore most nights they would even sleep together; and she became so fascinated with writing that all the time she was with him she was either writing or talking about writing; and when asleep she would always dream of writing.

After about two months of this, Ser Ugolino said to the lady: "I should like to instruct Baldina, so that when you go to Florence you can write to each other." She objected, but he insisted, saying: "If you won't consent to my teaching her, don't count on learning anything more from me." Finally she was forced to yield, as she was unwilling to forget what she had already learned. And thus, under pressure, she had to agree that one night he would teach her, and Baldina the next. Thus Madonna Chiara and Baldina pursued their studies till there was no woman in town who could write better than they. Anyone who could have seen them handle the pen in such dainty style and with such skilful flourishes, according to all the rules of penmanship, would have been amazed. And through their continual utilization the first pen, of an ostrich feather, was worn down almost to nothing, and it was necessary to substitute a goose-quill. And to keep the inkwell supplied and the pen-point firm with so much use, moderation had to be practiced.

Now there was a certain gallant notary in Prato, named Giovanni da Prato, who had an excellent notarial practice and who was a good friend of Ser Ugolino. He was much in love with Baldina. He revealed all, trustfully, to Ugolino, and earnestly begged him for help. So insistent was he that Ser Ugolino promised to arrange an evening visit with her in his bedroom. Thus it was settled that one Thursday evening, when the mayor was in bed, Ser Giovanni and Baldina met in Ugolino's bedroom for supper. The three supped very gayly. It was the season of the long nights, and the watch was beginning its rounds. A volume of Dante lay on the table; Ser Giovanni, who loved the author, picked it up and began to read. Said Ugolino: "I have to go out on patrol. You stay here; and if I should return too late, you can sleep here." He then went out. The door was shut, and Ser Giovanni went on reading, with Baldina by his side. This went on for some time. He read three *canti*, with commentaries, and was beginning the fourth, as if he had no concern for Baldina and was more interested in reading Dante than in her. Being very touchy, she fell into a fury, and said to herself: "I suppose this fellow is waiting for me to invite him in! It looks to me as if he came here to teach a Dante class! If that's it, let him stay with Dante!" She got up and opened the door. Ser Giovanni, hearing her, said: "Where are you going, my pretty darling?"

"I'll be back in a moment," said she. He took her at her word, while she went into Madonna Chiara's room, locked the door, climbed into bed with her, and so spent the night.

Ser Giovanni read the fourth canto while waiting for Baldina. He had plenty of time to wait. Finally, as she did not return, he realized that he had been fooled. And thus he departed, in great despondency.

Now I knew him well and was a close friend, for he had attended our university in Siena. When I visited him in Prato he told me the whole sad tale one morning, from beginning to end. In the course of it he complained bitterly of his ill luck, frequently exclaiming: "O Fortune, what have I done that you should be so adverse to me?" He made many accusations against Fortune, making no mention of himself, who was all to blame. . . .

# ❦ Fra Ieronimo and the Miraculous Arm

## by MASUCCIO

Tommaso Guardati of Salerno, commonly known merely as Masuccio (a diminutive of Tommaso), was born either in Salerno or Sorrento between 1410 and 1415. He was of upper-class, if not noble stock; his father was secretary to the Prince of Salerno. He grew up at the little southern court and succeeded in time to his father's post. He was on friendly terms with many of the great of Italy. He compiled a storybook, *Il Novellino*, which was completed apparently about 1470. He died in 1475. This story is Novella 4.

His stories carry on the erotic, anti-feminine, anti-clerical bias inherited from Boccaccio. His plots are drawn largely from anecdotes current in Naples and its neighborhood. He insists that his tales are all based on fact; but a fiction-writer's insistence on his truthtelling is hardly evidence.

IN THE time when King James the Frenchman, previously Count of the Marches, married the last of the Durazzo line,* a Minorite friar, Fra Ieronimo da Spoleto, landed in Naples. Giving every outward appearance of saintliness, he went about preaching not only in Naples but in all the neighboring cities, gaining a marvelous reputation and rousing great devotion. Hence it came about that, in a monastery of the Preaching Friars in Aversa, he was shown as a marvel the body of an eminent knight, dead for many long years. Whether this corpse had been remarkably well embalmed, or whether the body had been perfectly constituted in life, or for whatever other reason, it was so complete and sound that not only was every bone in its proper seat but the skin was so immaculate that if one merely touched the head the lower part of the body would wiggle. The friar, after

---

* Jacques de Bourbon espoused Queen Giovanna II of Naples in 1415; he was ousted after only a year.—Ed.

close inspection, suddenly conceived the plan of obtaining some member of this body, so that, by passing it off as a relic, he might extract from it hundreds and thousands of ducats, and thus not only live in idleness, but by its agency rise to some high rank in the Church, as is so often the case. One has only to look around to see how many have become great prelates at the expense of the poor stupid secular priests, one rising to be inquisitor of heretics, another collector for the crusades; and I won't mention those who with apostolic bulls, true or false, remit sins, and for cash land everyone in Paradise, while stuffing themselves, rightly or wrongly, with florins, although this is expressly forbidden in their holy rule.

But to return to our Fra Ieronimo. He suited his deed to the thought, and suborned the sacristan of the place, Dominican though he was, with the promised favor of the prior of Santa Croce, and thus he obtained the right arm and hand of the corpse. Not only were the skin and some hairs intact, but the nails were so sound and polished that they looked almost like those of a living man. Impatient of delay, the friar placed the holy relic, plentifully wrapped in sendal silk and sweetly perfumed, in a casket. He then departed and returned to Naples. There he found a faithful companion, an artist in his way like himself, named Fra Mariano da Savona. They decided to visit Calabria, a region inhabited by rude, unsophisticated people, there to try out their new weapon. And on this they made their pact.

Fra Mariano, prudently disguised as a Dominican, went to the harbor to take ship for Calabria. Meanwhile Fra Ieronimo with three companions with well-packed saddlebags set off alongshore. They happened on a boat from Amantea, and decided to take passage in her. They all went on board, but separately, each very chilly toward the others, like swindlers working country fairs or landing apparently by chance in roadside inns. The sailors hoisted the sails and pulled at their oars, and set off on their course. Suddenly, when they were not far from Capri, a squall came up, so black and ominous that the sailors agreed they could not withstand it. Unwillingly they had to make like castaways for a small beach near Sorrento. With much difficulty they hauled their vessel ashore. They all went up to the town, and decided to stay there until the weather should clear. Thus Fra Ieronimo with his companions went to the convent of the conventual friars, while Fra Mariano, who had turned himself into a Dominican, went with the other laymen to the inn. Recognizing that the turbulent sea was not likely to calm down soon, the worthy friar, impatient, decided to make there his first test of the false relic. He recalled hearing reports that this city of Sorrento was very ancient, very noble, so that its citizens were cankered with the rust of antiquity; his plan might succeed there as well as in Calabria.

He passed the word secretly to his Fra Mariano. And as the next day was Sunday, he sent the supervisor of the monastery to inform the archbishop that, with the prelate's blessing, he proposed to preach a pious sermon in the cathedral on the following day. And he begged the archbishop to announce the fact in the city and suburbs, so that if enough people, devout in spirit, should present themselves, he would display to them, for the honor and glory of God, a holy relic, the most precious that they had ever seen in their lives. The archbishop, who was himself one of the most ancient Sorrentines, received the word with unquestioning faith. He immediately had the announcement made throughout the city and its surroundings that everyone should come to hear the sermon and see the relic to be shown to the people of Sorrento by a holy servant of God. The news having been spread throughout the countryside, in the morning so many people gathered at the church that hardly half could be contained therein. At sermon time Fra Ieronimo, accompanied by many friars with the usual ceremonies, mounted to the pulpit, and uttered a long discourse on mercy and holy almsgiving. At the proper time he bared his head, and spoke somewhat as follows:

"Most reverend Monsignore, and you ladies and gentlemen, my fathers and mothers in Christ Jesus, I don't doubt that you have heard reports of my preaching in Naples, where, thanks to God and not to my own merit and virtue, I have had a constant and extraordinary reception. Being aware of the fame of your most noble city and of the humanity and devotion of its citizens, and as well of the beauty of this region, I have often thought of coming here to expound the word of God, and likewise to enjoy with you your delicious air, which in fact I find very beneficial to my constitution. Having received an order from my Father Vicar General to proceed to Calabria, to respond to summons made to me by certain cities, I was obliged to take my course whither I was commanded. And as I think you must know, our ship was caught in your gulf, beaten by contrary winds and tempestuous seas, and despite all the efforts and determination of the sailors, we were cast ashore here, having barely survived. But I think that my coming here was not caused by contrary winds, but by the divine disposition of my Creator, who answered in part my own desire. And that you too may be participators in His grace, I want to show to you, to augment your devotion, a marvelous relic, that is, a complete arm with the right hand of that most excellent and glorious Chancellor of our Savior Jesus Christ, Saint Luke the Evangelist. This was given by the Patriarch of Constantinople to our Father Vicar, and he is sending it by my hand to Calabria, since in that province there was never any body or member of any great saint. Therefore, my beloved, may God bless you; and let everyone devoutly uncover to see this treasure, which God himself has granted you to see, rather as a miracle than by any agency of mine. But first I must inform you that I have a bull from our Lord the Pope, by which he grants very great indulgences and remission of sins to any who will give alms to this relic, according to his means, to the end that these be collected to make a proper tabernacle, studded with jewels, as is fitting for so glorious an object."

Thereupon he drew from his sleeve a bull, counterfeited in his own style. Everyone accepted it without bothering to read it; and all pressed forward to make their offering. Fra Ieronimo, after telling his story in impressive manner, had his companions present him with the casket containing the holy arm. He had many candles lit, then knelt down, and holding the casket in his hands with great reverence, kissed it devoutly, with his eyes full of tears.

Then holding it solemnly, he turned to his companions, and they all sang pontifically a holy laud of Saint Luke. Then seeing all the people spellbound, he opened the casket, from which a delicious odor emerged, removed the silk wrappings, took out the relic and displayed the hand and part of the arm. Thus he spoke:

"This is the holy, blessed hand of the most faithful secretary of the Son of God! Here is the blessed hand that not only wrote the praises of the glorious Virgin Mary, but also often drew her face in its divine likeness!"

But when he was about to proceed with the praises of the saint, all of a sudden, at one side of the church, up spoke Fra Mariano da Savona, in his new Dominican habit! With great importunity he demanded to be heard. Shouting with a great voice against Fra Ieronimo, he cried:

"Impostor! Crook! Swindler of God and men! Aren't you ashamed to tell such tremendous great lies, saying that this is the arm of Saint Luke! I know for certain that his entire most holy body lies in Padua! You must have dug up that rotten arm from some grave in order to cheat the world! I am astounded at Monsignore and the other venerable clerical fathers. They should have stoned you, as you deserve!"

The archbishop and the people, startled by this interruption and stung by the monk's words, commanded him to be silent. But for all that he would not stop shouting; on the contrary he grew ever more furious, trying to persuade the congregation not to believe the preacher. While matters stood thus, it seemed to Fra Ieronimo that it was time to perform the prepared, pretended miracle. Apparently somewhat shaken, he raised his hand and imposed silence on the muttering throng. Having gained a moment's attention, he turned to the high altar, where hung a crucifix. He knelt before it and spoke, in a flood of tears:

"O my Lord Jesus Christ, redeemer of the human race, thou who hast formed me and made me in thy image, who hast set me here on earth through the merits of thy most glorious body and thy immaculate human flesh, and who hast redeemed me by thy bitter passion, I pray thee also by the miraculous stigmata which thou didst confer upon our seraphic Francesco that thou mayest be pleased to display an evident miracle, in the presence of this holy assemblage, with regard to this clever friar, who, as an enemy and rival of our religion, has come hither to contest my truthtelling. Therefore if I am lying, send down forthwith thy wrath upon me, and bid me die here and now. And if I say true, if this is indeed the genuine arm of Messer Saint Luke, thy most worthy Chancellor, then, my Lord, not out of vengeance but for the elucidation of the truth, impose thy judgment upon him, so that, however he will, he may not indicate his guilty thought by tongue or gesture."

Hardly had Fra Ieronimo pronounced this conjuration when Fra Mariano, according to plan, suddenly began to twist and writhe with hands and feet, howling loudly and gabbling, without voicing a recognizable word. His eyes rolling, his mouth twisting, his limbs flailing, he fell helplessly backward. And as everyone in church witnessed this manifest miracle, they all shouted "Mercy upon us!" so loudly that if it had thundered no one could have heard it. Fra Ieronimo, seeing the people properly hooked, to rouse them the more and make his swindle complete, began to shout loudly: "Praise be to God! Silence, my people!"

Having obtained silence by his words, he had Fra Mariano, who now lay as if dead, brought forward and deposited before the altar. He then addressed the assemblage:

"Ladies and gentlemen, and all you country people, I beg you by the holy passion of Christ, to kneel down, each of you, and devoutly say a paternoster in reverence of Messer Saint Luke; and through his merits may God not only return this poor man to life, but also restore to him the use of his limbs and his power of speech, that so his soul may not pass to eternal perdition."

No sooner had he given this command than all knelt in prayer; and he stepped down at the other side of the pulpit, pulled out a knife and shaved a scrap from the nail of the miraculous hand. He placed this in a glass of holy water, opened the mouth of Fra Mariano, and poured the precious liquid therein, saying: "I command you that by virtue of the Holy Spirit you rise up and return to your former state of health!"

Fra Mariano, who had so far only with great difficulty kept from laughing, swallowed the draught, and on hearing the conjuration jumped to his feet, opened his eyes, and with a bewildered air began to cry: "Jesus! Jesus!" When the company saw this manifest miracle, all, terrified and amazed, cried out together: "Jesus! Jesus!" Some ran to ring the church bell, others to touch and kiss the vestments of the preacher, and everyone seemed so to overflow with devotion, that one would have thought the Last Judgment had arrived.

Fra Ieronimo, who wanted to fulfill the purpose of his mission, again climbed, with no small difficulty, into the pulpit. He ordered that the relic should be placed before the altar, and around it he posted his companions, some carrying lighted candles, some directing the throng's movements, so that everyone might pray without impediment and conveniently make an offering to the holy arm. In addition to the great quantity of money, offered in the largest sums ever seen, some ladies were assailed by such a charitable frenzy that they pulled off their pearls and silver adornments and other precious jewels and offered them to the Holy Evangelist. All that day the holy relic was displayed. And when the friar judged it time to return to his quarters with his spoils he gave a cautious signal to his companions, and they deftly wrapped up everything and put it in the casket with the arm; and all went off together to the convent. The friar, generally honored and revered on a par with the saint, was reverently conducted to the house by the archbishop and all the people. The two notable miracles were recorded by Fra Ieronimo and attested in due form. And the next morning, as the weather had cleared, he embarked on his vessel with his considerable profits, accompanied by Fra Mariano and the other companions.

With a prosperous wind, they arrived shortly in Calabria. There they filled their pockets with money, by means of various novel swindling devices. Afterward they traveled both within and without Italy. Much enriched by their innumerable trickeries and the favor of the miraculous arm, they returned to Spoleto. There, seeming to be completely secure, Fra Ieronimo bought a bishopric by the agency of a lord cardinal. This was not simony, of course, oh no; but according to the new definition, it was by way of a "procuration-fee." He settled down, with his Fra Mariano, in great ease and comfort. And as long as they lived they had a very good time.

# ❧ A Quick-witted Cleric

by MASUCCIO

*This story is Novella 18 of Il Novellino.*

AS EVERYONE must know, the Little Brothers of Saint Anthony, with their base in Spoleto and Cerreto, constantly scour Italy, stimulating vows to their saint and collecting the proceeds. On this errand they go everywhere preaching and pretending to work miracles; and with every kind of sly trickery they fill their pockets with money and valuables, and then come back to idleness at home. More of them come daily to our kingdom of Naples than to any other place. And especially they take their course to Calabria and Apulia, where the people have plenty of charity and not much sense.

In January, last year, one of these Cerreto friars landed in Cerignola. He was on horseback, with an ass loaded with packs and a lackey on foot. They went throughout the countryside collecting alms and, as their custom is, making their horse genuflect at the name of the great baron Messer Saint Anthony.

They happened to notice, before the house of a rich peasant, two large pigs. As the farmer was absent, his wife gave them alms with more than usual devotion, thus indicating to the Brother that this was a good place to cast his nets. Overflowing with unction, he turned to his boy, and speaking low, but loud enough to be heard by the wife, he said: "What a pity that such beautiful pigs must so soon die suddenly!"

The woman pricked up her ears at this, and said: "Sir, what are you saying about my pigs?"

He replied: "I was merely saying that it seems to me a great fault of nature that they are to die in a few hours, without bringing profit to anyone."

Smitten to the heart by this, the woman said: "Oh dear! Man

of God, I beg you to tell me the reason for this curse, and to keep it off, if possible."

Said he: "Good woman, I can't give you any other reason than that this will take place, as I recognize by a certain sign in them. It could be perceived by no living person except our friars, who have this grace from our lord and master Saint Anthony. I could avert their fate, if I had with me one of our magic acorns."

"For God's sake see if you haven't got one," said she. "I will pay well for it."

The friar turned to his boy, who was very well schooled, and said to him: "Martino, look in our packs, and see if there isn't one there."

"Sir," said he, "there are just two. I have been saving them for our ass, who is often afflicted in this way."

Said the master: "Let us make a gift of them to this woman, so that she may not lose such noble pigs through our shortcoming. Surely she will be grateful enough to present to our hospital a pair of sheets for the poor patients."

"For the love of Christ's cross," said she, "save my pigs from such an evil fate, and I'll give you some very fine new cloth, enough to make not one pair of sheets but two for your hospital."

The friar immediately had Martino hand over the acorns. He called for a glass of water, put in it a good charge of bran and mixed in the magic acorns, with many prayers, in which his servant joined. Then he placed the mixture before the pigs, and they gobbled it down as if famished. Then the friar turned to the woman and said:

"Now you can be assured that your pigs are saved from a horrible death to which they were doomed. And may you, remembering the benefit received, now permit me to depart, since I must now bid you Godspeed and set forth on my way." His haste was caused by fear that the husband might appear and forbid him the hoped-for loot. But the woman willingly gave him the promised cloth. As soon as he obtained it he mounted his horse and left the town, taking the road to Tre Santi, to proceed to Manfredonia, where every year he made a good harvest.

Not long after his departure the farmer came home from the fields. His wife met him, and full of cheer told him how his pigs had been rescued from sudden death by virtue of the magic acorns of Saint Anthony, and how, in return for such a blessing, she had given her cloth to the hospital for the succor of the poor. The husband learned with great pleasure that his pigs had been saved from dreadful peril; but when he heard that the cloth had changed masters he was extremely cast down; and if his eagerness to recover the cloth had not prevented him he would have well massaged his wife's back with an oaken stick. But to do the necessary thing first, he said no word, except to ask her how long since the friar had departed and what road he had taken. She replied that he had left only a quarter of an hour before, and had taken the road to Tre Santi. The good man assembled six other young men, all with weapons; and they followed on the course the friar had taken. They had hardly gone a mile when they saw him in the distance. They whistled loudly to him, and yelled to him to stop, meanwhile hurrying to join him. At the shouts the Brother looked back, and seeing the band baying at his heels, well recognized the truth of the matter. And being a man of resource and sagacity, he quickly had Martino pass him the cloth. He placed it before the pommel of his saddle, and with his back to the enemy he pulled out his flint and steel, dropped a spark in a little pocket of tinder, and, hearing the pursuers near, wrapped the smoldering tinder in the middle of the many folds of the cloth. He then turned back to the men overtaking him, and said: "What do you want, my good men?"

The farmer stepped forward and said: "You dirty crooked loafer, I'd like to run this pike through your body! Didn't you have the gall to come to my house and to cheat my wife out of her cloth? Give it here, and a pox take you!"

The friar, without demur, put the cloth in his arms, saying:

"My good man, God pardon you! I have not robbed your wife of her cloth; she gave it of her own free will to the poor in our hospital. But take it, in God's name. I hope only in our baron Messer Saint Anthony, that he will shortly perform a manifest miracle, and that his fire will kindle not only within the cloth but upon all the rest of your possessions."

The farmer took the cloth, caring little or not at all for the friar's malediction. He turned homeward; but he hadn't gone far with his party when a smell of burning assailed him and he saw the cloth smoking: and his companions saw and smelt the same. So, in the greatest fear he had ever known, he threw the cloth on the ground, opened it up, and saw that it was all burning. In terror, and in fear of worse to come, he called to the friar, begging him for the love of God to return and pray to the miraculous Saint Anthony to revoke his cruel penalty, which had been put so quickly into action. The friar, in order not to see the cloth consumed, did not wait for much urging, but returned immediately. He ordered Martino to put out the fire, fell on his knees, and with simulated tears prayed most devoutly. Then he reassured the farmer that no offense was taken from his mistake; and all together went back to the town. When the news of this manifest miracle was spread, everyone, male and female, and even children, went to meet him, crying for mercy. And he entered the town in no less glory than was Christ received in Jerusalem. And he received so many gifts and offerings that ten sumpter-mules couldn't have carried them. He converted most of them into cash; and thus he left town rich and happy, and never returned there to fill his saddlebags.

# ❦ The Lovers among the Lepers
by MASUCCIO

This story is Novella 31 of *Il Novellino*.

FAME, THAT most truthful reporter of ancient deeds, has brought me a story from France, of the times when the Maid of Orleans convulsed that realm. In Nancy, the most important and noble city of the duchy of Lorraine, there were two very active and high-hearted knights, each the baron, from old times, of certain castles and villages set about that city. One was named the Sieur de Condi, the other the Sieur Jean de Brouchy. Fortune had granted to the Sieur de Condi only a single daughter, named Martine, of tender years but filled with singular virtues and graced with impeccable manners. The Sieur Jean had had many children, but only one remained living. His name was Louis; he was of about the same age as Martine, and was very handsome, noble-spirited, and abounding in every good quality. These gentlemen were distantly related, being of the same original stock. Their friendship and intimacy steadily increased, so that, what with their continual visits one to the other, it seemed that they held their vassals and properties in common, and there was rarely any disharmony between them.

By the time Louis came to manhood, his frequent contacts with Martine and their long familiarity brought it about that, being unsupervised and unsuspected, they fell deeply in love. Their inward ardors were such that neither could have any peace of mind save when they were together, taking solace in their conversation, under the impulsions of their youthful love. They happily spent several years in this amorous play, without ever indulging in any illicit acts. Although each longed to taste the ultimate and most delicious fruits of love, nonetheless Louis, somewhat the more sober of the two, wished to avoid any blame

*The Lovers among the Lepers*

on the part of the girl or her relatives. He had therefore made up his mind never to have carnal conjunction with her, except as authorized by the law of matrimony. He expounded often this firm, virtuous intention to Martine. She agreed heartily, and comforted him with the proposal that a formal request for their union should be made to their parents. Louis, who asked nothing better, persuaded his father to make such a request in due form to the Sieur de Condi. But the latter returned many sound reasons why this match should not be made; and courteously but firmly he required of Sieur Jean that, to preserve the honor of both houses, the association of the young people should be so restricted that Louis should be allowed in his house only in the case of urgent necessity. Thus not only was the proposal of marriage rejected, but all friendly intercourse was forbidden.

It would be endless and needless to recount what amorous plaints, bitter heartburnings, and fervent lamentations greeted this news. What chiefly afflicted poor Louis was the thought that, through insisting on following the path of virtue, he had been brought so low that he could hardly understand how body and soul did not part. He then determined that he would communicate by letter with his Martine, employing a faithful messenger; and he would earnestly beg her that if she knew any way to gain their common salvation she should so inform him. Having written the letter, he sent it to her in all secrecy. The girl, though plunged in intolerable grief, had had some thought of displaying the fortitude of her spirit. Weeping, she took the letter and read it. Though overcome with distress and hindered by the impossibility, in the circumstances, of writing an answer, she said to the messenger:

"You are the only one who knows of our hidden but virtuous passion. Assure the one who sent you of my love, and tell him that either will he be my husband and the only lord of my life, or of my own will I shall banish my soul from my afflicted body, by poison or by the sword. And although he, with superabundant virtue, has sought more my father's honor than the satisfaction of our youthful love, nevertheless, if he has the heart to come, with some of his followers, to the wall of our castle, just below the window of my bedroom, with a rope ladder and anything else needful for my descent, I will come down to him, and we will go to the castle of one of our common kin, and there we will contract our marriage. And when the news comes out, if my father is pleased, excellent; and if not, at least the thing will be done, and he might as well act sensibly and cover the accomplished fact with an air of virtuous concession. And if Louis is disposed to do this, let him come to me this very night, as I have said, without any further delay."

The faithful servant imprinted the message on his mind. Certain signals were agreed upon, to avoid mischances. He departed, returned to his master, and reported the conversation exactly. The latter needed no urging to comply with Martine's directions. He chose carefully some twenty gallant, high-spirited youths, his vassals and followers. When everything needful was in order and night fell, they set forth in perfect silence on their excursion, which was not long. And in a few hours they assembled under the designated window of the lady. He gave the agreed signal; she, who had been waiting impatiently, recognized it. She threw down a strong cord; this was tied to the rope ladder, which she pulled up and tied securely to the iron work at the edge of the window. And by it she descended, without any fear, as if she had often done it before. Her Louis received her in his arms, and after many kisses they were off to the highroad, where two fine riding horses awaited them. Their guide was instructed in the course to be followed; and the young men protected them, as advance guard and rear guard, to their great delight.

But a contrary fate frowned upon them and brought them to an evil, indeed incomparably horrible end. They had hardly gone a mile when a rainstorm burst upon them, so heavy and continuous, with lashing winds and hammering hail and frightful thunder and lightning, that all the reservoirs of heaven seemed to be opened. It was so dark, and the tempest so terrific, that the men on foot, most of them wearing only their jackets, lost their way, as did the guide. Some fled one way, some another, seeking whatever refuge;

the lovers, their hands tight-clasped, could hardly see each other. Both of them, fearful lest the sudden cloudburst should be a punishment sent by God for their elopement, unsure where they were or what way to take, conscious that all their companions were out of touch and making no answer to their loud repeated shouts, commended themselves to God, dropped the reins of their horses, and left the choice of the road—and their very lives —to the will of their steeds and to fate.

Having blundered here and there for several miles, like a ship without a steersman, seeming to be summoned by death itself, they perceived afar a little light. This reawakened their hope; they turned their horses' heads toward the gleam, while the savage storm did not for a moment relent. After much effort they reached the source of this light. They knocked at the door, which was opened to them. They discovered that the place was a lazar-house. Certain of the wasted creatures appeared, and asked them, with little charity, who had brought them there at such an hour. The two young people were so numb with cold and so weakened that they could hardly speak. With an effort Louis replied that the calamitous weather and their own evil fate had led them to the door. Then he begged them to grant the travelers a place at the fireside and some shelter for their weary horses. Although these lepers are a kind of damned folk, having no hope of cure, so that no humanity or charity exists among them, nevertheless they were moved by some feeble compassion. They aided the visitors to dismount, stabled the horses with their own asses, and led the guests to the kitchen and seated them before a good fire. And although the two young people instinctively recoiled from association with these rotten, polluted folk, still, having no alternative, they made the best of it.

Thanks to the warmth, Louis and Martine regained their native good looks so far that they seemed to have taken the shape of Diana and Narcissus. This transformation roused a wicked scoundrel among the lepers, who had served as a mercenary soldier in the late wars. He was more blemished and disfigured than any of the others. He was assailed by an overwhelming desire to carnally

possess the beautiful girl. Impelled by savage lust, he concluded
that by killing the young lover he could capture his noble prey.
Having made up his mind, he confided in a companion, no less
scoundrelly and inhuman than himself. The two went to the
stable; one untied the horses, made as much noise as possible, and
shouted: "Gentleman! Come and tend to your horses, and keep
them from bothering our asses!" The other stationed himself behind the door with a great axe in his hand, ready to commit his
horrible murder.

Alas, ribald Fortune, ever changeful, ill content with any long
felicity of any of your minions, with what cozening hopes have
you brought the two innocent doves to the net of cruel death! If
you were unwilling that the wretched lovers should prosperously
sail your serene and tranquil seas, had you not infinite other devices to separate them, in life and in death? Why did you decree
for them only this most horrible end? Truly I can do naught
else than protest against your detestable works, and proclaim
him a dupe who puts his faith and hope in you!

At the call, Louis, though reluctant to get up and leave the fire,
heeded the summons to tend to his horses. He dragged himself
out to the stable, leaving his lady with many other lepers, both
men and women. As he entered the stable, the fierce scoundrel
with his axe gave him such a blow on the head that he fell down
dead, without even time to say "Alas!" The attacker, though well
knowing that his victim was dead, continued landing many more
savage blows on his head. The assassins left him there and returned to the fireside; and as they were in a way the masters, they
ordered the rest of the party to return to their quarters to sleep.
And these immediately obeyed.

Unhappy Martine remained alone. She asked about her Louis,
but got no answer, till finally the killer approached her and said
in his hoarse broken voice: "My girl, you might as well be patient,
because I have just killed your man, and there is nothing you can
hope for from him. And I intend to enjoy your pretty person as
long as I live."

O pitiful ladies with tears to shed, who have deigned to read or hear my sad story of this strange and pitiable case, if any of you have loved a husband with your whole soul, or if any of you have been totally enamored of a lover—and you, maidens in love, in the heyday of your youthful bloom, if love has ever consumed your hearts with such a flame, I pray you, if any human pity dwells in you, to accompany my tale with your most woeful tears. No words can render the bitter, intolerable grief which that unhappiest of women felt. Now that I try to set down something of the tale, there appears before me the appalling picture of those lepers beside the wretched girl, with their red eyes, their hairless brows, their noses gnawed away, their puffed varicolored cheeks, their half-consumed inward-turning lips, their foul-smelling, contorted, paralyzed hands, so that the figures seem to be more of diabolic than of human form. The impression is so strong that it checks my trembling hand, barely able to continue the tale.

You who listen with pity in your hearts, imagine her thoughts, and with what terror as well as anguish she found herself between two savage dogs, so inflamed that it seemed that each demanded to be the first to mount her. Screaming, she beat her head against the wall. She fainted momentarily and recovered; she scratched her delicate face till it was covered with blood. And recognizing that she had no recourse or means of salvation, she fearlessly determined that as she had been Louis' companion in life, so would she follow and accompany him in death. Addressing the two rapacious beasts, she said: "O pitiless, inhuman creatures, since you have robbed me of the sole treasure of my life, I pray you by the one God in heaven that before you proceed to any other offense against my person you will grant me the singular grace to look for a moment on the dead body of my unhappy lord, and permit me to wash for a moment his bloody face with my bitter tears."

The men, who did not conceive what the lady had in mind to do, were persuaded to grant her plea. They led her to the place where the luckless Louis lay dead. When she saw him, in a kind of frenzy she uttered a heart-rending scream and flung herself heedless upon the body. Although she possessed a small knife sufficient for her purpose, nevertheless she looked at her lover's side and saw there his dagger, which the men had not removed. She thought that this would provide the quickest and most expeditious means for fulfilling her design. Surreptitiously pulling it out, and hiding it between her own body and that of the dead man, she cried: "Before the steel pierces my heart, I call upon you, gracious spirit of my lord, which has just escaped by violent means from your body! I pray you not to grieve at the delay of my own soul in joining you! May we be kept bound and conjoined by our eternal mutual love! And though it was not granted to our corruptible selves to live together their expected term in this life and to show forth our love to the world, may it be everlasting, may we be together forever in joy and possess one another eternally in whatever place! And do you, noble and beloved corpse, accept my body as a sacrifice; it hastens of its own will to follow you, wherever you may go. It was ordained for you not as a means of pleasure but as an offering. And let the incense of our funeral rites be composed of our blood, mingled and befouled in this evil spot, together with the tears of our cruel fathers!"

Thus she spoke; and although she would have liked to weep longer and bewail her lot, and though many pitiful words remained unspoken, she knew it was time to fulfill her destiny. She dexterously set the dagger's hilt on the breast of the dead man and the sharp point at her heart; and pressing upon it without concern or fear she let herself be transfixed by the cold steel, saying: "O pitiless dogs, you have lost the prey you longed for!" And closely embracing her dead lover, she departed from this grievous life. The men had hardly heard these last words, when they perceived more than a palm's breadth of the steel protruding from her back. Filled with anger and distress, and fearing for their own lives, they dug a deep hole beneath the stable and buried the two as they lay clasped together.

Such was the dolorous and grievous end of the loving pair, as I have recounted it with my sorrowing pen. There followed a savage, mortal war between their fathers, with many killed on both sides. And as God's justice could not let such an enormous crime go unpunished but rather demanded payment for murder, it happened that in time dissension arose among the lepers, and one of the inmates of the lazar-house revealed all that had taken place. When the two barons heard this, by common accord they sent a commission to the designated spot. The grave was dug up, and there were revealed the noble ill-starred lovers. And though they were decayed and corrupted, the dagger gave evidence of their cruel and pitiless death. They were rescued from that vile place, put in a coffin, and carried forth. Then the doors were locked, and fire was set within and without. And all its occupants, with their goods, their houses, even their chapel, were reduced to ashes in a few hours.

The dead bodies were carried to Nancy. Not only the parents, friends, and citizens, but all visitors put on mourning and gave vent to grief and woe. The bodies were laid in a single sepulcher with solemn, pious ceremonies. And thereon was written a worthy epitaph in antique lettering, in memory of the two unhappy lovers: "Envious and hostile fate brought to premature death the two lovers here buried, Louis and Martine, whose devotion ended in disaster. Thou who readest this, shed a tear for love come to a bitter end."

# ❧ The Jesting Inquisitor

## by SABADINO DEGLI ARIENTI

Giovanni Sabadino degli Arienti was born in Bologna in the mid-fifteenth century. He served as secretary to the ruling tyrants, and lived for a time at the court of Ercole d'Este, Duke of Ferrara, to whom his storybook is dedicated. He died in 1510.

*Le Porretane,* or "Tales Told at the Baths of Porretta" (which lies between Bologna and Florence), follows the Boccaccian formula. A group of ladies and gentlemen are presumed to meet at the baths, in 1475, and beguile their leisure with storytelling. The chief interest to the modern reader attaches to certain vivid anecdotes of contemporary life.

MOST EMINENT Count, most beautiful ladies, and you most elegant gentlemen: in the times of Eugenius, Nicholas, Calixtus, and Pius, popes by divine providence, the most reverend Cardinal of Saint Mark's, who later became Pope Paul II, was a gentleman of outstanding intelligence and of singular merit, as all of you can testify. As a man of religion and a cardinal of the Catholic Christian church, he had a suitable passage from Holy Scripture read aloud at his meals. Thus it happened one day that the life of the most holy and most patient Job was read. When dinner was over and the tables removed and grace rendered to God, the cardinal turned to his guests and remarked: "Certainly the patience of blessed Job was extraordinary and unexampled. Thus it is not surprising that God rewarded him lavishly, as his true friend." On hearing this Misser Francesco Malacarne, his auditor, a very sharp, witty, amusing man, who might well have been a robber captain if he hadn't been a university graduate with a doctor's degree, shot a keen glance at one of his companions, shook his head, and clapped his hand to his mouth, as if he wanted to swallow the cardinal's words in mockery. Said the prelate: "What do you mean by shaking your head and shutting up your mouth like a purse? Some of your usual nonsense, no doubt? Wasn't Job's patience a great virtue?"

Said Malacarne: "Most reverend Monsignore, I don't want to say any nonsense. But it does seem to me that Job's patience was not as great as Your Lordship says."

"And why?" said the cardinal.

"Please, Monsignore, let us drop this line of talk. Because, if I let myself go, I might say that the devil was not much of a tempter. In my own opinion, I could have tempted Job a lot better."

"What would you have done, Malacarne? Tell me."

"I can think of a thousand things. This would be one of the weakest methods—I would have got him into a good game of backgammon."

The cardinal began to laugh, in the style of his family. He said: "You idiot! Didn't I say that you would get off some nonsense?"

Malacarne rejoined: "My lord, you really shouldn't laugh so loud. Didn't I tell Your Lordship that this is just one way out of a thousand, and the weakest of the lot? But if playing backgammon shouldn't work to make him lose his patience, I would use one supreme method. But enough, enough, for God's sake. Let's say no more about it."

"What is that method, my good Malacarne? Tell me, I command you."

"I would rather not tell you now. Let the matter drop."

"You will tell me, on the spot," replied the cardinal. Malacarne demurring reluctantly, and the cardinal insisting and commanding, at length Malacarne said: "Since you force it out of me, I will tell you frankly, Monsignore. But please don't be angry. I would have put Job in the service of a master like Your Lordship."

At these words the cardinal, though considerably annoyed, chose not to reveal his irritation. He burst into loud laughter, together with all the others present. He went over to Malacarne, pinched his ear and pulled it a bit, and said: "You are well named Malacarne [Bad Meat]; it would take a lot of seasoning to make you fit for consumption." Then, ceasing to laugh and quitting the tone of comedy, he said: "Malacarne, you have such a subtle and ingenious mind that I am going to give you a responsible job. This very morning His Holiness the Pope commissioned me to go to the Castel Sant' Angelo to examine a heretic and hear his doubts about the Christian faith. Now I want you to go there in my place and perform this office with all possible diligence."

"Very gladly, Monsignore," said Malacarne, who found the task congenial.

Thus at the proper time he went to see the heretic. After the salutations, he said: "My good man, as you have been accused before His Beatitude, our lord, of heresy, a hateful thing to His Holiness and to the Christian religion, I have been ordered and commissioned in the name of His Holiness to hear from you the substance of your doubts. Such being the case, I should like to know what your heresy is and what doubts you have about our faith. If you tell me this freely, you will receive from me illumination that will assure your salvation and your liberation from this prison. Come then, brother; make a clean breast; don't be afraid; speak up sincerely and frankly. First off, how do you believe in the Christian faith?"

"Sir," replied the heretic, "I believe so much that I wonder if I don't believe too much."

At this reply Malacarne could hardly help laughing. Thinking that the man was more naïve than anything else, he decided to have some fun with him; he said: "Well, to put it briefly, I should like an answer to one question. Do you think that if a great fire should blaze up here it could be extinguished by divine power?"

"Without water?" said the heretic sharply.

"Without water," replied Malacarne.

"No, I don't believe that," said the heretic.

"To tell the truth, I don't either," said Malacarne, with a sudden shout of laughter. He continued: "Tell me, do you think one could walk on the water out to the middle of the sea without being drowned?"

"Without a boat?" said the heretic.

"Without a boat," repeated Malacarne.

"No, I don't believe that."

"Neither do I!" Continuing with his questions, though he was more inclined to laugh than anything else, he said: "Do you believe that God could satisfy many thousands of people with five loaves and that twelve basketsful remained over, as the holy Gospel reports?"

Said the heretic: "I should like to ask you first, sir, how big the loaves were, and then I will answer." Said Malacarne, chuckling: "I am assuming that the loaves were of normal size."

"Since you don't know anything surely, I don't know what to reply."

"Good! Well spoken!" said Malacarne. "But remember that with these five loaves there were two fish; now what do you think?"

"I believe everything, if the loaves were each made of a thousand bushels of grain, and if the fish were whales."

"That's too much to believe." Still laughing to himself, he said: "That's enough for now. I am amazed that anyone could have questioned your faith. So cheer up; you will be released soon, because you seem to me a very sensible man."

Thereupon Malacarne returned to his lord cardinal and said: "Most reverend Monsignore, I have examined that man accused of heresy with the utmost possible diligence."

"Good!" said the cardinal. "What is your opinion?"

"Monsignore, he seems to me a worthy man and a good Christian; in fact he believes exactly what I do; and indeed it seems to me a great injustice to hold him there."

The cardinal, laughing at Malacarne's comic manner, said: "My faith, he must be a worthy man, if he believes just what you do!" Malacarne, seeing his master in such good humor, went on: "You wanted to verify what I told you yesterday, that Job would have lost his patience in the service of Your

Lordship. Well, obviously that man you call a heretic and I too can believe more than you and the Pope." He developed this idea at length, and amusingly. And a few days later the imprisoned heretic was released. He left Rome; then Malacarne told his master how he had examined the man and his answers and everything. His Lordship was much diverted; he couldn't keep from recounting it in consistory. The Pope and his brother cardinals laughed so much that they are still laughing. But as a just and holy pastor he asked God's pardon therefor; he had Malacarne reprimanded, giving him to understand that the miraculous deeds of our heavenly King are to be reported only with the utmost reverence toward His divine glory.

# ❦ Belphagor

## by NICCOLÒ MACHIAVELLI

Niccolò Machiavelli was born in Florence in 1469. He held an important post in the Florentine civil service, and had plenty of oppportunity for observation as well as action. But something went wrong; he was disgraced, imprisoned, tortured, and eventually released to a life of obligatory leisure. He wrote histories and treatises on government, most noteworthily *The Prince*, an analysis of despotic rule and a manual for the ambitious, unscrupulous man who would engage in practical politics. He diverted himself also by writing comedies and occasional verse. He died in 1527.

*Belphagor* is his only extant short story, a development of a medieval theme. The translation is by Thomas Roscoe. It appeared in his *Italian Novelists* (London, 1825).

WE READ in the ancient archives of Florence the following account, as it was received from the lips of a very holy man, greatly respected by every one for the sanctity of his manners at the period in which he lived. Happening once to be deeply absorbed in his prayers, such was their efficacy that he saw an infinite number of condemned souls, belonging to those miserable mortals who had died in their sins, undergoing the punishment due to their offences in the regions below. He remarked that the greater part of them lamented nothing so bitterly as their folly in having taken wives, attributing to them the whole of their misfortunes. Much surprised at this, Minos and Rhadamanthus, with the rest of the infernal judges, unwilling to credit all the abuse heaped upon the female sex, and wearied from day to day with its repetition, agreed to bring the matter before Pluto. It was then resolved that the conclave of infernal princes should form a committee of inquiry, and should adopt such measures as might be deemed most advisable by the court

*Belphagor*

in order to discover the truth or falsehood of the calumnies which they heard. All being assembled in council, Pluto addressed them as follows: "Dearly beloved demons! though by celestial dispensation and the irreversible decree of fate this kingdom fell to my share, and I might strictly dispense with any kind of celestial or earthly responsibility, yet, as it is more prudent and respectful to consult the laws and to hear the opinion of others, I have resolved to be guided by your advice, particularly in a case that may chance to cast some imputation upon our government. For the souls of all men daily arriving in our kingdom still continue to lay the whole blame upon their wives, and as this appears to us impossible, we must be careful how we decide in such a business, lest we also should come in for a share of their abuse, on account of our too great severity; and yet judgment must be pronounced, lest we be taxed with negligence and with indifference to the interests of justice. Now, as the latter is the fault of a careless, and the former of an unjust judge, we, wishing to avoid the trouble and the blame that might attach to both, yet hardly seeing how to get clear of it, naturally enough apply to you for assistance, in order that you may look to it, and contrive in some way that, as we have hitherto reigned without the slightest imputation upon our character, we may continue to do so for the future."

The affair appearing to be of the utmost importance to all the princes present, they first resolved that it was necessary to ascertain the truth, though they differed as to the best means of accomplishing this object. Some were of opinion that they ought to choose one or more from among themselves, who should be commissioned to pay a visit to the world, and in a human shape endeavour personally to ascertain how far such reports were grounded in truth. To many others it appeared that this might be done without so much trouble merely by compelling some of the wretched souls to confess the truth by the application of a variety of tortures. But the majority being in favour of a journey to the world, they abided by the former proposal. No one, however, being ambitious of undertaking such a task, it was resolved to leave the affair to chance. The lot fell upon the arch-devil Belphagor, who, previous to the Fall, had enjoyed the rank of archangel in a higher world. Though he received his commission with a very ill grace, he nevertheless felt himself constrained by Pluto's imperial mandate, and prepared to execute whatever had been determined upon in council. At the same time he took an oath to observe the tenor of his instructions, as they had been drawn up with all due solemnity and ceremony for the purpose of his mission. These were to the following effect:—*Imprimis*, that the better to promote the object in view, he should be furnished with a hundred thousand gold ducats; secondly, that he should make use of the utmost expedition in getting into the world; thirdly, that after assuming the human form he should enter into the marriage state; and lastly, that he should live with his wife for the space of ten years. At the expiration of this period, he was to feign death and return home, in order to acquaint his employers, by the fruits of experience, what really were the respective conveniences and inconveniences of matrimony. The conditions further ran, that during the said ten years he should be subject to all kinds of miseries and disasters, like the rest of mankind, such as poverty, prisons, and diseases into which men are apt to fall, unless, indeed, he could contrive by his own skill and ingenuity to avoid them.

Poor Belphagor, having signed these conditions and received the money, forthwith came into the world, and having set up his equipage, with a numerous train of servants, he made a very splendid entrance into Florence. He selected this city in preference to all others, as being most favourable for obtaining an usurious interest of his money; and having assumed the name of Roderigo, a native of Castile, he took a house in the suburbs of Ognissanti. And because he was unable to explain the instructions under which he acted, he gave out that he was a merchant, who having had poor prospects in Spain, had gone to Syria, and succeeded in acquiring his fortune at Aleppo, whence he had lastly set out for Italy, with the intention of marrying and settling there, as one of the most polished and agreeable countries he knew.

Roderigo was certainly a very handsome man, apparently about thirty years of age, and he lived in a style of life that showed he was in pretty easy circumstances, if not possessed of immense wealth. Being, moreover, extremely affable and liberal, he soon attracted the notice of many noble citizens blessed with large families of daughters and small incomes. The former of these were soon offered to him, from among whom Roderigo chose a very beautiful girl of the name of Onesta, a daughter of Amerigo Donati, who had also three sons, all grown up, and three more daughters, also nearly marriageable. Though of a noble family and enjoying a good reputation in Florence, his father-in-law was extremely poor, and maintained as poor an establishment. Roderigo, therefore, made very splendid nuptials, and omitted nothing that might tend to confer honour upon such a festival, being liable, under the law which he received on leaving his infernal abode, to feel all kinds of vain and earthly passions. He therefore soon began to enter into all the pomps and vanities of the world, and to aim at reputation and consideration among mankind, which put him to no little expense. But more than this, he had not long enjoyed the society of his beloved Onesta, before he became tenderly attached to her, and was unable to behold her suffer the slightest inquietude or vexation.

Now, along with her other gifts of beauty and nobility, the lady had brought into the house of Roderigo such an insufferable portion of pride, that in this respect Lucifer himself could not equal her; for her husband, who had experienced the effects of both, was at no loss to decide which was the most intolerable of the two. Yet it became infinitely worse when she discovered the extent of Roderigo's attachment to her, of which she availed herself to obtain an ascendancy over him and rule him with a rod of iron. Not content with this, when she found he would bear it, she continued to annoy him with all kinds of insults and taunts, in such a way as to give him the most indescribable pain and uneasiness. For what with the influence of her father, her brothers, her friends, and relatives, the duty of the matrimonial yoke, and the love he bore her, he suffered all for some time with the patience of a saint. It would be useless to recount the follies and extravagancies into which he ran in order to gratify her taste for dress, and every article of the newest fashion, in which our city, ever so variable in its nature, according to its usual habits, so much abounds. Yet, to live upon easy terms with her, he was obliged to do more than this; he had to assist his father-in-law in portioning off his other daughters; and she next asked him to furnish one of her brothers with goods to sail for the Levant, another with silks for the West, while a third was to be set up in a goldbeater's establishment at Florence. In such objects the greatest part of his fortune was soon consumed.

At length the Carnival season was at hand; the festival of St. John was to be celebrated, and the whole city, as usual, was in a ferment. Numbers of the noblest families were about to vie with each other in the splendour of their parties, and the Lady Onesta, being resolved not to be outshone by her acquaintance, insisted that Roderigo should exceed them all in the richness of their feasts. For the reasons above stated, he submitted to her will; nor, indeed, would he have scrupled at doing much more, however difficult it might have been, could he have flattered himself with a hope of preserving the peace and comfort of his household, and of awaiting quietly the consummation of his ruin. But this was not the case, inasmuch as the arrogant temper of his wife had grown to such a height of asperity by long indulgence, that he was at a loss in what way to act. His domestics, male and female, would no longer remain in the house, being unable to support for any length of time the intolerable life they led. The inconvenience which he suffered in consequence of having no one to whom he could intrust his affairs it is impossible to express. Even his own familiar devils, whom he had brought along with him, had already deserted him, choosing to return below rather than longer submit to the tyranny of his wife.

Left, then, to himself, amidst this turbulent and unhappy life, and having dissipated all the ready money he possessed, he was compelled to live upon the hopes of the returns expected from his ventures in the East and the West. Being still in good credit, in order to support his rank he resorted to bills of exchange; nor was it long before, accounts running against him, he found himself in the same situation as many other unhappy speculators in that market.

Just as his case became extremely delicate, there arrived sudden tidings both from East and West that one of his wife's brothers had dissipated the whole of Roderigo's profits in play, and that while the other was returning with a rich cargo uninsured, his ship had the misfortune to be wrecked, and he himself was lost. No sooner did this affair transpire than his creditors assembled, and supposing it must be all over with him, though their bills had not yet become due, they resolved to keep a strict watch over him in fear that he might abscond. Roderigo, on his part, thinking that there was no other remedy, and feeling how deeply he was bound by the Stygian law, determined at all hazards to make his escape. So taking horse one morning early, as he luckily lived near the Prato gate, in that direction he went off. His departure was soon known; the creditors were all in a bustle; the magistrates were applied to, and the officers of justice, along with a great part of the populace, were despatched in pursuit. Roderigo had hardly proceeded a mile before he heard this hue and cry, and the pursuers were soon so close at his heels that the only resource he had left was to abandon the highroad and take to the open country, with the hope of concealing himself in the fields. But finding himself unable to make way over the hedges and ditches, he left his horse and took to his heels, traversing fields of vines and canes, until he reached Peretola, where he entered the house of Matteo del Bricca, a labourer of Giovanna del Bene. Finding him at home, for he was busily providing fodder for his cattle, our hero earnestly entreated him to save him from the hands of his adversaries close behind, who would infallibly starve him to death in a dungeon, engaging that if Matteo would give him refuge, he would make him one of the richest men alive, and afford him such proofs of it before he took his leave as would convince him of the truth of what he said; and if he failed to do this, he was quite content that Matteo himself should deliver him into the hands of his enemies.

Now Matteo, although a rustic, was a man of courage, and concluding that he could not lose anything by the speculation, he gave him his hand and agreed to save him. He then thrust our hero under a heap of rubbish, completely enveloping him in weeds; so that when his pursuers arrived they found themselves quite at a loss, nor could they extract from Matteo the least information as to his appearance. In this dilemma there was nothing left for them but to proceed in the pursuit, which they continued for two days, and then returned, jaded and disappointed, to Florence. In the meanwhile, Matteo drew our hero from his hiding-place, and begged him to fulfil his engagement. To this his friend Roderigo replied: "I confess, brother, that I am under great obligations to you, and I mean to return them. To leave no doubt upon your mind, I will inform you who I am"; and he proceeded to acquaint him with all the particulars of the affair: how he had come into the world, and married, and run away. He next described to his preserver the way in which he might become rich, which was briefly as follows. As soon as Matteo should hear of some lady in the neighbourhood being said to be possessed, he was to conclude that it was Roderigo himself who had taken possession of her; and he gave him his word, at the same time, that he would never leave her until Matteo should come and conjure him to depart. In this way he might obtain what sum he pleased from the lady's friends for the price of exorcising her; and having mutually agreed upon this plan, Roderigo disappeared.

Not many days elapsed before it was reported in Florence that the daughter of Messer Ambrogio Amedei, a lady married to Buonajuto Tebalducci, was possessed by the devil. Her relations did not fail to apply every means usual on such occasions to expel him, such as making her wear upon her head St. Zanobi's cap, and the cloak of St. John of Gualberto; but these had only the effect of making Roderigo laugh. And to convince them that it was really a spirit that possessed her, and that it was no flight of the imagination, he made the young lady talk Latin, hold a philosophical dispute, and reveal the frailties of many of her acquaintance. He particularly accused a certain friar of having introduced a lady into his monastery in male attire, to the no small scandal of all who heard it, and the astonishment of the brotherhood. Messer Ambrogio found it impossible to silence him, and began to despair of his daughter's cure. But the news reaching Matteo, he lost no time in waiting upon Ambrogio, assuring him of his daughter's recovery on condition of his paying him five hundred florins, with which to purchase a farm at Peretola. To this Messer Ambrogio consented; and Matteo immediately ordered a number of masses to be said, after which he proceeded with some unmeaning ceremonies calculated to give solemnity to his task. Then approaching the young lady, he whispered in her ear: "Roderigo, it is Matteo that is come. So do as we agreed upon, and get out." Roderigo replied: "It is all well; but you have not asked enough to make you a rich man. So when I depart I will take possession of the daughter of Charles, king of Naples, and I will not leave her till you come. You may then demand whatever you please for your reward; and mind that you never trouble me again." And when he had said this, he went out of the lady, to the no small delight and amazement of the whole city of Florence.

It was not long again before the accident that had happened to the daughter of the king of Naples began to be buzzed about the country, and all the monkish remedies having been found to fail, the king, hearing of Matteo, sent for him from Florence. On arriving at Naples, Matteo, after a few ceremonies, performed the cure. Before leaving the princess, however, Roderigo said: "You see, Matteo, I have kept my promise and made a rich man of you, and I owe you nothing now. So, henceforward you will take care to keep out of my way, lest as I have hitherto done you some good, just the contrary should happen to you in future." Upon this Matteo thought it best to return to Florence, after receiving fifty thousand ducats from his majesty, in order to enjoy his riches in peace, and never once imagined that Roderigo would come in his way again. But in this he was deceived; for he soon heard that a daughter of Louis, king of France, was possessed by an evil spirit, which disturbed our friend Matteo not a little, thinking of his majesty's great authority and of what Roderigo had said. Hearing of Matteo's great skill, and finding no other remedy, the king despatched a messenger for him, whom Matteo contrived to send back with a variety of excuses. But this did not long avail him; the king applied to the Florentine council, and our hero was compelled to attend.

Arriving with no very pleasant sensations at Paris, he was introduced into the royal presence, when he assured his majesty that though it was true he had acquired some fame in the course of his demoniac practice, he could by no means always boast of success, and that some devils were of such a desperate character as not to pay the least attention to threats, enchantments, or even the exorcisms of religion itself. He would, nevertheless, do his majesty's pleasure, entreating at the same time to be held excused if it should happen to prove an obstinate case. To this the king made answer, that be the case what it might, he would certainly hang him if he did not succeed. It is impossible to describe poor Matteo's terror and perplexity on hearing these words; but at length mustering courage, he ordered the possessed princess to be brought into his presence. Approaching as usual close to her ear, he conjured Roderigo in the most humble terms, by all he had ever done for him, not to abandon him in such a dilemma, but to show some sense of gratitude for past services and to leave the princess. "Ah! thou traitorous villain!" cried Roderigo, "hast thou, indeed, ventured to meddle in this business? Dost thou boast thyself a rich man at my expense? I will now convince the world and thee of the extent of my power, both to give and to take away. I shall have the pleasure of seeing thee hanged before thou leavest this place." Poor Matteo finding there was no remedy, said nothing more, but, like a wise man, set his head to work in order to discover some other means of expelling the spirit; for which purpose he said to the king, "Sire, it is as I feared: there are certain spirits of so malignant a character that there is no keeping any terms with them, and this is one of them. However, I will make a last attempt, and I trust that it will succeed according to our wishes. If not, I am in your majesty's power, and I hope you will take compassion on my innocence. In the first place, I have to entreat that your majesty will order a large stage to be erected in the centre of the great square, such as will admit the nobility and clergy of the whole city. The stage ought to be adorned with all kinds of silks and with cloth of gold, and with an altar raised in the middle. To-morrow morning I would have your majesty, with your full train of lords and ecclesiastics in attendance, seated in order and in magnificent array, as spectators of the scene at the said place. There, after having celebrated solemn mass, the possessed princess must appear; but I have in particular to entreat that on one side of the square may be stationed a band of men with drums, trumpets, horns, tambours, bagpipes, cymbals, and kettle-drums, and all other kinds of instruments that make the most infernal noise. Now, when I take my hat off, let the whole band strike up, and approach with the most horrid uproar towards the stage. This, along with a few other secret remedies which I shall apply, will surely compel the spirit to depart."

These preparations were accordingly made by the royal command; and when the day, being Sunday morning, arrived, the stage was seen crowded with people of rank and the square with the people. Mass was celebrated, and the possessed princess conducted between two bishops, with a train of nobles, to the spot. Now, when Roderigo beheld so vast a concourse of people, together with all this awful preparation, he was almost struck dumb with astonishment, and said to himself, "I wonder what that cowardly wretch is thinking of doing now? Does he imagine I have never seen finer things than these in the regions above—ay! and more horrid things below? However, I will soon make him repent it, at all events." Matteo then approaching him, besought him to come out; but Roderigo replied, "Oh, you think you have done a fine thing now! What do you mean to do with all this trumpery? Can you escape my power, think you, in this way, or elude the vengeance of the king? Thou poltroon villain, I will have thee hanged for this!" And as Matteo continued the more to entreat him, his adversary still vilified him in the same strain. So Matteo, believing there was no time to be lost, made the sign with his hat, when all the musicians who had been stationed there for the purpose suddenly struck up a hideous din, and ringing a thousand peals, approached the spot. Roderigo pricked up his ears at the sound, quite at a loss what to think, and rather in a perturbed tone of voice he asked Matteo what it meant. To this the latter returned, apparently much alarmed: "Alas! dear Roderigo, it is your wife; she is coming for you!" It is impossible to give an idea of the anguish of Roderigo's mind and the strange alteration which his feelings underwent at that name. The moment the name of "wife" was pronounced, he had no longer presence of mind to consider whether it were probable, or even possible, that it could be her. Without replying a single word, he leaped out and fled in the utmost terror, leaving the lady to herself, and preferring rather to return to his infernal abode and render an account of his adventures, than run the risk of any further sufferings and vexations under the matrimonial yoke. And thus Belphagor again made his appearance in the infernal domains, bearing ample testimony to the evils introduced into a household by a wife; while Matteo, on his part, who knew more of the matter than the devil, returned triumphantly home, not a little proud of the victory he had achieved.

# ❦ Romeo and Juliet

## by LUIGI DA PORTO

Luigi da Porto (1486–1529) was a gentleman of the old nobility of Vicenza. He undertook a military career in the service of Venice; when only twenty-five he was seriously wounded and permanently paralyzed. Out of mere ennui he became a poet and scholar.

He was not the first to tell the story of the star-crossed lovers of Verona, but his version was the best known of its time. Shakespeare may have read it in translation; it is more likely that he took the plot from Arthur Brooke's narrative poem, *The Tragical History of Romeo and Juliet*, published in 1562.

The translation is taken from Thomas Roscoe's *Italian Novelists* (London, 1825). The story is presumed to be told by one Pellegrino, a Veronese fellow-soldier of da Porto.

AT THE period when Bartolommeo della Scala, a gentle and accomplished prince, presided over the destinies of our native place, a fine and beautiful tract of country, I frequently remember hearing my father say that there flourished two noble but rival families, whose exasperation against each other was carried to the utmost extreme. The name of one of these was the Cappelletti, that of the other the Montecchi; and it is believed that the descendants of the latter faction are now residing in Udino in the persons of Messer Niccolò and Messer Giovanni, who settled there by some strange chance under the title of Monticoli of Verona. They would appear, however, to have retained little of their ancient splendour and reputation beyond their courteous manners and demeanour. And although, on perusing several ancient chronicles, I have met with the names of the families, who are mentioned as united in the same cause, I shall merely touch upon their history as it was told to me in the following words, without deviating from the original authority.

Both families, we are told, were equally powerful and wealthy, abounding in friends and relatives, and highly favoured in Verona, under the above-mentioned prince. Whether of a private or a public nature, the feud which arose between them was of a very ferocious and fatal character, various partisans on both sides falling victims to its rage. Nor was it until weary of mutual wrongs, and awed by the repeated commands and entreaties of their prince, that they were induced to enter into such terms as to meet or to address each other peaceably without apprehension of further violence and bloodshed. But daily becoming more reconciled, it happened that a festival was to be given by Messer Antonio, the head of the house of the Cappelletti, a man of gay and joyous character, who made the most magnificent preparations to receive all the chief families in the city. At one of these assemblies there one evening appeared a youth of the Montecchi family, who followed thither some lady whom he was desirous, as lovers often are, of accompanying in person (no less than in mind) upon such occasions of general festivity. He had a noble and commanding person, with elegant and accomplished manners; and he had no sooner withdrawn his mask, screening himself in the character of a wood-nymph, than every eye was turned with admiration on his beauty, which appeared to surpass even that of the most beautiful ladies present. But he more especially attracted the attention of an only daughter of Messer Antonio, whose charms both of mind and person were unrivalled throughout the whole city. Such was the impression she received at his appearance, that from the moment their eyes first met she found that she was no longer mistress of her own feelings. She saw him retire into a distant part of the assembly, seldom coming forward either in the dance or in converse with others, bearing himself like one who kept a jealous watch over some beloved object whom he would fain have held aloof from the joyous scene. Such a thought struck a chill to her heart, as she had heard he was a youth of warm and animated manners.

About the approach of midnight, towards the conclusion of the ball, was struck up the dance of the torch, or of the hat, whichever we choose to call it, usually proposed with us before the breaking up of the feast. While the company stand round in a circle, each dancer takes his lady, and the lady him, changing partners as they please. As it went round, the noble youth was led out by a lady who chanced to place him near the enamored daughter of Cappelletti. On the other side of her stood a youth named Marcuccio Guercio, whose hand, ever cold to the touch, happened to come in contact with the fair lady's palm; and soon after Romeo Montecchi, being on her left hand, took it in his, as was customary. On which the lady, anxious to hear his voice, said, "Welcome to my side, Messer Romeo"; and he, observing her eyes were fixed upon his awaiting his reply, and delighted at the tone of her voice, returned, "How! am I indeed then welcome?"

"Yes, and I ought to thank you," she returned, smiling, "since my left hand is warmed by your touch, whilst that of Marcuccio freezes my right."

Assuming a little more confidence, Romeo again replied, "If your hand, lady, feels the warmth of mine, my heart no less has kindled warm at your eyes."

A short bright smile was the only answer to this, except that in a lower tone, as fearful of being seen or heard, she half whispered back, "I vow, O Romeo, there is no lady here whom I think nearly so handsome as you seem to me."

Fascinated by her sweet address, Romeo, with still greater warmth, replied, "Whatever I may be, I only wish you, sweet lady, to hold me ever at your service."

When the festival broke up, and Romeo had retired to his chamber, dwelling on the harsh usage of his former love, from whose eyes he had drunk softness mixed with too much scorn, he resolved to give his soul wholly, even to the fair foe of his father's house. She, on the other hand, had thought of little else since she left him than of the supreme felicity she should enjoy in obtaining so noble a youth for her lord. Yet when she reverted to the deadly enmity which had so long reigned between the two houses, her fears overpowered the gentler feelings of her soul, and unable wholly to subdue them, she inveighed against her own folly in the following words: "Wretch that I am! what enchantment thus drags me to my ruin? Without hope or guide, O how shall I escape? for Romeo loves me not. Alas! he perhaps feels nothing but hatred against our house, and would perhaps only seek my shame. And were it possible he should think of taking me for his wedded wife, my father would never consent to bestow my hand."

Then revolving other feelings in her mind, she flattered herself that their attachment might become the means of further reconciliation between the houses, even now wearied with their mutual feuds; and, "Oh!" she exclaimed, "what a blissful means of changing foes into relatives!" Fixed in this resolve, she again met Romeo with eyes of softness and regard. Mutually animated with equal ardour and admiration, the loved image was fixed so deeply in their imagination, that they could no longer refrain from seeing each other; and sometimes at the windows and sometimes in the church, they sought with avidity every occasion to express their mutual passion through their eyes, and neither of them seemed to enjoy rest out of the presence of the beloved object. But chiefly Romeo, fired at the sight of her exquisite charms and manners, braved all risks for the pleasure of having her near him; and he would frequently pass the greatest part of the night around her house, beneath her windows, or, scaling the walls, force his way to the balcony that commanded a view of her chamber, without the knowledge either of herself or others; and there he would sit for hours, gazing and listening his soul away, enamoured of her looks and voice. He would afterwards throw himself listlessly to sleep, careless of returning home, in the woods or in the roads.

But one evening, as love would have it, the moon shining out more brightly than usual, the adventurous Romeo was discovered by his lady, as she opened the casement, on the balcony. Imagining that it might be someone else, he retreated, when, catching a glimpse of his figure, she gently called to him, "Wherefore, O Romeo, come you hither?"

"It is the will of love: therefore do I come," he replied.

"And if you should be found here, Romeo, know you it will be sudden death?"

"Too well I do, dear lady; and I doubt not it will happen so some night, if you refuse me your aid. But as I must at some time die, wherever I may be, I would rather yield my breath here as near you as I dare, with whom I would ever choose to live, did Heaven and you consent."

To which words the lady replied, "Believe me, Romeo, it is not I who would forbid thee to remain honourably at my side; it is thou, and the enmity thou and thine bear us, that stand between us twain."

"Yet can I truly aver," replied the youth, "that the dearest hope I have long indulged has been to make you mine; and if you had equal wishes, on you alone it would rest to make me for ever yours: no hand of man, believe me, love, should sunder us again" On saying this, they agreed on further means to meet again, and converse much longer some future evening; and they retired, full of each other, to rest.

The noble youth having frequently in this way held appointments with her, one winter's evening, while the snow fell thick and fast about him, he called to her from the usual spot: "Ah, Juliet, Juliet! how long will you see me thus languishing in vain? Do you feel nothing for me, who through these cold nights, exposed to the stormy weather, wait on the cold ground to behold you?"

"Alas! alas! I do indeed pity you," returned a sweet voice, "but what would you that I should do? often have I besought you to go away."

"No, no," returned Romeo, "not away: and therefore, gentle lady, deign to give me refuge in your chamber from these bitter winds."

Turning towards him with a somewhat scornful voice, the lady reproached him: "Romeo, I love you as much as it is possible for woman to love; therefore it is that you ask me this; your worth has led me further than I ought to go. But, cruel as you are, if you dream that you can enjoy my love by long prevailing suit in the manner you imagine, lay such thoughts aside, for you deceive yourself, Montecchi. And as I will no longer see you nightly perilling your life for me, I frankly tell you, Romeo, that if you please to take me as I am, I will joyfully become your wife, giving myself up wholly to your will, ready to follow you over the world wherever you may think best."

"And this," replied the gentle youth, "is all I have so long wished; now then let it be done!"

"So let it be, even as you will," cried Juliet; "only permit the Friar Lorenzo da San Francesco, my confessor, first to knit our hands, if you wish me wholly and happily to become yours."

"Am I to suppose, then, that Friar Lorenzo, my love, is acquainted with the secret of your breast?"

"Yes, Romeo," returned Juliet, "and he will be ready to grant us what we request of him"; and here, having fixed upon the proper measures, they again took leave of each other.

The friar, who belonged to the minor order of Osservanza, was a very learned man, well skilled no less in natural than in magical arts, and was extremely intimate with Romeo, in whom he had found it necessary to confide on an occasion in which he might otherwise have forfeited his reputation, which he was very desirous of maintaining with the vulgar. He had fixed upon Romeo in his emergency, as the most brave and prudent gentleman he knew to trust with the affair he had in hand. To him only he unbosomed his whole soul; and Romeo, having now recourse to him in his turn, acquainted him with his resolution of making the lovely daughter of Messer Antonio as quickly as possible his wedded wife, and that they had together fixed upon him as the secret instrument and witness of their nuptials, and afterwards as the medium of their reconciliation with her father.

The friar immediately signified his consent, no less because he ventured not to oppose or disoblige the lover, than because he believed it might be attended with happy results; in which case he would be likely to derive great honour from the heads of both houses, as the means of their reconciliation. In the meanwhile, it being the season of Lent, the fair Juliet, under semblance of going to confession, sought the residence of Friar Francesco, and having entered into one of the confessionals made use of by the monks, she inquired for Lorenzo, who, hearing her voice, led her along after Romeo into the convent. Then closing the doors of the confessional, he removed an iron grate which had hitherto separated her from her lover, saying, "I have been always glad to see you, my daughter; but you will now be far dearer to me than ever if you wish to receive Messer Romeo here as your husband." To which Juliet answered that there was nothing she so much wished as that she might lawfully become his wife, and that she had therefore hastened thither, in order that before Heaven and him she might take those vows which love and honour required, and which the friar must witness, as her trust in him was great.

Then in the presence of the priest, who performed the ceremony under the seal of confession, Romeo espoused the fair young Juliet; and having concluded how they were to meet each other again at night, exchanging a single kiss, they took leave of the friar, who remained in the confessional awaiting the arrival of penitents. Having thus secretly obtained the object of their wishes, the youthful Romeo and his bride for many days enjoyed the most unalloyed felicity, hoping at the same time for a favourable occasion to become reconciled to her father, in acquainting him with their marriage.

But Fortune, as if envious of their supreme happiness, just at this time revived the old deadly feud between the houses in such a way, that in a few days, neither of them wishing to yield to the other, the Montecchi and the Cappelletti, meeting together, from words proceeded to blows. Desirous to avoid giving any mortal hurts to his sweet wife's relatives, Romeo had the sorrow of beholding his own party either wounded or driven from the streets, and incensed with passion against Tebaldo Cappelletti, the most formidable of his adversaries, he struck him dead at his feet with a single blow, and put his companions to flight, terrified at the loss of their chief. The homicide had been witnessed by too many to remain long a secret, and the complaint being brought before the Prince, the Cappelletti threw the blame exclusively on Romeo, who was sentenced by the council to perpetual banishment from Verona. It is easier for those who truly love to imagine than it is here to describe the sensations of the young bride on receiving these tidings. She wept long and bitterly, refusing to hear any consolation; and her grief was deepened by the reflection that she could share it with no one. Romeo, on the other hand, regretted leaving his country on her account alone, and resolving to take a sorrowful farewell of the object of all his soul's wishes, he had again recourse to the assistance of the friar, who despatched a faithful follower of Romeo's father to apprise his wife of the time and place of meeting, and thither she eagerly repaired.

Retiring together into the confessional, they there wept bitterly over their misfortune. The young bride at length, checking her tears, exclaimed in an accent of despair, "I cannot bear to live! What will my life be without you? Oh, let me fly with you; wherever you go I will follow, a faithful and loving servant. I will cast these long tresses away, and by none shall you be served so well, so truly, as by me."

"No, never let it be said," replied Romeo, "that you accompanied me in other guise than in that of a cherished and honoured bride. Yet were it not that I feel assured that our affairs will soon improve, and that the strife between our two families will very shortly cease, indeed I could not bear, my love, to leave you. We shall not long be divided, and my thoughts, sweet Juliet, will be ever with you. And should we not be quickly restored to each other, it will then be time to fix how we are to meet again." So, after having wept and embraced each other again and again, they tore themselves asunder, his wife entreating that he would remain as near her as possible, and by no means go so far as Rome or Florence.

After concealing himself for some time in the monastery of Friar Lorenzo, Romeo set out more dead than alive for Mantua, but not before he had agreed with the servant of the lady that he was to be informed, through the friar, of every particular that might occur during his absence; and he further instructed the servant, as he valued his protection and rewards, to obey his wife in the minutest things which she might require of him. After her husband had departed, she gave herself up a prey to the deepest grief, a grief so incessant as to leave its traces on her beauty, and attract the attention of her mother. She tenderly loved her daughter, and affectionately inquiring into the cause of her affliction, she merely received vague excuses in reply. "But you are always in tears, my daughter," she continued; "what is it that can affect you thus? Tell me, for you are dear to me as my own life, and if it depend upon me, you shall no longer weep." Then imagining that her daughter might probably wish to bestow her hand in marriage, yet be afraid of avowing her wishes, she determined to speak to her husband on the subject; and thus, in the hope of promoting her health and happiness, she pursued the very means that led to her destruction.

She informed Messer Antonio that she had observed, for many days past, that something was preying on their daughter's mind, that she was no longer like the same creature, and that although she had used every means to obtain her confidence as to the source of her affliction, it had been all in vain. She then urged her suspicions that Juliet perhaps wished to marry, but that, like a discreet girl as she certainly was, she was averse to declare her feelings. "So I think, Messer Antonio, we had better without more delay make choice for our daughter of a noble husband. Juliet has already completed her eighteenth year, on St. Euphemia's Day; and when they have advanced much beyond this period, the beauty of women, so far from improving, is rather on the wane. Besides," continued her mother, "it is not well to keep girls too long at home, though our Juliet has always been an excellent child. I am aware you have already fixed upon her dower, and we have nothing to do but to select a proper object for her love." Messer Antonio agreed with his lady, and highly commended the virtues and the prudence of his daughter. Not many days afterwards they proposed and entered into a treaty of marriage between the Count of Lodrone and their daughter. When it was on the point of being concluded, the lady, hoping to surprise her daughter with the agreeable tidings, bade her now rejoice, for that in a very few days she would be happily settled in marriage with a noble youth, and that she must no longer grieve, for it would take place with her father's consent and that of all her friends.

On hearing these words, Juliet burst into a flood of tears, while her mother endeavoured to console her with the hope of being happily settled in life within the course of eight days. "You will then become the wife of Count Lodrone; nay, do not weep, for it is really true: will you not be happy, Juliet, then?"

"No, no, my dear mother, I shall never be happy."

"Then what can be the matter with you? What do you want? Only tell me; I will do anything you wish."

"Then I would wish to die, mother; nothing else is left me now." Her mother then first became aware that she was the victim of some deep-seated passion, and saying little more, she left her. In the evening she related to her husband what had passed, at which he testified great displeasure, saying that it would be necessary to have the affair examined into before venturing to proceed further with the Count. And fearful lest any blame might attach to his family, he soon after sent for Juliet, with the intention of consulting her on the proposed marriage. "It is my wish, my dear Juliet, to form an honourable connection for you in marriage. Will you be satisfied with it?"

After remaining silent for some moments, his daughter replied, "No, dear father, I cannot be satisfied."

"Am I to suppose, then, that you wish to take the veil, daughter?"

"Indeed I know not what"—and with these words out gushed a flood of bitter tears.

"But this I know," returned her father, "you shall give your hand to Count Lodrone, and therefore trouble yourself no further."

"Never, never!" cried Juliet, still weeping bitterly. On this Messer Antonio threatened her with his heaviest displeasure did she again venture to dispute his will, commanding her immediately to reveal the cause of her unhappiness. And when he could obtain no other reply than sobs and tears, he quitted the apartment in a violent passion, unable to penetrate into her motives, leaving her with her mother alone.

The wretched bride had already acquainted the servant intrusted with their secret, whose name was Pietro, with everything which had passed between herself and her parents, taking him to witness that she would sooner die than become the wife of any lord but Romeo. And this the good Pietro had carefully conveyed through the friar to the ears of the banished man, who had written to her, encouraging her to persevere, and by no means to betray the secret of their love, as he was then taking measures, within less than ten days, to bear her from her father's house. Messer Antonio and his lady Giovanna being unable in the meanwhile, either by threats or kindness, to discover their daughter's objections to the marriage, or whether she was attached to another, determined to prosecute their design. "Weep no more, girl," cried her mother, "for married you shall be, though you were to take one of the Montecchi by the hand, which I am sure you will never be compelled to do!" Fresh sobs and tears at these words burst from the poor girl, which only served to hasten the preparations for their daughter's nuptials.

Her despair was terrible when she heard the day named, and calling upon death to save her, she rushed out of her chamber, and repairing as fast as possible to the convent of the friar, in whom, next to Romeo, she trusted, and from whom she had received tidings of her husband, she revealed to him the cause of her anguish, often interrupted by her tears. She then conjured him, by the friendship and obligations which he owed to Romeo, to assist her in this her utter need. "Alas! of what use can I be," replied the friar, "when your two houses are even now so violently opposed to each other?"

"But I know, father, that you are a learned and experienced man, and you can assist me in many ways if you please. If you should refuse me everything else, at least, however, grant me this. My nuptials are even now preparing in my father's palace; he is now gone out of the city to give orders at the villa on the Mantuan road, whither they are about to carry me, that I may there be compelled to receive the Count, without a chance of opposition, as he is to meet me on my arrival at the place. Give me, therefore, poison, to free me at once from the grief and shame of exposing the wife of Romeo to such a scene. Give me poison, or I will myself plunge a dagger into my bosom!"

The friar, on hearing these desperate intentions, and aware how deeply he was implicated with Romeo, who might become his worst enemy were he not in some way to obviate the danger, turning to Juliet, said, "You know, my daughter, that I confess a great portion of the people here, and am respected by all, no testament, no reconciliation taking place without my mediation. I am therefore careful of giving rise to any suspicions which might affect me, and should especially wish to conceal my interference in an affair like the present. I would not incur such a scandal for all the treasure in the world. But, as I am attached both to yourself and Romeo, I will exert myself in your favour in such a way as I believe no one ever before did. You must first, however, take a vow that you will never betray to others the secret I now intrust you with."

"Speak, speak boldly, father," cried Juliet, "and give me the poison, for I will inform nobody."

"I will give you no poison," returned the friar; "young and beautiful as you are, it would be too deep a sin. But if you possess courage to execute what I shall propose, I trust I may be able to deliver you safely into the hands of Romeo. You are aware that the family vault of the Cappelletti lies beyond this church in the cemetery of our convent. Now I will give you a certain powder, which, when you have taken it, will throw you into a deep slumber of eight and forty hours, and during that time you will be to all appearance dead, not even the most skilful physicians being able to detect a spark of life remaining. In this state you will be interred in the vault of the Cappelletti, and at a fitting season I will be in readiness to take you away, and bring you to my own cell, where you can stay until I go, which will not be long, to the chapter; after which, disguised in a monk's dress, I will bear you myself to your husband. But tell me, are you not afraid of being near the corpse of Tebaldo, your cousin, so recently interred in the same place?"

With serene and joyful looks the young bride returned, "No, father; for if by such means I can ever reach my Romeo, I would face not this alone, but the terrors of hell itself."

"This is well; let it be done," cried the friar; "but first write with your own hand an exact account of the whole affair to Romeo, lest by any mischance, supposing you dead, he may be impelled by his despair to do some desperate deed; for I am sure he is passionately attached to you. There are always some of my brethren who have occasion to go to Mantua, where your husband resides: let me have your letter to him, and I will send it by a faithful messenger."

Having said this, the good monk, without the interference of whose holy order we find no matters of importance transacted, leaving the lady in the confessional, returned to his cell, but soon came back bringing a small vase with the powder in it, saying, "Drink this, mixed with simple water, about midnight, and fear not. In two hours after it will begin to take effect, and I doubt not but our design will be crowned with success. But haste, and forget not to write the letter, as I have directed you, to Romeo, for it is of great importance." Securing the powder, the fair bride hastened joyfully home to her mother, saying, "Truly, dear mother, Friar Lorenzo is one of the best confessors in the world. He has so kindly advised me that I am quite recovered from my late unhappiness." Overjoyed on perceiving her daughter's cheerfulness, the Lady Giovanna replied, "And you shall return his kindness, my dear girl, with interest; his poor brethren shall never be in want of alms."

Juliet's recovered spirits now banished every suspicion from the mind of her parents of her previous attachment to another, and they believed that some unhappy incident had given rise to the strange and melancholy disposition they had observed. They would now have been glad to withdraw their promise of bestowing her hand upon the Count, but they had already proceeded so far that they could not, without much difficulty, retreat. Her lover was desirous that some one of his friends should see her; and her mother, Lady Giovanna, being somewhat delicate in her health, it was resolved that her daughter, accompanied by two of her aunts, should be carried to the villa at a short distance from the city—a step to which she made no opposition. She accordingly went; and imagining that her father would immediately on her arrival insist upon the marriage, she took care to secure the powder given to her by the friar. At the approach of midnight, calling one of her favourite maids, brought up with her from her childhood, she requested her to bring her a glass of water, observing that she felt very thirsty; and as she drank it in the presence of the maid and one of her aunts, she exclaimed that her father should never bestow her hand upon the Count against her own consent. These simple women, though they had observed her throw the powder into the water, which she said was to refresh her, suspected nothing further and went to rest.

When the servant had retired with the light, her young mistress rose from her bed, dressed herself, and again lay down, composing her decent limbs as if she were never more to rise, with her hands crossed upon her breast, awaiting the dreaded result. In little more than two hours she lay to all appearance dead, and in this state she was discovered the next morning. The maid and her aunt, unable to awake her, feeling that she was already quite cold, and recollecting the powder, the strange expressions she had used, and, above all, seeing her dressed, began to scream aloud, supposing her to have poisoned herself. On this, the cries of her own maid, who loved her, were terrible. "True, too true, dear lady: you said that your father should never marry you against your will. Alas! you asked me for the very water which was to occasion your death. Wretch that I am! And have you indeed left me, and left me thus? With my own hands I gave you the fatal cup, which, with yours, will have caused the death of your father, your mother, and us all. Ah! why did you not take me with you, who have always so dearly loved you in life?" And saying this she threw herself by the side of her young mistress, embracing her cold form.

Messer Antonio, hearing a violent uproar, hastened, trembling, to ascertain the cause, and the first object he beheld was his daughter stretched out in her chamber a corpse. Although he believed her gone beyond recovery, when he heard what she had drunk, he immediately sent to Verona for a very experienced physician, who having carefully observed and examined his daughter, declared that she had died of the effects of the poison more than six hours before.

The wretched father, on hearing his worst fears confirmed, was overwhelmed with grief; and the same tidings reaching the distracted mother, suddenly deprived her of all consciousness. When she was at length restored, she tore her hair, and calling upon her daughter's name, filled the air with her shrieks. "She is gone! the only sweet solace of my aged days. Cruel, cruel! thou hast left me without even giving thy poor mother a last farewell! At least I might have drunk thy last words and sighs, and closed thine eyes in peace. Let my women come about me, let them assist me, that I may die! if they have any pity left, they will kill me; far better so to die than of a lingering death of grief. O God! in Thy infinite mercy take me away, for my life will be a burden to me now!" Her women then came round her, and bore her to the couch, still weeping, and refusing all the consolation they could offer to her. The body of Juliet was in the meantime carried to Verona, and consigned with extraordinary ceremonies, amidst the lamentations of a numerous train of friends and relatives, to the vault in the cemetery of San Francesco, where the last rites to the dead were discharged.

The friar, having occasion to be absent from the city, had, according to his promise, confided Juliet's letter to Romeo to the hands of one of his brethren going to Mantua. On arriving, he called several times at the house without having the good fortune to meet with Romeo, and unwilling to trust such a letter to others, he retained it in his own hands, until Pietro, hearing of the death of Juliet, and not finding the friar in the city, resolved to bear the

unhappy tidings to his master. He arrived in Mantua the following night, and meeting with Romeo, who had not yet received
the letter from the priest, he related to him, with tears in his
eyes, the death of his young bride, whose burial he had himself
witnessed. The hue of death stole over the features of Romeo as
he proceeded with the sad story; and, drawing his sword, he was
about to stab himself on the spot, had he not been prevented by
force. "It is well," he cried, "but I shall not long survive the lady
of my soul, whom I value more than life! O Juliet, Juliet! it is
thy husband who doomed thee to death! I came not, as I promised, to bear thee from thy cruel father, whilst thou, to preserve
thy sweet faith unbroken, hast died for me; and shall I, through
fear of death, survive alone? No, this shall never be!" Then,
throwing a dark cloak which he wore over Pietro's shoulders, he
cried, "Away, away! leave me!"

Romeo closed the doors after him, and preferring every other
evil to that of life, only considered the best manner of getting rid
of it. At last he assumed the dress of a peasant, and taking out a
species of poison which he had always carried with him, to use in
case of emergency, he placed it under the sleeve of his coat, and
immediately set out on his return to Verona. Journeying on with
wild and melancholy thoughts, he now defied his fate, hoping to
fall by the hands of justice, or to lay himself down in the vault
by the side of her he loved and die.

In this resolution, on the evening of the following day after her
interment, he arrived at Verona without being discovered by anyone. The same night, as soon as the city became hushed, he resorted to the convent of the Frati Minori, where the tombs of the
Cappelletti lay. The church was situated in the Cittadella, where
the monks at that time resided, although, for some reason, they
have since left it for the suburb of San Zeno, now called Santo
Bernardino, and the Cittadella was formerly, indeed, inhabited by
San Francesco himself. Near the outer walls of this place there
were then placed a number of large monuments such as we see
round many churches, and beneath one of these was the ancient
sepulchre of all the Cappelletti, in which the beautiful bride then

lay. Romeo approaching near not long after midnight, and possessing great strength, removed the heavy covering by force, and with some wooden stakes which he had brought with him, he propped it up to prevent it from closing again until he wished it; and he then entered the tomb and replaced the covering. The lamp he carried cast a lurid light around, while his eyes wandered in search of the loved object, which, bursting open the living tomb, he quickly found. He beheld the features of the beautiful Juliet now mingled with a heap of lifeless dust and bones, on which a sudden tide of sorrow sprung into his eyes, and amidst bitter sobs he thus spoke: "O eyes, which while our loves to Heaven were dear, shone sweetly upon mine! O sweeter mouth, a thousand and a thousand times so fondly kissed by me alone, and rich in honeyed words! O bosom, in which my whole heart lay treasured up, alas! all closed and mute and cold I find ye now! My hapless wife, what hath love done for thee, but led thee hither? And why so soon two wretched lovers perish? I had not looked for this when hope and passion first whispered of other things. But I have lived to witness even this!" and he pressed his lips to her mouth and bosom, mingling his kisses with his tears. "Walls of the dead!" he cried, "why fall ye not around me and crush me into dust? Yet, as death is in the power of all, it is a despicable thing to wish yet fear it too."

Then taking out the poison from under his vest, he thus continued: "By what strange fatality am I brought to die in the sepulchre of my enemies, some of whom this hand hath slain? But as it is pleasant to die near those we love, now, my beloved, let me die!" Then seizing the fatal vial, he poured its whole contents into his frame, and catching the fair body of Juliet in his arms in a wild embrace, "Still so sweet," he cried, "dear limbs, mine, only mine! And if yet thy pure spirit live, my Juliet, let it look from its seat of bliss to witness and forgive my cruel death; as I could not delighted live with thee, it is not forbidden me with thee to die"; and winding his arms about her, he awaited his final doom.

The hour was now arrived when, the vital powers of the slumbering lady reviving, and subduing the icy coldness of the poison, she would awake. Thus straitly folded in the last embraces of Romeo, she suddenly recovered her senses, and uttering a deep sigh, she cried, "Alas! where am I? in whose arms, whose kisses? Oh, unbind me, wretch that I am! Base friar, is it thus you keep your word to Romeo, thus lead me to his arms?" Great was her husband's surprise to feel Juliet alive in his embrace. Recalling the idea of Pygmalion, "Do you know me, sweet wife?" he cried. "It is your love, your Romeo, hither come to die with you. I came alone and secretly from Mantua to find your place of rest."

Finding herself within the sepulchre and in the arms of Romeo, Juliet would not at first give credit to her senses; but, springing out of his arms, gazed a moment eagerly on his face, and the next fell on his neck with a torrent of tears and kisses. "O Romeo, Romeo! what madness brings you hither? Were not my letters which I sent you by the friar enough to tell you of my feigned death, and that I should shortly be restored to you?"

The wretched youth, aware of the whole calamity, then gave loose to his despair. "Behold all other griefs that lovers ever bore, Romeo, thy lot has been! My life, my soul, I never had thy letters!" And he told her the piteous tale which he had heard from the lips of her servant, and that, concluding she was dead, he had hastened to keep her company, and had already drunk the deadly draught.

At these last words, his unhappy bride, uttering a wild scream, began to beat her breast and tear her hair, and then in a state of distraction she threw herself by the side of Romeo, already lying on the ground, and pouring over him a deluge of tears, imprinted her last kisses on his lips. All pale and trembling, she cried, "Oh, my Romeo! will you die in my sight, and I too the occasion of your death? Must I live even a moment after you? Ah, would that I could give my life for yours! Would that I alone might die!"

In a faint and dying tone her husband replied, "If my love and truth were ever dear to you, my Juliet, live, for my sake live; for it is sweet to know that you will then be often thinking of him who now dies for you, with his eyes still fixed on yours."

"Die! yes! you die for the death which in me was only feigned! What, therefore, should I do for this your real, cruel death? I only grieve that I have no means of accompanying you, and hate myself that I must linger on earth till I obtain them. But it shall not be long before the wretch who caused your death shall follow you"; and uttering these words with pain, she swooned away upon his body. On again reviving, she felt she was catching the last breath, which now came thick and fast, from the breast of her husband.

Friar Lorenzo, in the meanwhile, aware of the supposed death and of the interment of Juliet, and knowing that the termination of her slumber was near, proceeded with a faithful companion about an hour before sunrise to the monument. On approaching the place, he heard her sobs and cries, and saw the light of a lamp through an aperture in the sepulchre. Surprised at this, he imagined that Juliet must have secreted the light in the monument, and awaking and finding no one there, had thus began to weep and bewail herself. But on opening the sepulchre with the help of his companion, he beheld the weeping and distracted Juliet holding her dying husband in her arms, on which he immediately said, "What! did you think, my daughter, I should leave you here to die?"

To which she only answered with another burst of sorrow, "No! away! I only fear lest I should be made to live. Away, and close our sepulchre over our heads; here let me die. Or, in the name of pity, lend me a dagger, that I may strike it into my bosom and escape from my woes. Ah, cruel father! well hast thou fulfilled thy promise, well delivered to Romeo his letters, and wed me, and borne me safely to him! See, he is lying dead in my arms!" and she repeated the fatal tale.

Thunderstruck at these words, the friar gazed upon the dying Romeo, exclaiming with horror, "My friend, my Romeo! alas! what chance hath torn thee from us? Thy Juliet calls thee, Romeo, look up and hope. Thou art lying in her beauteous bosom and wilt not speak." On hearing her loved name, he raised his languid eyes, heavy with death, and fixing them on her for a short space, closed them again. The next moment, turning himself round upon his face in a last struggle, he expired.

Thus wretchedly fell the noble youth, long lamented over by his fair bride, till, on the approach of day, the friar tenderly inquired what she would wish to do. "To be left to die where I am," was the reply.

"Do not, daughter, say this, but come with me; for though I scarcely know in what way to proceed, I can perhaps find means of obtaining a refuge for you in some monastery, where you may address your prayers to Heaven for your own and for your husband's sake."

"I desire you to do nothing for me," replied Juliet; "except this one thing, which I trust, for the sake of his memory," pointing to the body of Romeo, "you will do. Never breathe a syllable to any one living of our unhappy death, that our bodies may rest here together for ever in peace. And should our sad loves come to light, I pray you will beseech both our parents to permit our remains to continue mingled together in this sepulchre, as in love and in death we were still one." Then turning again towards the body of Romeo, whose head she held sustained upon her lap, and whose eyes she had just closed, bathing his cold features with her tears, she addressed him as if he had been in life: "What shall I now do, my dear lord, since you have deserted me? What can I do but follow you? for nothing else is left me: death itself shall not keep me from you."

Having said this, and feeling the full weight of her irreparable loss in the death of her noble husband, resolute to die, she drew in her breath, and retaining it for some time, suddenly uttered a loud shriek and fell dead by her lover's side. The friar, perceiving that she was indeed dead, was seized with such a degree of terror and surprise, that, unable to come to any resolution, he sat down with his companion in the sepulcher bewailing the destiny of the lovers.

At this time some of the officers of the police, being in search of a notorious robber, arrived at the spot, and perceiving a light and the sound of voices, they straightway ran to the place, and seizing upon the priests, inquired into their business. Friar Lorenzo, recognising some of these men, was overpowered with shame and fear; but assuming a lofty voice, exclaimed, "Back, sirs, I am not the man you take me for. What you are in want of you must search for elsewhere."

Their conductor then came forward, saying, "We wish to be informed why the monument of the Cappelletti is thus violated by night, when a young lady of the family has been so recently interred here. And were I not acquainted with your excellent character, Friar Lorenzo, I should say you had come hither to despoil the dead."

The priests, having extinguished the lamp, then replied, "We shall not render an account of our business to you; it is not your affair."

"That is true," replied the other; "but I must report it to the Prince."

The friar, with a feeling of despair, then cried out, "Say what you please"; and closing up the entrance into the tomb, he went into the church with his companion.

The morning was somewhat advanced when the friars disengaged themselves from the officers, one of whom soon related to the Cappelletti the whole of this strange affair. They, knowing that Friar Lorenzo had been very intimate with Romeo, brought him before the Prince, entreating, that if there were no other means, he might be compelled by torture to confess his reason for opening the sepulchre of the Cappelletti. The Prince having placed him under a strict guard, proceeded to interrogate him wherefore he had visited the tomb of the Cappelletti, as he was resolved to discover the truth. "I will confess everything very freely," exclaimed the friar. "I was the confessor of the daughter of Messer Antonio, lately deceased in so very strange a manner. I loved her for her worth, and being compelled to be absent at the time of her interment, I went to offer up certain prayers over her remains, which when nine times repeated by my beads, have power to liberate her spirit from the pangs of purgatory. And because few appreciate or understand such matters, the wretches assert that I went there for the purpose of despoiling the body. But I trust I am better known. This poor gown and girdle are enough for me, and I would not take a mite from all the treasures of the earth, much less the shrouds of the departed. They do me great wrong to suspect me of this crime."

The Prince would have been satisfied with this explanation, had it not been for the interference of other monks, who, jealous of the friar, and hearing that he had been found in the monument, examined further, and found the dead body of Romeo, a fact which was immediately made known to the Prince while still speaking to the friar. This appeared incredible to every one present, and excited the utmost amazement through the city. The friar, then aware that it would be in vain further to conceal his knowledge of the affair, fell at the feet of his Excellency, crying, "Pardon, oh pardon, most noble Prince! I have said what is not truth, yet neither for any evil purpose nor for love of gain have I said it, but to preserve my faith entire, which I promised to two deceased and unhappy lovers."

On this the friar was compelled to repreat the whole of the preceding tale. The Prince, moved almost to tears as he listened, set out with a vast train of people to the monument of the family, and having ordered the bodies of the lovers to be placed in the Church of San Francesco, he summoned their fathers and friends to attend. There was now a fresh burst of sorrow springing from a double source. Although the parties had been the bitterest enemies, they embraced one another in tears, and the scene before them suddenly wrought that change in their hearts and feelings which neither the threats of their Prince nor the prayers of their friends had been able to accomplish. Their hatred became extinguished in the mingled blood of their unhappy children. A noble monument was erected to their memory, on which was inscribed the occasion of their death, and their bodies were entombed together with great splendor and solemnity, and wept over no less by their friends and relatives than by the whole afflicted city. Such a fearful close had the loves of Romeo and Juliet, such as you have heard, and as it was related to me by Pellegrino da Verona.

# ❦ An Adventure of Francesco Sforza

## by STRAPAROLA

Giovanni Francesco Straparola came from Caravaggio, a village not far from Milan. The name Straparola (the Gabbler) may have been a pseudonym or a nickname. The date of his birth is unknown.

His *Piacevoli notti* ("Jolly Evenings") was printed in 1550; Straparola died in 1557. The book reports the diversions of a house-party in Murano, an island in the bay of Venice, during the carnival of 1536. The ladies and gentlemen amused themselves with music, dance, puzzle-solving, and storytelling. Many of the stories are traditional; others are new, at least to us. The translations, by W. G. Waters, appeared in London in 1894. This story is the third *novella* in the "Ninth Evening."

IN THESE our times there lived in Milan Signor Francesco Sforza, the son of Lodovico Moro, the ruler of the city, a youth who, both during the lifetime of his father and after his death suffered much from the bolts of envious fortune. In his early youth Signor Francesco was of graceful figure, of courtly manners, with a face which gave fair token of his righteous inclinations, and when he was come to that age which marks the full bloom of youth—his studies and all the other becoming exercises being finished—he gave himself up to the practice of arms, to throwing the lance and following the chase, gathering from this manner of life no little pleasure. Wherefore, on account of his converse and of his prowess in manly exercises, all the young men of the city held him in great affection, and he, on his part, was equally well disposed towards them. In sooth, there was no youth at all in the city who did not partake in a share of his bounty.

One morning the Signor Francesco gathered together for his pleasure a goodly company of young men, of whom not one had yet reached his twentieth year, and, having mounted his horse, rode away with them to follow the chase. And when they had come to a certain thicket, which was well known as the haunt of wild animals, they surrounded it on all sides, and soon it chanced that, on the side of the wood where Signor Francesco was keeping a vigilant watch, there broke forth a very fine stag, which, as soon as it beheld the hunters, fled away from them in terror. Francesco, who had the heart of a lion, and was likewise a perfect horseman, no sooner marked how rapid was the flight of the stag than he struck his spurs deep into his horse's sides and dashed away impetuously in pursuit, and so long and so far did he follow it that, having outridden all his companions, he found he had missed his way. Then, because he had lost sight of the stag, he gave up the pursuit, not knowing where he was or whither he should turn. Finding himself left alone and far away from the high road, and wotting nought as to how he should make his way back thereto—seeing that the dark shadows of night were fast gathering around—he lost his wits somewhat, and was in no small fear lest there should happen to him some mischance which would not be to his taste. And so indeed it fell out.

Signor Francesco took his way onward and onward through the dubious paths, and finally came upon a small cottage with a roof of straw, and of very mean and ill aspect. Having ridden into the yard he got down from his horse, which he made fast to the fence which was built around, and straightway went into the cottage, where he found an old man, whose years must have numbered ninety at least, and by his side was a young peasant woman, very fair to look upon, who held in her arms a five-year-old child, to whom she was giving nourishment. Signor Francesco, having made polite salutation to the old man and the young peasant woman, sat down with them and asked them whether of their kindness they would be willing to give him shelter and lodging for the night, not letting them know, however, who he was.

The old man and the young woman, who was his daughter-in-law, when they saw that the youth was of high station and of graceful seeming, willingly made him welcome, putting forth many excuses the while that they had no place for his accommodation at all worthy of his condition. Francesco, having thanked them heartily, went out of the cottage to have care for his horse, and after he had duly seen to its wants he entered once more. The child, who was very lovesome, ran up to the gentleman's side with all manner of affectionate greeting and covered him with caresses, and Francesco on his part kissed the little one with many soft words and blandishments. While Signor Francesco was standing talking in familiar wise with the greybeard and his daughter-in-law, Malacarne, the son of the old man and the husband of the young woman, came home, and having entered the cottage, espied the gentleman who was chatting with the old man and caressing the child. He bade Signor Francesco good evening, getting a courteous return of his greeting, and gave orders to his wife that she should forthwith get ready the supper.

The master of the house then addressed Signor Francesco and begged to know what was the reason which had brought him into so savage and desert a place, and to this question the youth by way of explanation replied, "Good brother, the reason why I have come to this place is simply because, finding myself alone upon my journey at the fall of the night, and not knowing whither to betake myself through being somewhat ill-informed as to the features of this country, I discovered by good luck this little cottage of yours, into which this good old father and your wife in their kindness bade me enter." Malacarne, as he listened to the speech of the youth and marked how richly he was attired, and how he wore a fine chain of gold about his neck, of a sudden conceived a design against Francesco, and made up his mind, at all hazard, to first slay and then despoil him. Therefore, being firmly set upon carrying out this diabolical project of his, he called together his old father and his wife, and, having taken the child in his arms, went forth from the cottage. Then, when he had drawn them aside somewhat, he made with them a compact to slay the youth, and after they should have taken off from him his rich raiment to bury his body in the fields, persuading themselves that, when this should be done, no further report would ever be heard of him.

But God, who is altogether just, would not suffer these wicked schemings to come to the issue the miscreants desired, but brought all their secret design to light. As soon as the compact was finally made and their evil plans fully determined, it came into Malacarne's mind that he by himself alone would never be able to carry out the plan they had formed. And, besides this, his father was old and decayed, and his wife a woman of little courage, and the youth, as Malacarne had already remarked, seemed to be gifted with a stout heart, and one who would assuredly make a good fight for his life, and perhaps escape out of their hands. On this account he resolved to repair to a certain place, not far distant from his cottage, and to enlist the services of three other ruffians well known to him who dwelt there, and then, with their aid, fully carry out his design. As soon as these three worthies understood what he would have them do, they at once consented to follow him, greedy of the gain he promised them, and having caught up their weapons, they all went to Malacarne's cottage.

There the child, having left the place where her mother and grandfather were together, returned to Francesco and gave him greetings and caresses more lovesome even than before, whereupon the young man, observing the very loving ways the little one used towards him, took her in his arms and caressed her tenderly and kissed her again and again. The child, seeing the glitter of the chain of gold about his neck, and being greatly delighted therewith (as is the manner often with children), laid hands upon the chain and showed that she would fain have it round her own neck. Signor Francesco, when he saw what great delight the child took in the chain, said to her as he caressed her, "See here, my little one, I will give you this for your own." And with these words he put it about her neck. The child, who had by some means or other become privy to the business that was afoot, said to Francesco without further words, "But it would have been mine all the same without your having given it to me, because my father and mother are going to kill you and to take away all you have." Francesco, who was of a shrewd and wary temper, as soon as he realized from the words of the child the wicked designs which were being woven against him, did not let the warning pass unheeded, but prudently holding his peace he rose up from his seat, carrying the child in his arms, having the collar about her neck, and laid her down upon a little bed, whereupon she, because the hour was now late, forthwith fell asleep. Then Signor Francesco shut himself close in the cottage, and, having made secure the entrance by piling up against the door two large chests of wood, awaited courageously to see what the ruffians without might do next. Then he drew from his side a small firearm, having five barrels, which might be discharged all together or one by one, according to will.

As soon as the young gentlemen who had ridden a-hunting with Signor Francesco found that he had strayed away from their company without leaving any trace to tell them whither he might be gone, they began to give signal to him by sounding their horns and shouting, but no reply came back to them. And on this account they began to be greatly afeared lest the horse he rode might have fallen amongst the loose rocks, and that their lord might be lying dead or perhaps eaten by wild beasts. While the young courtiers were thus standing all terror-stricken, and knowing not which way to turn, one of the company at last cried out, "I marked Signor Francesco following a stag along this forest path, and taking his course towards that wide valley, but, seeing that the horse he rode was swifter in its pace by far than mine, I could not hold him in sight, nor could I tell whither he went." As soon as the others heard and understood this speech, they at once set out on their quest, following the slot of the stag all through the night in the anticipation of finding Signor Francesco either dead or alive.

While the young men were thus riding through the woods, Malacarne, accompanied by the three villains his comrades, was making his way back towards his house. They deemed that they would be able to enter therein without hindrance, but on approaching the door they found it fast shut. Then Malacarne kicked at it with his foot and said, "Open to me, good friend. Why is it you keep thus closed the door of my house?" Signor Francesco kept silence and gave not a word in reply; but, peeping through a crevice, he espied Malacarne, who carried an axe upon his shoulder, and the three other ruffians with him fully armed. He had already charged his firearm, and now, without further tarrying, he put it to the crevice of the door and let off one of the barrels, striking one of the three miscreants in the breast in such fashion that he fell dead to the ground forthwith, without finding time to confess his sins. Malacarne, when he perceived what had happened, began to hack violently at the door with his axe in order to bring it down, but this intent he was unable to carry out, seeing that it was secured on the other side. Francesco again discharged his pistolet with such good fortune that he disabled another of the band by shooting him in the right arm. Whereupon those who were yet left alive were so hotly inflamed with anger that they worked with all their force to break open the door, making the while such a hideous rout that it seemed as if the world must be coming to an end. Francesco, who felt no small terror at the strait in which he was placed, set to work to strengthen yet further the door by piling up against it all the stools and benches he could find.

Now it is well known that, the brighter and finer the night, the more still and silent it is, and a single word, though it be spoken a long way off, may at such times be easily heard; wherefore on this account the hurlyburly made by these ruffians came to the ears of Francesco's companions. They at once closed their ranks, and, giving their horses free rein, quickly arrived at the spot from whence came the uproar, and saw the assassins labouring hard to break down the door. One of the company of young gentlemen at once questioned them what might be the meaning of all the turmoil and uproar they were making, and to this Malacarne made answer: "Signori, I will tell you straightway. This evening, when I came back to my cottage weary with toil, I found there a young soldier, a lusty fellow full of life. And for the reason that he attempted to kill my old father, and to ravish my wife, and to carry off my child, and to despoil me of all my goods, I took to flight, as I was in no condition to defend myself. Then, seeing to what sore strait I was reduced, I betook myself to the dwellings of certain of my friends and kinsmen, and besought them to give me their aid; but, when we returned to my cottage, we found the door shut and so strongly barricaded within that there was no making entrance, unless we should first break down the door. And not satisfied with outraging my wife, he has also (as you may well see) slain with his firearm one of my friends and wounded another to death. Wherefore, finding it beyond my endurance to put up with such ill-handling as this, I have made up my mind to lay hands on him dead or alive."

The young men in attendance upon Signor Francesco, perceiving what had happened, and believing Malacarne's tale to be true on account of the dead body lying on the ground before them and of the other man gravely wounded, were moved to pity, and having dismounted from their horses, cried out loud, "Ah, traitor and enemy of God, open the door at once! What is it you are doing? In sooth you shall suffer the penalty due to your misdeeds." To this Francesco answered nought, but carefully and dexterously went on strengthening the door on the inside, knowing not that his friends stood without. And while the young men went on with their battering without being able, in spite of all the force they used, to open the door, a certain one of them, having gone a little apart, espied in the yard a horse tied to the fence, and, as soon as he had drawn anigh thereto, he knew it to be the horse of Signor Francesco, so he cried out in a loud voice, "Hold off, my comrades, and let go the work you are about, because our master is surely within there"; and with these words he pointed out to them the horse tied to the fence. The young men, as soon as they saw and recognized the horse, were at once convinced that Signor Francesco was shut up within the cottage, and straightway they called upon him by name, rejoicing greatly the while. Francesco, when he heard himself thus called, knew that his friends were at hand, and, being now freed from all dread of his life, he cleared away his defences from the door and opened it.

And when they heard the reason why he had shut himself up so closely, they seized the two ruffians, and, having bound them securely, carried them back to Milan, where, after they had first been tormented with burning pincers, they were torn in quarters, while living, by four horses. The little child by whose agency the nefarious plot was found out was called Verginea, and her Signor Francesco gave in charge to the duchess, in order that she might be well and carefully brought up. And when she had come to an age ripe for marriage, as a reward for the great service she had rendered to Signor Francesco she was amply dowered and honourably given in marriage to a gentleman of noble descent. And after this they gave her in addition the castle of Binasio, situated between Milan and Pavia, which in this our day has been so sorely vexed by continual broils and attacks that of it there hardly remains one stone on another. And in this sad and terrible fashion the murderous thieves made a wretched end, while the damsel and her husband lived many years in great happiness.

# ❦ The Will of the Wicked Usurer
by STRAPAROLA

This story is the fourth *novella* of the "Tenth Evening" of
the *Piacevoli notti*. The translation of this, as of the preceding
story, is by W. G. Waters.

THERE IS a well-used proverb that a bad end waits upon
every bad life, and for this reason it is far wiser to live pi-
ously, as a good man should, than to give a loose rein to one's
conscience, and, without forethought, to work one's will unre-
strained, as did a certain noble citizen who, when nearing his latter end, bequeathed his soul to the enemy of mankind, and then
in despair (as was the will of divine justice) made an evil end.

In Como, one of the lesser cities of Lombardy, not far distant
from Milan, there once dwelt a citizen called Andrigetto di Val
Sabbia, who, though he was rich beyond any other man in Como
in goods and heritages and land and cattle, paid so little heed to
his conscience that he was ever prompt to rise early in the morning to undertake some fresh wickedness. His granaries were filled
with all sorts of corn, the product of his farms, and it was his custom to peddle this away to the neighbouring peasants, in lieu of
selling it to the merchants or to those who came with money in
their hands; not being urged to this course by any compassion towards the poor, but rather designing thereby to snatch away
from them any little bit of land which yet remained to them, and
add it to his own, seeking always to gain his end in order that he
might, little by little, get all the land round about into his own
possession.

One certain year it happened that the country was afflicted by
a grievous famine, so that in many places men and women and
children died of hunger, and for this reason peasants from all the
neighbouring parts, both from the mountains and the plains, be-

took themselves to Andrigetto, this one offering to let him have a meadow, that one a ploughed field, and the other a track of woodland, in exchange for corn and other provisions to serve their present need. And the crowd of people about Andrigetto's house, coming from all parts, was so great that one might well have believed the year of Jubilee was come.

There was living at that time in Como a notary, Tonisto Raspante by name, a man highly skilled in his calling, and one who far out-distanced all others of his craft in the address he showed in wringing the last coin out of the peasant's purse. Now one of the laws of Como forbade a notary to draw up any instrument of sale unless the money for the same should first have been counted over in his presence and in the presence of divers witnesses, and for this reason Tonisto Raspante, who had no mind to bring himself within reach of legal penalty, had more than once remonstrated with Andrigetto when the old usurer had required him to draw up contracts of sale which were contrary to the form of the statute of Como; but Andrigetto would heap foul abuse upon him, and even threaten his life if he persisted in his refusal. And because the usurer was a man of weight, a leading citizen, and one moreover who frequented assiduously the shrine of Saint Moneybags, the notary dared not run counter to his will, but drew up the illegal contracts as he was commanded.

Just before the advent of a certain season when Andrigetto was wont always to go to confession, he sent to his confessor enough good cheer to give himself a sumptuous feast, and fine cloth enough to make hose for himself and for his servant as well, bidding him at the same time to keep himself in readiness on the morrow at the confessional. The priest, for the reason that Andrigetto was a man of wealth and of great weight in the city, took due heed of these words, and when he saw his penitent approaching made him dutiful obeisance, and prepared to receive his confession; whereupon Andrigetto, kneeling down and charging himself narrowly with divers transgressions, at last stumbled upon the sin of avarice, and laid bare in detail the history of all those illegal contracts he had made. The priest, who had read enough to know that these contracts were unlawful and usurious, began respectfully to take Andrigetto to task, pointing out to him that it was his duty to make restitution; but Andrigetto, who took his interference in very ill part, replied that the priest knew not what he was talking about, and that it behoved him to go and learn his duty. Now it was Andrigetto's habit often to send presents to the priest, who, fearing he might lose custom should the usurer resort to some other confessor, forthwith granted him absolution, with a light penance therewith, and Andrigetto, having thrust a crown into his hand, took his leave and departed with a light heart.

It chanced that soon after this Andrigetto was smitten with a malady so severe that he was given up by all the physicians. His relations and friends, perceiving by the report of the doctors that his disease was incurable, urged him to make his will, to regulate his affairs, and to confess himself according to the ways of all good Catholics and Christians; but he, who was altogether given up to avarice, and was accustomed night and day to think of nought else than how he might pile up more riches, took no thought of death, and put far away from him all those who would talk of such matter, causing rather to be brought to him now this and now that of his prized possessions, and taking delight in the handling thereof. But his friends were very pressing on his account; so to content them he let them summon Tonisto Raspante, his notary, and Messer Pre Neofito, his worthy confessor, in order that he might confess and settle his worldly affairs. When these two had come into his presence they saluted him, and asked him how he was, and prayed to God to give him back his health, exhorting him at the same time to take courage, for with God's help he might soon be himself again; but the sick man replied that he felt much worse, for which reason he desired now to make his will and to confess. Then the priest, turning his discourse to matters of faith, admonished him that he should be mindful of God and bow to His holy will, by which means there would be granted to him the restoration of his bodily health.

This done, Andrigetto directed them to bring in seven men to be witnesses of his will. When these were come he said to the notary, "Tonisto, how much do you charge for every will you draw?"

"The law allows us a florin," Tonisto answered; "but we receive sometimes more, sometimes less, according to the wish of the testator."

Then Andrigetto went on: "See, here are two florins, which I give you on condition that you set down everything I direct you to write."

The notary agreed to these terms, and, having invoked the name of God, and inscribed the year, and the month, and the day, according to the manner of his calling, began to write in these terms: "I, Andrigetto di Val Sabbia, being of sound mind though infirm of body, bequeath and recommend my soul to God my creator, whom I thank with all my heart for the many benefits which He has showered upon me during this life."

But Andrigetto, interrupting him, said: "What is it you have written there?" whereupon the notary replied, "I have written this and that," and told him word for word what he had set down. Then Andrigetto, in a passion of rage, cried out, "And who told you to write in such terms? Why do you not keep the promise you made me? Now write down what I tell you—I, Andrigetto di Val Sabbia, infirm of body but sound in mind, bequeath and recommend my soul to the devil of hell."

The notary and the witnesses, when they heard these words, stood aghast, and, turning to the testator, said to him: "Alas! Signor Andrigetto, what has become of your good sense and your ordinary prudence? Surely these are the words of a madman. Have done with such folly, for the love of God, as well as with such sins against your good name, which must bring scandal and disgrace upon all your family. Remember also that all those who up to this time have rated you as a wise and prudent man will set you down as the most wicked and mischievous traitor nature ever brought forth, if you thus cast behind you all your well-being and salvation; and, indeed, if you thus despise your own welfare and profit, how much more will you despise the welfare and profit of others!"

In answer to this Andrigetto, whose rage was now as hot as a burning brazier, replied, "How? Have I not commanded you to write exactly what I shall tell you, and have I not paid you beyond your due to do this?" To this question the notary replied affirmatively. "Then put down," said the testator, "the things I tell you, and not those I have no mind for."

The poor notary would fain have been quit of the whole business, seeing how savage was the old man's humour; nevertheless, fearing lest he might die in a fit brought on by his anger, he wrote all that was dictated to him. Then said Andrigetto to the notary, "Write this—Item, I leave to the devil also the soul of Tonisto Raspante, my notary, in order that I may have company when I depart from this world."

"Ah, Messer Andrigetto," cried the notary, "you are doing me a great injury, and putting an affront on my honour and good name."

"Go on with your writing, rascal," cried the testator, "nor trouble me more than I am troubled already. I have given you double fee to write according to my wish; so write as I shall direct you. 'For if he had not so readily endorsed my knavish suggestions, and drawn up so many unlawful and usurious contracts, but had driven me from his presence forthwith, I should not now find myself taken in this snare. And because in time past he set more store on my payments to him than on my soul, or his own, I once more give and commend him to Lucifer.'"

The poor notary, fearing that yet worse might befall him, wrote down all the foregoing words, and then Andrigetto went on: "Write now—Item, I bequeath now the soul of Pre Neofito, my confessor, to be tormented by sixty thousand devils."

"What is this you say, Signor Andrigetto?" interrupted the priest. "Are these the words of a sober man such as you have always been held to be? Good God, recall what you have said. Know you not that our Lord Jesus Christ is merciful, with arms of pity always open, provided that the sinner be convinced of his offences, and repents and acknowledges his transgressions. Acknowledge, therefore, the grave and enormous sins you have committed, and pray God for His mercy, and He will plentifully pardon you. The means are at hand, and you have yet time to re-

store what you have of other men's goods; and, if due restitution
be made, God, who is all merciful and willeth not the death of a
sinner, will pardon you, and receive you into paradise."

Then Andrigetto answered, "Wicked apostate priest, destroyer
of my soul and of your own as well, man full of greed and simony! Fine counsel this, to give at such a time! Write, notary—
I consign his soul to the centre of the pit; because, had he not
been such a pestilential avaricious knave, he would not have been
ever ready to absolve me from my sin, and then I should not have
committed so many offences, nor should I find myself brought
to my present state. What? does it seem honest and fitting that I
should now strip myself of my wealth, ill-acquired though it be,
and leave my children vagabonds and poor? No! keep counsel
such as this for those whom it may profit. I will have nought to
say to it. And, notary, write this also—Item, I leave to Felicita,
my mistress, my farm in the village of Comachio, in order that
she may be furnished with sustenance and raiment, and be able,
from time to time, to take pleasure with her lovers as she has always done hitherto, and, when her life shall be finished, to come
to me in the pit of hell and be tormented eternally with us three.
And as to all my other goods, personal or otherwise, present or
to come, I give them to my two legitimate sons, Comodo and
Torquato, exhorting them to waste nothing of my estate in paying for masses, or matins, or vigils, or de profundises on my
behalf, but rather to pass their time in gambling, wenching, drinking, brawling, fighting, and in all other nefarious and detestable
courses, so that my goods, having been badly gotten, may in
brief time be spent in like manner, and that my sons, when they
shall be left bare, may hang themselves in despair. And this I declare to be my last will, and I call upon you all to witness it."

When the will was written and executed, Andrigetto turned
his face to the wall, and, with a roar like that of a bull, gave up
his soul to Pluto, who had long been waiting for it. Thus the
wretched sinful man, unconfessed and impenitent, made an end
to his foul and wicked life.

# ❧ Friar Stefano's Resurrection

## by GIROLAMO PARABOSCO

Girolamo Parabosco (1524–1557) was born in Piacenza; he lived and died in Venice. A professional musician, he was organist of the ducal chapel of San Marco. His book *I Diporti* ("Diversions") takes as its scheme an excursion of Venetian gentlemen to hunt and fowl in the marshes. Bad weather keeps them indoors and prompts them to pass the time in storytelling. This story is Novella 3, slightly abridged.

IN THE Tuscan city of Arezzo once dwelt a shysterish friar, called Maestro Stefano, since he was a preacher. He came from Mantua, but most people, indeed practically everyone, thought he was a native Aretine. He was about thirty-eight, a handsome fellow, uncommonly bold and eloquent, and very amorous, like most of his fellows. (I am speaking of the knavish ones, who are so lacking in love and charity toward their neighbors that they are forever flaying the sins of others.) . . .

Our Maestro Stefano was one of those who was always on the prowl, as they say. He fell in love with a very beautiful and respectable young woman, named Emilia, the wife of a worthy young man named Girolamo de' Brendali. It would never have entered her head that Fra Stefano, whom she took to be a man of pure and saintly life, would have been driven by carnal appetite to fall in love with her. Thus she gave him a most cordial greeting whenever he called at her house, partly because she respected him, partly because her husband liked him very much. And besides she had long been in the habit of confessing to him at least twice a year.

The friar, tortured by amorous flames, decided one day to declare his love, accustomed as he was to easy conquests. He then thought it best to wait till carnival time, when she was accus-

*Friar Stefano's Resurrection*

tomed to make her confession. The place would provide more security for his reputation than would her own home. Thus, a week after the carnival, the lady came to confess, as was her habit, to the church where the friar lived and where he was preaching that year. She sent for him, and told him that she would like to make confession, if it were agreeable to him. The friar asked nothing better. He summoned her to one of the darkest and most secluded parts of the church. After some proper words and ceremonies he began to interrogate her. He passed very casually over all the mortal sins, except the sin of the flesh. On this he dwelt at length; partly because of the great pleasure he found, like many others of his kind, in hearing how, and with whom, and all the details. (They think they profit much by such talk; but often, when they should chastise and expel sin, by their babbling they merely teach and increase the modes of sinning—so little are they ashamed of their indecent interrogations!) Thus the friar lingered upon the sin of the flesh, from the pleasure he took in talking about it and also because it was an excellent expedient for him to reveal his love for Emilia. Finally, heaving a great sigh, he said: "Madame, God knows that often I have been much in doubt whether to give you absolution after your confessions; and that because I have found you, according to your own words, too chaste, too sincere, with regard to this sin of the flesh."

"What, Father!" exclaimed the lady. "Is it perhaps a sin to be virtuous and faithful to one's husband?"

The friar replied: "I find it hard to believe that you, so beautiful, charming, and desirable, don't have a great number of suitors, and that you haven't been able eventually to resist them all. And I have often wondered whether, out of shame, you haven't told me all, possibly from fear that I tell your husband (though God forbid!), or perhaps from fear that I wouldn't give you the customary absolution. But in fact you would be unworthy of absolution only if you had concealed from me some of your deeds. So now dispose yourself to tell me everything; don't let shame or fear hold you back. And though perhaps you expect that I will reprove and chastise you, I promise that I shall rather praise and soothe you. I think it a much greater sin to let a man die who deserves a thousand lives for his affection and love than to infringe a law which was perhaps imposed only to bring some order into our lives. The law would be needless, if all things were held in common. Perhaps also the rule of chastity is designed to make those things appear better to us which we would prize but little if they were granted to us otherwise or more readily."

The lady was much amazed at these words, and being no fool, suspected somewhat the purpose of the friar's remarks. But she kept a good countenance, and decided to carry on, and not to frighten him off so that he would refrain from saying what was on his mind. So she said, with a half smile: "Dear me, Father! So you don't believe that I am the virtuous, respectable woman that I am in fact?"

"Rather," said the friar, "I think you are perversely virtuous and respectable; for it is not a virtuous thing to let another languish and die, just to preserve one's virtue."

"Alas!" said the lady. "God save us, who do you think I'm letting die? Who has ever looked me in the face with amorous intent?"

"Oh, who could look you only once in the face and not thereafter yield to you his heart? In my own case—pardon me if I offend you—since I first met you, not a day or a night has passed that I didn't think of your beauty and beg the god of love to grant me an opportunity—even though I should die of it—to demonstrate to you the love I bear you. And if by ill luck I offend you therein, lay the blame and seek the pardon in your divine beauty and your winning ways, which have brought me to such a pass that I can no longer live unless you come to my rescue. And though you delay ever so little in saving me, it will be too late, for I shall be dead."

Emilia, decent woman that she was, and answering her husband's love with her own, was so offended by the friar's words that she thought he deserved punishment. She told him that she did not believe in miracles, nor in her own amazing beauty, nor in the friar's devotion. She left him however rather hopeful than otherwise, though neither in word nor in deed did she reveal any impropriety. Thus she took her leave, went home, and told the whole story to her husband Girolamo. But first she bound him by the most solemn oaths to take only a mild vengeance, and afterward to forbid the house to the priest, as a person unworthy to associate with decent people.

Girolamo reflected on what he could do to the wanton friar that would cover him with the utmost shame but do him no serious hurt. He then conceived a very pretty trick. He told his wife to contrive that the preaching father should come some night to sleep with her, and he set forth what he had in mind to do, to her great pleasure. The better to entangle the friar and to put in operation the scheme that both husband and wife desired, a few days later she sent by the hand of a servant-girl some presents of small value, that is, some perfume and flowers arranged and bound up with dark-green silk, such as loving ladies often send to their swains. The lusty priest happily received the present, and promptly sent back the double by one of the brothers; and in her turn she doubled the gift. Now the friar thought that he was riding high. He proposed to pay her a visit on the Saturday, because he had that day off from preaching; and he looked forward to bringing matters to a happy issue.

Thus, without his companion friar, he betook himself to Emilia's house on Saturday, which was, as it happened, the day before Saint Lazarus' day. And by happy chance, in accordance with his ardent desire, he discovered that the husband Girolamo was not at home. Beaming, he mounted the stairs, and had it announced to Emilia that he wished to visit her. She received him with a cheery countenance and made him a cordial welcome. After a little conversation the friar judged that the time had come; he recalled to her his sufferings and his great need. Emilia, who had been schooled by her husband how to act and answer, thus replied: "Father, God knows that I have always thought it a very serious sin in a woman to surrender to any other person than her husband. But since you have assured me that there is no sin in so doing, and since you have told me how profound is your love for me, I am willing to give you the reward you deserve, on condition only that you promise to keep everything secret. And so that you won't think that I am merely putting you off with words, let me say that if you didn't have to preach tomorrow on Saint Lazarus' day, I would tell you to come here about midnight, and I would be sure to open the door to you, because this evening my husband is riding off to our country house, and by then all the servants would be asleep."

The good friar, who had never longed for anything so much and who felt that every moment's delay lasted a century, rejoined: "My lady, since this is your pleasure and the opportunity presents itself, don't worry about my preaching; for if I could spend the whole night with you I would be in the mood to make a most satisfactory sermon. All I need is that you should put me out a little before daybreak, so that I won't be seen emerging during your husband's absence."

Thus the pact was made for the approaching night. The friar left, to douse himself with perfume, the better to please the lady and to banish that stale smell that so afflicts most of those fellows that even a corpse would be preferable. Emilia, on her part, told her husband the whole story. He again laid down her course of action, and went off to dine with a close friend.

When the trysting hour arrived the good friar presented himself at Emilia's door. She admitted him, according to plan, and led him silently up to the room where she and her husband slept. Once there, she told him to undress; and she went out with the excuse of making some preparations before joining him. This she did in such a way that he could not even steal a kiss from her. Hardly had the poor fellow stripped to his shirt than Girolamo, who had lain on watch at the house door with his dinner companion, taken fully into confidence, pounded violently on the door. At this noise Emilia, simulating terror, appeared on the balcony and demanded to know who was there. Girolamo bade her open up—it was her husband. Crying that she was undone, she ran into the bedroom, where the friar, his head in a whirl, stood half-dead. Said she: "Alas and alack, Father, we are done for! I don't know how it happened—I thought my husband was ten miles away, but now he's knocking at the door, as you must have heard. For God's sake, there's only one way out!" She pointed to a great chest, and said: "Get in there, and stay there until I can see what's to be done. I will hide your clothes somewhere, the best way I can. God knows I care more for Your Worship than for my own life!"

The poor fellow, who found himself in a very sorry plight, did as the lady instructed him. Meanwhile the servants were aroused and opened the door to the master. And he told a story how he and his companion had been attacked by brigands outside of Arezzo; he said that they had returned and had succeeded in getting the city gate opened by giving a crown to the guardian. But the guardian had had to go to the Palace for the keys, and he had made the gentlemen wait more than three hours. Then Girolamo commanded a bed to be made for his friend in another room, and he climbed into bed with his wife, and took his solace with her, within the hearing of the friar, shut in his chest.

In the first light of day the bell for the service sounded from the cathedral where the good friar preachified. Girolamo and his friend had two servants, brought in from the country house the previous day, carry the chest on their backs. These were ordered to make their way, in the name of the preacher, through the assembled throng, and deposit the chest in the very middle of the cathedral, saying that this was by command of the preacher. Then they should discharge their burden and leave it there, without raising the chest's lid. These commands the men promptly fulfilled. The congregation was amazed; bewildered, some made one conjecture, some another. Finally, the church bell having long ceased to ring and no one appearing in the pulpit or elsewhere, a young man stood up and said: "Surely our preacher has left us too long in the lurch. Let's see what he has delivered in this chest." Then with everyone clustering about, he raised the chest lid, peered inside and saw the good brother in only his shirt, pale and terrified, as if he had already died and been buried in the chest. As soon as he found himself uncovered and revealed he collected his wits as best he could, and sat upright, to general amazement. Remembering that the day was dedicated to Saint Lazarus, he thus addressed the people: "My faithful flock, I am no whit surprised to see you marveling and amazed at my appearance before you in this guise, or better at my delivery before you in this chest. Well you know that this is the day when our holy mother church commemorates the stupendous miracle which our Lord performed upon the person of Lazarus, resuscitating him when he had already been buried for four days. It was my desire, similarly, to impersonate most exactly, for your edification, the dead Lazarus. Thus, seeing me in this chest, which symbolizes the tomb in which he was laid when dead, you may be moved with greater inwardness to consider the wretched lot of mankind; and seeing me only in my shirt, you may realize that we can take nothing else with us of all our worldly possessions. Now if you give earnest thought to this, perhaps you will undergo a total change in your lives. Will you believe that, base creature that I am, since last night at this hour I have, like Lazarus, died and been resuscitated more than a thousand times? This is absolutely true. Think then that every living man must die; have recourse to Him who alone can restore life. But first die to concupiscence, to avarice, to thievery, in short to all those sins to which you may be led by the corporal senses, cruel enemies of our souls. And above all refrain from tempting the wives of others; for God saves but few of such offenders from the grave —I mean those who wickedly meddle with women."

With many such admonishing words the good friar finished his sermon. He was much applauded for his object-lesson by all the Aretines, and especially by Girolamo and his friend, who had betaken themselves there to see the outcome of the story. They acclaimed his marvelous quickness of wit, and privately laughed consumedly at his discouragement of the people from tempting the wives of others. In recognition of this Girolamo refused to take any further revenge; but from then on he never allowed the friar or any of his rascally kind to set foot in his house.

# ❧ *Spanish Revenge*

## by MATTEO BANDELLO

Matteo Bandello was born near Tortona, at the eastern limit of Piedmont, in 1485. He entered the Dominican order, chiefly, one supposes, because his uncle was master-general. He knew the courts better than the cloisters. He was employed in important confidential posts by the rulers of Milan and Mantua; he attached himself to a celebrated mercenary soldier in France. For his political services he was rewarded with the bishopric of Agen, in southern France. He died in 1561.

Bandello was a compulsive writer. He composed scholarly works, and quantities of secular poetry, including love-sonnets. Chiefly he lives as a storyteller. His collections, totaling almost a million words, appeared in 1554 and 1573. They continue to amuse and delight; incidentally they provide a vivid picture of Italian life in the Renaissance. The first story is translated by Percy Pinkerton in his *Matteo Bandello* (London, 1895), the others by Morris Bishop. This story is Novella 42 of Part I of his *Novelle*.

VALENCIA, in Spain, is deemed a most noble and pleasant city, where, as Genoese merchants have often told me, beautiful and gracious women abound, who by their charms have such power to captivate men that in all Catalonia no more voluptuous city exists. Indeed, if by chance they should happen upon some inexperienced youth, they give him such a trimming that, as cunning barbers, not the Sicilians themselves can beat them. Here, in this city, was the home of the Centigli, a house long famed for its many noble and opulent scions. One of these, Didaco by name, lived there not many years ago. He was twenty-three years of age, and very wealthy. He ranked as the most liberal and courteous of all the knights of Valencia, and it was he who at bullfights, tourneys, and other festivals made the bravest show. Meeting one day a damsel of low degree, yet of great beauty and unusual charm, he fell passionately in love with her. The girl had a mother, and two brothers, who were goldsmiths, while she herself broidered stuffs with admirable skill. The knight, who so burned with love that he had neither happiness nor rest save when he thought of her or spoke with her, used often to pass by in front of the house, and with messages and letters importune her. Pleased beyond measure to be thus wooed by the first nobleman of the town, she gave to his pleadings neither too much heed nor too little regard, holding him, as it were, between the two. He, who craved other food than mere words and glances, fell ever deeper in love, hoping to achieve his end with gold. At length he was able to persuade the damsel to grant him an interview wherever it pleased her best, he pledging his word of honour that she should receive no harm nor insult at his hands. The girl told all to her mother, who, yielding to entreaty, agreed to allow the lover to hold the desired interview at her house. Having gained thus much, the knight came thither, and in the mother's presence spoke at much length with Violante, for so the damsel was named. Yet, though he was eloquent, and in fact a fine spokesman, and though he made many promises to both mother and daughter, offering to pay, not only a good sum of money now, but also, if the girl should marry, to give her a suitable and handsome dowry, from Violante he got no other answer save this, that she was greatly indebted to him for the love that he said he bore for her, and that in matters honourable she would readily oblige him, but that she was firm in her resolve to die rather than to lose her good name. And with many words the mother upheld her daughter's decision.

The luckless lover, good-natured as he was, when he perceived that by no arts that he might use could he win Violante for his mistress, resolved to make her his wife. He saw that she had beauty, grace, pleasant manners, and was endowed with every charm, and he judged that, though of base lineage, if he took her to wife, she might rank with the noblest dames of Valencia. Moreover, he bethought him that he had neither father nor mother who could cry out at his bringing to them such a kins-woman. Then, too, he was spurred on to this choice by the great love which he bore for Violante; and this made him feel in duty bound to wed her, since the main thing in this world is to content oneself; and though in buying a horse a friend's judgment will serve, when it comes to choosing a wife it is best to take one after one's own heart.

He also remembered to have heard that, not long since, a King of Aragon espoused the daughter of one of his vassals. Thus, after much thought, being unable to overcome his great love, which, as it seemed to him, grew ever stronger, he at length de-clared his resolve by saying, "Signora Violante, in order that you may know my love for you to be true, and that the words I spoke came from my heart, if you will be mine, so long as I live I will be yours, and I will make you my lawful wife." Hearing this, the mother and her daughter grew joyful, and thanked God for His bounty in giving them such good fortune. And Violante modestly replied—

"Signor Didaco, although I know myself to be unworthy of such a cavalier as yourself, you being of ancient lineage and one of the great nobles of the land, whereas I am but of poor and base parentage, yet to requite honourably your honourable love, I will always be to you a loyal consort and a faithful servant." In this fashion, then, it was agreed that the knight should wed Violante in the presence of her mother and her brothers. The nobleman was well pleased with the compact, and soon after, having kissed the damsel's hand, he returned to his home.

Violante's mother lost no time in telling her sons of all that had been arranged with Signor Didaco, whereupon the two young men rejoiced greatly, as it seemed to them a fine thing that their sister should make such a grand match, without their having to give her a dowry. Two days had not passed before the knight re-turned, and then in the presence of the mother and the two brothers, as well as of a trusted servant, whom he brought with him, he solemnly took his beloved Violante to wife. He besought them all, however, to keep the marriage a secret until such time as

he could make it public, there being certain reasons for this con-
cealment. Having wedded his bride, he passed the night in her
company, and the marriage was duly consummated to their mutual content.

For more than a year his love for Violante remained steadfast,
and almost every night he came to her bed. He provided her with
rich dresses and jewels, giving to her brothers a handsome sum
of money. This caused many who were ignorant of the actual
facts to think that the knight had bought the girl's love, and took
his pleasure of her as of a mistress, and this seemed to them more
likely to be true, when they saw how frequent were his visits to
her house, and how thoroughly at home he appeared to be there.
The girl, though she heard somewhat of all this gossip, gave it no
heed, knowing how matters really stood, and hoping before long
to announce her marriage, thus undeceiving every one. The
mother and the brothers shared this hope, and often urged
Violante to persuade her husband to make the marriage public.
And when he came to her she repeatedly besought him to fulfil
his promise to take her back with him to his home. This he said he
would do, but made no further sign of keeping his word.

Thus a year had passed since the secret marriage, when the
knight, being either ashamed of Violante's plebeian origin, or
tired of her, began to pay court to a daughter of Signor Ramiro
Vigliaracuta, a member of one of the first families in Valencia.
The courtship continued in this way for some time, until a
dowry had been mutually agreed upon, when the knight publicly
wedded this lady of high degree. The event became known
throughout Valencia, and when on that very day Violante
heard the news, she was as one stunned, for, needless to say, it
troubled her much. She loved him who was her lord and master
with an ardent and illimitable love, and now, after hoping for so
long to win for herself a place of honour in the world, but finding
herself despised, no way seemed open to her that might bring
comfort. At nightfall the two brothers came home, who had also
heard of this new marriage, and finding their sister disconsolate
and weeping bitterly they tried their best, as also did the mother,

to calm her and to make her refrain from tears. Yet she, being mindful only of her great sorrow, paid no heed to their exhortations, but with sighs and bitter lamenting bewailed her disgrace.

So, for well nigh three days, she remained in this state, neither eating nor sleeping, and wasting gradually away. When forced at length by nature to take food and rest, she began to perceive that weeping availed naught, and, being loth to submit to the shame which Signor Didaco had brought upon her, she bethought herself of some scheme of vengeance which should make others bear a part of the punishment—vengeance meet for such villainy, so that for the future it should be less easy for men to betray unfortunate women. And, while disclosing nothing to any one of her fell purpose, she waited for some opportune moment when the knight should fall into her hands. Being resolved to wreak her vengeance upon him, she brooded over the way that this could best be done, and she resolved to give up grieving, and lead as merry a life as might be.

In the house with her there lived a slave, a tall powerful woman of about thirty years of age, who was greatly attached to Violante, having nursed her as a child. She could not bear to see the girl scorned after this fashion, and sincerely condoled with her in her sorrow. It was to this woman that Violante proposed to reveal her plan, knowing that by herself she could not accomplish that which had to be done. Moreover, there was no one more fitted to help, so she told the slave of her cruel scheme, who not only consented to be a partner thereto, but highly praised her for inventing it. Having both settled that which they meant to do, they only waited for an opportunity; and as they say, opportunity is the mother of all things.

A fortnight had hardly passed since the cavalier had married his second wife, when one day, while out riding, he went by Violante's house. She was at the window, as if greatly surprised at not seeing the knight for so long in this part of the town. When she saw him, she blushed deeply, and waited to hear what he would say. The nobleman, when aware of her presence, also changed colour somewhat, but putting a bold face on matters reined up his steed, and with a bow called out, "Good morrow, my lady! How goes it with you? It seems a year since I saw you."

At this the girl smiled, and replied, "You give me good day with your lips, but in truth you have already given me a very sad day; and how it goes with me you know as well as I. But God guard you, since it cannot be otherwise. You have forsaken me for good and all; and then you say that it seems a year since you saw me! It is plain to me that you no longer care for me, and I fain would tell you that this was my constant fear, for I was not so blind nor so witless as not to perceive that my base birth could never sort with your exalted rank. Yet I pray you still to be mindful of me and to remember that I am, and always shall be, yours."

When the knight heard this and saw that Violante made no further protest, he thought he had got a cheap bargain, and replied, "That which I have done, my lady, I was obliged to do, in order to make a lasting peace between my family and the Vigliaracuta, instead of a bloody feud, and by this marriage all has now been set right; yet this will not cause me to forsake you, but whatever may be of benefit to you, that I will gladly do with all my heart, and be sure that my love for you is in no wise changed." To which Violante answered, "I shall take note if at times you choose to find enjoyment in my company."

The knight assured her that this was his intention; and he had hardly gone fifty paces past the house when, summoning his trusty servant, who knew all, he said to him, "Go back and tell Signora Violante that, if it put her to no trouble, in proof of my love and regard for her, I will come tonight and stay with her for a while." The servant brought this message to Violante, who seemed to be greatly delighted at the news. She saw that her plan began to shape itself in the way she wished, and she at once called the slave, to whom she gave orders for the achievement of her design.

When night came, Signor Didaco supped with his bride and stayed for some time, until, she being willing, he took leave of her. Then he dismissed all his servants except the one who knew the secret, and went to Violante's house, where he was gladly welcomed. The servant, having accompanied his master thus far, found lodging at a neighbouring inn. The hour was late, and the lovers soon sought their couch, conversing much about the new marriage, the girl being apparently desirous of nothing, save that the knight should care for her in the future. And he, who really loved her, for she was very beautiful, made large promises that he would always keep her as his minion. Then the knight, who was weary, fell into a sound sleep.

Seeing this, Violante rose silently from the bed, and opening the chamber door let in the slave, who was waiting outside. Together they took a rope which had been got ready, and fortune so far favoured them that, before he was ware of it, they had bound the wretched knight with a thousand adamantine knots. Then, as he woke, dazed from sleep, the two audacious women thrust a gag into his mouth, so that he could not call out for help. There was in the room a beam which served as a prop for the floor above; and to this beam they tightly bound the knight, he standing on his feet, all naked as at the day of his birth. The fiendish slave then fetched a sharp knife, a pair of small pincers, and other instruments for cutting. What fears and anguish must then have seized the unhappy knight as he saw these two women display such deadly tools and eagerly prepare for their work, just as a butcher in the slaughter-house prepares to rip off the skin from an ox! Verily I think he must have felt greatly grieved that ever he offended Violante; but to repent too late avails naught—that is, with men, though with God, so I have often heard it said, heartfelt repentance ever avails much.

The young man being thus bound, Violante, grown desperate, took the pincers, and with them seized her trembling victim's tongue, exclaiming, "Ah! false, perfidious, base, and cruel knight, whose wicked conduct makes you no longer knight, but the vilest of men, how sorry am I that, publicly, in the sight of the whole city, I cannot wreak on you that vengeance which your villainy deserves! Yet I will so punish you that you shall be an example to those who, coming after, will take care how they cheat simple incautious maids, and remember that, when of their own will they have done a thing before God, they must keep their word. Traitor, do you forget that here, in this place, with a pretence of words, you gave me the wedding-ring, and with further false speeches robbed me of my honour! See, yonder, faithless one, is the nuptial-bed that you so lightly have stained with infamy. Ah me! how many lies, all told to my cost, has not this false tongue spoken! Yet, God be praised, it shall deceive no one more!"

So saying, with a pair of shears, she cut off more than four inches of his tongue. Then seizing his hand with the pincers, she cried, "O traitor of traitors! why, with this hand, did you give me the nuptial ring? Why did you wed me? Why, too, were these arms clasped about my neck, if they were afterwards to offer another an unlawful ring?" With this she cut off the tips of all his fingers; then, taking a sharp dagger, she looked into his eyes, and said, "I know not what to say of you, oh! traitorous eyes, that once were the tyrants of my own. You met my gaze with an infinite tenderness, a love that seemed immense—a burning desire always to please me. Where are those false tears that you fain would have had me think you shed for my sake? How often were you at pains to make me think that you could look on no beauty but mine, since mine was matchless, the very mould and mirror of all that was gracious and lovely? Ah! let your false light be now put out!" So saying, she thrust the sharp dagger into both his eyes, so that they might never again behold the light of the sun. Then she cut off other parts of his body, which for decency's sake I forbear to name, with her gleaming knives, and after this turned to his heart.

Owing to these wounds the hapless knight was now more dead than alive; and, though he writhed in agony, it availed nothing, they having bound him so tightly to the beam. An awful sight in truth was this, to see a strong man thus tortured, with his limbs torn, and powerless to save himself, or to cry for mercy! Violante, being now wearied rather than appeased by the cruel revenge that she had taken upon her faithless husband, spoke thus to him who, it may be, could not hear, "Didaco, such revenge as was possible for me to take I have taken upon you, though it was not that which you deserved, for your sin should have been punished in the sight of all people with burning flames. It is your boast at least to have died by the hand of a woman whom you loved, and who loved you with a love that had no limit. What befalls me matters little, but if it had been possible I would willingly have died at your hands. Since this cannot be, God will do with me that which seems to Him fittest. I will torture you no longer." Hereupon she plunged the bloody knife up to the hilt three times in his heart, when the wretched man, shuddering, expired.

Then the women wiped up the blood that had been spilled upon the floor, and, having untied the corpse, they placed it, with all the mutilated limbs, in a large basket, which they covered over with a linen cloth and put under the bed. Violante then turned to Giannica the slave, and said, "Giannica, I can never thank you enough for the help that you have given me in carrying out my longed-for revenge, which, without you, I could never have accomplished. Now that my great desire is appeased, all that remains for me is to provide for your safety, while at the same time I make it plain to the world in what way I revenged myself; so that I am desirous for you to leave me, and to find some means of going to Africa; and this will be easy enough, for I will give you money to travel thither in comfort, and you will always keep me in your memory." Then, opening a coffer, she said, "I have here much money, with gold and jewels worth over fifteen hundred ducats; take them all, for I give them to you gladly; lose no time in saving yourself. I will keep the thing hidden for the whole day, and will wait until you have made good your escape."

Hearing these kind words, the slave began to weep bitterly, and would on no account consent to leave Violante, declaring that she would share her fate, whatever it might be, and that love for her mistress made her careless of life. She could not be persuaded to go; and Violante, seeing that her efforts were in vain, and that the slave wished to die with her, proposed that they should sleep

there in the room during the short space of night that still remained.

When morning came, Violante again besought Giannica to
flee, but in vain. Some while before midday the servant of the unfortunate knight came, as was his custom, to accompany his
master to the house of the bride. When Violante saw him, she
said—

"If you would know where your lord has gone, go and bring
hither, if it please you, his Highness the Viceroy, for I am commissioned to tell the news to him and to none other. It will be a
vain task for you to try and learn the truth in any other way."

The servant went out, and meeting by chance the knight's
uncle and cousin, he told them what Violante had said. They
knew of Didaco's love for the girl, but not of the marriage, for
the servant had been strictly charged to reveal this to no one. The
two relatives never thought that a dreadful deed had been done,
but went on together to see Violante, who met them with a smiling face, and said, "My lords, whom do you seek?" and they replied, "We would have you tell us whither Signor Didaco has
gone."

"Pardon me, my lords, but I may not disobey his order; bring
hither the Viceroy, and you shall know all, for so he charged me
to act." At that time the Viceroy was my Lord Duke of Calabria,
son of King Frederick of Aragon, who died at Torsi in France.
"It is not convenient," said these gentlemen, "that my lord the
Viceroy should come hither." "Then do you see to it," answered
Violante, "that either he come here, or that he send for me."

Being unable to get more news from the girl than this, they
went to inform the Viceroy. Violante, who, with her accomplice,
foresaw all that was likely to happen, donned forthwith her
richest and most sumptuous robes, making Giannica do the same,
and then awaited the coming of a messenger from the Viceroy.
Her mother, seeing the two gentlemen arrive, had asked Violante what this might mean, who put her off with a false tale, saying not a word as to the crime. Soon there came a sergeant from
the Viceroy, who commanded Violante to appear before him.

She, who expected this summons, told nothing to her mother, but straightway went with Giannica to speak to the Viceroy, who at that time had with him most of the lords and gentlemen of the land. When she had arrived, after the usual salutation, the Viceroy asked Violante what it was that Signor Didaco had charged her to say concerning him. Then the girl spoke, not as some timid sorrowful woman might speak, but with spirit and a bold front, giving answer thus—

"My Lord Viceroy, you must know that more than a year since Signor Didaco Centiglia, seeing that by no other way could he have my love, resolved to make me his wife, and in the presence of my mother, my brothers, and Pietro his servant, who is now here, wedded me at my own home, and for more than fifteen months shared my couch as my lawful husband. Then he, regardless of the fact that I was his lawful wife, only lately, as all Valencia knows, espoused the daughter of Signor Ramiro Vigliaracuta, though wife of his she is none, seeing that I was first legally married to him. Nor did this suffice him, for, as if I had been his trull and common harlot, yesterday he impudently visits me and pours out a flood of lies into my ear, being at pains to make me believe that what was black was white. Hardly had he gone, than he sent Pietro, whom you see here, to tell me that he would spend the night now past in my company. To this, as Pietro can testify, I agreed, for the way seemed now open for me to take such revenge upon him as I was able. Therefore, O most just Viceroy, have I come here, that you may know all from my lips. With denials and entreaties I have nothing to do, deeming it too great a piece of cowardice to fear punishment for an act done wilfully and deliberately. Thus, by boldly and frankly confessing the truth, I shall protect my reputation, so that those who in the past had no reason to think ill of me, may now know surely and certainly that I was Signor Didaco Centiglia's lawful wife, and not his harlot. That my honour is safe suffices me, come what may. Last night, my Lord Viceroy, helped by this slave here, and spurred thereto by the injury received, I took such revenge upon my husband as seemed to me meet for the wrong which out of all reason he did me, since it was not I who was the offender; and with these hands I drove out from his vile body his viler soul. He took my honour; I have taken his life; yet how far more honour should be esteemed than life is all too plain."

Then she told exactly the manner in which she had murdered Didaco, and how she had tried to prevail upon the slave to escape.

At the recital of this tragedy, all the lords and gentlemen present were deeply moved, judging the woman to have greater courage than is wont to belong to her sex. The knight's pitiable corpse was exposed in a tower, presenting a hideous sight to all who viewed it. Violante's mother, the brothers, and the servant were in turn examined, when it was found of a truth the noble-man had no right to wed his second wife. After a strict and careful inquiry, Violante and Giannica were alone found guilty, and they were publicly beheaded. They went joyously to their death, as if going to some festival; and, as report has it, the slave, being care-less for herself, besought her mistress to meet death calmly, since thus nobly had she gotten her revenge.

# ❦ Love Is Blind, and Lovers Too

## by MATTEO BANDELLO

This story is Novella 31 of *Novelle*, Part II.

IN MILAN, that rich city, abundant in all good things, filled with a distinguished and courtly nobility, there was, not long since, a young man named Gian Battista da Latuate. By the death of his father he was left very rich; he was brought up under the watchful eye of his mother, a most noble lady of the Caimi family. She devoted all her diligent care and solicitude to the training of her only son, to school him in letters and in manners. The young man developed; already when he was fifteen or sixteen he gave every promise of becoming an accomplished gentleman; he associated with other young men of rank, practicing horsemanship, ball-playing, and fencing, and displaying great skill in handling all sorts of weapons.

His paternal home was in Brera Street, where indeed it still stands. Often he would go riding for pleasure through the city, either on a mule, or on one of his spirited horses. Now it happened that, passing down the Borgo Nuovo, he caught a glimpse of a girl at a window, behind a Venetian blind; she stood there watching people pass on the street below. It seemed to Gian Battista that he had never seen such a beautiful and charming girl; he was so dazzled and enthralled at first sight that he could think of nothing else. That same day he passed two or three times before her house; the more he looked at her the more her beauty and charm seemed to increase. He sent one of his servants to inquire about her father, whom he found to be a gentleman, not very rich but worthy and of good repute. All that day and the following night the enamored youth thought only of the girl he had seen; and all his thoughts blended into a single one—to find a way to speak to her. Thus he began every day, on foot or on horseback, as circumstances permitted, to capture her favor. Every time he saw her—which was nearly every time he went down the street—he bowed to her, cap in hand, with his eyes fixed so fondly upon her that any observer would have recognized that he was in love. And as she was a courteous and mannerly girl, every time that the young man doffed his cap she modestly inclined her head a little and with a smile acknowledged the honorable salute, so that Gian Battista felt a marvelous consolation, under the impression that she would not reject his love.

This went on for some time. Every day the youth became more enamored, and could find no ease of mind except when he was looking at her. With an old woman as go-between he found a means of delivering to her a love-letter, in which he told her how fervently he loved her, using those affectionate, cajoling words that young men readily discover when they write to their inamoratas. The girl accepted the letter and read it, but made no reply. The smitten youth wrote a second letter full of impassioned words and ardent entreaties, importuning her to deign to grant him a secret interview, because he had many things to tell her, not to be set down in writing, which would rejoice her. The girl was by no means displeased to be loved and courted by such a rich and noble young man; and though she was not his social equal she hoped that he might fall so deep in love that he would marry her. She was an intelligent girl, by no means naïve; she knew very well what his talk of a secret interview meant. She wrote back then, thanking him for the love which he claimed to feel for her, and saying that she loved him as much as was proper for a respectable girl; but as for a secret interview, he was never even to think of such a thing, since such interviews could be granted only to the man her father might choose as her husband. When Gian Battista received this sage reply he was bitten the more deeply by love's tarantula; the poison penetrated the more deeply and inflamed him the more. His state was all the worse since whenever the girl saw him she smiled upon him happily and seemed to enjoy his inspection.

Having reached this pass and finding no cure for his love, he decided to speak to her father and ask her hand in marriage. He seized an opportunity, sought out the father, and after the proper salutations came to the point. "Messer Ambrogio," he said, "not to engage in any jungle of fine words and ceremonies, I wish to speak to you frankly. I know that you are well aware who I am and that you will not have to go hunting for information about my circumstances. If and when you should be pleased to give me your daughter Laura to wife, I will marry her gladly, because for a long time I have been captured by her, and I have formed a firm determination to marry her."

Messer Ambrogio was much amazed at this offer. Knowing the young man's nobility and wealth, and recognizing that he might readily find in Milan a partner of much greater rank and property, he reflected for a moment, and then replied: "Signor Gian Battista, I have no need to seek information about your situation, since I know very well who and what you are. Therefore I cannot help being much surprised at your proposal, to learn that you wish to condescend to marry my daughter. For although she is born of noble stock, nevertheless she is the child of a poor father, and my resources are not such that I can by any means give her a dowry suitable for you."

"Don't mention dowry," said the lover. "Because, thanks be to God, I have money enough for her and for me. I am not asking you for a dowry or for anything else except Laura herself. I will give her a suitable dowry, befitting my own station. Make up your mind then to give me your daughter, and don't worry about anything else. I should prefer that for the present my mother should know nothing about it. But to set you at ease I shall marry Laura in the presence of four or five of your closest relatives."

Messer Ambrogio replied: "In a case of such importance it would be best that you should think it over for five or six days more, and on my part I shall give it full consideration."

"Assume that the six days have already passed," said the young man. "For I have been thinking it over at great length, and I have made up my mind what I want to do."

"Come, come!" said Messer Ambrogio. "Another day we'll talk it all over more at ease."

Each then went his own way, and the ardent, urgent lover

wrote to his beloved, reporting all his discussion with her father, whereat she was mightily pleased. But Messer Ambrogio, thinking over the young man's proposal, wondered whether, in the belief that he was contracting bonds of friendship and alliance, he might not in fact contract an everlasting hostility. He was conscious of the inequality between the two parties, and he concluded that such a marriage should not take place. Having pondered the matter at great length, he found means to speak to Madonna Francesca—such was the name of the enamored youth's mother—and recounted to her exactly the conversation he had had with the young man. Madonna Francesca was much shocked at the news; nevertheless she thanked Messer Ambrogio heartily for reporting to her her son's intention. She urged him to lose no time in marrying off his daughter Laura. The poor man shrugged his shoulders and demurred, saying that this was impossible; Laura was still a girl and the time was not ripe. Madonna Francesca asked him what dowry he was accustomed to give his daughters. Said he: "Signora, I have married two of them and I have given each of them a thousand ducats. Now Laura alone remains; I want to give her the same sum when the time arrives. But if I should marry her now I wouldn't be able to pay a hundred florins."

Said Madonna Francesca: "Messer Ambrogio, that you may know how precious to me is the warning you have given me of my son's purpose, look out a suitable match for your daughter, and the sooner the better. And I will lend you the full thousand ducats of the dowry; you will repay them to me at your convenience in five or six years. All I ask of you is a signed acknowledgment."

At this offer, so courteous and generous, Messer Ambrogio thanked her most profusely. He promised Madonna Francesca that he would use all diligence to arrange Laura's marriage. Thus the two remained in accord.

Meanwhile Gian Battista pursued Laura with letters and messengers. Every time he had a chance to pass down her street, and every time he saw her at her window he thought he saw a new paradise open before him, and felt a marvelous inward consolation at the sight. Madonna Francesca, who was terrified lest her son marry Laura, had a secret rendezvous with her brother, Monsignor Abbot Caimo, a man of authority and reputation, and with others of her kinsmen. She spoke likewise to some uncles and blood-relations of her son. To all of them she revealed his amorous enterprise and her dealings with Messer Ambrogio, and she asked aid and counsel, so that with the least possible hurt Gian Battista could be effectively prevented from marrying Laura. There was a great deal of talk; everyone offered his own opinion and a thousand schemes were proposed. Finally all came to this conclusion: the best remedy would be to get Gian Battista out of Milan for some time and meanwhile to marry Laura. All agreed, although Madonna Francesca, a gracious, tender mother, was reluctant. She loved her only son passionately and thought she could not live without him. Indeed if she passed two or three hours without seeing him she felt her heart die in her breast. Nonetheless she was exhorted by her brother, relatives, and friends, and made to realize that this was the only promising way to extricate her son from his amorous adventure; and so she fell in with the rest. So they all agreed on this course: Monsignor Abbot Caimo would invite Gian Battista and some other relatives, with two of his tutors, to dinner on the following day; and after dinner they would urge him to leave Milan and go for a time to the court of Rome.

The invitation was sent; the party dined at the Abbot's house. After the meal one of the tutors said to the young man: "Tell me, Gian Battista, how do you like the life in our city?"

"Very much," said the boy. The tutor added: "I won't say it isn't good; but if you should once make acquaintance with the court of Rome, perhaps you wouldn't want to return here right away."

"I don't know much about Rome," replied Gian Battista; "but it seems to me that we have all the pleasures in the world right here at home."

Everybody spoke up on this theme; and the Abbot said, "Look here, nephew; if you want to go and spend a few months in

Rome, I shall take it on myself to calm down my sister and to arrange that you will be fittingly supplied with funds. I can assure you that you will come back a changed man. If you are an accomplished young gentleman now, you will become very much more accomplished. You will learn the finest of manners and you will see the most beautiful things on earth. If you once make that visit, you will think the experience worth all the money in the world."

Finally the youth said he would be willing to go there, with his mother's permission. Then the whole party adjourned to call on Madonna Francesca, and begged her to approve this trip. Though she displayed the greatest reluctance, in the end she yielded, saying she was willing that her son might go wherever he wished for five or six months. When the journey was arranged, the young man informed his Laura of everything, begging her to keep him forever in mind and be constant in her love, for he would soon return and contrive that her father would consent to her marriage. The needful preparations being made, the young man left Milan with an honorable train and set forth for Rome.

As soon as he left, Madonna Francesca summoned Messer Ambrogio and asked him how matters stood for the marriage of his daughter. He replied: "I have three suitors for her hand, Madonna. All three are of suitable standing; they appeal to me about equally. But since, in your great goodness, you deign to advance me the money, I propose to choose as son-in-law the one that seems to you most fit." He informed her of the names and families of the three and of the state of their property. And after much talk they settled on one of them. Thereat Madonna Francesca, according to her promise, lent the thousand ducats to good Messer Ambrogio, and by her agency the marriage of his daughter was settled in two or three days. The betrothal and the wedding took place; the bridegroom, who lived on the Via Bigli, took the spouse to his home. As I have already told, before Gian Battista left, he wrote often to Laura and passed constantly before her house, weeping bitterly and making deep bows, as if he were taking leave of her at her window. He had then commissioned a servant, who was in the know, to watch over her solicitously and learn all the news of her.

Well, Gian Battista went to Rome and on his way saw many beautiful cities and beautiful ladies. In Rome he saw many more, but none who seemed to him as beautiful as Laura. After Laura's marriage his mother immediately wrote him to return. He awaited no further message, but came home with all speed. He dismounted, embraced his mother, then went to his room to take off his riding clothes and dress properly. He asked his servant the news of Laura.

"Bad news," said he. "She has married so-and-so; the ceremony is over." At this Gian Battista thought he would die. But he plucked up courage, got on his horse, and went to find Laura. He found her standing in her doorway with a woman relative of her husband. When he saw her, though he recognized her, he was amazed to see that she was blinded in one eye. He dismounted and greeted her. "Welcome back!" said she. He said that he was glad to hear of her marriage and that he wished her every happiness. Then he said that he sympathized deeply with her for her accident.

"What accident?" said she.

"The accident to your eye. I see you have lost it."

Said the young lady, who was no fool: "And I am overjoyed that you have recovered the sight of both your eyes." For Laura had been blind in one eye since childhood. But whether the young man had been too blinded by love for her, or whether the window-blind had blocked his vision, he had never noticed it. Thus Love puts out the eyes of incautious lovers.

# ❦ The Pertinacious Captain

## by MATTEO BANDELLO

This story is Novella 26 of *Novelle*, Part III.

SIGNORA CONTESSA and you courtly gentlemen, all of you here present must know the name of Captain Biagino Crivello. You must be aware that he was very valiant in arms, and during the rule of Duke Lodovico Sforza of Milan he played a very honorable part in all the wars. Now he asks nothing better than to live in retirement, and to visit daily all the Milan churches, devoting himself totally to the health of his soul. He enjoyed the highest credit with Duke Lodovico, and was on such familiar terms with him that he seemed rather the Duke's brother than his subject. He had a comfortable competence; and after the death of his wife, who left him only one daughter, he chose not to remarry and not to accumulate possessions. All the income from his pay as captain-general of the ducal crossbowmen he spent in providing good cheer for his companions. Similarly he laid out in hospitality the considerable gifts that the Duke gave him.

Now you must know that the stock of the Crivelli, in Milan and throughout the district, is immense. Some of the members are very poor, as is so often the case in big families. So there was one of the clan, a good deal of a scholar; he would have liked to become a priest, if he had had any way to obtain a benefice. It occurred to him that Captain Biagino would be an excellent intermediary, if he should be willing. Knowing him to be very affectionate and kindly, the young man visited him and told him of his ambition. At this the good captain, who liked to do good to everyone, and especially to his relatives, made lavish promises that he would take up the matter with the Duke and would do everything to promote the young man's purpose. Delaying not a moment, he called that same day on Messer Giacomo Antiquario, the Duke's secretary, who had general supervision over all the ecclesiastical benefices of the dukedom. Antiquario was a scholar of exemplary life, highly esteemed by all for his character and conduct.

Antiquario heard Biagino's request, and well knowing the Duke's fondness for him, he said: "Captain, I don't think there is any benefice now vacant; if there were any such, I would surely be informed, thanks to my office. It seems to me that you should speak to my Lord the Duke and get him to promise you one of the first vacancies. But don't lose any time; the Duke has already made many promises."

The captain thanked Antiquario profusely, and seized an opportunity to speak to the Duke. The Duke, on hearing his request, gave him many encouraging words, and urged him to keep his ears open, to learn if any beneficed priest should die, and then to inform his master. With this response in mind, the captain waited eagerly for some priest to enter Paradise. While he was in this expectation, an archpriest in Lomelina, in the domain of Count Antonio Crivello, happened to die. As soon as the captain heard of this, he went to the Duke to ask for the benefice. The Duke had heard of the archpriest's death, and wished to confer the archpresbytery on another. He said: "Captain Biagino, pardon us if we don't comply with your request; but only half an hour ago we were constrained to promise it to another."

Captain Biagino took this in good faith; he shrugged his shoulders, and settled down to await another chance. Not long after another priest died; and the captain got from the Duke the same reply as before. But he did not give up; he refused to be discouraged or dismayed. Many other livings fell vacant; the Duke forever excused himself, saying that he had already granted them; and Captain Biagino began to realize that he was being made a fool of. He said to the Duke: "My Lord, evidently you are playing me for a fool. By the body of Saint Ambrogio, you will drive me to something desperate. Give me a benefice and don't torture me any longer."

The Duke laughed and said he would take care of it. But nothing changed; whenever a prebendary fell vacant and Biagino asked for it, the Duke always replied that it had already been granted. The captain was furious at such treatment, and said to himself: "By God I'll play him a trick that will work!" Now it happened about that time that in the village of Merate in the Brianza hills he saw a decrepit priest, who held a very good living in the region. Thereat the captain, hardly giving the matter a second thought, killed him; he then went with all speed to find the Duke, who was at Cusago, only three or four miles from Milan. As soon as he arrived he asked for the benefice. The Duke, as was his wont, replied that he had bestowed it some time before. Then the captain shouted: "Body of Christ! That's impossible, because I killed him only three hours ago, and I have come here with the post-horses at a gallop!" The Duke was dumbstruck at this remark; and Biagino immediately mounted his horse and set off for the loop of the Adda River and thus passed into Venetian territory. He then made his peace with the relatives of the dead man, recovered the good graces of the Duke, and finally obtained a benefice for his kinsman. All this was brought about by the excessive familiarity of the good captain with his lord.

# ❧ Savoir-vivre in a Courtesan's Parlor

by MATTEO BANDELLO

This story is Novella 42 of *Novelle*, Part III.

I THINK that most of us have either known or heard of Imperia, the Roman courtesan, of her beauty in her heyday, and of the love borne her by the rich and great, for many here present were in Rome in those days. Among her other captives was Signor Angelo dal Bufalo, valiant of person, kindly, noble, and very rich. He protected her for many years and was most fervently loved by her, as was demonstrated in her declining days. And since he was very liberal and courtly, he kept her in a house most splendidly equipped, with many servants male and female, most solicitous in her service. Her house was elegant and elaborately furnished, so that any visiting stranger, at the sight of the splendor and the servant staff, thought some princess must live there. Among other things there were a parlor, a bedroom, and a boudoir so magnificently decorated that there was nothing but velvets and brocades on the walls and the richest carpets on the floor. In the boudoir to which she resorted when visited by some grand personage the wall-hangings were all of cloth of gold, elaborately festooned and curlicued, most magnificent work. There was also a side table inset with gold and ultramarine blue, a masterpiece of cabinet-making, and on it stood very beautiful vases made of various precious materials, with alabaster, porphyry, serpentine, and a thousand other substances. One observed also many chests and caskets, superbly carved, evidently of the utmost value. In the center of the room stood a most exquisite table covered with green velvet. On this were always disposed a lute or lyre and other instruments, with books of music. There were also books in Italian and Latin, sumptuously bound. She was particularly fond of Italian poetry, wherein she had as teacher and stimulator our most genial friend Domenico Campana, called Strascino. She profited so much by his instruction that she composed and set to music, very agreeably, some sonnets and madrigals. But really I have no reason to rehearse all this, for I would fall far short of the facts, both with regard to her personal charm and to the decoration of her house.

Well then, one day Signor Angelo introduced into this glorious boudoir the ambassador of the King of Spain, attracted by the fame of Imperia. She met him at the door of the parlor and led him into the bedroom and the boudoir. He marveled at the lady's beauty and at all the pomp and splendor of the surroundings. And after a time the ambassador felt a sudden need to spit. He turned to his manservant and spat full in his face, remarking: "I am sorry, but the ugliest thing in the room is your face."

Although the action was uncivil, it delighted Imperia, for it seemed to her that her beauty and the décor of her room could receive no higher praise. Therefore she thanked the ambassador for his tribute, observing however that he should have spat on the carpet, since it was laid down for that purpose.

Some say, it is true, that this episode occurred many years before in another place. But both stories are true; this is how. When King Peter of Aragon captured the island of Sicily he sent to the King of Tunis in Africa an ambassador named Cheraldo di Valenza. He was admitted one day to the King's chamber, where all was velvet and gold, with carpets underfoot of the finest silk worked in the Moorish style. And to please the King, who was very avid of praise for his possessions, he spat in the face of an African slave of the King. And when the Saracen demanded justice of his King, Cheraldo said: "My Lord, when I saw the immaculateness of this room, which is beyond all praise, I thought that you must have brought here this ugly face on purpose to be spat on, since it is the ugliest thing here present." The King was overjoyed at this fine remark, and the matter passed off in laughter.

Both of these expectorators were Spanish; make of that what you will. Let it suffice that an uncivil act is sometimes to be applauded, according to the circumstances.

# ❧ The Moor of Venice
## by G. B. GIRALDI (CINTHIO)

Giovanni Battista Giraldi, often called Cinthio or Cinzio, was born in Ferrara in 1504. At twenty-one he was appointed professor of natural philosophy, or physics, in the local university; twelve years later he moved to the chair of belles-lettres. Losing the favor of the ruling Este family in a literary controversy, he emigrated, and ended as professor of rhetoric at the University of Pavia. He died in 1573.

Giraldi produced nine tragedies, an interminable and unterminated epic poem, a *Discourse on the Composition of Romances,* and a collection of stories, the *Hecatommithi,* published in 1565. Contained therein is the tale of the Moor of Venice; it may well have been read by Shakespeare in a French translation.

Our version, by John Edward Taylor, appeared in London in 1855. It is Novella 7 of Decade III of the *Hecatommithi.*

THERE ONCE lived in Venice a Moor, who was very valiant and of a handsome person; and having given proofs in war of great skill and prudence, he was highly esteemed by the Signoria of the Republic, who in rewarding deeds of valour advanced the interests of the State.

It happened that a virtuous lady of marvellous beauty, named Disdemona, fell in love with the Moor, moved thereto by his valour; and he, vanquished by the beauty and the noble character of Disdemona, returned her love; and their affection was so mutual that, although the parents of the lady strove all they could to induce her to take another husband, she consented to marry the Moor; and they lived in such harmony and peace in Venice that no word ever passed between them that was not affectionate and kind.

Now it happened at this time that the Signoria of Venice made a change in the troops whom they used to maintain in Cyprus, and they appointed the Moor commander of the soldiers whom they dispatched thither. Joyful as was the Moor at the honour proffered him—such dignity being only conferred on men of noble rank and well-tried faith, and who had displayed bravery in arms—yet his pleasure was lessened when he reflected on the length and dangers of the voyage, fearing that Disdemona would be pained at his absence. But Disdemona, who had no other happiness in the world than the Moor, and who rejoiced to witness the testimony of his valour her husband had received from so powerful and noble a Republic, was all impatient that he should embark with his troops, and longed to accompany him to so honourable a post. And all the more it vexed her to see the Moor so troubled; and not knowing what could be the reason, one day, when they were at dinner, she said to him "How is it, O Moor, that when so honourable a post has been conferred on you by the Signoria, you are thus melancholy?"

The Moor answered Disdemona, "My pleasure at the honour I have received is disturbed by the love I bear you; for I see that of necessity one of two things must happen—either that I take you with me to encounter the perils of the sea, or, to save you from this danger, I must leave you here in Venice. The first could not be otherwise than serious to me, for all the toil you would have to bear and every danger that might befall you would cause me extreme anxiety and pain, yet, were I to leave you behind me, I should be hateful to myself, since in parting from you I should part from my own life."

Disdemona, on hearing this, replied: "My husband, what thoughts are these that wander through your mind? Why let such things disturb you? I will accompany you whithersoe'er you go, were it to pass through fire, as now to cross the water in a safe and well-provided ship; if indeed there are toils and perils to encounter, I will share them with you. And in truth I should think you love me little were you to leave me here in Venice, denying me to bear you company, or could believe that I would liefer bide in safety here than share the dangers that await you. Prepare then for the voyage with all the readiness which the dignity of the post you hold deserves."

The Moor, in the fulness of his joy, threw his arms around his wife's neck, and with an affectionate and tender kiss exclaimed, "God keep you long in such love, dear wife!" Then speedily donning his armour, and having prepared everything for his expedition, he embarked on board the galley with his wife and all his troops, and, setting sail, they pursued their voyage, and with a perfectly tranquil sea arrived safely at Cyprus.

Now amongst the soldiery there was an Ensign, a man of handsome figure, but of the most depraved nature in the world. This man was in great favour with the Moor, who had not the slightest idea of his wickedness; for, despite the malice lurking in his heart, he cloaked with proud and valorous speech and with a specious presence the villainy of his soul with such art that he was to all outward show another Hector or Achilles. This man had likewise taken with him his wife to Cyprus, a young, and fair, and virtuous lady; and being of Italian birth she was much loved by Disdemona, who spent the greater part of every day with her.

In the same Company there was a certain Captain of a troop, to whom the Moor was much affectioned. And Disdemona, for this cause, knowing how much her husband valued him, showed him proofs of the greatest kindness, which was all very grateful to the Moor. Now the wicked Ensign, regardless of the faith that he had pledged his wife, no less than of the friendship, fidelity, and obligation which he owed the Moor, fell passionately in love with Disdemona, and bent all his thoughts to achieve his conquest; yet he dared not to declare his passion openly, fearing that, should the Moor perceive it, he would at once kill him. He therefore sought in various ways, and with secret guile, to betray his passion to the lady; but she, whose every wish was centred in the Moor, had no thought for this Ensign more than for any other man; and all the means he tried to gain her love had no more effect than if he had not tried them. But the Ensign imagined that the cause of his ill success was that Disdemona loved the Captain of the troop; and he pondered how to remove him from her sight. The love which he had borne the lady now changed into the bitterest hate, and, having failed in his purposes, he devoted all his thoughts to plot the death of the Captain of the troop and to divert the affection of the Moor from Disdemona. After revolving in his mind various schemes, all alike wicked, he at length resolved to accuse her of unfaithfulness to her husband, and to represent the Captain as her paramour. But knowing the singular love the Moor bore to Disdemona, and the friendship which he had for the Captain, he was well aware that, unless he practised an artful fraud upon the Moor, it were impossible to make him give ear to either accusation; wherefore he resolved to wait until time and circumstance should open a path for him to engage in his foul project.

Not long afterwards it happened that the Captain, having drawn his sword upon a soldier of the guard, and struck him, the Moor deprived him of his rank: whereat Disdemona was deeply grieved, and endeavoured again and again to reconcile her husband to the man. This the Moor told to the wicked Ensign, and how his wife importuned him so much about the Captain that he feared he should be forced at last to receive him back to service. Upon this hint the Ensign resolved to act, and began to work his web of intrigue. "Perchance," said he, "the lady Disdemona may have good reason to look kindly on him."

"And wherefore?" said the Moor.

"Nay, I would not step 'twixt man and wife," replied the Ensign, "but let your eyes be witness to themselves."

In vain the Moor went on to question the officer—he would proceed no further; nevertheless, his words left a sharp, stinging thorn in the Moor's heart, who could think of nothing else, trying to guess their meaning and lost in melancholy. And one day, when his wife had been endeavouring to pacify his anger toward the Captain, and praying him not to be unmindful of ancient services and friendship for one small fault, especially since peace had been made between the Captain and the soldier he had struck, the Moor was angered, and exclaimed, "Great cause have you, Disdemona, to care so anxiously about this man! Is he a brother, or your kinsman, that he should be so near your heart?"

The lady, with all gentleness and humility, replied, "Be not angered, my dear lord; I have no other cause to bid me speak than sorrow that I see you lose so dear a friend as, by your own words, this Captain has been to you; nor has he done so grave a fault that you should bear him so much enmity. Nay, but you Moors are of so hot a nature that every little trifle moves you to anger and revenge."

Still more enraged at these words, the Moor replied, "I could bring proofs—by heaven it mocks belief! but for the wrongs I have endured revenge must satisfy my wrath."

Disdemona, in astonishment and fright, seeing her husband's anger kindled against her, so contrary to his wont, said humbly and with timidness, "None save a good intent has led me thus to speak with you, my lord; but to give cause no longer for offence, I'll never speak a word more on the subject."

The Moor, observing the earnestness with which his wife again pleaded for the Captain, began to guess the meaning of the Ensign's words; and in deep melancholy he went to seek that villain and induce him to speak more openly of what he knew. Then the Ensign, who was bent upon injuring the unhappy lady, after feigning at first great reluctance to say aught that might displease the Moor, at length pretended to yield to his entreaties, and said, "I can't deny it pains me to the soul to be thus forced to say what needs must be more hard to hear than any other grief; but since you will it so, and that the regard I owe your honour compels me to confess the truth, I will no longer refuse to satisfy your questions and my duty. Know, then, that for no other reason is your lady vexed to see the Captain in disfavour than the pleasure that she has in his company whenever he comes to your house, and all the more since she has taken an aversion to your black-ness."

These words went straight to the Moor's heart; but in order to hear more (now that he believed true all that the Ensign had told him) he replied, with a fierce glance, "By heavens, I scarce can hold this hand from plucking out that tongue of thine, so bold, which dares to speak such slander of my wife!"

"Captain," replied the Ensign, "I looked for such reward for these my faithful offices—none else; but since my duty, and the jealous care I bear your honour, have carried me thus far, I do repeat, so stands the truth, as you have heard it from these lips; and if the lady Disdemona hath, with a false show of love for you, blinded your eyes to what you should have seen, this is no argument but that I speak the truth. Nay, this same Captain told it me himself, like one whose happiness is incomplete until he can declare it to another; and, but that I feared your anger, I should have given him, when he told it me, his merited reward, and slain him. But since informing you of what concerns you more than any other man brings me so undeserved a recompense, would I had held my peace, since silence might have spared me your displeasure."

Then the Moor, burning with indignation and anguish, said, "Make thou these eyes self-witnesses of what thou tell'st or on thy life I'll make thee wish thou hadst been born without a tongue."

"An easy task it would have been," replied the villain, "when he was used to visit at your house; but now that you have banished him, not for just cause, but for mere frivolous pretext, it will be hard to prove the truth. Still, I do not forego the hope to make you witness of that which you will not credit from my lips."

Thus they parted. The wretched Moor, struck to the heart as by a barbed dart, returned to his home, and awaited the day when the Ensign should disclose to him the truth which was to make him miserable to the end of his days. But the evil-minded Ensign was, on his part, not less troubled by the chastity which he knew the lady Disdemona observed inviolate; and it seemed to him impossible to discover a means of making the Moor believe what he had falsely told him; and, turning the matter over in his thoughts in various ways, the villain resolved on a new deed of guilt.

Disdemona often used to go, as I have already said, to visit the Ensign's wife, and remained with her a good part of the day. Now, the Ensign observed that she carried about with her a handkerchief, which he knew the Moor had given her, finely embroidered in the Moorish fashion, and which was precious to

Disdemona, nor less so to the Moor. Then he conceived the plan of taking this kerchief from her secretly, and thus laying the snare for her final ruin. The Ensign had a little daughter, a child three years of age, who was much loved by Disdemona, and one day, when the unhappy lady had gone to pay a visit at the house of this vile man, he took the little child up in his arms and carried her to Disdemona, who took her and pressed her to her bosom; whilst at the same instant this traitor, who had extreme dexterity of hand, drew the kerchief from her sash so cunningly that she did not notice him, and overjoyed he took his leave of her.

Disdemona, ignorant of what had happened, returned home, and, busy with other thoughts, forgot the handkerchief. But a few days afterwards, looking for it and not finding it, she was in alarm, lest the Moor should ask her for it, as he oft was wont to do. Meanwhile, the wicked Ensign, seizing a fit opportunity, went to the Captain of the troop, and with crafty malice left the handkerchief at the head of his bed without his discovering the trick, until the following morning, when, on his getting out of bed, the handkerchief fell upon the floor, and he set his foot upon it. And not being able to imagine how it had come into his house, knowing that it belonged to Disdemona, he resolved to give it to her; and waiting until the Moor had gone from home, he went to the back door and knocked. It seemed as if fate conspired with the Ensign to work the death of the unhappy Disdemona. Just at that time the Moor returned home, and hearing a knocking at the back door, he went to the window, and in a rage exclaimed, "Who knocks there?" The Captain, hearing the Moor's voice, and fearing lest he should come down stairs and attack him, took to flight without answering a word. The Moor went down, and opening the door hastened into the street and looked about, but in vain. Then, returning into the house in great anger, he demanded of his wife who it was that had knocked at the door. Disdemona replied, as was true, that she did not know; but the Moor said, "It seemed to me the Captain."

"I know not," answered Disdemona, "whether it was he or another person."

The Moor restrained his fury, great as it was, wishing to do nothing before consulting the Ensign, to whom he hastened instantly, and told him all that had passed, praying him to gather from the Captain all he could respecting the affair. The Ensign, overjoyed at the occurrence, promised the Moor to do as he requested, and one day he took occasion to speak with the Captain when the Moor was so placed that he could see and hear them as they conversed. And whilst talking to him of every other subject than of Disdemona, he kept laughing all the time aloud, and, feigning astonishment, he made various movements with his head and hands, as if listening to some tale of marvel. As soon as the Moor saw the Captain depart, he went up to the Ensign to hear what he had said to him. And the Ensign, after long entreaty, at length said, "He has hidden from me nothing, and has told me that he has been used to visit your wife whenever you went from home, and that on the last occasion she gave him this handkerchief which you presented to her when you married her."

The Moor thanked the Ensign, and it seemed now clear to him that, should he find Disdemona not to have the handkerchief, it was all true that the Ensign had told to him. One day, therefore, after dinner, in conversation with his wife on various subjects, he asked her for the kerchief. The unhappy lady, who had been in great fear of this, grew red as fire at this demand; and to hide the scarlet of her cheeks, which was closely noted by the Moor, she ran to a chest and pretended to seek the handkerchief, and after hunting for it a long time, she said, "I know not how it is—I cannot find it; can you, perchance, have taken it?"

"If I had taken it," said the Moor, "why should I ask it of you? but, you will look better and another time."

On leaving the room the Moor fell to meditating how he should put his wife to death, and likewise the Captain of the troop, so that their death should not be laid to his charge. And as he ruminated over this, day and night, he could not prevent his wife's observing that he was not the same toward her as he had been wont; and she said to him again and again, "What is the matter? What troubles you? How comes it that you, who were the most light-hearted man in the world, are now so melancholy?"

The Moor feigned various reasons in reply to his wife's questioning, but she was not satisfied, and, although conscious that she had given the Moor no cause, by act or deed, to be so troubled, yet she feared that he might have grown wearied of her; and she would say to the Ensign's wife, "I know not what to say of the Moor; he used to be all love toward me; but within these few days he has become another man; and much I fear that I shall prove a warning to young girls not to marry against the wishes of their parents, and that the Italian ladies may learn from me not to wed a man whom nature and habitude of life estrange from us. But as I know the Moor is on such terms of friendship with your husband, and communicates to him all his affairs, I pray you, if you have heard from him aught that you may tell me of, fail not to befriend me." And as she said this, she wept bitterly.

The Ensign's wife, who knew the whole truth (her husband wishing to make use of her to compass the death of Disdemona), but could never consent to such a project, dared not, from fear of her husband, disclose a single circumstance: all she said was, "Beware lest you give any cause of suspicion to your husband, and show to him by every means your fidelity and love."—"Indeed I do so," replied Disdemona, "but it is all of no avail."

Meanwhile the Moor sought in every way to convince himself of what he fain would have found untrue, and he prayed the Ensign to contrive that he might see the handkerchief in the possession of the Captain. This was a difficult matter to the wicked Ensign; nevertheless, he promised to use every means to satisfy the Moor of the truth of what he said.

Now, the Captain had a wife at home who worked the most marvellous embroidery upon lawn, and seeing the handkerchief, which belonged to the Moor's wife, she resolved, before it was returned to her, to work one like it. As she was engaged in this task, the Ensign observed her standing at a window, where she could be seen by all the passers-by in the street, and he pointed her out to the Moor, who was now perfectly convinced of his wife's guilt. Then he arranged with the Ensign to slay Disdemona and the Captain of the troop, treating them as it seemed they both deserved. And the Moor prayed the Ensign that he would kill the Captain, promising eternal gratitude to him. But the Ensign at first refused to undertake so dangerous a task, the Captain being a man of equal skill and courage; until at length, after much entreating and being richly paid, the Moor prevailed on him to promise to attempt the deed.

Having formed this resolution, the Ensign, going out one dark night, sword in hand, met the Captain on his way to visit a courtesan, and struck him a blow on his right thigh, which cut off his leg and felled him to the earth. Then the Ensign was on the point of putting an end to his life, when the Captain, who was a courageous man and used to the sight of blood and death, drew his sword, and, wounded as he was, kept on his defence, exclaiming with a loud voice, "I'm murdered!" Thereupon the Ensign, hearing the people come running up with some of the soldiers who were lodged thereabouts, took to his heels to escape being caught: then turning about again, he joined the crowd, pretending to have been attracted by the noise. And when he saw the Captain's leg cut off, he judged that, if he was not already dead, the blow must, at all events, end his life; and whilst in his heart he was rejoiced at this, he yet feigned to compassionate the Captain as he had been his brother.

The next morning the tidings of this affair spread through the whole city, and reached the ears of Disdemona; whereat she, who was kind-hearted and little dreamed that any ill would betide her, evinced the greatest grief at the calamity. This served but to confirm the Moor's suspicions, and he went to seek for the Ensign, and said to him, "Do you know that my wife is in such grief at the Captain's accident that she is well nigh gone mad?"

"And what could you expect, seeing he is her very soul?" replied the Ensign.

"Ay, soul forsooth!" exclaimed the Moor; "I'll draw the soul from out her body; call me no man if that I fail to shut the world upon this wretch."

Then they consulted of one means and another—poison and daggers—to kill poor Disdemona, but could resolve on nothing.

At length the Ensign said, "A plan comes to my mind, which will give you satisfaction and raise cause for no suspicion. It is this: the house in which you live is very old, and the ceiling of your chamber has many cracks; I propose we take a stocking, filled with sand, and beat Disdemona with it till she dies; thus will her body bear no signs of violence. When she is dead we can pull down a portion of the ceiling, and thus make it seem as if a rafter falling on her head had killed the lady. Suspicion cannot rest on you, since all men will impute her death to accident."

This cruel counsel pleased the Moor, and he only waited for a fitting time to execute the plot. One night, when he and Disdemona had retired to bed, the Ensign, whom the Moor had concealed in a closet which opened into the chamber, raised a noise in the closet, according to a concerted plan; whereat the Moor said to his wife, "Did you not hear that noise?"

"Indeed I heard it," she replied.

"Rise," said the Moor, "and see what 'tis."

The unhappy Disdemona rose from bed, and the instant she approached the closet, out rushed the Ensign, and being strong and of stout nerve, he beat her cruelly with the bag of sand across her back; upon which Disdemona fell to the ground, scarce able to draw her breath; but with the little voice she had left, she called upon the Moor for aid. But the Moor, leaping from bed, exclaimed, "Thou wickedest of women, thus has thy falseness found its just reward, the recompense to wives who, counterfeiting love, place horns upon their husbands' brows."

The wretched lady, hearing these words, and feeling that she was near her end (for the Ensign had given her another blow), appealed to the justice of Heaven, since justice here had failed her, in proof of her fidelity and truth; and as she was thus calling Heaven to witness, the wicked Ensign inflicted a third blow, under which she sank lifeless on the floor.

Then the Ensign and the Moor, laying Disdemona on the bed and wounding her head, pulled down part of the ceiling of the chamber, as they had arranged; whereupon the Moor began to call aloud for help, exclaiming that the house was falling. Hearing this uproar, the neighbours all came running up, and there found Disdemona lying dead beneath a rafter—a sight which from the good life of that poor lady, did fill all hearts with sorrow.

On the following day Disdemona was buried, followed to the grave by the universal grief of the people. But Heaven, the just regarder of all hearts, willed not that so wicked a deed should go unpunished. Ere long the Moor, whom Disdemona had loved more than her own life, began to feel such sorrow at her loss that he went wandering about as one bereft of reason, searching in every part of the house. And reflecting in his thoughts that the Ensign had been the cause that he had lost, with Disdemona, all joy in life, he conceived so deep a hatred to that wicked man he could not bear to set eyes on him, and had it not been for his fear of the inviolable justice of the Signoria of Venice, he would have slain him openly. But being unable to do this with safety, he deprived him of his rank, and would not allow him to remain in his Company; whereat such an enmity arose between the two that no greater or more deadly can be imagined.

The Ensign, that wickedest of all bad men, now turned his thoughts to injuring the Moor; and seeking out the Captain, whose wound was by this time healed, and who went about with a wooden leg in place of the one that had been cut off, he said to him, " 'Tis time you should be avenged for your lost limb; and if you will come with me to Venice, I'll tell you who the malefactor is, whom I dare not mention to you here for many reasons; and I will bring you proofs."

The Captain of the troop, whose anger returned fiercely, but without knowing why, thanked the Ensign, and went with him to Venice. On arriving there the Ensign told him that it was the Moor who had cut off his leg, on account of the suspicion he had formed of Disdemona's conduct with him; and for that reason he had slain her, and then spread the report that the ceiling had fallen and killed her. Upon hearing which, the Captain accused the Moor to the Signoria, both of having cut off his leg and killed his wife, and called the Ensign to witness the truth of what he said. The Ensign declared both charges to be true, for that the Moor had disclosed to him the whole plot, and had tried to persuade him to perpetrate both crimes; and that having afterwards killed his wife out of jealousy he had conceived, he had narrated to him the manner in which he had perpetrated her death.

The Signoria of Venice, when they heard of the cruelty inflicted by a barbarian upon a lady of their city, commanded that the Moor's arms should be pinioned in Cyprus, and he be brought to Venice, where, with many tortures, they sought to draw from him the truth. But the Moor, bearing with unyielding courage all the torment, denied the whole charge so resolutely that no confession could be drawn from him. But, although by his constancy and firmness he escaped death, he was, after being confined for several days in prison, condemned to perpetual banishment, in which he was eventually slain by the kinsfolk of Disdemona, as he merited. The Ensign returned to his own country, and, following up his wonted villainy, he accused one of his companions of having sought to persuade him to kill an enemy of his, who was a man of noble rank; whereupon this person was arrested and put to the torture; but when he denied the truth of what his accuser had declared, the Ensign himself was likewise tortured to make him prove the truth of his accusations; and he was tortured so that his body ruptured, upon which he was removed from prison and taken home, where he died a miserable death. Thus did Heaven avenge the innocence of Disdemona; and all these events were narrated by the Ensign's wife, who was privy to the whole, after his death, as I have told them here.

# ❧ II
# FRANCE

*Little Jehan de Saintré*

# ❧ Little Jehan de Saintré

## by ANTOINE DE LA SALE

Antoine de La Sale was born in Provence in 1388. He had a court education and a distinguished army career; he then became tutor in princely families. Literature was a diversion of his elder years. *Le petit Jehan de Saintré* was evidently completed in 1456, when the author was nearly seventy. He died about 1462.

The book has been called, with good reason, the first modern novel. It is also, like *Don Quixote*, a mockery of the chivalric romances then in vogue. In the first part of the story Little Jehan is educated in the household of the kindly Dame des Belles-Cousines. He vows to her undying devotion, and, when grown, leaves her court to try his prowess, and gains fame as an intrepid knight. During his long absence the Lady falls in with a sturdy Abbot, as will now be told in this excerpt. (The translation, by Alexander Vance, was first published in London in 1862.)

T HE LADY'S principal seat was at a league from a principal city, and at another league from the said seat was an Abbey, being at a like distance from the city; so that the said city, Madame's hotel, and the Abbey may be said to have lain in a triangle. . . .

This Abbey, which is nameless, was founded by the ancestors of Madame, who had so bountifully endowed it, that, at this day, it is accounted one of the ten richest in France; and Damp * Abbot of it, for the time being, was the son of a rich burgess of the town, who, in consideration of a timely word in the ear of the King, and from his friends at the Court of Rome, so judiciously placed his money to account, that said son at length was made Abbot. And now, at the age of twenty-five, our Abbot was big

* Damp: Dom (Dominus), Lord.—Ed.

and brawny; and whether to wrestle, jump, vault, throw, pitch the sledge, or put the stone; at tennis, or what you will, there was not a monk, knight, squire or citizen alive, who, when Damp Abbot had chosen to do his best, had ever proved his match; and if on the one hand he kept himself in condition with all sorts of exercises and sports; on the other, he spent his money with so good a grace, so handsomely, that he was exceedingly beloved and praised of all. And when Damp Abbot heard of the arrival of Madame, he was wonderfully pleased; and he immediately ordered one of his carts to be filled with haunches of venison, boars' heads, hares, conies, pheasants, partridges, fat capons, pullets, pigeons, etc.; and all this he sent to Madame, together with a pipe of wine *de Beaune;* praying of her to be good enough to accept it, as it was meant, at his hands. And when Madame saw all this fine present, you need hardly ask if she was flattered! So she ordered the party who brought it to be well provided for, sending back her compliments to Damp Abbot.

And the time when all this happened was not far from Lent; and in the Abbey, the greater pardons were to be had on the Mondays, Tuesdays, Wednesdays, and Fridays of Lent. Now Madame, in a spirit of deep devotion, as became that holy season, determined to be there. But in order to allow the press of the common sort to be over, she refrained for some fifteen days. Then she sent word to Damp Abbot, that the next day she would attend a high mass; and after, procure her pardons.

On hearing this, Damp Abbot, who had never seen her, was delighted. So he gave orders to have all the holy reliques laid out on the grand altar, in the oratory of the chapel, where all her ancestors lay interred. And, in addition to this, he sent a requisition to the good town for whatever was to be found in the way of lampreys, salmon, or other fresh or salt water fish. Then he had stabling provided for all her equipage, and viands got together of every sort; and besides, he had fires lighted in all the rooms, for the season was such as required them. And when at length Madame was come, and had alighted at the door of the monastery, she was there met by all the officers, and the noblest churchmen of the same, who, on their knees, with Damp Abbot at their head, presented to her the keys, with all the choicest of their ornaments, as also the tender of their humble duties; for all which Madame thanked them greatly. And when she had made her offering at the great altar, she was conducted to her chapel to hear mass. Then, as she was leaving, after prayers, she was met by Damp Abbot and all his convent, on their knees; the said Damp Abbot saying to her, "Ever, and our most redoubted Lady, deign to accept your welcome from your own hall; and truly joyful and thankful are we, God has vouchsafed to us the grace to see, and to receive you in it. Into your hands, Lady, as at once our patron and our founder, we resign and offer up the Abbey with all that is in it, our bodies as our goods." Then said Madame to him, "Abbot, from our heart we thank you; and if there is anything we can either do for you or for your convent, you may count upon us." Then, Madame asked if she could see the holy reliques. On this, Damp Abbot, who was on his knees, got up, and diving his great fist into the chest, brought up arms and bones by the dozen, which were in it, of holy Saints deceased. And then he harangued Madame as follows, telling her, "Madame, yonder lies the body of that most valiant Prince, your ancestor, our first founder, who, on his return from the Holy Land, brought back with him this skull, this hand, and other bone of Such and Such a blessed saint, martyr, or holy woman. My Lord, his brother, who lies near him, it was, who gave us these thumbs, with the under jaw, and the toenail. They once belonged to So and So, and So and So; blessed virgins and sufferers, now with God. And, not to weary you; one or other of your progenitors have presented us with, I may say, all these reliques, and made this church, and much of all you see attached to it, what they are. The remainder has been the work of my predecessors, the Abbots, and the divers Lords and Ladies of the country, whose monuments you see around."

And when Madame had kissed these most precious reliques, she offered a cope, and two tunics, with a covering for the great altar, of rich crimson velvet, all wrought with gold. And when Madame thought to return, and her people were baiting the horses, or hurrying on their bridles, Damp Abbot led her into his room, to warm herself; which said room was all neat, and trim and carpeted, and it had glass windows in it; brief, was such as became a good fellow, like himself, and one who knew how to take his ease. Then he said to all, "Let us retire, and leave Madame alone, that she may warm and refresh herself."

And so they did. And when Madame, and the Ladies and Gentlewomen who were with her, had warmed and rested themselves, Madame sent word to know if the chariots were ready.

Then Damp Abbot, who had already told his maître-d'hôtel that Madame was to dine with him, when everything was ready, came and said to her that if she must go, he hoped she would accept his arm. And so saying, Damp Abbot stepped up to Madame, and taking her by the hand, led her into his dining-room, for all the world like an audience-hall, so nicely was it hung, carpeted, and glazed. And he had had a good fire put in it. And in the hall were three tables, each covered with the whitest of linen; and on the cupboards was show plate of every sort. And when Madame saw the tables laid, she said to Damp Abbot, "And is this your dinner-hour?"

"And is it not time?" said he: "it must be twelve by this."

But he had had the clock put on; and as he spoke it struck. And when Madame heard it strike, she was for hurrying away. And when Damp Abbot saw that she was determined to go, he said to her, "Madame, by the fealty I owe you, you are not going to leave us till you have had your dinner!"

"Dinner!" said Madame, "it is not to be thought of. I have too much to do elsewhere."

Then said Damp Abbot, "Ha, maître-d'hôtel; and you, my Ladies, will you stand by, and see me denied in this manner?"

Then the maître-d'hôtel, and the Ladies and Gentlewomen, who were all fasting, and as hungry as could be, thinking, besides, that they would get a better dinner by dining with Damp Abbot than they might at home, began to nudge one another for each to appeal to Madame. And at last, on their telling her that it was the first prayer Damp Abbot had ever made her, she consented.

Then Damp Abbot, all bowing, smiles, and gracious, fell on his knees, and humbly thanked Madame, and the other Ladies and Gentlewomen. Then the horses were sent back to the stables, and all were restored to good humour.

Then said Damp Abbot to Madame, "Madame, we are now in the holy season of penitence, so you are not to be surprised with the miserable fare before you. Besides, it was only late last evening that I heard of your intention to visit our Abbey."

"Abbot," said Madame, "we are sure we shall want for nothing."

Then Damp Abbot called for water, that they might wash their hands. And when it came, it was rose-water, with the chill off; an attention which pleased Madame and the other Ladies greatly. Then Madame required Damp Abbot, as Prelate, to wash after: which he would on no account do: so, to let the chaplains of Madame proceed, he withdrew to the sideboard, as if to see to something. And when the table was all ready, Madame desired Damp Abbot to be seated.

Then said Damp Abbot to her, "Madame, you are the Lady, and the Abbess of this house: it is for you to sit, leave me to take care of myself."

And at the foot of the table, where Madame presided, sat Madame Jehanne, Madame Katharine, and the Lord de Gency, who had come with her. And at the second table were the Prior of the convent, Isabelle, and the other Gentlewomen, and two or three Squires; and Sir Geoffrey de Sainct-Amant was opposite the said Isabelle. Then Damp Abbot, with his napkin before him, went to the cupboard, where was the wine, and brought to Madame a sop of white ypocras; * then handing it about to the other tables. Then he carried round the Lenten fruits, then the sweetmeats. Madame, all this time, was begging him to be seated; but he would only answer, "Madame, you must allow me this once to keep the company of maître-d'hôtel; and show him how his Lady should be served."

* Sop of white ypocras: piece of bread dipped in hippocras, spiced wine.—Ed.

But when the first dishes were on the table, and she still found Damp Abbot standing before them, Madame said to Damp Abbot, "Really, Abbot, if you will persist this way in standing, we will get up too."

"Sooner than that, Madame," said Damp Abbot, "I will obey you."

Madame was then going to bid some of them rise, to make way for him. But Damp Abbot said, "Let everybody sit still: God forbid that any should be disturbed for such as I."

Then he got a stool, and sat himself down, opposite Madame, only a little lower down. Then he had white wine, *de Beaune*, handed round; and after it red, of three or four kinds; and all had of them. What need I tell you of all their good cheer, or of how they all encouraged one another to eat and to drink? To be short, for many a long day Madame had never found herself so well entertained. So that soon it came, that the eyes, those archers of the heart, as well on the part of Madame as of Damp Abbot, began to launch their fiery darts: those of Madame at Damp Abbot; and those of Damp Abbot at Madame. Brief, so quickly came they to an understanding, that under cover of the cloth and napkins, which were long and trailing, first, from as if unintentionally touching one another with their feet, they got, at length, to treading on each other's toes. So that, so passionately were they absorbed with this new, below-board pastime, that what was upon it was quickly forgotten. However, Damp Abbot, who, on this new insight into the virtues of Dame Abbess and Foundress, was the more joyous of the two; though he might not eat, never once ceased drinking, now to one, now to another. What need I say more? Never, in his life, had Damp Abbot been in better spirits. One moment he was up, and had his stool placed before the Ladies; and when he had sat a little with them, he would be off to the Gentlewomen, telling them they had lost their appetites, or that they were in love; and that they must eat away heartily and be merry. Then he would make for Madame's women, and when he had had a jolly good laugh with them, return to Madame, and gloriously plant himself down by her side. Then would begin the archers to shoot again, more hard than ever; and those tender interpreters, the toes, to press the mutual ardour of their flames. And of all the sorts of wines, the viands, the lampreys; the fish, as well fresh as salt: in a word, how they were regaled and entertained, I will, at present, say nothing more; turning rather to the sequel of our tale, which, in all conscience, is rich enough.

And when the tables were removed; and the maître-d'hôtel and all the rest had gone to dine, Madame thanked Damp Abbot for the kindly entertainment she had met with; and so, talking, or walking about the hall, they amused themselves as best they could, whilst their people were dining. And Madame had given order, that by the time maître-d'hôtel had done, the horses and carriages were to be at the door. But Damp Abbot, so that Madame might repose herself, had had his own best bed new made with fair fresh linen. So he said to her, "How, Madame, surely you are not going to make so little of the good old customs of the place?"

"And what, Abbot," inquired Madame, "are the good old customs?"

"Madame," said he, "they are, that whenever any Ladies of condition, or Gentlewomen, have dined at the Abbey, they and their attendants should accept of a bed, either to sleep or rest themselves, as they please; and this as well in winter as in summer; and that they stay supper. So, Madame, for this afternoon, I make over to you my own room, and will sleep, myself, somewhere else. It is a usage has never yet been departed from in our Abbey; so I hope, Madame, you are not going to break in upon it."

At length, such were the prayers of Damp Abbot and the Ladies, that Madame became gracious, and said she would keep up the good old customs.

Then Madame withdrew to her apartment; and there she found wine and dessert on the cupboard. Then the door was closed, and Madame was left by herself, with her Ladies, to repose till the time of vespers.

And when the Ladies and Gentlewomen were all left to themselves, first Isabelle began to open, and said, "And how, Madame, have you had nothing to say, nor the rest of you, sots, of Damp Abbot's good cheer, and the reception he has given us? Certainly, I never saw such a table; more on one, or drunk better wine."

"Certainly," said Madame, "the man seems a respectable one enough."

"And is that all you have to say for him!" said Madame Jehanne. "A more engaging man I never came across."

"And yet you, Madame," said Katharine, "were not for staying, if we had not made you!"

"Ha!" said Isabelle, "I knew from the first he would carry his point: he was in earnest about it."

Then they all fell to together, as women will do, when alone. to praise the magnificence, the jolliness, and the fine proportions of Damp Abbot, and all with such a relish and a gusto, one would fancy they would never cease. However, Madame, whose great griefs were now beginning to abate, and who, besides, was more taken with Damp Abbot than she cared them to see, allowing them to jabber, simply confined herself to saying, at intervals, "The man seems a respectable one enough."

And while they were all still busy belauding Damp Abbot, the bell rung for vespers, so that they were forced to rise, without having so much as closed an eye.

And as soon as vespers were over, and when Madame was thinking to mount, Damp Abbot took her by the hand, on which Madame said to him, "Hey, Abbot, where next?"

Then said Damp Abbot, "Permit me, Madame, to lead you to a slight collation, for it is high time."

And as he said this, he placed Madame's arm under his, and gently pressing her hand, he led her into a lower hall, which was well hung, and where was a great fire, and the tables were spread. And on them were salads and vinegar, and lampreys, roasted and in pies, and sauces; and roaches, and barbels, and salmon, cut in steaks, griddled and boiled; and fat carp, and great dishes of crawfish, and huge river eels, swimming in their fat; and, besides these, there were dishes and plates of various devices, covered with dessert; jellies, white, carnation, and of gold; tarts *à la bourbonnoise*, cheese-cakes, flawns, sugar-plums, white almonds, rose-water crackers; together with figs from Melique, Allegarde, and Marseilles, raisins from Corinth, and with abundance of other things, all laid out in the order of a banquet.

Madame who, though hungry, had no idea of taking anything save a cup of wine or a biscuit, found the tables, however, groaning with all these good things. For the traitor, God of love, had so furiously assailed her with his arms during all the time of dinner that either to eat or to drink she had had no heed. But as nature seldom fails, sooner or later, to make her wants to be attended to, Madame's appetite was now so much restored, that, to stay, she required but little pressing. And when the rest of the company saw Madame seated, and Damp Abbot at the middle of the table opposite to her, with very little prayers on the part of Damp Abbot, they consented to fall into their places. And, by Madame's orders, and to be better company to one another, it was enjoined them all to sit as well on each side, as at the ends of the table. And that nothing should be wanting, and all might pass more pleasantly, four of five monks of the more jovial of the fraternity were sent for and introduced. And thus the table was full.

What need I tell you more? The mirth and jollity was such, that among the like number of persons, greater was never seen. However, at length, the hour arrived when Madame and Damp Abbot, to their great regret and sorrow, were obliged to part. And as she was stepping into her chariot, there were Damp Abbot and Prior, most humbly thanking Madame for the great honour that she had done them, and recommending to her the church and convent. Then Madame said to them, "We shall often see you, for we hope, from henceforth, more frequently to be sharers of your pardons than hitherto we have been able." On hearing which they were well pleased. Presently she continued, "But as for you, Abbot, we have to request that there may be a truce to all this prodigality; for, assuredly, to-day's feasting has been altogether out of all conscience, and it is not our wish to see the like repeated."

"At least, Madame," said Damp Abbot, "you will not decline or forbid me to offer you, after mass, a morsel, *à la poudre de duc,** with either white wine, or ypocras, or grenasche, or malmsey, or Greek wine, as you would prefer?"

"But I will," said Madame: "at such a season as this it is our business to fast."

"To fast!" said Damp Abbot; "it is not to be thought of. I can always give you absolution."

And after, Damp Abbot mounted on his horse, and conducted Madame a good way, and then took his leave.

And as soon as Damp Abbot had left them, and gone back to his Abbey, then commenced his praises, and it was who loudest could extol him. And Isabelle, who was the most rattling, began to say, "Ha, Madame, Madame, you are much to blame to refuse a good thing when it falls in your way."

Then Madame Jehanne said to her, "Isabelle, you are mistaken; Madame often intends to go, and she will dine each time she does."

To this said Madame Katharine, "You are both in the wrong. There is no occasion whatsoever that Madame should dine every time she goes to the convent; but I certainly think she is perfectly warranted in accepting, once in a way, the civilities of Damp Abbot; for, as far as one can judge, they are offered out of real good nature, and without any afterthoughts. He can well afford it, or it would be another thing. What say you, Madame; am I not in the right?"

Then Madame, when she had heard them all round, said, "Of his mutton we will be content with the wool. So we will confine ourselves to his snatch, *à la poudre de duc*, white wine, ypocras, grenasche, malmsey, or other rich or rarer sort; that will be quite sufficient. But, seriously, it is our intention to acquire for ourselves all these pardons, or, at any rate, most of them; for we hardly know when again we may be in these parts, or able to procure them."

And by this they had gotten to their hotel. Madame, into whose

---

* *A la poudre de duc*: with sugar and cinnamon.—Ed.

breast this new flame had now wormed its way, was unable, all this night, to sleep, doing nothing but sigh and mourn, and toss and turn; planning with herself how, soonest, she could get again to see Damp Abbot, and open herself to him more fully; whilst Damp Abbot, on his side, tormented with the like imaginations, and who had not yet forgotten all the pleasant earnest had been interchanged between them, either above or below the board, had not another thought but "When will Madame be coming for her pardons?"

And when the long-wished-for day was come, Madame said to her women that, in order the better to prepare herself to receive, fitly and worthily, the pardons, she had resolved to confess herself unfeignedly to Damp Abbot, who was a prelate, and, so far as she could judge of him, a man of a deep devotion.

Then said Madame Jehanne to Madame, "Madame, you will do very rightly; I was with him yesterday myself."

Then Madame bid the little Perrin, of her bedchamber, to get on a horse, and go and tell Damp Abbot that Madame would be glad to see him presently.

On hearing this, Damp Abbot lost no time, as he was anxious to show his great respect for Madame. Then Madame, after he had made his reverence, present all her Ladies, openly said to him, "Abbot, the more worthily to be constituted partakers of your pardons, we have determined to confess ourselves."

"Ah, Madame," said Damp Abbot, "how stand you with God? And, Madame, who purpose you to be your confessor, so that I may give him dispensation, if unhappily unprovided?"

"Then," said Madame, "There is none here more able or sufficient than yourself."

To which Damp Abbot replied, "Ah, Madame, if there is any good or efficacy in me, it is in virtue of my staff; deprive me of it, and I am no more worthy than is another."

With these words, Madame retired into her dressing-room, in which there was a good fire, Damp Abbot devoutly following her. And when the door was closed, for two hours she poured out before him, in all humbleness and penitence of spirit, all the little

kindnesses, and the amorous mercies, in which, from her youth
up, she had indulged herself; in all honour, however, and without
any sort of villainy, and, for all which, Damp Abbot gave her
absolution, as tenderly as he could. And before they separated,
Madame went to her coffer, and took from it a very large and
splendid ruby ring, all set in gold, and putting it on his middle
finger, said to him, "Sweetheart, my only thought, my soul's desire, this day I elect you as my only friend, and with this ring I
wed you."

Then Damp Abbot, as humbly as he could find words, thanked
her, all the while muttering to himself the good old saw, which
says,

> He who a chance refuses,
> Deserves when he loses.

Then he gave Madame absolution, and kissing her as softly as he
could, with the holy kiss of charity, he took his leave. And as he
was returning through the hall, he said, feelingly, to the Ladies
and Gentlewomen present, "Till she calls let none of you, my
sisters and my friends, disturb her. May God be with you; Madame I leave to your care."

Whilst Madame, to recover a little the colour which her
mortification had withdrawn from her cheeks, remained so long
behind, that, at last, her Ladies and her people heard the clock
announce the hour for prayers, on which Madame, who heard it
too, called for Jehanne, and when she had put on some of the
plainest things she had, and, the better to cover her face, a handkerchief over her head; in this simple and unpretending manner,
her eyes and her face toward the ground, she went, in deep con-
trition, to hear mass; and after that to dinner, and so the day
passed. And the one following, Wednesday, pardons being again
to be dispensed, Madame having signified her intention to be
present, Damp Abbot, in the greatest spirits, had all sorts of good
things prepared; ypocras, and other foreign wines, of various
kinds, decanted; white and red herrings and more substantial
victuals for the companions, besides good stabling and provender

for the horses. And when Madame had heard mass, Damp Abbot took Madame under his arm, and led her into his apartment, where there was a good fire, and breakfast laid out. And when Madame had plentifully breakfasted, Damp Abbot took her by the hand, saying, "Madame, while all your people are finishing and regaling themselves, allow me to show you our new buildings."

Then they both left the room, and had quickly wandered so far out of one chamber and into another, that her Ladies lost all trace of her. And before they came out of the secret closet, Damp Abbot gave Madame a piece of fine black velvet, which afterwards she quietly sent for. Then Madame returned into the dining-hall, where the company were, and when her Ladies came in from looking for her, Madame, as if in a rage, was down upon them, saying, "I told you to come after me, and I thought, all the time, you were; but you would rather sit here, the lot of you, cramming yourselves with Abbot's good things, and roasting your toes at the fire, than have a thought or care for your mistress!"

"Ah, Madame," said they, "though we went almost immediately after you, do what we would we could not find you!"

On this, Damp Abbot put in a word, saying, "Ah, Madame, do for this once let them be forgiven."

Then Madame, relenting, began to praise Damp Abbot's fine buildings, which she said she had been through. Then she made for her chariot, on which Damp Abbot took his leave of her. What need I say more? Hardly a week of Lent went over in which she did not succeed, with a no less assiduous attendance, in gaining for herself the pardons, etc., as often as not remaining, along with one or two others, banqueting, dining, and supping. And after she got up, it was frequently to hunt, with Damp Abbot, stags, foxes, pheasants, and the like game. And in this manner the season of Lent slipped heedlessly and joyously away. . . .

[Little Jehan de Saintré, now the Lord de Saintré, after fighting valiantly for the king, returns to the court in Paris. He and his companions are most cordially received by royalty.]

And, not to be tedious, as soon as they had all made their reverences, and the first congratulations were over, and the excitement, on seeing them, had begun a little to subside, the Lord de Saintré, amazed beyond all conception that he could no where see Madame, whom above all the world he was longing most to have a word with, at once concluded that something surely must have happened to her. So, making for Madame de Sancte-More, his cousin; and first having chatted of one thing, then another, he presently said to her, carelessly, and as if he was thinking of something else, "But, Goody, what has become of Madame? I see most of the old faces; is she about, or is she ill?

"Faith," said she, "ill or not ill, she is ill enough in the graces of the Queen. For about three weeks after you left, something unaccountable came over her: so that, visibly, she was wasting away. And from what the Queen's physician said, she would certainly be very shortly either dead or in a consumption, supposing her native air to fail to bring her round. So, of course, the Queen told her, by all means, to go; but to come back in two months. But, as at the end of the two months, and a half to the back of it, no Madame was making her appearance, the Queen wrote to her by Master Julien de Bray, reminding her that her time was up; and since, she sent to her again. But all the answer she could ever get was, '*Coming, Madame; coming*'; but with all her coming, she has never come."

And when the Lord de Saintré heard tell how Madame was ill, incontinent flashed upon him all she had ever told him, how she never would know peace of mind again till she had seen him returned in safety. And surely, said he to himself, it was to hide herself, since her sorrow she could not, that she went. But, presently, comforting himself, he recollected, that if it was sorrow for his departure had driven her away, the tidings of his return, as assuredly, would bring her back. However, on reflection, he came to the conclusion, that, considering everything, he could not do better than be, himself, the herald of his own right-glorious self. And continuing, some ten or twelve days, in the same opinion, he then said to the King, "Sir, if it would be your good pleasure to allow me to absent myself for some few days, I should feel myself very greatly indebted to you. My Lady-Mother is solicitous to see me."

To which the King replied, "How, Saintré; off again? But if your mother really does wish to see you, by all means go, and you may remain for a month."

And when the Lord de Saintré had thanked him, he set to work, and never stopped, day or night, till he had got himself, and all his people, and his horses, and everything about him in the sprucest order, the better to delight Madame, and take her by surprise. And when he had taken his leave of the King, the Queen, and my Lords, he got on his horse, nor ever once halted, but to rest, till he had got to the good town, at one league from the hotel where Madame stayed, and there he dined. And then he dressed and refreshed himself. And when he had put on a doublet of satin, trimmed with gold, with scarlet stockings, all worked in the device and colours of Madame, with a natty little cap upon his head, as was the fashion of those times, with a brooch in it; thus arrayed, accompanied by two Knights and seven Squires, all in a no less costly attire, with the like robes and devices, he set out for the hotel of Madame. And when they had got to the door, and had knocked, the porter inquired of them what it was they wanted.

To which the Lord de Saintré replied that he was anxious to see Madame, and that he might say, the Lord Saintré was there.

"She is out, then," said the porter; "she went this morning to the Abbey to hear mass; and she was to stay dinner."

So, from that he went to the Abbey. And when he got there, he found that they had already dined; and that, after dinner and bed, Madame and Damp Abbot had gone out hawking. Then, having first inquired in what direction he was most likely to fall in with them, he told four or five of his people to put their spurs to their horses, one this way, one that; and that, as soon as they should see any Ladies in the fields, they were to come back at once, and tell him. And so they all dispersed about; and, in a very few minutes, one of them came riding in post haste to tell him that he had seen a party of at least twenty, on horseback; and that seven or eight of them appeared Ladies, and evidently persons of condition.

Then this faithful Knight, who, till the instant after, never so much as suspected or dreamt of the falseness of his Lady, clapping spurs to his horse, made, as fast as its legs would carry him, for the presence of her whom above all the world he longed the most to feast his eyes upon. And as soon as he saw her, his heart began to bound within him; half conscious to himself of the pretty and the noble fellow he looked. And with this, he rode right up to her. But before he had reached her, one of the monks of Damp Abbot, who had been observing Saintré and his party, coming up to Damp Abbot, who was alongside of Madame, told him to look, for he strongly suspected there must be strangers about, or something wrong. And when Damp Abbot looked closer, and saw the strange faces, and horsemen all galloping about the country, he was not too much at his ease, for he thought with himself, surely these are Madame's brothers and people, who have heard all about our carryings on, and they have now come down to make mince-meat of poor Damp Abbot. Then, on the instant, he wheeled his mule round, leaving Madame to her fate, and made off; his hawk upon his fist, and his three monks after him, their big-bellied bottles, and their prog-baskets * dangling to the wind. However, Madame, her hawk upon her wrist, and seated on her good stout cob, and who was not so easily to be frightened out of her presence of mind, quietly stood her ground, to see who in the world it could be. And as soon as her people perceived it to be the Lord de Saintré, and had told her so; turning on them, she said in a fury, "May the devil seize the lot of you! And is that any reason why, for one man, you should all scamper off like that?"

And as she was yet speaking, the Lord de Saintré, now breathless with emotion, was alighting from his horse. And when

* Prog-baskets: picnic baskets.—Ed.

Madame saw him on the ground, she said, aloud to him, so that all might hear, "Sir, Sir, a more unwelcome guest may it never be my part to entertain!"

This, however, so little reached the ears of Saintré, that, in an instant, he was down upon his knee; and, taking her by the hand, had already begun, "Ha, and how are you, my ever-to-be-redoubted Lady; and what are you doing?"

"How am I?" said she; "and cannot you look for yourself? Doing? do you not see that I have my hawk on my hand, and that I am sitting in my saddle?"

And without more ado, she turned her horse's head, and calling to her people, told them to lead on, for that there was no occasion for their stopping; letting them plainly see how little account she made of Saintré.

Saintré, who, this time, heard Madame clear enough, did not exactly know either what to think of it or what to do. However, as the Ladies and Gentlewomen came up, he shook them by the hand, and kissed them, and embraced them. Then he mounted again on his horse, and went after Madame. And when he got alongside of her, in a distressed tone he said to her, "Hey, Madame; can you possibly have meant it, when you spoke to me the way you did; or was it only done to try me? How had you the heart to speak so cruelly to one who has loved you so long, and never yet, in his life, disobeyed you? Hey, Madame, some one has been imposing upon you. If it be so, depend upon it, time and I will clear all up."

To this, Madame, who all the while was wishing him far enough, only replied, "Is there no other string but that you have to harp upon? if not, you may just as well give over at once."

And by the time all this had passed, Damp Abbot had begun to be a little recovered of his fright; so calling to him one of his monks, he bade him ask the maître-d'hôtel who this strange Lord was. And when Damp Abbot heard that it was the Lord de Saintré; now reassured, he came to him at once, and paid him his respects, saying, "Most honoured Lord, be you the very welcome; you, and all your honourable company; for, I can assure you, there is not a noble in the land I have longer wished to lay my eyes on than yourself."

The Lord de Saintré comprehending, on hearing this, and seeing him, that he was an Abbot, and his people were monks; said to him, "Damp Abbot, you are welcome, as are all with you."

"Sir," said Damp Abbot, who was now himself again, "and what think you of the condescension of this noble Lady; thus deigning to honour with her presence the parlour of her poor confessor; to hunt with an unfortunate monk like myself?"

"Madame," said the Lord de Saintré, " is a Lady of all honour, and none of more discernment. There is no pleasanter pastime; and Madame has been ever a friend to the church."

These compliments interchanged, Damp Abbot gradually fell back, leaving Madame and the Lord de Saintré together. And as the vesper bell was now heard, and they were approaching the convent, Damp Abbot sent one of his monks to the maître-d'hôtel, bidding him to sound Madame, as to whether she would wish the Lord de Saintré to be invited to remain for supper. Then the maître-d'hôtel came to Madame, and asked her if she would wish the Lord de Saintré to sup with her.

To which, Madame, who had not distinctly heard him, only rejoined, by ordering him to speak up, that she could hear.

So he asked her the same thing again, and, this time, loud enough for Saintré to overhear.

And when Madame understood what he wanted, after a moment's reflection, she replied, "Ask him, if you have a mind; but if he wants to go, he need not be under any ceremony on my account."

On hearing this, which he did clearly enough, the Lord de Saintré thought he had better decline at once, without exposing himself to any sort of pressing. Whilst Madame, now sick of him and his prayers, kept telling every one that she was tired, and to get home as quick as they could.

Now, Damp Abbot, who knew well what became a gentleman, had already gone on before, so as to have all things in readiness.

And when they were come, the Lord de Saintré got off his horse, offering his assistance to Madame to do the same. But she called for one of her own people. And when they had both alighted, the Lord de Saintré was about to take his leave of Madame. And as she was holding out her hand to him, Damp Abbot, to show him his respect, said to Madame, "Madame, and is he then to go? It remains with you."

"With him," said Madame.

Then Damp Abbot said to him, "Ha, my Lord de Saintré; bear a little with Madame. Be entreated to stay."

Then the Lord de Saintré said to Damp Abbot, "Ha, Damp Abbot; your first request it would be uncivil and ill-natured to decline."

Then the Lord de Saintré kept with him two Squires, a varlet, and a page only, sending the remainder of his people to the good town to get their supper; and telling the maître-d'hôtel that they were all to come back to him, after, to Madame's. And by this time, the tables were laid, and supper all ready. Then Madame washed her hands first; and next, Damp Abbot and the Lord de Saintré. And then on account of his position and his dignity, Damp Abbot was placed at the middle of the table, with his face turned toward Madame, who was at the other side, and with her back to the wall. And, after Madame came the Lord de Saintré, then Madame Jehanne, and Madame Katharine next. Then salad was first handed round; of which Madame and Damp Abbot ate freely. Then came the larger dishes, all full of young rabbits, partridges, pigeons, of which they all ate, and then washed well down with the best of wines; Beaune, de Tournon, Saint-Poursain. And when all their bellies began to be pretty well filled, it was not long after till their tongues commenced to wag; and, incontinent, Damp Abbot began to be facetious. And anon he said, "Ho! my Lord de Saintré; ho! wake up, Sir, wake up; I see well by your manner, and your half-lined guts, that you are either half asleep or dreaming!"

Then the Lord de Saintré said to him, "Far from it, my Lord Abbot; really, all these good things of yours, and these excellent wines I find before me, are keeping me so busy, that, to tell you the truth, I have room to think of little else."

Then said Damp Abbot, "My Lord de Saintré, do you know, it has often occurred to me, in a quiet way, that, occasionally, it may have happened among you others, Noblemen, Knights, and Squires, to be capable of putting tricks on us, poor stick-at-homes; telling us how you were the conquerors at this or that tilt or tournament, when, God knows, things went a very other way." Then turning himself to Madame, he appealed to her, demanding of her if it was not so.

"Faith, Abbot," said Madame, "it is no more than the truth, and likely enough. Good sir, say on, for you seem to me perfectly to understand the matter."

"Madame," said he, "if I do, remember, it must be by your orders, and with your consent; for, possibly, my Lord de Saintré may not be equally disposed to take it all in like good part; but since you have put it on me, Madame, my opinion is this: There is a certain sort of Knight and Squire, for the most part to be found, as well in the King's Court, as the Queen's, and those of great Lords and Princes, generally, who give themselves out to the world, to be the devoted champions of the Ladies. And to work themselves the better into your good graces, if not in them already, they will ever have tears at their command, and so sigh and mourn, and rave, and come the disconsolate that out of sheer commiseration, you, poor Ladies, whose hearts are naturally but too tender and compassionate, inch by inch, are encompassed in their toils; so that, at last, they have their pleasure of you. And then they go to a second, and then a third. And they will take for their badge a garter, or a bracelet, a smock, a turnip, or a pig, or God only knows what trumpery; and then they will tell some dozen of them, sighing, one after the other, 'Ah, Madame, it is for your sake I am wearing this token!' So, goodness only knows how the unfortunate wretches are gammoned of their lovers; one, one way; one, another. As for sincerity, it is a word their mothers never taught them. And then, as if it was not enough to gull their Ladies; for their further recreation, they must worm themselves into the good graces of King, Queen, and all the world and his wife; at whose expense they fig themselves out. What say you, Madame; is it not the case?"

Madame, to whom all this lecture suited most wonderfully, smiling, said to him, "Abbot, how came you to have learned all this? Methinks, however, you are not far from the mark." And as she spoke, she put her foot on Damp Abbot's toes.

"And farther than this, Madame," said Damp Abbot, "you may not be aware, that when these famous Paladins, Knights and Squires, are about to set out on some wonderful exploit or other, and they have taken their leave of the King, no matter for where; let it but happen to be cold, and they take the way of Germany, there to pass the winter, chaffing with the girls over good hot stoves. But if it happens to be summer, they will be off to the delicious realms of Sicily, or of Aragon; there, amid the fragrant groves, by purling fountains, the orange and the lime, to bask the hours away, surrounded by the lovely houris of the land. And glad enough are the gentry of the same to see them; and the best of wine, and fruit, and cheer is theirs. And then, when they think they have been long enough away, they get some Trumpet or other, or a Herald, with a sign-board on his back, and sticking one of their old cloaks upon his shoulders, they give him an écu *  to shout about the country, '*My Lord, as the most valiant, has gained the prize of Arms!*' Poor Ladies, how easily are you imposed upon! and, from my soul, I pity you."

Madame, who, on hearing this, was so delighted, that more she could not be, turning her head a little round, said to the Lord de Saintré, who was excedingly displeased to hear so injurious an affront thus laid to the door of his order, "My Lord de Saintré, what have you to reply to this?"

But before he could speak, Damp Abbot went on to say, "Madame, you have all your life lived among them; if it is not as much, you must know it."

Then said Madame, "We must certainly allow we have met

* Ecu: crown (coin).—Ed.

with some who were capable of better things, but we are far
from being able to answer for all. However, as a general principle,
we think, Damp Abbot, you are not far off the truth."

And as she said it, she kept winking and nodding to Damp
Abbot, and then she would touch him with her foot. On seeing
this the Lord de Saintré said, "Ha, Madame, you are saying this
on purpose; however, I pray God you may yet return to another
mind, and be better informed."

"And how would you have Madame better informed?" said
Damp Abbot, "she cannot know better than she does already."

"As to knowing," said the Lord de Saintré, "I have nothing to
say; Madame is at liberty to express the opinions she thinks proper;
but as to yourself, and the licence you have permitted your
tongue, in declaring your notions of Knights and noble men, I
have to tell you, that if you were a party to whom it would become me to reply, you should not long be wanting for an answer.
But mindful as well of my own dignity, as of who and what
you, Damp Abbot, are, I am now silent. It may so hap, however,
that on some other and more fitting occasion, the subject will
prove such as I shall return upon."

Damp Abbot, now head and tail alike on fire, as if determined
to affront the Lord de Saintré, appealing to Madame, said, "Madame, you have been the means of having me insulted in your
own house!"

And as he said it, the war of toes went on more hard than ever.
And when he saw Madame continue to nod, and wink, and smile,
and encourage him, he well knew the sport was to her mind; so
he said, "Ho, my Lord de Saintré! ho, my Lord de Saintré! I
am no man of war, or man of blood; I am but a poor simple
beadsman,* with my all upon my back. For the love of God, Sir,
is it for the like of me to fight with you? But should there be any
one, and I care not one fico for the Who, who will undertake to
contradict me in this quarrel, and to wrestle me upon it, I'm his
man!"

* Beadsman: cleric bound to pray for founders of his house.—Ed.

"Would you, then," said Madame, "would you really?"

"Madame," said he, "at the worst, I can but be thrown; but please God, who will be on my side, and the truth and justice of my cause, I will get the better of him, be he the biggest butcher of the lot of them."

All this while the Lord de Saintré, who could not but see at whom all these outrages were aimed, hearing such encouragement on the part of Madame, was feeling as if his very heart would split, and was wishing himself a thousand times dead. Madame, who saw all this well, without appearing, however, to take any sort of notice of it, said to him, "Ha, my Lord de Saintré, you, the conqueror, as they tell us, of so many a hard-fought field, fear you to wrestle with Damp Abbot? Certainly, if you do not, I shall be forced to think as he does of the matter."

"Ah, Madame," said he, "you know well that I never was taught to wrestle, and that these Lords of churchmen are adepts at the art, as at tennis, hurl-bat, pitch-bar, and every pastime of the sort. They are their only recreations when among themselves, and, for this reason, I know well, Madame, that I would not have a chance with him."

"At least try," said she, "you can do your best; and you have my word for it, that if you do not, you shall be posted in every place I go, for a false and craven-hearted Knight."

"God, Madame!" said he, starting up, "and this to me! One would think I had done enough to satisfy any woman; but since such is your pleasure, you shall be obeyed."

"What's that he says?" said Damp Abbot.

"He says, Abbot," said Madame, "that he will accept your challenge, for that he has been in greater scrapes in his time, yet come out of them triumphant."

"He has, then, has he?" said Damp Abbot, "we'll see for that, presently."

Then, without waiting another second, or till a single thing was removed, Damp Abbot jumped up in an ecstacy, and next Madame rose, and then the Lord de Saintré, to the amazement of all the rest of the company. And the sun was now about setting.

Then Damp Abbot took Madame by the arm, and led her into a fair smooth green, and placing her under a spreading pine, bade her be seated, and to be their judge.

Then Madame sat down, more joyous than she had ever been before in all her life, calling to her women to sit down by her. But they, to see all this, however much they might dissimulate, for Madame's sake, their feelings, at heart were not over-well pleased. Then went Damp Abbot through a ceremony, which neither Saint Benoist, Saint Richard, Saint Augustin, Saint Bernard, nor any other Saint or Father of Holy Church was ever known to have performed in his living; for, there and then, before them all, he stripped himself to his doublet, and letting down his stockings to his knees, fastened them, with a wisp, at the same. Thus arrayed, he was the first to make his appearance before Madame. And when he had paid her his reverence, for her farther gratification, and that of the company, he next threw a great somersault, displaying his great big brawny arms and thighs, all hairy over like any bear. And after him came the Lord de Saintré, who, at a little distance, had undressed himself, his stockings all richly sown in pearl and gold. And he, too, came to pay his respects to Madame, smothering, as best he could, the mortification and humiliation of his soul. And presently they were facing one another; but before either of them had time to lay hold, Damp Abbot all of a sudden wheeled about, and throwing himself imploringly on his knees before Madame, said to her, with uplifted hands, "Ah, Madame, entreat for me to the Lord de Saintré!"

Then Madame, who was well acquainted with Damp Abbot's powers, laughing, said to the Lord de Saintré, "Hey, my Lord de Saintré, we recommend to you our Abbot; do not, for our sake, be too hard with him."

To which the Lord de Saintré, who too well saw through all this raillery, only said, "Alas, Madame, it is he who will have to spare me."

And when he had said this, Damp Abbot and the Lord de Saintré closed, and made a feint or two. Then Damp Abbot put out his leg, and by a twitch of his foot sent the Lord de Saintré flying head over heels; the said Lord falling on the grass, on the flat of his back, with his legs in the air. Then Damp Abbot, striding across him, as he lay there, cried out, as in distress, to Madame, "Ah, Madame, recommend me to the Lord de Saintré!"

Then Madame, laughing as if she would burst, said to him, "Ah, Lord de Saintré, hear Damp Abbot's prayer!" but for the way she was tickled, she could not add another word.

Then Damp Abbot got up on his legs, and said aloud, so that all might hear, "Madame, what I have done, was out of love; the God of heaven, and the God of love have fought on my side, and avenged my quarrel. And if the Lord de Saintré should now be disposed to assert that he loves his lady better than I do mine, here am I, all simple and naked as I am, ready and willing to attest the contrary."

"You are, are you?" said Madame.

"Aye, against him, or any other man," said Damp Abbot.

Then said Madame, smiling, to the Lord de Saintré, "What say you to this, my Lord de Saintré? Surely as a gentleman and a man of honour, you are bound to take it up."

"Madame," replied he, "and as a gentleman, had it been toward a gentleman, I had taken it up, and in such a manner too as gentlemen alone are privileged to take such matters up."

"That is but an idle evasion," said Madame, "to get out of it. It should be taunt enough to raise the spirit of any gentleman, to be told that he dare not stand up in defence of his Lady; but faith, methinks whoever looks for spirit in you will have to look hard before he finds it."

"Alas, Madame," said the Lord de Saintré, "and why should you say that?"

"I say it," said Madame, "because I cannot help saying it. Do not I see you this moment afraid?"

Then said the Lord de Saintré, " I see clearly, Madame, there is nothing for it but to commence again; and that there is no sort of excuse, however reasonable, to which you are disposed to lend an ear. So, since it is your determination, I bow to it."

Then Damp Abbot, as soon as he had caught his words, by way of farce, said, "Ha, Madame, pardon me this once; for if, by any chance, I have not justice on my side, he will certainly get the better of me, so sorely was I put to it in our last encounter. Madame, it is true all they say of him, nor does it at all surprise me. However, since I have brought it on myself, I suppose I must go through with it."

Then they each stepped back a few paces. Then Damp Abbot, who was by this, with excitement, half wild and out of his wits, began to cry, at the top of his voice, "Ha, Fidelity, guard now thy faithful slave!" And with this, he came a trick which had well nigh laid the Lord de Saintré sprawling. However, by a sort of miracle, he recovered his feet, but it was only to find himself, at the end of one or two closes, where, from the first, he too well knew he would have to come—the flat of his back.

Then said Damp Abbot to Madame, "Madame, you are our judge. It is for you to say, have I acquitted myself as became me? Which of us is the most loyal?"

"Which!" echoed Madame; "it is you that have gained."

Whilst the poor Lord de Saintré, broken-hearted to perceive not only that he had got the worst of it, but that his discomfiture was an occasion of triumph to Madame, could not so much as find a word to say. Then they both retired to dress.

All this while, the two Squires that Saintré had retained about him had like to die with grief and spite, thus to see Madame and Damp Abbot twitting and laughing at the Lord de Saintré, than whom, in all the realm of France, there lived not, that day, a gallanter gentleman, or a nobler Knight. So, as he was coming away, they said to him, "Our Lord, it will be more than human in you if you forbear to revenge this day's brutality."

But he only said to them, "My friends, do not be distressing yourselves. Keep quiet; never fear, I'll put all this to rights."

Then the Lord de Saintré, who had now for ever extinguished in his breast all love or hope of Madame, indignant at such treatment from one whom he had so passionately loved and faithfully served, feigning to take it all in good part, carried himself as though he had not, in any way, taken his defeat to heart. So, good-humouredly, and as if half talking to himself, he said to Madame, "Alas, Madame, it is a thousand pities such a man as my Lord Abbot, of such a build and strength, should never have been brought up to the noble science of arms. Such a man should have been defending the marches of our Lord, the King. I much question if there are above one or two men in all this realm who would dare to meet him in an open field."

Then Damp Abbot, on hearing so handsome a tribute to his prowess, scarcely now knowing whether he was on his head or his heels, turned another great somersault, to the no small entertainment of Madame and the remainder of the company. Then he sent for wine and cherries to refresh them all.

[Later, Jehan de Saintré gets Damp Abbot into armor, and, fighting with knightly weapons, discomfits him; and Madame is shamed before the court.]

# ❦ The Bailiff and the Scrupulous Curate

## by NICOLAS DE TROYES

Of the author we know no more than he tells us, that he was a saddler, born in Troyes in Champagne, and established at the time of writing in Tours; further that in 1535 he began setting down good stories that he had heard or read. His best gifts are his ear for savory speech and his eye for bourgeois behavior. His book, *Le Grand Parangon des nouvelles nouvelles*, was not printed until 1869. Our story is Nouvelle 28.

DOWN IN Poitou there was a bailiff, a very good fellow, quartered in a village there. One Easter time he came to confess to his curate, and he did so very properly. After he had confessed to a few sins, the curate asked him if he had broken his marriage vows, for, they say, a minstrel never forgets his music. The bailiff said to the priest: "Monsieur, I have not broken them; I assure you they are intact."

"What!" said the curate. "You think you can fool God?"

"No, by God!" said the bailiff.

"Haven't you had anything to do with other women than your wife?"

"No, sir; I swear to you."

"Well then," said the priest, "haven't you felt unlawful desires? Haven't you seen other women you would rather have gone to bed with than with your wife?"

"Oh dear, yes," said the bailiff. "It is quite true that not long ago I saw a very beautiful woman, the kind who appeals to me. I kept staring at her; she seemed to me so beautiful that I would have loved to go to bed with her. I tell you straight, I would have embraced and kissed her with the greatest of pleasure, and so would you, Monsieur le curé, if she had appealed to you."

"All right, all right," said the curate. "But you didn't do anything to her?"

"No, sir."

"But you had this will, that if you had been in bed with her, you would have done it to her?"

"By gad, yes, sir; I sure would."

"Now let me tell you, my friend," said the curate; "the will is taken as equivalent to the deed. Therefore for this sin of yours I impose this penance, that on Friday next you will fast on bread and water."

"Now wait a minute," said the bailiff. "But sir, I didn't do anything!"

"I don't care," said the priest. "The will is equivalent to the deed."

"Monsieur, if I had done anything, I grant you a little fasting wouldn't do me any harm; but——"

"But, but, but!" said the curate. "If you don't fast and if I find out about it, I won't admit you to communion on Easter."

"Oh very well, Monsieur le curé, I will fast, if that's what God wants. But——"

"No more buts!"

"Well, on my faith, Monsieur le curé, I think that if this had happened to you, you wouldn't have much liked to fast for it. But let it go; drop it; who cares? The good God will take care of everything."

"Look here," said the priest; "do you know what you've got to do? You will fast just as bravely as you would have slept with the lady."

"All right, I'll do it," said the bailiff. Then the priest absolved him, and our man went off, but still grumbling about the fast.

Some time after came the month of May, when the wheat stood high. You must know that the curé owned several cows, and one of them was pastured next to a big wheat-field protected by a hedge. The cow longed to eat this wheat, but couldn't reach it. She kept thrusting out her long tongue, trying to get at the wheat through the hedge, but could never come at it. Now you must know that the bailiff came there and watched the cow, waiting for her to get into the wheat so that he could carry her off to prison. He asked a bystander whose cow it was; he was told that she belonged to the curé. "To the curé!" he said. "You'll go to jail!" He then led off the cow, a prisoner. The priest was informed; he sought out the bailiff and told him he had no right to carry off his cow, since she had done nothing wrong. "What!" said the bailiff. "Monsieur, she wanted to eat the wheat; and the will is equivalent to the deed. By God, you'll pay the fine for her! Don't you remember how you made me fast on bread and water one Friday because I wanted to go to bed with a beautiful young woman, but I never did? And you made me go through with it. Well, I haven't forgotten, no, no; and you will go through with it for your cow."

So the curé had to pay the fine.

# ❦ The Too Clever Fox

## by BONAVENTURE DES PÉRIERS

Bonaventure des Périers was a Burgundian, born about 1510. A good scholar, drawn to the humanism of the Protestant reformers, he aided in a famous translation of the Bible and published versions of Greek and Roman classics. He entered the service of the famous patroness of liberal causes, Margaret of Navarre, in 1536; but his increasing skepticism cost him his post. In despair, he committed suicide in 1544 by casting himself on his sword.

In the intervals of scholarly activities and polemics he wrote a collection of stories, *Les Nouvelles récréations et joyeux devis*, published posthumously, in 1558. The first of our two animal stories is Nouvelle 31. Like Nicolas de Troyes, he took many of his themes from provincial life, and presented them with delightful realism and gayety.

IN THE city of Maine-la-Juhés,* in the lower part of the province of Maine, there was a magistrate, a hearty good fellow like his countrymen, and of a whimsical turn of mind. He kept a number of tamed animals in his house as pets; among them was a fox, which he had brought up from a cub. He had cut off the fox's tail; hence the creature was called Stumpy. Stumpy was naturally clever, by inheritance; but he had improved upon his native endowment by association with human beings. He had such a fine foxy wit that if he had been able to speak he would have put a lot of people to shame. And certainly he gave every sign of trying to talk in his own comical fox-language. When he was with the house-boy or the chambermaid, who coddled him in the kitchen, you would have sworn that he was trying to call them by name. He knew very well when the magistrate was

* Evidently Mayenne, in western France, midway between Le Mans and Rennes.—Ed.

going to have a big dinner, by the activity of the whole household, and especially of the cook. Then he would run off to the town's poultry-yards, and he never failed to bring back rabbits, hares, capons, pigeons, partridges, as circumstances offered. He captured them so cunningly that he was never caught in the act; and he supplied his master's kitchen marvelously well.

However, he did so much mischief that he fell under the suspicion of the poultrymen and others, whose treasures he stole. Little he cared for that, just invented new tricks and increased his robberies, until his victims laid plans to kill him. They didn't dare to do so openly, for fear of his master, one of the city's bigwigs; but they took counsel together, to surprise him by night.

Well, old Stumpy, on the prowl, would enter sometimes by a cellar ventilator, sometimes by an upper window. Or again he would wait till someone opened a door, without a light, and slip in as secretly as a rat. And as he had devices for getting in, he had others for getting out with his prey. Often the chicken-fanciers would discuss ways to kill him, and he would hide and listen to the plotters, thinking: "You'll never get me!" Sometimes a poultryman would set out a chicken as a tempting bait, while standing watch to kill the marauder, with a cocked crossbow and the bolt in place. But the clever fox could smell the deception far off, like roasting meat; and he would not come near while the watcher lay in ambush. As soon as the guard nodded and closed his eyes, Stumpy leaped on his prey. And if men laid traps for him he avoided them as if he had set them out himself. Thus the chicken-raisers were never vigilant enough to catch him. All they could do was to keep their charges locked up tight where Stumpy could not get at them. Even at that he managed occasionally to seize some stray; but not often. All this annoyed him a good deal, partly because he was no longer able to make offerings to the cook, and partly because fasting disagreed with him.

Thus, as he grew older, he turned sulky, and began to think that people held him cheap. Perhaps in fact he was not so much petted as before, for old age is a sad business at best. So he developed un ugly streak; he started even to eat the chickens belonging to his master. When everyone was asleep he would go to the hen-roost and pick off now a capon, now a hen. For a long time no one suspected him; they blamed some weasel or marten. But finally—as all wickedness comes eventually to light—he returned so often that a little girl who slept in the woodshed noticed him and told all. Then came poor Stumpy's downfall. It was reported to the magistrate that Stumpy was eating his chickens. Now the fox ran about everywhere to hear what people were saying about him. It was his custom always to attend his master's dinner and supper, for the magistrate loved him, fed him at table, and always tossed him a bit of the roast. But when the master heard that his pet was eating his own chickens, he looked very sour. At dinner Stumpy hid behind the servants, and heard the magistrate say: "What do you know about my Stumpy? He's eating my chickens! I'll bring him to justice before three days are up!"

When Stumpy heard this he realized that town life was no longer healthy for him. Without waiting for the three days to pass he went into voluntary exile; he fled to the wild, where lived the other foxes. You may imagine that he tried all his blandishments upon them; but poor Stumpy had plenty of trouble making peace with them. For during his stay in the town he had learned good dog-language and dog-manners. He had hunted with the pack and lured the poor wild foxes with a false show of friendship, and had delivered them over to the dogs. The foxes remembered this; they did not trust him, and would not receive him into their company. But he used all his rhetoric, now making excuses, now asking pardon; and then he gave them to understand that he could enable them to live royally, since he knew the best hen-yards in the region and the best times to raid them. Thus finally the foxes yielded to his fine talk and made him their captain.

For a while everything went well. He led his foxes to the best places, where they found plenty of booty. But the trouble was that he was too eager to organize them, keeping them always on the go, so that the countrymen, seeing them hunting in packs, called out their dogs; and some of the foxes were constantly falling victim. Nevertheless Stumpy always escaped, for he remained with the rear-guard, and while the dogs attacked the leaders he had time enough to escape. Even, he would never enter the foxhole except in company with other foxes; and when the dogs burrowed in he would nip his companions and force them to come out, so that the dogs would chase them and let him escape.

But in spite of all his cleverness poor Stumpy was caught in the end. For since the peasants well knew that he was responsible for all the depredations, they hated him and went after him alone, all of them swearing that sooner or later they would get him. To this end they convened all the parishes round about, each of which deputed a churchwarden to go and beg help from the local gentlemen, asking them, for the common good, to lend some dogs to rid the country of that scoundrelly fox. The gentlemen cordially assented, and gave a favorable answer to the ambassadors. Indeed, most of the gentlemen had been lending their efforts to the same end without success.

In short, the community marshaled so many dogs that there were more than enough for Stumpy and his army. In vain he bit and harassed his companions; when they were captured he had to share their fate. He was taken alive, backed up in a fox-hole, by dint of digging and excavating; for the dogs could never drive him out of the hole, whether because he was always playing some new trick on them, or whether—as is more credible—because he talked with them in good dog-language, and made some sort of a deal with them.

At any rate, poor Stumpy was carried alive into the city of Maine, and there was brought to trial. He was publicly convicted of thefts, larcenies, pillages, misappropriations, treasons, deceptions, assassinations, and other outrageous and iniquitous crimes by him committed and perpetrated. And he was executed before a great assembly of the people, for everyone ran to the ceremony as to a fire, because he was known for ten leagues round about as the most villainous fox the earth ever bore. It is also said, however, that some enlightened individuals expressed pity for him, because he had done such amusing tricks so deftly. They said it was too bad that such an intelligent fox should die. But after all, these dissenters could not have prevailed, even if they had drawn their swords to save Stumpy's life; for he was hung and strangled at the castle of Maine.

Thus we see how there is no low cunning and mischievousness that is not, in the end, punished.

## ❧ *The Sagacious Monkey*

### by BONAVENTURE DES PÉRIERS

This animal story is Nouvelle 91 of *Les Nouvelles récréations et joyeux devis.*

A N ABBÉ had a pet monkey, marvelously clever. Not to mention his tricks and comicalities, he knew men's characters by their faces. He recognized sober, decent folk by their beards, their dress, their expression; he would come and caress them. But a page, never! Though the page might be dressed as a girl, the monkey would discern him among a hundred. He could smell a page on his entry into a room, though he had never seen the fellow before. When people were discussing something he listened intently, as if he understood the speakers; and he made certain unmistakable signs to indicate that he understood. Though he uttered no word, you may be sure that he thought none the less. In short, I think he was of the same race as that monkey in Portugal who was such a fine chess-player.

Monsieur l'Abbé was very proud of his monkey and often talked about him at dinner or supper. One day he had a fine company in his house—the court was visiting the city that day—and he began to sing the praises of his pet. "Isn't he really a very remarkable creature?" he said. "I think that Nature really started out to make a man, when she created him; but being so overworked, she forgot that man had already been made. For look you, she made his face just like that of a man, and his fingers and hands and even the characteristic lines of the palms, just like a man's. What do you think of that? To be a man, all he needs is speech. But wouldn't it be possible to teach him to speak? We do indeed teach birds to talk, who haven't as much understanding or reasoning power as that creature. I would gladly give a year's income to make him talk as well as my parrot. I don't think it's impossible at all. For even when he complains, or when he laughs, you would say he is a human being, trying only to explain himself. And I think that if someone should attempt to develop Nature's resources, he would succeed."

Now it chanced that an Italian was among those present. Observing that the Abbé was so fond of his pet and that he was so near to believing that the monkey might learn to talk, he presented himself with all the assurance natural to his nation, and addressed the Abbé with a wealth of "Your Reverences, Your Excellencies, Your Magnificences." "Sir," said he, "you are in the right of it. Since Nature has made this animal so like man in face and figure she has surely not ruled out the possibility that artifice could achieve the little that remains. Surely she has deprived him of language only to spur on man to prove that there is nothing that may not be done by following her indicated course. Do we not read of talking elephants? And of a talking ass? (Pray pardon me; I meant no jest.) I am amazed that no king, prince, or lord has so far made a test of this creature. I hold that such a one who will first make the experiment will gain immortal praise."

The Abbé listened eagerly to this philosophical discourse, the more so as it was of Italian origin (for the French have always had, among other defects, the character of favoring and listening to foreigners more readily than to their own nationals). He looked wide-eyed at the Italian, and said: "Really, I am delighted to find a man who shares my opinion. I have had this idea in mind for a long time."

To make short of it, after further arguments proposed and examined, the Abbé concluded that the Italian knew what he was talking about. He said to the visitor, with a significant look: "See here—would you undertake the task of teaching him to talk?"

"Yes, Monseigneur," said the Italian. "I would be willing to undertake it. I have already accepted some rather important challenges, with full success."

"How long would it take?" said the Abbé.

"Monsieur, you must realized that this is no short-term affair. I should like to have ample time for such an enterprise as this, without precedent. To bring it to pass, the monkey must be fed at fixed hours, on choice, rare, and precious foods; and I should have to be in attendance day and night."

"Well," said the Abbé, "we won't argue about the cost. I will pay it, whatever it may be. Tell me only how long it will take."

Finally the Italian stipulated a term of six years. The Abbé agreed. He turned over the monkey; the Italian asked a handsome fee for board and lodging, and took the monkey into his charge. You may well imagine that this conversation much amused some of those present, but they postponed their laughter to a later occasion, as they did not wish to offend the Abbé. But the Italian friends of the entrepreneur were much annoyed (for this was the time when the Italian vogue in France was beginning, and they were afraid that by this simiagogy—or monkey business—they would lose their reputation). For this reason some of them sharply blamed the new tutor, pointing out to him that he was dishonoring the whole Italian nation by the folly of his undertaking, that he had no right to befool the Abbé; and if the king should hear of the matter it would be the worse for him. When the Italian had heard them out, he replied: "Let me tell you, you are all in the wrong. I have contracted to teach a monkey to talk in six years. The term is fair, and so is the pay for the term. Lots of things can happen in six years. Before the end, either the Abbé will die, or the monkey, or possibly I myself. Then I will have nothing to worry about."

You see what it is to be a bold venturer. They say that everything turned out wonderfully well for this Italian. The Abbé having lost the company of his monkey, fell into despondency, so that he no longer found pleasure in anything. (You must know that the Italian took the beast away, insisting that he must have a change of air; also, the educator wanted to employ certain secrets that no one must see or learn about.) Hence the Abbé, seeing that the Italian, not he, had all the pleasure of the monkey's company, repented of his bargain and demanded the monkey back. Thus the Italian was quit of his promise, and at the same time made a great splash with the Abbé's golden crowns.

# ❧ The Virtuous Widow

## by MARGARET OF NAVARRE

Margaret of Navarre (1492–1549) was the elder sister of King Francis I of France. An intellectual from the first, she learned Latin, Italian, Spanish, and some Greek and Hebrew. Her second husband was Henri d'Albret, King of Navarre; the two held court at Pau and Nérac, just north of the Pyrenees. There Margaret, a religious liberal, received and protected free-thinking writers and scholars, noteworthily Bonaventure des Périers and Clément Marot. Though sympathetic with much Protestant doctrine, she remained in the Catholic Church.

The *Heptameron*, a frank imitation of Boccaccio's *Decameron*, was begun in 1546. It has been called "the most characteristic book of the early French Renaissance, the book which gives us the best picture of its social and intellectual atmosphere, of that curious mixture of coarseness and refinement, of cynicism and enthusiasm, of irreverence and piety, of delight in living and love of meditation on death, which characterised that period of transition between the mediaeval and the modern world" (Arthur Tilley. *The Literature of the French Renaissance* [Cambridge, England, 1904], I, 109). Our translation, by Arthur Machen, first appeared in London in 1886. According to a not unlikely tradition, the story, Nouvelle 4, recounts an actual adventure of Margaret, in her first widowhood, and Admiral Bonnivet.

THERE WAS in the land of Flanders a lady of a most illustrious house, who had been twice married and was now a widow without any children. In the time of her widowhood she lived retired with her brother, who was a great lord, and married to a daughter of the King, and this brother loved his sister exceedingly. Now this prince was a man somewhat enslaved to pleasure, having great delight in hunting, games, and women, as his youth led him, but, having to wife one of a peevish disposition, to whom none of her husband's contentments were pleasing, he would always have his sister with him, for she was of a most joyous nature, and a good and honourable woman withal. And there was in the house of this prince a gentleman whose beauty and grace did far surpass that of his fellows; and he beholding the sister of his master that she was joyous and always ready for a laugh, thought that he would assay how the offer of an honourable love would be taken by her. But her reply was by no means favourable to him; yet though it was such as became a princess and a woman of honour, she, seeing him to be a handsome man and of good address, easily pardoned to him his great boldness in speaking to her after such a fashion. And moreover she assured him that she bore him no displeasure for what he had said, but charged him from henceforth to let her have no more of it. This he promised, that he might not lose the delight he had in her company, but as time went on his love grew even more and more, so that he forgot the promise he had given. Not that he made a second trial of what words could do, for he had found out the manner of her replies; but he thought that since she was a widow, young, lusty, and of a pleasant humor, she might perchance, if he came upon her in a fitting place, take compassion on him and her own flesh.

To which end, he said to his master that hard by his house there was most excellent hunting, and that if in Maytime he would be pleased to come and chase the stags, he could promise him as good contentment as he could desire. The prince, as much for the love he bore him as for his delight in hunting, granted his request, and going to his house found it most bravely ordered, and as good as that of the greatest lord in the land. And the gentleman lodged his lord and lady on one side, and opposite to them he appointed a room for her whom he loved better than himself. And so bravely was this room decked out with tapestry above and matting below, that no one could discover a trap-door contrived in the wall by the bed, which led to where his mother was lodged. And she, being an old dame with an obstinate rheum, and troubled with a cough, had made an exchange of chambers with her son, so as not to annoy the princess. And before curfew-time in the evening this good lady would carry sweetmeats to the princess for her supper, in which service she was assisted by her son, since being well-beloved of the prince, it was not refused to him to be present at her *levée* and *couchée*, at which times he got fresh fuel for the fire that was in him. And so late one night did he tarry there that she was well nigh asleep before he left her for his own room. And having put on him the finest and best scented shirt he had, and a night-cap of surpassing device, he was well persuaded, on looking himelf over, that there was not a lady in the world hard enough to refuse a man of such a grace and beauty. Wherefore, promising to himself a good issue of his adventure, he lay down on his bed, hoping not to make thereon a long stay, but to change it for one more pleasant and honourable. And as soon as he had dismissed his servants he got up and shut the door behind them, and afterwards listened for a long while if he should hear any noise in the room of the princess. So when he was satisfied that all was quiet, he was fain to begin his pleasant travail, and little by little let down the trap-door, which, so well was it carpeted over, did not make so much as the least noise. And so he got into the room by the bed of the princess, who was now asleep. And straightway, heeding not the duty he owed her or the house from which she came, without with your leave, or by your leave, he got into bed with her, who felt herself in his arms, before she knew he was in the room. But she, being strong, got from between his hands, and having required of him who he was, fell to beating, biting, and scratching with such hearty good will that, for fear of her calling out, he would have stopped her mouth with the blanket; but in this he was foiled, since the princess, seeing that he spared none of his resources to rob her of her honour, spared none of hers to defend it. So she called at the top of her voice to her maid of honour, an ancient and prudent dame, who slept with her, and she, clad only in her nightgear, ran to the help of her mistress.

And when the gentleman saw he was discovered, so great a fear had he of being recognised, that as fast as might be he departed by his trap-door; and in like degree, as he had been desirous and well assured of a good reception when he was going, so now did he despair as he went back in such evil case. He found his mirror and candle upon the table, and beholding his countenance, that it was all bloody from the bites and scratches she had dealt him, he began to say: "Beauty! thou has received a wage according to thy deserving; for by thine idle promise I attempted an impossible thing, and which, moreover, in place of increasing my happiness, hath made my sorrow greater than it was before; since I am well assured that if she knew that I, against my solemn undertaking, had done this foolish thing, I should be cut off from that close and honourable commerce I aforetime had with her. And this I shall have well deserved, for to make my beauty and grace avail me anything, I should not have hidden them in the darkness; I should not have attempted to carry that chaste body by assault; but striven to gain her favour, till by patience and long service my love had gained the victory; for without love all the power and might of men are as nothing."

So, in such wise that I cannot tell, passed the night in tears, and regrets, and griefs; and in the morning, so torn was his face, that he made pretence of great sickness, saying that he could not bear the light, even until the company was departed.

The lady who had come off conqueror knew that there was none other in the prince's court who durst set about such an enterprise save her host, who had already had the boldness to make a declaration of love to her. So she, with her maid of honour, made search around her chamber to find how he could have made an entry. And not being able to find any place or trace thereof, she said to her companion in great wrath: "Be assured that it was none other than the lord of the house, and in such sort will I handle him on the morrow with my brother, that his head shall bear witness to my chastity." The maid of honour, seeing her so angered, said to her: "My lady, I am well pleased at the price you set on your honour, since the more to exalt it you would make sacrifice of the life of one who, for his love of you, has put it to this risk. But in this way one ofttimes lessens what one would fain increase. Wherefore, my lady, I do entreat you to tell me the whole truth of this matter." And when the princess had made a full account of the business, the maid of honour said to her: "Do you verily assure me that he had nothing from you but only scratches and fisticuffs?" "I do assure you," said the lady, "and if he find not a rare mediciner, I am much mistaken if to-morrow his face do not bear evident witness to what I say." "Well, my lady," said the maid of honour, "if it be as you say, it seems to me that you have rather occasion to thank God than to imagine vengeance; for you may conceive that since this gentleman had a heart daring enough to attempt such a deed, you can award to him no punishment, nay, not death itself, that will not be easier to bear than his dolour at having failed therein. If you are fain to be revenged on him, leave him to his love and to his shame, and from them he will suffer more shrewdly than at your hands; and if you have regard for your honour, beware lest you fall into the same pit as he, for in place of gaining the greatest delight he could desire, he is in the most shameful case that may hap to a gentleman. So you, good mistress, thinking to exalt your honour, may haply bring it to the dust; for if you make advertisement of this affair, you will cause to be blazed abroad what no one would ever know, since the gentleman, trust me, will throw but little light on the matter. And when my lord, your brother, shall do justice on him at your asking, and the poor gentleman goes forth to die, it will be noised abroad that he had his pleasure of you, and men will say that it is not to be believed a man could make such an attempt, if he had not before had of you some good matter of contentment. You are young and fair, living gaily amongst all, and there is no soul at court who has not seen your commerce with this man you have in suspicion, so all will determine that if he finished the work you began it. So your honour, which hitherto hath been mightily extolled, will become common matter of dispute wherever this story is related."

The princess, considering the fair conclusions of the maid of honour, perceived that she had spoken the truth, and that with just cause would she be blamed, since both openly and privily she had always given a good reception to the gentleman, and so would have her woman tell her what was best to be done. And she answered her: "Good mistress, since it is your pleasure, seeing the love from whence they come, to give ear to my counsels, I think that you should be glad at heart, for that the bravest and most gallant gentleman I have ever seen hath not been able to turn you from the path of true virtuousness. And for this you should humble yourself before God, confessing that it is not your own strength or virtue, for women leading, beyond compare, straiter lives than you, have been brought to the dust by men less worthy of love than he. And henceforth, do you avoid proposals of love and the like, for many that at the first got off scot-free, the second time have fallen into the pit. Be mindful that Love is blind, and a causer of blindness, for it makes believe the path is sure, when in truth it is most slippery. And it is my mind that you should give him no sign as to what has taken place, and if he say anything on the matter, feign to understand him not, and so be quit of two perils; the one of vainglory for your victory, the other of recalling to mind things that are pleasant to the flesh, ay, so pleasant are they that the chastest have much ado to quench all sparks of that fire they are most fain to avoid. And moreover, I counsel you, that he think not he hath done you any sort of pleasure, that you do, by small degrees, put a close to your intimacy with him, so he may perceive your misliking to what he hath done, and yet understand that so great is your goodness that you are content with the victory God hath given you, and desire no farther vengeance. And may God grant you to abide in your virtuousness of heart, and seeing that all good things are from Him, may you love and serve Him in better sort than afore." And the princess, determined to abide by these conclusions, gave herself to a sleep as joyful as her lover's wakefulness was sad.

And on the morrow, the prince being about to depart, asked for his host, but they told him he was so sick as not to endure the daylight, or to speak with any one, whereat the prince was astonished and would have seen him, but being advised that he slept, he went forth from the house without so much as good-bye, and took with him his wife and sister. But she, hearing the put-offs of the gentleman, and that he would see neither the prince nor the company, was assured that he was the man who had so troubled her, and would not show the marks she had stamped upon his face. And though his master ofttimes sent for him, he would by no means return to court till he was healed of his wounds; save those indeed that love and shame had made upon his heart. And when he did return, and found himself before his victorious foe, he blushed; nay, he who was most bold-faced of all the company, was in such case that often in her presence he was struck dumb. At this, being quite persuaded that her suspicion was truth, she by little and little severed herself from him, yet not by such slow degrees that he was not aware of it, but could say nothing lest he should fare worse, and patiently bore this punishment which he so well deserved.

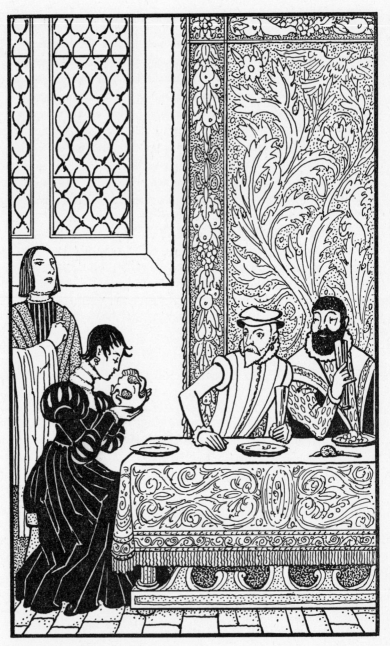

*A Lesson to Errant Wives*

# ❧ *A Lesson to Errant Wives*
## by MARGARET OF NAVARRE

This story is Nouvelle 32 of the *Heptameron*. The translation is by Arthur Machen.

KING CHARLES, the Eighth of his name, sent into Germany a gentleman named Bernage, lord of Sivray, near Amboise, who to make good speed spared not to journey by day nor night, and so one evening came very late to a house and asked there for lodging. At this great difficulty was made, but when the master understood how great a king he served, he entreated him not to take in bad part the churlishness of his servants, since, by reason of certain kinsfolk of his wife, who were fain to do him a hurt, it was necessary that the house should be under strict ward. Then the aforesaid Bernage told him the reason of his embassage, which the gentleman offered to forward with all his might, and led him into his house, where he honourably lodged and entertained him.

It was now supper-time, and the gentleman brought him into a large room, bravely hung with tapestry work. And as the meats were set upon the table there came a woman from behind the tapestry, of a most surpassing beauty, but her head was shorn and the rest of her body was clothed in black gear of the German fashion. After that the gentleman had washed his hands with Bernage, water was borne to the lady, who when she had washed her hands sat herself down at the bottom of the table, without a word from her or to her. My lord de Bernage looked at her very attentively, and she seemed one of the comeliest women he ever had beheld, save that the manner of her countenance was pale and melancholic. And when she had eaten a little she asked for drink, and this was brought her by a servant in a most marvellous vessel, I would say a death's-head with the eyes closed up with silver, and so from this she drank three or four times. And her supper hav-

ing come to an end she washed her hands, and with a reverence
to the lord of the house she returned behind the tapestry without
a word to anyone. Bernage was so astonished to see so strange a
case that he fell into a thoughtful melancholy, which being perceived of the gentleman, he said to him: "I know well that you
marvel within yourself at what you have seen done at this table;
and for that I judge you to be an honourable man, I will not conceal the affair from you, to the intent that you may not think
there is so great cruelty in me without a weighty cause. The lady
you have seen is my wife, whom I loved as man never loved before, so much indeed that to wed her I forgot all fear and brought
her here by force against the will of her kinsfolk. And she in like
manner gave me so many evident proofs of her love that I would
have risked ten thousand lives to bring her here as I did, to the
delight of the pair of us, and we lived awhile in such quietness
and contentment that I esteemed myself the most fortunate gentleman in all Christendom. But while I was away on a journey
made for the sake of my honour, she so far forgot her virtuousness, her conscience, and the love she had for me, that she fell in
love with a young gentleman whom I had brought up in my
house, and this I perceived upon my coming home. Yet I loved
her so well that I was not able to distrust her till experience gave
belief unto my eyes, and with them I saw what I feared more
than death. Then was my love turned to madness and my trust to
despair; and so well did I play the spy upon her that one day,
feigning to go out, I hid myself in the room which is now her
dwelling-place. And very soon after she saw me go, she went
away and made the young man come to her, and him I beheld
handling her in such fashion as belonged to me alone. But when I
saw him get upon the bed beside her, I came forth from my hiding-place, and, taking him between her very arms, there put him
to death. And since the offence of my wife seemed to me so great
that death would not suffice for her punishment, I appointed one
that I deem is much more bitter than death to her: namely, to
shut her up in the room where she had her greatest pleasures of
him she loved more than me, where I have set all the bones of her

lover in an aumbry,* as a precious thing and worthy of safe keeping. And to the end that in eating and drinking she may not lose
the memory of him, I have made serve her at table, with the head
of that villain in place of a cup, and this in my presence, so that
she may see living him whom she has made through her sin a mortal enemy, and dead for love of her him whom she preferred before me. And so at dinner and supper she beholds the two things
which should most make her to despair; the living enemy and
the dead lover; and all through her own sin. For the rest, I treat
her as myself, save that she goes shorn, for an array of hair doth
not belong to a woman taken in adultery, nor the veil to an harlot.
Wherefore her hair is cut, showing that she has lost the honour
of virginity and purity. And if it be your pleasure to see her, I
will take you there."

To this Bernage willingly agreed; and they went down the stair
and found her in a fine room, sitting alone before a fire. Then the
gentleman drew a curtain that was before a high aumbry, and in
it were hanging all the bones of the dead man. Bernage had a great
desire to speak with the lady, but for fear of the husband durst
not do it. He, perceiving this, said to him: "An it please you to
say anything to her, you shall see how admirably she talks."
Forthwith Bernage said: "Mistress, your long-suffering and your
torment are alike great. I hold you for the most wretched of all
women." The lady, with tears in her eyes, graciously yet most
humbly answered him: "Sir, I confess my sin to be so great that
all the ills the lord of this place (for I am not worthy that I should
call him husband) can bestow upon me, are as nothing compared
with my sorrow that I have done him a displeasure." So saying
she fell to weeping bitterly; and the gentleman took Bernage by
the arm and led him away. And very early on the morrow he
went on to execute the charge given him of the King. But, in
bidding the gentleman farewell, he could not refrain from saying
to him: "Sir, the love I bear you, and the honour and privity you
have used towards me in this your house, constrains me to tell

* Aumbry: a chest or wardrobe.—Ed.

you that, in my opinion, seeing the repentance of your poor wife, you should have compassion on her. Furthermore, you being still young have no children, and it would be a great pity that such a brave line as yours should come to an end, and they for whom, perchance, you have no great love, should be your heirs." The gentleman, who had resolved never again to speak to his wife, thought for a long while on what my lord de Bernage had said to him, and finding him to be in the right, promised that if she continued in her humble repentance he would one day have compassion on her. And so Bernage went forth on his embassage. And when he was returned to the King his master, he told him the whole matter, which the prince, having made inquiry, found to be as he had said. And among other things, Bernage having spoken of the lady's beauty, the King sent his painter, John of Paris, thither, that he might draw her to the life. This he did, and with the consent thereto of the husband, who, beholding her long repentance, and having a great desire for children, took pity on his wife, who with such humbleness had borne her punishment, and, taking her back to him, had of her many brave children.

# ❦ A Case of Sacred and Profane Love

by MARGARET OF NAVARRE

This story is Nouvelle 35 of the *Heptameron*. The translator is Arthur Machen.

IN THE town of Pampeluna there lived a fair and virtuous lady, as chaste and devout as any in the land. So well did she love and obey her husband that he entirely put his trust in her: at divine service and at hearing of sermons she was always to be found, and would persuade her husband and children to go there with her. And on a certain Ash-Wednesday, she having come to the age of thirty years, when ladies are content to put by the name of fair for that of discreet, she went to church to take the ashes which are for a memorial of death. And the preacher was a Grey Friar, a man held by all the people as holy on account of the great goodness and austerity of his life, which, though it had made him to be thin and pale, yet hindered him not from being as comely a man as one could desire to see. The lady listened to his sermon, with eyes fixed upon his venerable person, and eyes and mind ready to hear what he said. And the sweetness of his words passed through her ears even unto her soul; and the comeliness and grace of his body passed through her eyes and smote her so at heart that she was as one in a dream. When the sermon was finished she was careful to look at what altar the preacher was to say mass, and there she presented herself to take the ashes from his hand that was as fine and white as any lady's. And to this hand the devout woman paid more attention than to the ashes it gave to her. So being assured that this manner of spiritual love and certain pleasures she felt therein could do her conscience no harm, she failed not to go every day and hear the sermon, taking her husband; and so great praise did both of them give the preacher that at table or elsewhere they spoke of nought else. Then did this fire named spiritual become so carnal that it burnt up first the heart and next the whole body of this poor lady; and as she was slow to feel it, so swift was it to spread, and, before she knew she was in love, she felt all love's delights. And as one altogether surprised by Love her enemy, she resisted none of his commands; but it was sore grief to her that the physician for all her sickness was not so much as ware of it. Wherefore, setting aside all fear of showing her foolishness to a man of wisdom, and her wickedness and vice to a man of virtue and goodness, she set down as softly as she could the love she bore him in a letter, and gave it to a little page, telling him what he had to do, and above all enjoining him to have a care lest her husband should see him going to the Grey Friars.

The page, seeking for the shortest way, passed through a street where was his master sitting in a shop; whereupon the gentleman, seeing him go by, came out to discover whither he was going, and when the page saw him, much affrighted, he hid himself in a house. At this his master followed him, and taking him by the arm asked whither he went, and finding no sense or meaning in his excuses, and the face of him terrified, he threatened to beat him shrewdly if he would not say whither he was going. The poor page said to him: "Alas, sir, if I tell you the dame will kill me"; so the gentleman, suspecting that his wife was treating for some commodity in which he should have no share, assured the page that if he told the truth he should have no evil but rather all good, but if he lied he should be put in gaol for life. The little page, so as to have the good and avoid the evil, told him the whole matter, and showed him the letter his mistress had written to the preacher, which gave the husband as much astonishment as anger, since he had altogether trusted his whole life in his wife's faithfulness, and had never found in her any fault. But being a prudent man, he concealed his wrath, and entirely to discover what his wife was minded to do, he counterfeited a reply as if the preacher had written it, thanking her for her goodwill toward him, and declaring that on his side there was no less. The page, having sworn to conduct the matter discreetly, carried to his mistress the counterfeited letter; and so great gladness did it give her that her husband plainly perceived the manner or her countenance to be altered, since in place of being thin, as is fitting in the Lenten Fast, she was fairer and more ruddy than in the Carnival.

And now it was Mothering Sunday,*yet did she not cease to send the preacher by letters her mad ravings, nor for the matter of that during Passion and Holy Week. For it seemed to her, when he turned his eyes to that part of the church where she was, or spoke of the love of God, that love of her was at the bottom of it; and as far as her eyes could tell him her mind, she did not spare them. And to all these her letters the husband failed not to reply after the same sort, and after Easter he wrote to her in the preacher's name praying her to devise some means of speaking with him privily. She, who for this hour waxed weary, counselled her husband to go see some lands he had in the country, to which he agreed, and went and hid himself in the house of one of his acquaintance. The lady failed not to write to the preacher that the time was come for him to see her, since her husband was in the country; and the gentleman, willing to sound his wife's heart to the very bottom, went to the preacher, praying him for the love of God to lend him his habit. But the monk, who was a good man and an honest, told him his rule forbade him, and by no means would he lend it for masquerading in; yet the gentleman, assuring him that he would make no ill use of it, and that it was necessary to his well-being, the friar, who knew him for a good and devout man, lent it him.

And putting the habit on him, and drawing the hood over his face so that his eyes could not be seen, the gentleman got him a false beard and a false nose like to the friar's, and with cork in his shoes made himself of the fitting height. In this gear he betook himself, when evening was come, to his wife's room, where she awaited him with much devotion. And the poor fool stayed not for him to come to her, but, as a woman out of her wits, rushed to throw her arms around him. He, with his face lowered, so as

* Mothering Sunday: mid-Lent Sunday, Mother's Day of old.—Ed.

not to be known, began to draw away from her, making the sign of the cross, and saying the while only one word: "Temptation! temptation!" The lady said: "Alas, father, you are in the right, for there is none stronger than what comes from love. But since you have promised to be the cure, I pray you now we have time and leisure to have compassion upon me." So saying she strove by force to throw her arms around him, but he, flying round the room, making great signs of the cross, cried all the while: "Temptation! temptation!" But when he saw she pressed him hard, he took a stout stick he had under his habit, and so entreated her with it that her temptation was overcome, and he not known of her. This done he forthwith gave back the habit to the preacher, assuring him he had done him a great kindness.

And on the morrow, making a pretence of returning from afar, he came to his house and found there his wife in bed, and, as if he knew it not, asked what ailed her, and she replied that it was a rheum, and, moreover, that she could not stir hand nor foot. The husband, though exceeding desirous to laugh, feigned to be much grieved; and, as a matter of consolation, told her he had bidden the good preacher to sup with them that very evening. But to this she instantly answered: "Be it far from you, sweetheart, to ask such folk hither, for they work ill in every house they enter."

"Why, sweetheart, how is this?" said the husband; "you have always mightily praised this man. I, for my part, think that if there be a holy man on this earth it is he."

The lady replied: "They are good at the altar and in the pulpit, but in houses they are Anti-Christ. Prithee, sweetheart, let me not see him, for with this my sickness it would be the very death of me."

The husband said: "Since you wish it not you shall not see him, but for all that he must sup with me."

"Do as you will," said she, "so long as I do not see him, for I hate the monks like the devil."

The husband, having given the good monk his supper, said to him as follows: "Father, I esteem you so beloved of God that He will not refuse you anything you ask Him, wherefore I entreat you have compassion on my poor wife, who these eight days hath been possessed of an evil spirit, in such sort that she endeavours to bite and scratch whomsoever she sees. Of cross or holy water she makes no account, but I firmly believe that if you put your hand on her the devil would come out; and this I pray you to do."

The good father said: "My son, to a believer all things are possible. Do you steadfastly believe that the goodness of God refuses no grace to him who asks it faithfully?"

"I do believe it, father," answered the gentleman.

"Be then also assured, my son," said the friar, "that God is able to do what He wills, and is as all-mighty as He is good. Let us go, then, strengthened by faith, to resist this roaring lion, and snatch from him his prey, that God hath won for Himself by the blood of His dear Son, Jesus Christ."

So the husband led the good man to the room where his wife lay on a small bed; and she, thinking she saw him who had beaten her, fell into great astonishment and wrath; but for that her husband was also present, lowered her eyes and was dumb. Then said the husband to the holy man: "While I am with her the devil no longer tormenteth her, but as soon as I am gone forth, do you cast holy water upon her, and you will see the evil spirit do his work." So saying he left the friar alone with his wife, but stayed by the door, so as to observe the fashion of their discourse. And when she saw herself alone with the friar, she began as one mad, to cry out at him, calling him wretch, villain, murderer, deceiver. The good father, thinking that of a very truth she was possessed of an evil spirit, would have taken her by the head to say his exorcisements over it, but she scratched and bit him in such wise that he was fain to parley with the devil from afar; and while he cast the holy water on her very plentifully, said many a devout orison. And the husband, thinking him to have done his duty, entered the room and thanked him for the pains he had taken, and as he came in his wife ceased her cursing and abuse, and for her fear of her husband, kissed the cross with much meekness. But the holy friar, who had seen her before so furiously enraged, firmly believed that by his prayer to Our Lord the devil had come out of her, and went his way praising God for this mighty work. The husband, seeing his wife to have been well chastised for her brainsick folly, would not declare to her what he had done; for he was content to have conquered her desire by his wisdom, and to have taken such order with her that she mortally hated what aforetime she had loved, and so gave herself up more than before to her husband and her household.

# III
# SPAIN

*Marriage à la Mode*

# ❧ Lazarillo de Tormes

La Vida de Lazarillo de Tormes was published in 1554. Its authorship has never been settled, although it has often been ascribed to the scholar-diplomat Diego Hurtado de Mendoza. The little book is the first picaresque novel, or romance of roguery, or realistic depiction of low life on the edge of criminality. Its distant ancestor was Petronius' *Satyricon;* its progeny is innumerable. *Lazarillo* recounts the life of a waif in Salamanca, trying merely to exist by attaching himself to a succession of masters. His story is a small saga of hunger. Our excerpt is from the translation by Thomas Roscoe, which appeared in London in 1881.

[Lazarillo has just suffered starvation and maltreatment at the hands of a niggardly priest.]

NOTWITHSTANDING the weak state to which I was reduced, I was obliged to take heart, and with the assistance of some kind people, I gradually made my way to the famous city of Toledo, where, by the mercy of God, I was shortly cured of my wounds.

While I laboured under sickness there were always some well-disposed persons who were willing to give me alms; but no sooner was I recovered than they said, "Why do you stay idling here? Why don't you seek a master?" On which the reply would rise to my lips, "It is very easy to talk, but it is hard to find one."

In this manner I went on seeking my living from door to door, and a mighty poor living it was, for Charity has left us mortals here to take a flight to heaven long since. But one day I accidentally encountered a certain esquire in the street; he was of a good appearance, well dressed, and walked with an air of ease and consequence. As I cast my eyes upon him, he fortunately took notice of me, and said, "Are you seeking a master, my boy?" I replied that I was. "Then follow me," said he; "you have reason to thank your stars for this meeting: doubtless you have said your prayers with a better grace than usual this morning."

I followed him, returning thanks to Providence for this singular good turn of fortune, for, if one might judge from appearances, here was exactly the situation which I had so long desired. It was early in the morning when I was engaged by this kind master, and I continued to follow him, as he desired, till we made the tour of a great part of the city. As we passed the market, I hoped that he would give me a load to carry home, as it was then about the hour that people usually made their purchases of that nature; but he passed by without taking the slightest notice. "Per-adventure," quoth I to myself, "these commodities are not exactly to his taste; we shall be more fortunate in some other quarter."

It was now eleven o'clock, and my master went into the cathedral to hear prayers, where I likewise followed him. Here we stayed until the whole service was finished and the congregation were departed; and then my master left, and proceeded towards one of the back streets of the city. Never was anybody more de-lighted than I, to find my master had not condescended to trou-ble himself about supplying his table, concluding, of course, that he was a gentleman whose means enabled him to consign to oth-ers such inferior domestic cares, and that on our arrival at home we should find everything in order—an anticipation of great de-light to me, and, in fact, by this time almost a matter of necessity. The clock had struck one, when we arrived at a house before which my master stopped, and throwing his cloak open, he drew from his sleeve a key with which he opened the door.

I followed my master into the house, the entrance of which was extremely dark and dismal, so much so as to create a sensa-tion of fear in the mind of a stranger; and when within found it contained a small courtyard and tolerably sized chambers. The moment he entered, he took off his cloak, and inquiring whether I had clean hands, assisted me to fold it, and then, carefully wip-ing the dust from a seat, laid it thereon. He next very composedly seated himself, and began to ask me a variety of questions, as to who I was, where I came from, and how I came to that city; to all which I gave a more particular account than exactly suited me at that time, for I thought it would have been much more to the purpose had he desired me to place the table and serve up the soup, than ask me the questions he then did.

With all this, however, I contrived to give him a very satisfactory account of myself, dwelling on my good qualities, and concealing those which were not suitable to my present auditory. But I began now to grow very uneasy, for two o'clock arrived, and still no signs of dinner appeared, and I began to recollect that ever since we had been in the house I had not heard the foot of a human being, either above or below. All I had seen were bare walls, without even a chair or a table—not so much as an old chest like that I had such good occasion to remember. In fact, it seemed to me like a house labouring under the influence of enchantment.

"Boy, hast thou eaten anything to-day?" asked my master at last. "No, sir," I replied, "seeing that it was scarcely eight o'clock when I had the good fortune to meet your honour."

"Early as it was," returned my master, "I had already breakfasted, and it is never my custom to eat again till the evening; manage as you can till then; you will have the better appetite for supper."

It may be easily supposed that, on hearing this, my newly raised hopes vanished as rapidly as they had risen; it was not hunger alone that caused me to despond, but the certainty that fortune had not yet exhausted her full store of malice against me. Already I saw in perspective my troubles renewed, and I turned to weep over my unhappy anticipation. The consideration which prevented my taking an abrupt departure from the priest arose to my remembrance—that of falling from bad to worse—and I beheld it, as I feared, realised. I could not but weep over the incidents of my past unfortunate career, and anticipate its rapidly approaching close; yet withal, concealing my emotion as well as possible, I said, "Thank God! sir, I am not a boy that troubles himself much about eating and drinking; and for this quality I have been praised even to this very day by all the masters whom I have ever served."

"Abstinence is a great virtue," returned my master, "and for this I shall esteem thee still more; gormandising is only for swine, men of understanding require little to allay their appetite."

"I can understand that sentiment right well," quoth I to myself; "my masters have all advised the same course; though the devil a bit do *they* find the virtues of starvation so very pleasant, by all that I have seen."

Seating myself near the door, I now began to eat some crusts of bread which I had about me; they were part of some scraps I had collected in my career of charity. "Come here, boy," said my master; "what are you eating?"

I went to him and showed him the bread. He selected from the three pieces which I had, the best and largest, and said, "Upon my life, but this seems exceedingly nice bread."

"Yes, sir," I replied, "it is very good."

"It really is," he continued; "where did you get it? was it made with clean hands, I wonder?"

"That I can't answer for," I replied, "but the flavour of it does not come amiss to me."

"Nor to me either, please God!" said my poor devil of a master; and, having finished his scrutiny, he raised the bread to his mouth, and commenced as fierce an attack on it as I quickly did on the other.

"By heavens! but this bread is beautiful!" exclaimed he; and I, beginning to see how matters stood with him, redoubled my haste with the remainder, being well assured that if he finished first, he would have little hesitation in assisting me: but luckily we finished together. He then carefully picked up the crumbs which had fallen, and entering a small chamber adjoining, brought out an old jar with a broken mouth. Having drank therefrom he handed it to me, but to support my character of abstemiousness, I excused myself, saying, "No, sir, I thank you; I never drink wine."

"The contents of the jar will not hurt you," he said; "it is only water!" I took the jar, but a very small draught satisfied me, for thirst was one of the few things from which I suffered no inconvenience.

Thus we remained till night, I anticipating my supper, and my master asking me many questions, to all of which I answered in the best manner I was able. Then he took me into the chamber whence he had brought the jar of water, and said, "Stay here, my boy, and see how to make this bed, as from henceforth you will have this duty." We then placed ourselves on each side of this bed, if such it can be called, to make it; though little enough there was to make. On some benches was extended a sort of platform of reeds, on which were placed the clothes, which, from want of washing, were not the whitest in the world. The deuce of anything was there in the shape of feather-bed or mattress, but the canes showed like the ribs of a lean hog through an old covering which served to lie upon, and the colour of which one could not exactly praise.

It was night when the bed was made, and my master said, "Lazaro, it is rather late now, and the market is distant; likewise the city abounds with rogues; we had better therefore pass the night as we can, and to-morrow morning we will fare better. Being a single man, you see, I don't care much for these things, but we will arrange better in future."

"Sir, as to myself," I replied, "I beg you will on no account distress yourself. I can pass a night without food with no inconvenience, or even more indeed, if it were necessary."

"Your health will be all the better for it," he said, "for take my word for it, as I said to-day, nothing in the world will ensure length of life so much as eating little."

"If life is to be purchased on such terms," said I to myself, "I shall never die, for hitherto I have been obliged to keep this rule, whether I will or no; and, God help me, I fear I shall keep it all my long life."

My master then went to bed, putting his clothes under his head instead of a pillow, and ordered me to seek my rest at his feet; which I accordingly did, though the situation precluded all hope of sleep. The canes of which the bedstead was composed, and my bones, which were equally prominent, were, throughout the night, engaged in a continual and most unpleasant intimacy; for considering my illness and the privations which I had endured, to say nothing of my present starving condition, I do not believe I had a single pound of flesh on my whole body. Throughout that day I had eaten nothing but a crust of bread, and was actually mad with hunger, which is in itself a bitter enemy to repose. A thousand times did I curse myself and my unhappy fortunes—the Lord forgive my impiety; and what was a sore addition to my misery, I dared not to move, nor vent my grief in audible expressions, for fear of waking my master. Many times during this night did I pray to God to finish my existence!

As the morning appeared, we arose, and I set about cleaning my master's clothes, and putting them in order; and helped him to dress, very much to his satisfaction. As he placed his sword in his belt, he said, "Do you know the value of this weapon, my boy? The gold was never coined that should buy this treasure of me. Of all the blades Antonio ever forged, he never yet made its fellow." And then drawing it from the scabbard and trying the edge with his fingers, he added, "With this blade I would engage to sever a bale of wool."

"And I would do more than that with my teeth," said I to myself; "for though they are not made of steel, I would engage to sever a four-pound loaf, and devour it afterwards."

He then sheathed his sword and girded it round him, and with an easy, gentlemanlike carriage, bearing himself erect, and throwing the corner of his cloak over his shoulder, or over his arm, placing his right hand on his side, he sallied forth, saying, "Lazaro, see to the house while I go to hear mass, and make the bed during my absence; the vessel for water wants filling, which you can do at the river which runs close by; though take care to lock the door when you go, lest we should be robbed, and put the key on this hinge, in case I return before you, that I may let myself in."

He then walked up the street with such an air of gentility, that a stranger would have taken him for a near relation of the Count of Arcos, or at least for his valet de chambre.

"Blessed be the Lord!" said I to myself, "who, if He inflicts misfortunes, gives us the means of bearing them. Now who, on meeting my master, would dream but that he had supped well and slept well; and, although early in the morning, but that he had also breakfasted well? There are many secrets, my good master, that you know, and that all the world is ignorant of. Who would not be deceived by that smiling face and that fine cloak? and who would believe that such a fine gentleman had passed the whole of yesterday without any other food than a morsel of bread, that his boy had carried in his breast for a day and a night? To-day washing his hands and face, and, for want of a towel, obliged to dry them with the lining of his garments—no one would ever suspect such things from the appearance before them. Alas! how many are there in this world who voluntarily suffer more for their false idea of honour, than they would undergo for their hopes of an hereafter!"

Thus I moralised at the door of our house, while my master paced slowly up the street; and then, returning within, I lost no time in making the tour of the house, which I did, though without making any fresh discovery whatever, or finding anything of a more consolatory nature than my own gloomy thoughts.

I quickly made our bed, such as it was, and taking the water-jar, went with it to the river. There I saw my gay master in one of the gardens by the river side, in close conversation with two ladies, closely veiled, for there were many who were in the habit of resorting thus early in the morning to enjoy the fresh air, and to take breakfast with some of the gentlemen of the city, who likewise frequented the spot. There he stood between them, saying softer things than Ovid ever did; while they, seeing him apparently so enamoured, made no scruple of hinting their wish to breakfast. Unfortunately his purse was as empty as his heart was full, therefore this attack on his weaker position threw him somewhat suddenly into disorder, which became evident from his confusion of language and the lame excuses of which he was obliged to avail himself. The ladies were too well experienced not to perceive, and that quickly, how matters stood; it was not long, therefore, before they exchanged him for a more entertaining gallant.

I was all this time slily munching some cabbage-stalks, for want of a better breakfast, which I despatched with considerable alacrity, and then returned home, without being seen by my master, to await his orders respecting breakfast on his return.

I began to think seriously what I should do, still hoping, however, that as the day advanced my master might return with the means to provide at least for our dinner, but in vain. Two o'clock came, but no master; and, as my hunger now became insupportable, without further consideration I locked the door, and, placing the key where I was told, sallied out in search of food. With a humble subdued voice, my hands crossed upon my breast, and the name of the Lord upon my tongue, I went from house to house begging bread. The practice of this art, I may say, I imbibed with my mother's milk; or rather that, having studied it under the greatest master in all Spain, it is no wonder that I was so great an adept in all its various branches.

Suffice it to say, that although in this city there is no more charity than would save a saint from starvation, yet such was my superiority in talent, that before four o'clock I had stowed away nearly four pounds of bread in my empty stomach, and two pounds more in my sleeves and in the inside of my jacket. Passing then by the tripe market, I begged of one of the women that keep the stalls, who gave me a good-sized piece of cow-heel, with some other pieces of boiled tripe.

When I got home, I found my good gentleman already arrived, and having folded and brushed his cloak, he was walking about the courtyard. As I entered he came up to me, as I thought, to chide me for my absence, but, thank God, it was far otherwise. He inquired where I had been, to which I replied, "Sir, I remained at home till two o'clock; but when I found that your honour did not return, I went out, and recommended myself so well to the notice of the good people of this city, that they have given me what you see." I then showed him the bread and the tripe which I had collected. At the sight of these delicacies his countenance brightened up. "Ah!" said he, "I waited dinner for you some time; but as it grew late I finished. You have nevertheless acted very properly in this matter; for it is much better to ask, for the love of God, than to steal. I only charge you on no account to say you live with me, as such proceedings would not exactly redound to my honour, although I hardly think there is any danger, seeing that I am known so little in this city."

"Do not alarm yourself, sir, on that head," said I, "for people thought as little of asking who was my master as I of telling them."

"Eat away, then, you young rogue," said he, "and with the blessing of God we shall not long have need of such assistance, though I must say since I have been in this house good fortune has never visited me. There are houses, from some reason or other, so unlucky that every one who occupies them becomes infected with their ill-fortune, and this is without doubt one of them; but I promise you that directly the month is up I will leave, even if they should offer it to me for nothing."

I seated myself on the end of the bench, and commenced my supper with the tripe and bread. My poor unhappy master all the time eyed me askance, and never once took his eyes from my skirts, which at that time served me instead of a dinner-service. Providence had that day so favoured me, that I resolved my master should partake of my abundance, for I could well understand his feelings, having experienced them of old, and to that very day, indeed, I was no stranger to them. I began to think whether it would exactly become me to invite him to my repast, but as he had unfortunately said he had dined, I feared lest he might take it amiss. However, I very much wished that the poor sinner might have the benefit of my labour, and break his fast as he had done the day before, particularly as the food was better and my hunger less. My good wishes towards him were speedily gratified, as they happened to jump with his own humour, for directly I commenced my meal he began walking up and down the room, and approaching me rather closely—

"Lazaro," said he, "I really cannot help remarking the extreme grace with which you make your meal. I don't think I ever saw any one eat with more natural elegance; certain it is, that an observer might benefit by your example."

"Doubtless, my good sir," thought I, "it can only be to your extreme amiability that I am indebted for this compliment." Then, in order to give him the opportunity which I knew he longed for, I said, "Good materials, sir, require good workmen. This bread is most delicious, and this cow-heel is so well cooked and seasoned that the smell alone is sufficient to tempt any one."

"Cow-heel, is it?" said he.

"It is, sir," I replied.

"Ah!" said he, "cow's heel is one of the most delicate morsels in the world, there is nothing I am so fond of."

"Then taste it, sir," said I, "and try whether this is as good as you have eaten." He seated himself on the bench beside me, and laying hands on the cow-heel, with three or four pieces of the whitest bread, commenced in such good earnest that one might easily see his rations were not disagreeable to him—grinding every bone as ravenously as a greyhound. "With a nice sauce of garlic," said he, "this would be capital eating."

"You eat it with a better sauce than that, my good sir," thought I.

"By heavens," said he, "anybody would think, to see me eat, that I had not touched a morsel to-day."

"I wish I was as sure of good luck as I'm sure of that," said I to myself. He asked me for the water-jug, and I gave it to him, which, by the way, was a sure proof he had eaten nothing, for it was as full as when I brought it from the river. After drinking we went to bed in the same manner as on the night before, though it must be confessed in a much more contented mood.

Not to dwell too much on this part of my story, I shall only say that in this manner we passed eight or ten days, my worthy master taking the air every day, in the most frequented parts, with the most perfect ease of a man of fashion, and returning home to feast on the contributions of the charitable, levied by poor Lazaro.

Many times did the reflection suggest itself, that, when with former masters I prayed so heartily to be released from such miserable service, my desire was certainly gratified, though with this difference, that not only did my present one decline feeding me, but expected that I should maintain him.

With all this, however, I liked him very much, seeing he had not the ability to do more—in fact, I was much more sorry for his unfortunate condition than angry at the situation in which his deficiencies placed me; and many times I have been reduced to short commons myself, that I might bring home a certain share for my unlucky master. But he was poor, and nobody can give what he has not got—an excuse which I cannot make for the old scoundrels I served before—though, as God is my witness, to this very day I never see a gentleman, like my master, strutting along as though the street was hardly wide enough for him, without marking the singular way in which Fortune apportions her favours. I pitied him from my heart, to think, that with all his apparent greatness he might at that moment suffer privations equally hard to endure. But with all his poverty I found greater satisfaction in serving him than either of the others, for the reasons I have stated. All that I blamed him for was the extravagance of his pride, which, I thought, might have been somewhat abated towards one who, like myself, knew his circumstances so intimately. It seems to me, however, that the poorest gentlefolk are always the most proud; but there is consolation in the thought that death knows no distinction, but at length most generally places the commoner in higher ground than it does the peer. I lived for some time in the manner I have related, when it pleased my miserable fortune, which seemed never tired with persecuting me, to envy me even my present precarious and unhappy condition.

It appeared that the season in that country had been unfavourable to corn, therefore it was ordained by the magistracy that all strangers who subsisted by alms should quit the city, or risk the punishment of the whip. This law was enforced so rigidly that, only four days after its promulgation, I beheld a procession of miserable wretches who were suffering the penalty through the streets of the city; a sight which so alarmed me that I did not dare for the future to avail myself of my accustomed means of subsistence. It can hardly be possible to imagine the extreme necessity to which our house was reduced, or the mournful silence of those who were expiring within; for two or three days we neither spoke a word nor had we a mouthful to eat. With regard to myself, there were some young women, who earned their living by cotton-spinning and making caps, and with whom, being near neighbors of ours, I had made some slight acquaintanceship—out of their pittance these poor girls gave me a morsel, which just served to keep life within me.

I did not, however, feel my own situation so keenly as I did that of my poor master, who, during the space of eight days, to the best of my knowledge, never touched a mouthful; at least, I can say, the deuce a morsel ever entered our door. Whether he ever got anything to eat when he went out I cannot determine; but I know well that he sallied out every day with a waist as fine as a greyhound of the best breed; and the better, as he thought, to evade suspicion, he would take a straw from the mattress, which could even ill spare the loss, and go swaggering out of the house, sticking it in his mouth for a toothpick! He continued to attribute all his ill-fortune to the unlucky house in which we were lodged. "The evils we have to bear," he would say, "are all owing to this unfortunate dwelling—as you see, it is indeed sad, dark, and dismal: nevertheless, here we are, and, I fear, must continue awhile to suffer; I only wish the month was past, that we might well be quit of it."

It happened one day, suffering, as I have described, this afflicting persecution of hunger, that, by some extraordinary chance, I know not what, nor did I think it dutiful to inquire, there fell into my poor master's poverty-stricken possession the large sum of one rial, with which he came home as consequentially as though he had brought the treasure of Venice, saying to me, with an air of extreme satisfaction and contentment, "Here, Lazaro, my boy, take this—Providence is at last beginning to smile on us —go to the market and purchase bread, meat, and wine; we will no longer take things as we have done. I have other good news likewise. I have taken another lodging, so that there will be no occasion to remain in this wretched place longer than the end of the month. Curse the place and him who laid the first brick; by the Lord, since I've been here not a drop of wine have I drunk, nor have I tasted a morsel of meat, neither have I enjoyed the smallest comfort whatsoever; but everything has been, as you see, miserable and dismal to the last degree. However, go, and quickly, for to-day we will feast like lords."

I took my rial and jar, and without another word set out on my errand with the utmost speed, making towards the market-place in the most joyous and light-hearted mood imaginable. But alas! what enjoyment could I expect, when my adverse fortune so preponderated that the slightest gleam of sunshine in my career was sure to be overtaken by a storm? I was making my way, as I said, in extremely good spirits, revolving in my mind in what manner I should lay out my money to the best advantage, and returning heartfelt thanks to Providence for favouring my master with this unexpected stroke of fortune, when I saw a great crowd at the other end of the street, among whom were many priests; and I soon found to my horror that they were accompanying a corpse. I stood up against the wall to give them room, and as the body passed I beheld one, who, as I supposed, from the mourning she wore, was the widow of the deceased, surrounded by friends. She was weeping bitterly, and uttering in a loud voice the most piteous exclamations. "Alas!" she cried, "my dear husband and lord! whither are they taking you? To that miserable and unhappy dwelling; to that dark and dismal habitation; to the house where there is neither eating nor drinking!" Good heavens! never shall I forget the moment when I heard those words; it seemed in my fright as though heaven and earth were coming together. "Miserable and unhappy wretch that I am," I exclaimed in an agony of mind, "it is to our house then that they are bearing this body!"

I rushed from the place where I stood, through the crowd, forgetting in my fright the object of my errand, and made with all speed towards home. The instant I arrived, I closed the door, barred and bolted it, and cried out to my master with the utmost earnestness of manner to help me to defend the entrance. He, greatly alarmed, and with the impression that it was something else, called to me, "What is the matter, boy? why do you slam the door with such fury?"

"O master," said I, "come here and assist me, for they are bringing a dead body here! I met them in the street above, and I heard the widow of the dead man crying out, 'Alas! husband and master, whither do they take you? To the dark and dismal house; to the house of misery and misfortune; to the house where they neither eat nor drink.' To what other house, then, can they be bringing him than this?" Directly my master heard these words, albeit in no merry humour, he burst out into such a fit of laughing that it was some time before he could utter a word.

During this time I was holding fast the door, placing my shoulder against it for better security. The crowd passed with the body, though still I could not persuade myself but that they intended to bring it in. When my master was more satiated with mirth than with food, he said to me, in a good-tempered manner, "It is very just, Lazaro; according to what the widow said, you were right in thinking as you did; but as they have thought better of it and passed on, open the door and go on your errand." "Stop a little longer, sir," said I, "let them pass the end of the street, that we may be sure"; but he would not wait, and coming to the street door, he opened it and forced me away, for I hardly knew what I did with fright, and so he despatched me again to the market.

We dined well that day, though my appetite was but indifferent; and it was some time before I recovered from the effect of that misadventure, though it was an excellent source of mirth to my master whenever it was brought to his recollection.

In this manner I lived some little time with my third and poorest master the esquire, having great curiosity to know what could possibly have induced him to come to that part of the world, for I knew he was a stranger on the first day I lived with him, from the fact of his not knowing a single soul in the city. At last my wish was gratified; for one day, when we had feasted pretty well, and were consequently in good humour, he told me a little of his history. He was a native of Old Castile, and had quitted his country because he had refused to salute a neighbouring gentleman of consequence by taking off his hat first, which, according to punctilio, was construed into an insulting mark of disrespect. My honourable master wished to convince me that, being a gentleman, the other, though superior, had an equal right to doff his bonnet to him; "for," said he, "though I am, as you see, but an esquire, I vow to God, if the count himself were to meet me in the street, and did not take off his hat to me, ay, and entirely off, the next time we met I would turn into some shop, pretending business, rather than pay him the least mark of respect. And though you see me here but poorly off, yet in my own country I have an estate in houses in good condition and well rented, only sixteen leagues from the place where I was born, worth at least two hundred thousand maravedis; so you see that they must be of good size and in good repair. I have likewise a dovecot, which if it were taken care of, which it is not, would furnish upwards of two hundred young birds annually; and many other things I possess, which I have relinquished solely because I would not have the slightest imputation cast upon my honour, by yielding precedence to one who was in fact no better than myself; and I came to this city hoping to obtain some honourable employment, though I have not succeeded so well as I could have wished."

In this manner my master was going on with his narrative, giving me an account of the honourable proceedings by which he had suffered, when he was interrupted by the appearance of an old man and woman; the former came to demand the rent of the house, and the latter that of the bed. They brought the account, and claimed for two months more than he could raise in a year; I think it was about twelve or thirteen rials. He answered them very courteously, that he was then going out to change a piece of gold and should return in the evening. But he made his exit this time for good; and when the good people came for their money, I was obliged to tell them that he had not yet returned. The night came, but without my master, and, being fearful of remaining in the house by myself, I went to our neighbours, to whom I related the circumstance, and they allowed me to remain with them.

Early in the morning the creditors returned and inquired of the neighbours. The woman replied that his boy was there, and the key of the door ready for them. They then asked me about my master, and I told them that I knew not where he was, and that I had not seen him since he went out to change the piece of gold; but that I thought it was most likely he was gone off with the change.

On hearing this news they sent for a lawyer and a constable, and called me and others to witness their taking possession of my master's effects in payment of their demands. They went all over the house, and found just as much furniture as I have recounted before, when they demanded of me, "What has become of your master's property? where are his trunks? and where is his household furniture?"

"I am sure I don't know," I replied.

"Doubtless," said they, "the property has been removed during the night. Señor Alguazil,* take that boy into custody; he knows whither it has been taken." On this up came the Alguazil, and, seizing me by the collar, said, "Boy, thou art my prisoner, if thou reveal not where thy master hath hid his effects." I, as if quite new to this sort of thing, expressed the utmost surprise and terror, and promised to state everything I knew, which seemed a little to disarm his anger.

"That is right," exclaimed all, "tell all you know, and fear nothing." The man of law seated himself at a desk, and desired me to begin.

"Gentlemen," I continued, "my master is in possession of a good stock of houses and an old dovecot."

"So far well," was the reply; "however little worth, it will meet the debt he owes us. In what part of the city do they lie?"

"On his own estate, to be sure," was my answer.

* Alguazil: police officer.—Ed.

"That is all the better," they exclaimed; "and where is his estate?"

"In Old Castile," I replied, "as he told me." Both Alguazil and notary laughed out at hearing this, exclaiming, "Quite enough—quite enough to cover your claim, though it were even greater." The neighbours who had gathered round us now said, "Gentlemen, this here is a very honest boy; he has not been long in the 'squire's service, and knows no more of him than does your worship; the poor little sinner came knocking at our doors, and for charity's sake we gave him something to eat, after which he has gone to sleep at his master's."

Seeing that I was innocent they let me go free; but the notary and the Alguazil now came on the owners for the taxes, which gave rise to no very friendly discussion and a most hideous din; the man and woman maintained very stoutly that they had neither the will nor the means to pay them. The others declared they had other business in view of more importance; but I left them without stopping to see the issue of the affair, though I believe the unfortunate owner had to pay all; and he well deserved to do it, for when he ought to have taken his ease and pleasure, after a life of labour, he still went on hiring out houses to increase his gains.

It was in this way that my third and poorest master took leave of me, by which it seems I put the seal to my bad fortune, which, while exercising its utmost rigour against me, had this singularity in it that, though most domestics are known to run away from their masters, it was not thus in my case, inasmuch as my master had fairly run away from me.

## ❧ Portrait of Father

### by MATEO ALEMÁN

Mateo Alemán was born in Seville in 1547. His father, the city's prison doctor, took the boy on his tours of duty, giving him an early introduction to low life. Mateo studied at Spanish universities, and obtained a post in the Treasury. A poor guardian of money, he was imprisoned for debt and suspected malversations. Eventually he emigrated to Mexico, and vanished from the records, some time after 1613.

His one important book, *Guzmán de Alfarache*, appeared in two parts, the first in 1599. It is a picaresque novel, the autobiography of a crook.

The translator, James Mabbe, was one of those spirited Elizabethans who made an art of their drudging task. *The Rogue*, his translation of *Guzmán*, was published in 1622. The spelling and punctuation have here been modernized, and the abundant moralizing digressions omitted.

MY FATHER and his kinsmen were a certain kind of upstart gentlemen that came out of the Levant, who having no certain abiding came at length to reside and settle in Genoa, where they were engrafted into the nobility, and had many large and goodly privileges granted unto them. And although they were not naturals of that place, yet we shall here put them under that style, as if they had been born there. His traffic and income, whereby he maintained himself, was according to the common custom of that country, the which, for our sins' sake, is grown now into ours. Which infection of late hath spread itself through the world, to wit, usury, money-banks, and profitable exchange of gold and silver. Even for this was he persecuted and reviled, defaming him with that foul name "usurer." Many times he himself heard that reproachful word as he passed along the streets; it could not escape his ear; yet he was of that good nature and gentle condition that he took no notice of it, but slightly passed it over. . . .

My father had a fair large mass-book with the full number of David's 150 psalms, wherein he had been taught to pray (I mean in the Spanish tongue), and a great pair of beads, whereof every one of them was as big as a hazel nut. These my mother gave him, which she had inherited from her own mother. These he always carried with him; you should never see them out of his hand. Every morning he heard his mass, humbly kneeling with both his knees on the ground, his hands joining themselves together at his breast, lifting them up toward heaven, on the top whereof his hat hung. Some malicious people, by way of reproach, did not stick to say that he did pray in this manner because he would not hear the priest, and that he held his hat so high because he would not see him. But of this let them judge who find themselves free from passion, and let them tell me whether it be not a perverse and rash censure, proceeding from a profane kind of people that have no care of their souls, and without any conscience at all. But the very truth is that the main cause and first beginning of their murmuring against him was that a partner of his in Seville, being broken and turned bankrupt and having carried away with him great sums of money that were his, he pursued after him, as well to remedy himself as well as he could of so great a loss, as also to order and settle some other necessary businesses which did much concern him.

The ship he went in was set upon and taken, and he, together with the rest that were in her, taken captives and carried to Algiers; where, what out of fear and what out of despair—fear, for that he knew not how or which way to recover his liberty; and despair, for that he never looked to get again his moneys— for quietness' sake, as one that had not the spirit of contradiction or that was wont to gainsay anything, he renounced his religion and turned Turk. There he married a Moor, a woman of perfect beauty and principal rank, with whom he had good store of wealth. . . .

It afterward so fell out that my father's partner, to secure himself from after-claps and to live out of danger, labored to take order with his creditors and to compound for his debts upon fair and reasonable conditions, requiring such rates and days of payment as that he might both be able to live well himself as also to pay his debts.

When this came to my father's ear, that had certain and assured notice of it, he had a great desire to come away with all the secrecy and diligence he could possibly devise. And the better to deceive the Moor his wife he told her that he purposed to employ himself in matters of merchandise, which would turn much to their profit. He made money of most that he had, and putting it into sequins (a certain coin that is made of fine Barbary gold), taking with him all the jewels he could finger, and so leaving her alone and very poor, he came this way with all the speed he could. And not making anyone acquainted therewith, neither friend nor foe, reducing himself to the faith of Jesus Christ, repenting himself of his fault, with tears in his eyes, being his own promoter,* he accused himself, craving pardon for his offense, and that some favorable penance might be inflicted upon him. Which being enjoined him and fully performed by him, he afterward went about to recover his debts. And this was the chief cause why they would never afterward trust him, nor have any charitable opinion of him, were his works never so good, never so pious. . . .

That which I saw with my own eyes, for that time that I knew him and was conversant with him, I am able to tell thee what manner of man my father was. He was of a fair complexion, ruddy, well colored; clean and soft was the grain of his skin, and his hair curled, which on my conscience was natural unto him. He had a full eye, and that full of life, resembling in color the watery turquoise. He wore a foretop, and those his locks which overspread his temples, to give them the greater grace, curled themselves into rings of hairs. . . .

I told you before that, having performed his penance, my father came to Seville for to recover his debt; whereupon law

---

* Promoter: ecclesiastical defender.—Ed.

was waged, many offers made either to give or to take—some demands and some answers. And if he had not thoroughly purged himself for his health and found an evasion—that is, if he had not well cleared himself of being a renegado—it would have broken out upon him into the scurf of his head, or the scratches in the pasterns; * all the fat had lain in the fire, and he had been quite blown up. But he had wrought such a cure upon himself and handled the business so handsomely that they could not catch hold of him for having the leprosy, or the dry scab.† All things were so well made up that they could not find a hole in his coat, or make any mark or white ‡ to shoot at him, so well was he provided for all comers. Means were used on both sides, composition offered but not accepted; the one being unwilling to pay all, the other as loth to lose all. Of this spilt water he gathered up as much as he could, making the best of a bad bargain. And with that which came to his share, be it what it will, it so well served his turn that the cards once more were dealt round again, and he come into very good play. His incomes were such and his luck so great that in a very short time he gained not only wherewithal to dine, but also to sup. He built him a pretty handsome house; he sought to plant and settle himself in those parts; he bought him land of inheritance.§ He had a garden in San Juan de Alfarache; a neat one it was, and of much recreation and pleasure, distant from Seville little more than half a league; whither many days, especially in the summertime, he went for his pastime, and made many banquets.

It happened that the merchants made a bourse or money-market for their contractations at the stairs of the great church, like that of San Felipe at Madrid, with a place to walk in which went round about it, having a parapet or wall breast-high on the outside of it to separate it from the open street, girt in with great

* I.e., he would have been soundly beaten.—Ed.
† Leprosy: apparently ephemeral slang for "heresy."—Ed.
‡ White: bull's eye.—Ed.
§ Land of inheritance: land conferring heritable noble or gentle rank on the holder.—Ed.

marble pillars and strong chains of iron. My father walking there with other merchants, there chanced a christening to pass by. And as the talk there went, this child was said to be the secret son, or, to speak plain English, bastard to a certain person, that shall be nameless. My father followed in the tail of the troop and entered in after them even to the very font, for to see and view my mother, who with a certain old knight of the military habit (who for to maintain the honor of his order lived by the rents of the Church) were partners in this ceremony. It was a metaled * thing, a lusty lively wench, yet grave enough withal. Her carriage was very graceful and full of courtesy, her self young, beautiful, discreet, modest, and of a well-composed and settled behavior. Her handsome feature needs no other commender than itself. He stood steadily looking upon her all the while that the exercise of that sacrament gave him leave so to do, being astonished for to behold so rare a beauty, if not besotted with it. For to that her natural beauty of face and feature of body (without any tricking or painting at all), all was so curious and fitly placed through that whole frame of nature that one part helping another and all put together into one piece did make such a delicate contexture that no pencil can reach to express its perfection, nor imagination conceive how to make it better. The parts and fashion of my father I have already largely laid open to you; this goodly creature (for they seem gods and not men, who are not touched with natural affections) began to perceive his earnest eying of her and did not a little rejoice in it, howsoever she did dissemble it. . . . For that time there passed no more betwixt them, nor aught else done, save only that he came to know that she was that knight's pawn, his jewel, his delight, a morsel that he kept for his own mouth, over whom he was wondrous wary, and so tenderly affected that he could scarce endure to have her out of his sight. In fine, this gentlewoman went directly home to her house, and my father was at his wit's end, not knowing in the

* Metaled: spirited.—Ed.

world how to put her out of his mind. He used, that he might come to the sight of her again, many extraordinary diligences; but, unless when she went forth to mass upon some solemn feast days, he could not otherwise see her for a long time together.

The often falling drop hollows the hardest stone that is, and steadfast perseverance still gets the victory; for continuance crowneth our actions and disposeth them to their intended ends. He plodded so long on the matter that he found out a trick to serve his turn, using the means of a good old beldame, a reverend matron forsooth, an honest bawd, one of my charitable aunts. For such ministers as these doth the devil set awork and employ in his service; with which secret mines he overturns the strongest towers of the chastest women. . . . This good creature then, being courted by him with words and rewarded by him with deeds, went and came to and fro with papers. And because the principles, as they are the first, so are the hardest to learn, and because the greatest difficulty consists in the beginning, and for that loaves go aside if they be not well set into the oven, she molded the business well, using the best sleights she had. And because my father had heard of old that money leveleth the greatest difficulties and makes all things plain and easy, he did ever manifest his faith by his works, because they should not condemn it to be dead and fruitless. He was never negligent, nor yet no niggard. He began, as I told you, by this woman's hand to sow the seeds of his love and prodigally to spend upon my mother; and they both very willingly and very cheerfully are ready to receive all. . . . As we see many times, jesting turned into earnest, and things full often do end in sober earnest, which at the first were but begun in jest.

My mother, as ye have already heard, was a discreet woman; fain she would, but durst not. She had a good mind to the business, but yet she was afraid. She was sometimes on, sometimes off. Her own heart was the oracle of her desires; with that she consulted often what were best to do. . . . In conclusion, whom will not silver win? Whom will not gold corrupt? This knight was an elderly man, much given to spitting, spalling,* and coughing. He was troubled with the stone, with sharpness of his urine, and other the like infirmities. She had seen him full oft by her sweet side in the naked bed, where he did not appear the man my father was; he had not that vigor, nor liveliness, nor that handsomeness of shape and proportion. And besides, observe it while you live and you shall evermore find it to be true that long acquaintance and much conversation (where God's fear is not) breeds wearisomeness, and loathsomeness at the last. Novelties please all, especially women, who are lovers of flimflam tales, and for the receiving and returning of news—like unto *materia prima*, which never ceaseth to desire and seek after new forms. She was resolved to have forsaken the old knight, to shift her of her old clothes, to change her smock, and was fully bent to fly out and to break loose, whatsoever came of it. But her great wisdom and long experience, which was hereditary unto her and sucked from her mother's teat, opened the way and presented unto her an ingenious resolution. And questionless, the fear of losing her pension kept her aloof off, the thought whereof much perplexed her for the present, who otherwise was of herself well egged forward, and had a good mind to the game. For what lesson my father read but once unto her the devil repeated the same ten times over; so that it was no such great matter now to win Troy; there was likelihood enough to take it in less than ten years. . . .

Having taken these things into her consideration, she treated with this her bawdy ambassadress how and when it might be: the manner, how; and the time, when. But finding, after long consultation, that it was impossible to effect her desires in her own house, and that there was no good to be done at home for to enjoy each other freely, and to take that fulness of content which must satisfy the hungry maws of greedy lovers, amongst many other shifts and tricks and very good and witty devices and strange plots, which they had laid their heads about for the better success in the business, they made choice of this which followeth.

* Spalling: spitting.—Ed.

The spring had so far advanced itself that May was in its ending and the summer was now making his entrance. And the village of Gelves and that of San Juan de Alfarache are now the sweetest and the pleasantest of all that bordering territory; none thereabouts was like unto them. Besides, the fertileness and goodness of the soil (which is all one with that of Seville, as next neighbor unto it) which that river of Guadalquivir makes the more famous, whose watery gullets purling along the banks enrich and adorn all those gardens and fields that confine thereupon, so that with reason, if there may be a known paradise upon earth, sure the name thereof properly appertains to this particular seat—so fairly is it set forth with shadow-casting trees, so beautiful with curious bowers, so richly enameled with sundry sorts of flowers, so abounding with savory fruits, so accompanied with silver-running streams, with clear springs, glass-labor-saving fountains, fresh airs, and delightsome shades, whereinto the beams of the sun are at that time denied their entrance and have not permission so much as once to peep in. At one of these retiring rooms of recreation, my mother agreed with her marriage-maker, her *sine qua non*, and some of the people of her house to come one day thither to make merry. And albeit the place whither they were to go was not that which my father was owner of, but was somewhat beyond it, nearer unto Gelves, yet of force they must, to go thither, pass close by our door.

Upon this care taken, and former agreement concluded between them, just about the time that she was to come near unto our garden gate, my mother began presently to complain of a sudden and grievous pain in her stomach, imputing the cause thereof to the coldness of the morning and the freshness of the weather, and did so cunningly dissemble the pangs and gripings she endured that they were fain to take her down from her xamuga,* which for her more ease in her journey was borne by a pretty, little, but sure-footed Sardinian ass. She feigned such extremities of torture, made such pitiful faces and such woeful ges-

* Xamuga: a chairlike saddle for ladies.—Ed.

tures—holding her hands as hard as she could for her life upon her belly, crushing and wringing them with all the might and main she could, then would she let them loose again, then clasp them together and wring each finger through anguish of her pain. Otherwise she would hang the head as if she were fainting and ready to swoon; and that fit past, fetching a deep sigh or two, she fell to unlacing and unbracing herself, that all that were about her, save those that were privy to the plot, did verily believe that she was wonderfully and mightily tormented, that she made them to melt into tears and to have a compassionate feeling of this her affliction. Divers passengers chanced in the interim to come by, and everyone proposed his remedy—so many men, so many medicines. But because they knew not for the present where to have the things that should be applied, nor where to have a fit place for to minister unto her, their medicines were impertinent and to no purpose in the world. To go back unto the city, it was impossible; to go further forward, dangerous; and to abide thus in the highway, not commodious. Her fits increased; all stood amazed, as not knowing what to do, nor what course to take. At last, one amongst the rest that was there, who was laid there for the purpose, breaks me in amongst them, and as he passes the press cries: "Room, for the passion of God! Make way there, stand farther off, lest you stifle her for want of air! Come, let us take her and remove her out of the highway; it were cruelty not to seek to cure her, and a thousand pities that so sweet a creature should be cast away for want of care and looking after! Come, let us take her in our arms and put her into this garden-house here hard by; in this case we must be content to take that which comes next to hand."

All approved what he said; his motion was applauded and so generally well liked that it was presently concluded amongst them that until that fit were overpassed they should crave leave of those that kept the house to give her entrance, not doubting but she would be much the better if they could be but so happy as once to get her within the doors. They knocked hard and thick, as men use to do when they are in haste. The good woman that kept the house made show as if she thought her master had been there; and as she came waddling along bawled to herself: "O good God, is it you, master? O sweet Jesus! I pray be not angry that I came no sooner, I was very busy, I could not do withal, I came as soon as I could." These and the like excuses her unprofitable chaps mumbled to herself. . . .

My good old woman had by this time opened the gate, and either not well remembering, or making show as if she had not known them, full of dissimulation, she fell thus upon them: "What a stir, what a knocking is here! The devil take you all for me! Beshrew me if I did not think it had been our master. The very fear whereof, lest I might have stayed too long before I let him in, hath not left me one drop of blood in all my body. It's very well; what's the matter now, I pray? What would you with me? What is your worship's pleasure? Have you any things to say to me? If you have, let me know your mind, that I may make an end and go about my business; for I have something else to do than stand thus idly here."

Then the old knight answered and said: "Good woman, I pray afford us some place in your house where this gentlewoman may rest herself awhile, for a grievous pain in her stomach hath befallen her here upon the way."

She that kept the house, seeming to resent her pain and to be much grieved for it, in her rude rustic manner sorrowfully replied: "Now a mischief on all such ill luck! Oh what a grief it is to see that any pain should prove so unhappy as to be thus ill employed upon so sweet a face, such a dainty bed of red and white roses! Come in, a' God's name, come in, I pray, for all the house is at your service." My mother, all this while, said not so much as one word, only she complained of her grief.

The good old wench of the house, using her with all the kindness her country fashion could afford, gave them the liberty of the whole house, bringing them into a lower room, where, in a well-furnished bed, there were certain *colchones*, or mattresses. These she presently unfolded, and having spread them forth and made all things fit and handsome, she presently opened a chest, whence she took out a very fine pair of sheets that were neat and sweet, a fair quilt and a couple of pillows, wherewith she dressed up a bed and made it ready for her to take her rest in. Well might the bed have been made, the room kept clean, all places sweetened with the burning of perfumes, breathing forth pomanders and other the like odoriferous scents, and a breakfast provided and many other dainties and delicacies put in a readiness for to entertain them withal. All these things, I say, might well have been made ready beforehand, but it was thought that some of them should not be prepared, as also that the woman that kept the house should not come at the first knocking, as likewise that the gate should be shut against them and not be opened until they called, that it might not seem to be a set match, and lest it might chance to breed some suspicion, and so the stratagem might be discovered and the maskers made known—for this day's plot was merely no other thing.

My mother, in this her pitiful pain, put off her clothes, got her to bed, and called ever and anon for warm cloths; which being brought unto her, making as if she had laid them to her belly, she thrust them lower beneath her knees and somewhat apart from her, because the heat of them did somewhat offend her, fearing lest they might cause some remotion or alteration in her body, whereby qualms might arise and weaken her stomach. With the help of these warm napkins she found herself much eased, and feigned she had a desire to sleep, hoping she could be the better after she had taken some rest.

The poor old knight, whose chiefest joy consisted in giving her content, having placed all his happiness in her welfare, was (honest cuckold as he was) wonderfully glad of this, and left her all alone in her naked bed. And having made fast the door after him, that none could get in to trouble her, he went forth to recreate himself in those gardens belonging to the house, charging his people to make no noise and that none should come near the door, enjoining stillness and silence, and that none of them should dare to open it till they had farther order from him or that he came himself. And for that honest woman of the house, he willed her that she should watch by her till she awaked, and that then she should come and call him.

My father in the meanwhile was not asleep, but stood with attention hearkening to what was said, and lay peeping out through the keyhole (like one that lies in ambuscado) of a certain back door belonging to a little close closet, whither he had retired himself till he could spy his time of advantage for to sally forth and surprise that desired fort, which he had long since so cunningly undermined.

Now, when all was hushed and quiet, and that her own nurse that came with her and that other old bawd of the house stood like two sentinels upon their watch, ready upon all occasions to give quick advice by a certain secret sign which might serve instead of a watchword, when the old knight should make head that way, then did my father issue out of that postern or little back door of his, that he might see and confer with his mistress. And at that very instant did her feigned pangs cease, and those truer ones of love began to manifest themselves, giving other kind of twinges, and those kinder for the place affected. In this swelling kind of sport they continued two long hours, two years being not sufficient to express those passages that were betwixt these two new lovers in this their merry fit.

Now the day began to grow hot, and was entering more and more into his heats, which forced the knight to make his retreat toward the house. Which he did the more willingly, out of the desire which he had to know how his sick saint did, whether she were any better, and whether they should stay there or go forward, or what they were best to do. These were the lines that led him along to visit her. Upon his marching thitherward, the sentinels shot off a warning piece; and my father with great sorrow of heart forsook the fort where he had set up his standard and retired back to his court of guard, and shut himself up close where he was before.

Upon the entering in of her old gallant, she made show as if she had been fast alseep, and was awakened with the noise that he had made. And with a bended brow and angry look, casting her eye askew upon him with a coyness of language, she turned aside from him, accenting her words in a pretty kind of mournful fashion, pitying as it were and bemoaning herself: "Ay me, God help me! Why, alas, have they opened the door so quickly? Was there no care, no love to be shown unto me, in letting me sleep a little longer? I thought you, of all others, would not have put me out of so sweet a slumber. But 'tis no matter; I shall one day." And with that she sighed and stopped, as if she had something else to say, studying more to amuse him than to declare herself.

This good old knight of ours, this patient piece of flesh, gently made answer: "By those eyes of thine, than which I adore nothing more, I did not think to wake thee. It grieves me, pretty soul, that I have done thee that wrong; yet hast thou slept full two hours and more."

"Two hours?" replied my mother. "No, nor yet half an hour. Methinks it is but even now that I began to shut mine eyes; and in all my life I never had so quiet and contented a nap, for that little while that it lasted." Nor did she lie in all that she said, for she gulled him with a matter of truth. And looking with some-what a more cheerful countenance upon him, she much commended the remedy which they had given her, telling them that they had given her her life.

The old knight was glad to see so much comfort come from her. And by consent of both parties they agreed to celebrate their feast there, and to pass away as merrily as they could the remainder of that day, for that garden was no less pleasant than that whither they intended to have gone. And because their people were not far off that had charge of their provision (for the other house was hard by), they sent to them to bring back their dinner thither and such other things as they had brought along with them.

Whilst this business was a-doing, my father found fit opportunity to get out secretly at the other gate and to return back to Seville, where every hour was a thousand years, a moment an age, and the time of his absence from his new love a present hell.

Now, when the sun was in his declining, which was about five in the evening, mounting upon his jennet, as if it had been his ordinary walk, he came to visit this his house, wherein he found these gallants. He bid them welcome and told them he was very glad to see them there, only he was sorry for the mishap which caused their stay. For he no sooner came in but they told him all that had passed. His carriage was courteous, his voice loud and shrill, but not very clear. He made them many discreet and fair offers, for he had learned a little courtship; and they on the other side remained no whit in his debt for kind words. So that in the end there was a great league of friendship professed and confirmed between them in public, but a stricter tie in secret betwixt my father and his mistress, for the good pawns and pledges of love that had lately passed between them. . . .

The conversation went forward. Cards are called for, and to play they go. Their game was primera at three hands; my mother, she got the money, for my father was willing to lose to her. And it beginning now to wax night they gave off play, and went out into the garden to take the air. In the meanwhile the cloth was laid and their supper brought in and set on the board. They sit down, they eat, and have supped. And having given order against after supper that a barge should be made ready for them and tricked up with fresh flags and green boughs, when they came to the waterside they took boat, and were no sooner launched forth into the channel but they might hear from other vessels, which went to and fro upon the river, sundry consorts of all sorts of music, which made a most melodious sound—being an usual and ordinary thing with them in such a place and such a time as that was, being in that season of the year that was fittest for it. In this manner they were brought along till at last they landed. And being now come into the city, they took their leaves, everyone betaking himself to his own home and his own bed, save only my father's contemplative pate, whose roving head was so full of fancies that it could take no rest. My mother too, like another Melisendra, full of musing and thoughtful love, slept with her bedfellow, her old consort, "her body being prisoner in Sansuena and her soul a slave in Paris," * her corps in one place and her mind in another.

From that day forward such a strong knot of friendship was there knit between them, and continued with so much discretion and good cunning (considering their overventurousness and the danger they might run into) as could possibly be presumed from the quaint wit and close conveyance of an Easterling † dyed into a Genoese dipped in the vat of usury, who knew well enough how to put out his money to the best profit; who could clear you any account, could liquidate and divide you to a hair, how much loss there was in measure from the wastings that arose from the winnowing and cleansing of corn, how many grains lost in the refining of such a proportion or quantity of metal; nay, he could tell you to a crumb how much loss there was in a hundred dozen between the bread that was broken with the hand and that which was cut with the knife. As likewise from a woman of that good talent and those gifts and conditions which I have heretofore acquainted you withal, it is enough, if I say no more, that she was an Andaluz, born in the town of Seville and bred up in that good school, where she proved so good a proficient that she ran through the whole course of her art and did all her exercise for her degree of a whore, which she had laudably taken by making her appointments between the two choirs and the naves, or aisles, of the old church. Now my mother had her fits and flings before this time. This was not her first flying out, insomuch that not having at her outset anything of her own in her hands that was worth the keeping, that very day that she compounded with this old knight for her company and had driven her bargain with him, she swore unto me that she put over in trust above three thousand ducats only in jewels of gold and plate, besides the movables of her house and her change of apparel for the setting forth of her person. . . .

[Guzmán is born, and is recognized by each gentleman as his son.]
* A quotation from a popular ballad.—Ed.
† Easterling: Levantine.—Ed.

The good old knight, as formerly you have heard, was an ancient man, and of a feeble body; my mother young, fair, and full of wit, and knew so well how to provoke his appetite upon all occasions that his disorder opened the door to his death; for the old lad, by overdoing himself, hastened his own end. First his stomach began to fail him; then was he taken with a pain in his head; after that followed a burning fever, which after some few fits began to leave him. But though that ceased, he had never a whit the more mind to his meat—he could eat nothing. So by little and little he consumed away, and after some few pulls, he died. My mother not being able to restore him to life, though she would ever swear unto him that she was his life, and he hers —but all that protestation proved to be but a lie, for he was buried, yet she still lived.

The old knight left many kinsmen behind him in the house when he died, but none of them of the same suit with myself, though they colored for it. Only my mother and I sorted well together. As for the rest, they were *pan de diezmo, cada uno de la suya;* like the bread that the people offer up to the priest, "every one with a different device or contrary mark, that his loaf may be known from others." That good old gentleman (God be with him and have mercy on his soul) had but little comfort in this life; and at the time of his death, they on the one side, my mother on the other, while the breath was yet in his body pulled the linen from under him, leaving him a soul in his body but not a sheet in his bed, so that the sacking of Antwerp, which for the cruelty thereof is grown into a proverb, compared with this was not half so rigorous nor half so inhumane as this. And all, forsooth, for fear of a sequestration to have the goods deposited! But my mother, as she churned the milk, so she was her own carver; she was the tailor to cut her own coat and the worker of her own fortune. She found a time not long after to put her hands there where her heart was long before, and fell to fingering of his money. For she had the chiefest of all his goods in her own keeping under lock and key, and was mistress of all that was worth the having. But seeing herself in danger, and fearing to be put to her jumps, she thought it better to steal than to beg, and like a thief to make a start out of a bush than hereafter to ask an alms for God's sake. They were so nimble on all hands that there was scarce enough left wherewithal to bury him.

Some few days were scarce overpast but many diligences were used for to make these his goods appear. They set up excommunications at the churches and upon men's doors, to try if that would do any good, and make the purloiners to bring in the goods; but all to small purpose, for he that steals seldom returns to make restitution. But my mother made her excuse, saying that the knight (God be with him!) would still tell her, when he came to visit his moneys, and ran over his coffers and his cabinets: "This is thine, sweetheart; it is all for thee." So the lawyers were of opinion that with this she might very well satisfy her conscience. Besides, they affirmed that it was a due debt and properly belonged unto her; for though she gained it ill, yet it was not received ill. And howbeit the act were not lawful, yet the compact was justifiable. It was not lawful for her to play the whore, yet might she by law have whatsoever was promised her for the use of her body. . . .

But I return to my first station, whence I have digressed; for my mother looks for me, now being the widow of him that first possessed her; and dearly beloved and wonderfully made much of by this second owner. In this change and alteration of things, between these and those other nuptials, I was between three and four years old. And by the reckonings and rules of your feminine knowledge, I had two fathers; for my mother was so well learned in her art that she knew very well how to father me on them both. She had attained to the knowledge of working impossibilities, as plainly was to be seen, since she had the cunning to serve two masters and to please two husbands, to both of them giving good contentment. Both of them did acknowledge me to be their son. The one said I was his; so did the other. And when the knight was alone by himself, my mother would tell him that I was like him as if I had been spit out of his mouth, and that two eggs were not liker one another than I was like him. When, again, she talked with my father, she would tell him that I was his alter ego, that he and I were one, and so would have seemed if our heads had been cut off and laid in a charger, and that I was himself made less, and did so truly resemble him as if my head had stood upon his shoulders. But I wonder, a' God, in this resemblance of mine, which a blind man might discern at first blush, that the mystery thereof was not discovered, that they found not out her craft and searched not out the secret of this her deceit. But what with the blindness wherewithal they loved her and the confidence which each of them had, it was not perceived, nor any the least suspicion made thereof. And so both their beliefs were good, and both made exceeding much of me. The only difference was that in the time the good old man lived, he was my true father in public, and the stranger in secret. And so my mother certified me afterward, making large relations of these things unto me. . . .

My father did love us both with that true love, as his actions shall sufficiently declare. For by the force of this his love he did tread underfoot the idolatry of that which men style by the name of popular voice and common opinion. For they knew no other name that she had save the Commendadora, and to that she would answer, as if she had some commendam * conferred upon her. But he not regarding any of these things nor making any reckoning of the one or the other, setting as light by them as the least hair of his head, kept company with her and in the end took her to wife. I would have thee likewise to understand that he did not enter upon this business *a humo de pajas,* suddenly and unadvisedly, without having first well bethought himself of what he did. Every man knows his own estate best; and a fool understands more in his own than a wise man in another man's house.

In this intermedium, albeit this his *quinta* or garden-house which he had purchased was a place of pleasure and delight, yet it was his undoing, it was his overthrow—the profit little, and loss much; the cost great, as well for the keeping of it neat and hand-

* Commendam: a church living, held by her spouse.—Ed.

some as for the feastings and banquetings, which were very frequent. . . .

What with suits in law, what with making love to my mother and other expenses, one charge drawing on another, a great part of my father's state was consumed, all was almost gone. He was upon the point of breaking and ready to turn bankrupt, as he had often done before, so that it would have been no strange or new thing unto him.

My mother was a storer, a thrifty wench, one that could hold her own. She was no waster, but lay still on the saving hand. What with that which she gained in her youthfuller days and what she had scraped up in the knight's lifetime, as likewise at his death, amounted almost to ten thousand ducats. This was her dowry, and so much had he with her.

This money did somewhat refresh his drooping estate; it made him hold up his head again, who was before upon fainting and ready to swoon. It was unto him like a piece of wick or cotton in a lamp, dipped in oil. He began to give light afresh; he spent bravely, got him a carriage and a *silla de manos*, a little chair to carry with hands, borne with girths upon men's shoulders, as well for ease as state. Not so much for any longing that my mother had thereunto as for his own ostentation and glory, that the world might not take notice of the weakness of his estate, or that he was going down the wind. In this kind of fashion did he live, to uphold his credit; and rubbed out as well as he might with his means. But his gains did not equal his expenses. There was but one to get, and many to spend; but one pair of hands, and a great many mouths. The times were hard, the years dear, dealings small and bad, little or no trading. What was well gotten is wasted and gone; and what was ill gotten hath not only consumed itself but his owner too. So that at last all was brought to nothing. Sin brought it in; and sin, on my conscience, sent it packing. For of all that was left, nothing appeared. The light was now quite out, and my father, being taken with a grievous sickness, was arrested by death within five days after, and so shut up his shop-windows and departed this world.

# ❧ Marriage à la Mode

## by CERVANTES

Miguel de Cervantes Saavedra was born in Alcalá de Henares, near Madrid, in 1547. His father was an apothecary surgeon. He entered the army, served gallantly in Italy, and lost permanently the use of his right hand when wounded in the great sea-battle at Lepanto in 1571. On his way back to Spain he was taken by Barbary corsairs and spent five years as a slave in Algiers. Eventually ransomed, he attempted the literary life, writing plays and a pastoral novel, without much success. He got a government job, collecting tax-money in rural districts. Accused of peculation, he was jailed and then dismissed from his post, to live in poverty. The first part of the great book, *The Ingenious Hidalgo Don Quixote de la Mancha*, appeared in 1605 and brought him fame but not ease. He died in 1616.

The *Exemplary Novels,* written at various times and published in 1613, is a collection of novellas and short stories, varied in style and subject. *Marriage à la Mode (El Casamiento engañoso)* exemplifies one of the author's manners—a romanesque frame enclosing a picture of ugly, even brutal, realism. Critics all talk of Cervantes' bubbling gayety; he could also express a cynic's view of human behavior.

FROM THE door of Resurrection Hospital * in Valladolid, outside the Puerta del Campo, emerged a soldier. His dependence on his sword as a cane, the weakness of his legs, his yellow hue, indicated that, though the weather was not very warm, he had sweated out in three weeks all the humors he had no doubt contracted in an hour. He took short steps and stumbled like a convalescent.

Entering in at the city gate, he encountered a friend whom he

* This charitable hospital specialized in the treatment of syphilis.—Ed.

had not seen in more than six months. The friend crossed himself as at the sight of a ghost; then came up and said: "What is all this, Lieutenant Campuzano? Is it possible that you are actually here? 'Pon my life, I thought you were in Flanders, trailing the puissant pike, rather than dragging a sword along here. You look sick, you're a shadow! What's happened to you?"

"As to my being here or elsewhere, Licentiate * Peralta, your seeing me is a sufficient answer. And for your other question, I need not tell you that I am making my exit from that hospital, where I sweated out some fourteen colonies of buboes, implanted on my back by a woman I took to wife—a serious error."

"So you were married!" said Peralta.

"Yes, sir."

"It must have been love. Such marriages have repentance built into them."

"I can't be sure if it was love," rejoined the lieutenant. "But I can assure you it was to my sorrow, since my wedlock, or my deadlock, brought me so many afflictions of body and soul that those of the body have cost me some forty sweat-treatments, and for those of the soul I haven't yet found any remedy. But as I am not fit for a long conversation in the street, please pardon me. Some other time I will tell you of my adventures, which are as novel and peculiar as any you have ever heard of."

"Not at all, not at all!" said the licentiate. "I beg you to come to my quarters, and there we will do penance together. They make a fine stew for invalids. I pay for two portions, but I'll give my servant a pie. And if your convalescent diet permits, we'll have some slices of Rute ham to tickle the appetite, and season it with my good will, which I offer to you now and on all other occasions."

Campuzano thanked him and accepted the invitation gratefully. The two went to San Lorenzo and heard mass. Then Peralta took the lieutenant home and supplied the promised meal. At its conclusion the host again asked for an account of the ad-

---

* Licentiate: holder of a higher degree; lawyer.

ventures which the guest had so magnified. Campuzano acceded willingly, and thus began: "You will remember, my dear Licentiate Peralta, that I was a good friend, in this city, of Captain Pedro de Herrera, who is now in Flanders."

"I remember it well," replied Peralta.

Well then (continued Campuzano), one day we were just finishing lunch in that Solana inn where we were living, when in came two women of a genteel appearance, with two menservants. One of the ladies started to talk to the captain; they stood in the window-bay. The other sat in a chair near me, dropping her veil to her chin, letting me see only what the flimsy substance revealed. Though I begged her to be so kind as to do me the favor of unveiling, she could not be persuaded. And to stimulate me the more, whether by accident or design, the lady thrust out a very white hand, sparkling with fine jewels. I was then dressed in the height of fashion, wearing that big chain which you certainly remember, a hat with feathers and a jeweled band, a bright-colored tunic of military style. In my own foolish eyes I cut such a figure that I thought I could turn any woman's head. Thus I again urged her to show her face. She replied: "Don't be so pressing. I have my own house. Tell a page to accompany me; and although I am more respectable than would appear from the freedom of my reply, I shall be glad to admit you to my acquaintance and to learn if your discretion corresponds to your gallant show."

I kissed her hands in gratitude for her kindness, and promised her mountains of gold in recompense. The captain's conversation came to an end. The two ladies departed, followed by my manservant. The captain told me that his lady wanted him to take some letters to Flanders for another captain, whom she alleged to be her cousin, though the captain well knew him to be her lover. I was excited by the snow-white hands I had glimpsed and by the face that I longed to see. Thus next day, guided by my servant, I presented myself and was welcomed in. The house was well furnished. I found there a woman of about thirty; I recognized her by her hands. She was not remarkably beautiful, but was sufficiently so to capture a man, and her speaking voice was so sweet that it passed readily through one's ears to touch one's very soul. I made to her long, loving discourses; I boasted, I lunged and parried, I made offers, I promised; I went through all the ritual that seemed to me necessary to attract her regard. But as she was used to hearing similar or superior offers and arguments it seemed that she was rather lending an ear to them than giving them complete credit. In short, our dealings, during four days of constant visits, consisted mostly of flowery words, without my attaining the fruit of my desires.

In all my calls I found the house ever unoccupied, with no hint of the presence of pretended relatives or of actual friends. My lady was served by a maid, rather sly than simple. Finally, pursuing my suit in the manner of a soldier awaiting transfer abroad, I pressed the Señora Doña Estefanía de Caicedo—that is the name of my captor—for a decision. She replied: "Señor Lieutenant Campuzano, it would be silly for me to try to pass myself off as a saint. I have been a sinner—indeed I am one still—but not in such a way that the neighbors are scandalized and that the generality of men point me out. I inherited not a penny from my parents or other relatives; nevertheless my household furnishings are worth a good two thousand five hundred crowns; they are of such a quality that they would hardly be put up at auction and would take time to dispose of for cash. With this property in hand I am on the lookout for a husband to whom I may submit. With him I may reform my life; and at the same time I shall expend upon him a notable care in serving and tending him. For no prince has a more accomplished chef than I am, nor one who better understands the fine points of gourmet cooking than I, when I set myself to domestic tasks. I know how to be a first-class housekeeper, a servant in the kitchen and a lady in the parlor. In fact, I can command others and compel obedience. I don't waste anything; I take in much. My housekeeping funds bring in not less, but much more, when they are spent at my order. My linen, plentiful and of good quality, does not come out of a shop or stall; it was stitched by my own hands and those of my maids. It would have been woven at home, if that were possible. I speak in my own praise; don't blame me, since I am forced to do so. In short, I am trying to say that I am looking for a husband who will protect me, command me, and honor me, not a lover who will serve me—and abuse me. If you should choose to accept this proposal, I am ready and willing, submissive to your orders, without putting myself up for sale—which is equivalent to putting oneself in the hands of matchmakers. The best contracting agents are the parties concerned."

My wits, I fear, resided not in my head but in my heels. My pleasure exceeded the bounds of imagination. Picturing the quantity of furniture, which I reckoned up at cash value, I made no more discourses than my pleasure suggested, which held my judgment enchained. I told her that I was the luckiest of men, in that heaven had granted me, almost miraculously, such a mate, whom I could make mistress of my will and of my property— which was no small matter, what with the chain about my neck and my other precious stones at home, and some military adorn- ments, which could be cashed in. These would be worth more than two thousand ducats; added to her two thousand five hun- dred, there was enough to permit our retirement to my native village, where I had some property. This could be exploited with the money; and by selling the products in season we could lead a cheerful and comfortable life.

In short, that day we settled our engagement. We attested that we were unmarried, and during the three festival days that fol- lowed the banns were published, and on the fourth we were married. Present at the ceremony were two friends of mine and a young man whom she presented as her cousin, and whom I wel- comed as a kinsman with the utmost cordiality. Indeed, cordiality had marked all my speeches so far to my new wife; though I cherished a secret, treacherous intention that I prefer not to reveal. For though I am telling nothing but the truth, it is not exactly confessional truth, which must be stated in full.

My manservant carried my trunk from the inn to my wife's

house. In her presence I locked up in it my magnificent chain. I showed her three or four others, not so big, but of better workmanship, with three or four rings of various sorts. I displayed to her my finery and feathers, and handed over four hundred reals for household expenses. For six days I fed on wedding dainties; I luxuriated like a wanton son-in-law in the home of his rich father-in-law. I trod on sumptuous carpets, rumpled sheets of Holland linen, lighted my leisure with silver candlesticks. I breakfasted in bed, rose at eleven, lunched at one, and at two took my siesta on the parlor sofa. Doña Estefanía and her maid waited on me hand and foot. My servant, whom I had theretofore regarded as lazy and stupid, was transformed into a paragon. When Doña Estefanía was not at my side she was to be found in the kitchen, busy confecting dishes to tease my appetite and please my palate. My shirts, collars, and handkerchiefs were like the gardens of Aranjuez in bloom, so sweet they smelt, with the angel-water and orange-flower she sprinkled on them.

The days sped by, like the years under the command of time. And seeing myself so tended and coddled, I began to renounce my wicked intentions and turn them into good ones. And when these days were past, one morning—I was still in bed with Doña Estefanía—there was a loud knocking on the street door. The maidservant ran to the window; then, turning around, she said: "A good welcome to her! You see, she has come sooner than she promised in her letter."

"Who is it that has come, girl?" said I.

"Who? Why, my mistress, Doña Clementa Bueso, and Señor Don Lope Meléndez de Almendárez is with her, and two menservants, and the duenna, Hortigosa."

"How nice! Run, my girl, and open the door," said Doña Estefanía. "And you, my dear, don't get upset and answer, in my defense, anything you may hear against me."

"Why, who could say anything to offend you, especially in my presence? Tell me, who are these people, who seem to have disturbed you by their coming?"

"I haven't time to answer now," said Doña Estefanía. "You

must know merely this, that everything that is going to happen is only a put-up job, and that it is part of a certain scheme to bring about something which you will learn of later on."

Although I wanted to answer this, I was forestalled by the entry into the room of Señora Doña Clementa Bueso. She wore a gown of glossy green velvet with many gold trimmings and a short jacket of the same material, with like adornments. Her hat bore green, white, and red feathers, with a rich golden band. A delicate veil covered half her face. She was accompanied by Señor Don Lope Meléndez de Almendárez, wearing an equally rich and stylish traveling costume. The duenna Hortigosa was the first to speak: "Dear God! What is this? The bed of my lady Doña Clementa occupied! And by a man! Marvels I see today in this house! This Señora Estefanía has certainly made herself at home, trusting in my lady's friendship!"

"You are quite right, Hortigosa," said Doña Clementa, "but the fault is mine. You won't catch me again making friends with people who know only how to take advantage of me!"

Doña Estefanía put in: "Don't make a grievance of it, Señora Doña Clementa Bueso. Be assured that whatever you see in this house covers a mystery. When you learn the facts you will acquit me of all blame and will find nothing to complain of."

Meanwhile I had pulled on my breeches and jacket. Doña Estefanía took my hand and led me into another room. There she told me that her friend was playing a trick on Don Lope, her companion. She was trying to marry him; and her trick was to persuade him that she owned the house and all its contents, which she would bring him as a legal dowry; and after the marriage, she cared little for his discovery of the cheat, trusting in his great love for her. "And then," she said, "she will give me back my own; and no one will think the worse of her, or of any other woman, for trying to capture a worthy husband, even at the cost of a little deceit."

I replied that her project was carrying friendship pretty far, and that she had better be careful, for afterward she might have to go to law to get back her property. But she overwhelmed me with arguments, detailing all her obligations toward Doña Clementa, even in matters of greater importance; so that in spite of myself I abdicated my better judgment and was driven to fall in with Doña Estefanía's wishes. She assured me that the plot could only last a week, which we would spend in the house of another lady friend. We finished dressing; then she went in to take leave of Señora Doña Clementa Bueso and of Señor Don Lope Meléndez de Almendárez, and ordered my man to shoulder my trunk and follow her. I trailed behind, taking my leave of nobody.

Doña Estefanía stopped at her friend's house. Before we entered she held a long conversation with that lady; after which a servant-girl came out and told me to enter with my servant. She led us to a tiny room, containing two beds so close together that they seemed one; there was no intervening space, and the sheets of both kissed one another.

We stayed there, in fact, six days, during which not an hour passed without a quarrel. I kept pointing out my lady's idiocy in leaving her house and property, even if it were to oblige her own mother. I constantly harped on this theme, so that one day when Doña Estefanía went off (to check up on her affairs, she said), the lady of the house asked me what made me wrangle perpetually with my wife, and what she had done that made me so reproach her and call her actions mere madness, not a manifestation of perfect friendship. I recounted the whole story; when I came to tell her of my marriage to Doña Estefanía and of her dowry, and of her simple-mindedness in turning over her house and goods to Doña Clementa, although with the honorable purpose of capturing an eminent husband like Don Lope, the lady began to bless and cross herself so actively and with so many cries of "Jesus! Jesus! The wicked woman!" that she cast me into great distress of mind. Finally she said: "Lieutenant, I don't know if I may offend my conscience in revealing to you what would lie heavy upon it if I should keep silent. But God's will be done and come what may, let truth prevail and down with falsehood! The truth is that Doña Clementa Bueso is the real owner of the house and furnishings which were given to you as dowry; the falsehood is everything that Doña Estefanía has told you. She owns no house, no property, no other gown than the one she has on. The reason she had time and opportunity for this fraud is that Doña Clementa went to visit some relatives in the city of Plasencia; from there she went to make a nine-day devotion to Our Lady of Guadalupe. Meanwhile she left Doña Estefanía in her house, to take charge for her—since in fact the two are great friends. And if you really go to the bottom of things, you should not blame the poor lady, since she was able to capture a gentleman like yourself for husband."

Thus her speech ended; and I fell into a crisis of despair. No doubt I would have totally surrendered to it if my guardian angel had been inattentive. But he came to my aid, telling me inwardly that I should remember I was a Christian and the greatest sin of mankind is despair; it is the sin of demons. This consideration, or good inspiration, comforted me somewhat, but it did not prevent me from taking my cloak and sword and issuing forth in search of Doña Estefanía. It was my purpose to impose on her an exemplary punishment. But fate decreed—I cannot say whether it bettered or worsened my affairs—that I should not find Doña Estefanía anywhere that I searched. I went to San Llorente, commended myself to Our Lady, and sat down on a bench. In my depression I fell into a sound sleep, so sound that I would never have awakened of my own accord. But being roused, and harried by my thoughts and sorrows, I went to Doña Clementa's house. I found her well established as mistress of the household. I dared say nothing because Don Lope was with her; so I returned to my landlady's. She told me that she had reported to Doña Estefanía that I knew all her tricks and stratagems. The lady had asked how I had taken the news. "Very badly," the landlady had replied, adding that I had gone out with a grim purpose and fixed determination to seek her out. The good lady told me finally that Doña Estefanía had carried off all the contents of my trunk, leaving me only one traveling suit.

This was the last straw. Again God had struck me down! I went to look at my trunk; I found it yawning open, like a grave awaiting a corpse, properly my own, if I had had intelligence enough to appreciate and weigh my disaster.

At this point Licentiate Peralta interrupted: "Indeed it was a disaster, if Doña Estefanía carried off your fine chain and your jeweled ornaments. As the saying goes, misfortunes never come singly."

"That didn't bother me so much," replied the lieutenant. "I could quote, in my turn: 'Don Simueque fobbed off his one-eyed daughter on me, but by God, I am deformed on one side.' "

"I don't see how that applies," said Peralta.

"The application is that the heap of glittering chains, ornaments, and trinkets would bring at most ten or twelve crowns."

"Impossible!" exclaimed the licentiate. "That chain about your neck was clearly worth more than two hundred crowns."

"It would have been, if truth always matched appearances. But as all is not gold that glitters, the chains, ornaments, jewels, and trinkets were no more than alchemists' work. However, they were so well made that their falsity could be detected only by a touchstone or by fire."

"So then you and the Señora Doña Estefanía came out quits!"

"So much quits," said the lieutenant, "that we could call for a new deal. But, my dear licentiate, the difficulty is that she can get rid of my chains, but I can't be quit of her falsity. Damn it all, she is still my wife, my property!"

"You should thank God, Señor Campuzano, that she is movable property. She has walked out on you, and you aren't obliged to run after her."

"Quite right. But even so, without my pursuing her, I can't get rid of her. Wherever I am, her offense against me is present in my mind."

"I don't know what to answer," said Peralta, "unless to recall to you two lines of Petrarch:

> Che chi prende diletto di far frode
> non s'ha di lamentar s'altro l'inganna.

Or, in good Castilian, 'Whoever finds his pleasure in trickery cannot complain if another cheats him.' "

"I don't complain," replied the lieutenant. "But I do lament my case. A guilty man may recognize his guilt, but he can't help feeling the pangs of punishment. I can see clearly that I tried to cheat and was cheated, caught in my own toils. But I can't control my feelings to the point of suppressing all my murmurs. In sum, to come to what is the nub of my history, as this record of events may well be called, I learned that Doña Estefanía was carried off by the cousin who, I told you, was present at the wedding. He had been for a long time her devoted lover.

"I made no effort to seek her out. I was smitten by the one affliction I had missed. Within a few days I changed my lodging and also my hair. My eyebrows and lashes began to drop out, then the hair of my head. So I became untimely bald, with an illness called alopecia, or, more exactly, the pox. I found myself absolutely plucked, for I had no longer any hair to comb or money to spend. My illness got worse along with my finances; and poverty is a foe to honor—it brings some men to the gallows, others to the hospital, and others to surrender and beg at the doors of their enemies. This is one of the greatest humiliations of a luckless man. Thus, not to sell for my cure the very clothes which would cover me decently in health, when the time came for the free sweating-treatments at the Resurrection Hospital, I entered there for a course of forty sweats. They say I will recover my health if I take care of myself. I still have my sword; for the rest may God provide!"

# IV
# GERMANY

*Dr. Faustus*

# ❦ The History of the Damnable Life and Deserved Death of Dr. John Faustus

The story-theme of the man who sells his soul to the devil appears in ancient Jewish and other Semitic literatures; it was popular in the European Middle Ages. Various current tales were gathered and imposed upon Dr. John Faustus, an actual professional magician who plied his trade in Germany, about 1500. The clustering stories expressed the common man's mingling of horror at deviltry with admiration for the intrepid character who braves the very devil.

The first Faust book was printed in Germany in 1587. It has a Protestant cast; Mephistopheles wears a Franciscan robe, and Faust is presented as a rebel against divine authority. In later times Goethe made his Faust a skeptical philosopher, who learns to submerge his intellectual arrogance in beneficence.

The translation, by "P. R., Gent.," whom the editor has not identified, appeared in 1589 or thereabouts. It is reproduced here, abridged and with some modernization, from William J. Thoms, *Early English Prose Romances* (London, 1858).

JOHN FAUSTUS, born in the town of Roda, being in the province of Weimar, in Germany, his father a poor husbandman, and not able well to bring him up, yet having an uncle at Wittenberg, a rich man, and without issue, took this Faustus from his father, and made him his heir, insomuch that his father was no more troubled with him, for he remained with his uncle at Wittenberg, where he was kept at the university in the same city, to study Divinity; but Faustus being of a naughty mind and otherwise addicted, plied not his studies, but betook himself to other exercises, which his uncle oftentimes hearing, rebuked him for it; as Eli oftentimes rebuked his children for sinning against the Lord, even so this good old man laboured to have Faustus apply his study to Divinity, that he might come to the knowledge of God and his law. But it is manifest that many virtuous parents have wicked children, as Cain, Reuben, Absalom, and such like, have been to their parents. So Faustus having godly parents, who seeing him to be of a toward wit, were desirous to bring him up in those virtuous studies, namely, of Divinity; but he gave himself secretly to necromancy and conjuration, insomuch that few or none could perceive his profession.

But to the purpose—Faustus continued at study in the university, and was by the rectors, and sixteen masters afterward, examined how he had profited in his studies, and being found by them, that none of his time were able to argue with him in Divinity, or for the excellency of his wisdom to compare with him, with one consent they made him Doctor of Divinity. But Dr. Faustus, within short time after he had obtained his degree, fell into such fantasies and deep cogitations, that he was mocked of many, and of the most part of the students was called the Speculator, and sometimes he would throw the scriptures from him, as though he had no care of his former profession, so that he began a most ungodly life, as hereafter more at large may appear, for the old proverb saith, "Who can hold what will away?" So, who can hold Faustus from the devil, that seeks after him with all his endeavours; for he accompanied himself with divers that were seen in those devilish arts, and that had the Chaldean, Persian, Hebrew, Arabian, and Greek tongues, using figures, characters, conjurations, incantations, with many other ceremonies belonging to those infernal arts, as necromancy, charms, soothsaying, witchcraft, enchantment, being delighted with their books, words, and names so well, that he studied day and night therein, insomuch that he could not abide to be called Doctor of Divinity, but waxed a worldly man, and named himself an astrologian, and a mathematician, and for a shadow sometimes a physician, and did great cures, namely with herbs, roots, waters, drinks, receipts and glysters; * and without doubt he was passing wise and excellent

* Glysters: enemas.—Ed.

perfect in Holy Scriptures. But he that knoweth his master's will, and doth it not, is worthy to be beaten with many stripes. It is written, "No man can serve two masters, and thou shalt not tempt the Lord thy God." But Faustus threw all this in the wind, and made his soul of no estimation, regarding more his worldly pleasures than the joys to come; therefore at the day of judgment, there is no hope of his redemption.

You have heard before that all Faustus' mind was to study the arts of necromancy and conjuration, the which exercise he followed day and night, and taking to him the wings of an eagle thought to fly over the whole world, and to know the secrets of heaven and earth, for his speculation was so wonderful, being expert in using his vocabula, figures, characters, conjuration, and other ceremonial actions, that in all haste he put in practice to bring the devil before him, and taking his way to a thick wood near to Wittenberg, called in the German tongue, Spisser Holt, that is in English, the Spisser's Wood, as Faustus would oftentimes boast of it among the crew, being in jollity, he came into the wood one evening into the cross-way, where he made with a wand a circle in the dust, and within that many more circles and characters; and thus he passed away the time until it was nine or ten of the clock in the night; then began Dr. Faustus to call on Mephistopheles the Spirit, and to charge him in the name of Beelzebub, to appear there presently, without any long stay. Then presently the devil began so great a rumour in the wood, as if heaven and earth would have come together, with wind, and the trees bowed their tops to the ground, then fell the devil to roar, as if the whole wood had been full of lions, and suddenly about the circle run the devil, as if a thousand waggons had been running together on paved-stones. After this, at the four corners of the wood it thundered horribly, with such lightning, as the whole world to his seeming had been on fire. Faustus all this while, half amazed at the devil's so long tarrying, and doubting whether he were best to abide any more such horrible conjurings, thought to leave his circle, and depart, whereupon the devil made him such music of all sorts, as if the nymphs themselves had been in place: whereat Faustus revived, and stood stoutly in his circle, expecting his purpose, and began again to conjure the spirit Mephistopheles in the name of the Prince of Devils, to appear in his likeness: whereat suddenly over his head hung hovering in the air a mighty dragon. Then calls Faustus again after his devilish manner, at which there was a monstrous cry in the wood, as if hell had been open, and all the tormented souls cursing their condition. Presently, not three fathom above his head, fell a flame in manner of lightning, and changed itself into a globe; yet Faustus feared it not, but did persuade himself that the devil should give him his request before he would leave. Oftentimes after to his companions he would boast that he had the stoutest head under the cope of heaven at command. Whereat they answered, they knew no stouter than the Pope or Emperor. But Dr. Faustus said, "The head that is my servant, is above all upon earth"; and repeated certain words out of St. Paul to the Ephesians, to make his argument good, "The Prince of the World is upon earth and under heaven."

Well, let us come again to his conjuration, where we left him at the fiery globe. Faustus vexed at his spirit's so long tarrying, used his charms, with full purpose not to depart before he had his intent; and crying on Mephistopheles the spirit, suddenly the globe opened, and sprung up in the height of a man, so burning a time, in the end it converted to the shape of a fiery man. This pleasant beast ran about the circle a great while, and lastly, appeared in the manner of a Gray Friar, asking Faustus what was his request. Faustus commanded, that the next morning at twelve of the clock, he should appear to him at his house; but the devil would in no wise grant it. Faustus began to conjure him again, in the name of Beelzebub, that he should fulfil his request; whereupon the spirit agreed, and so they departed each on his way.

Dr. Faustus, having commanded the spirit to be with him, at his hour appointed, he came and appeared in his chamber, demanding of Faustus what his desire was: Then began Dr. Faustus anew with him, to conjure him, that he would be obedient unto him, and to answer him certain articles, to fulfil them in all points:

1. That the spirit would serve him, and be obedient unto him in all things that he asked of him, from that hour until the hour of his death.

2. Further, any thing that he desired of him, he should bring him.

3. Also that in all Faustus' demands and interrogations, the spirit should tell him nothing but that which was true.

Hereupon the spirit answered, and laid his case forth, that he had no such power of himself, until he had first given his prince (that was ruler over him) to understand thereof, and to know if he could obtain so much of his lord: "Therefore speak farther, that I may do thy whole desire to my prince; for it is not in my power to fulfill without his leave."

"Shew me the cause why," said Faustus.

The spirit answered Faustus, "Thou shalt understand, that with us it is even as well a kingdom, as with you on earth; yea, we have our rulers and servants, as I myself am one; and we have our whole number the legion, for although that Lucifer is thrust and fallen out of heaven, through his pride and high mind, yet he hath notwithstanding a legion of devils at his command, that we call the Oriental Princes, for his power is infinite, also there is a power in meridie, in septentrio, in occidente,* and for that Lucifer hath his kingdom under heaven, we must change and give ourselves to men, to serve them at their pleasure. It is also certain, we have not as yet opened to any man the truth of our dwelling, neither of our ruling, neither what our power is, neither have we given any man any gift, or learned him any thing, except he promise to be ours."

Dr. Faustus upon this arose where he sat, and said, "I will have my request, and yet I will not be damned."

The spirit answered, "Then shalt thou want thy desire, and yet art thou mine notwithstanding. If any man would detain thee, it is but in vain, for thy infidelity hath confounded thee."

Hereupon spake Faustus, "Get thee hence from me, and take

* Meridie, septentrio, occidente: south, north, and west.—Ed.

St. Valentine's farewell; * yet I conjure thee, that thou be here at evening, and bethink thyself of what I have asked thee; ask thy prince's counsel therein." Mephistopheles the spirit thus answered, vanished away, leaving Faustus in his study, where he sat pondering with himself how he might obtain his request of the devil, without the loss of his soul, yet he was fully resolved in himself, rather than to want his pleasure, to do what the spirit and his lord should condition upon.

Faustus continued in his devilish cogitations, never moving out of the place where the spirit left him, such was his fervent love to the devil; the night approaching, this swift-flying spirit appeared to Faustus, offering himself with all submission to his service, with full authority from his prince, to do whatsoever he would request, if so be Faustus would promise to be his. "This answer I bring thee, an answer must thou make by me again: yet I will hear what is thy desire, because thou hast sworn to me to be here at this time." Dr. Faustus gave him this answer, though faintly for his soul's sake, that his request was none other but to become a devil, or at the least a limb of him, and that the spirit should agree to these articles following:

1. That he might be a spirit in shape and quality.

2. That Mephistopheles should be his servant at his command.

3. That Mephistopheles should bring him any thing, and do for him whatsoever he desired.

4. That all times he would be in the house invisible to all men, except only to himself, and at his command, to shew himself.

5. That Mephistopheles should at all times appear at his command, in what form or shape soever he would.

Upon these points the spirit answered Dr. Faustus. That all this should be granted him, and fulfilled, and more if he would agree unto him upon certain articles as followeth:

1. That Dr. Faustus should give himself to the lord Lucifer, body and soul.

---

* Take St. Valentine's farewell: May a sore illness carry thee off; a pox take thee.—Ed.

2. For confirmation of the same, he should make him a writing written in his own blood.

3. That he would be an enemy to all Christian people.

4. That he would deny the Christian belief.

5. That he let not any man change his opinion, if so be any man should go about to dissuade or withdraw him from it.

Farther the spirit promised Faustus to give him certain years to live in health and pleasure, and when such years were expired, that then Faustus would be fetched away; and if he would hold these articles and conditions, that then he should have whatsoever his heart would wish or desire; and that Faustus should quickly perceive himself to be a spirit in all manner of actions whatsoever. Hereupon Dr. Faustus' mind was inflamed, that he forgot his soul, and promises Mephistopheles to hold all things as he mentioned them: he thought the devil was not so black as they use to paint him, nor hell so hot as the people say.

After Dr. Faustus had made his promise to the devil, in the morning betimes, he called the spirit before him, and commanded him, that he should always come to him like a friar, after the order of St. Francis, with a bell in his hand like St. Anthony, and to ring it once or twice before he appeared, that he might know of his certain coming: then Faustus demanded of his spirit what was his name. The spirit answered, "My name is as thou sayest, Mephistopheles, and I am a prince, but a servant to Lucifer, and all the circuit from septentrio to the meridian, I rule under him." Even at these words was this wicked wretch Faustus inflamed, to hear himself to have gotten so great a potentate to serve him. Forgetting the Lord his Maker, and Christ his Redeemer, he became an enemy to all mankind; yea, worse than the giants, whom the poets said to climb the hills to make war with the gods, not unlike the enemy of God and Christ, that for his pride was cast into hell; so likewise Faustus forgot, that high climbers catch the greatest falls and sweet meats have oft sourest sauce.

After a while Faustus promised Mephistopheles to write and make his obligation with all assurance of the articles in the chapter before rehearsed: a pitiful case, Christian reader, for certainly this letter or obligation was found in his house, after his most lamentable end, with all the rest of his damnable practices used in his whole life.

Wherefore I wish all Christians to take example by this wicked doctor, and to be comforted in Christ, concerning themselves with that vocation, whereunto it hath pleased God to call them, and not so esteem the vain delights of this life as did this unhappy Faustus in giving his soul to the devil: and to confirm it the more assuredly, he took a small penknife, and prickt a vein in his left hand, and for certainty thereupon were seen on his hand these words written, as if they had been written in his own blood, "O homo fuge"; * whereat the spirit vanished, but Faustus continued in his damnable mind.

Dr. Faustus set his blood in a saucer on warm ashes, and writ as followeth: "I John Faustus, doctor, do openly acknowledge with mine own hand, to the great force and strengthening of this letter, that since I began to study, and speculate the course and nature of the elements, I have not found, through the gift that is given me from above, any such learning and wisdom that can bring me to my desire, and for that I find that men are unable to instruct me any farther in the matter; now have I Dr. Faustus, to the hellish prince of Orient, and his messenger Mephistopheles, given both body and soul, upon such conditions, that they shall learn me, and fulfill my desires in all things, as they have promised and vowed unto me, with due obedience unto me, according to the articles mentioned between us.

"Farther, I do covenant and grant with them by these presents, that at the end of twenty-four years next ensuing the date of this present letter, they being expired, and I in the mean time, during the said years, be served of them at my will, they accomplishing my desires to the full in all points as we are agreed: that then I give to them all power to do with me at their pleasure, to rule, to send, fetch or carry me or mine, be it either body, soul, flesh, blood or goods, into their habitation, be it wheresoever:

* "O homo fuge": Flee, O man.—Ed.

and hereupon I defy God and his Christ, all the Host of Heaven, and all living creatures that bear the shape of God; yea, all that live. And again I say it, and it shall be so, and to the more strengthening of this writing, I have written it with my own hand, and blood, being in perfect memory: and hereupon I subscribe to it with my name and title, calling all the infernal, middle, and supreme powers to witness of this my letter and subscription.

"John Faustus, approved in the elements, and the spiritual doctor."

Dr. Faustus sitting pensive, having but one only boy with him, suddenly there appeared his spirit Mephistopheles in likeness of a very man, from whom issued most horrible fiery flames, insomuch that the boy was afraid, but being hardened by his master, he bid him stand still, and he should have no harm: this spirit began to bleat as in a singing manner. This pretty sport pleased Dr. Faustus well; but he would not call his spirit into his counting house until he had seen more: Anon was heard a rushing of armed men, and trampling of horses, this ceasing, came a kennel of hounds, and they chased a great hart in the hall, and there the hart was slain: Faustus took heart, came forth and looked upon the hart, but presently before him there was a lion and a dragon together, fighting so fiercely, that Faustus thought they would have thrown down the house; but the dragon overcame the lion, and so they vanished. After this came in a peacock and peahen, the cock bruising of his tail, turning to the female, beat her, and so vanished. Afterward followed a furious bull, that with a full fierceness ran upon Faustus, but coming near him vanished away. Afterward followed a great old ape. This ape offered Faustus the hand, but he refused; so the ape ran out of the hall again. Hereupon fell a mist in the hall, that Faustus saw no light, but it lasted not; and so soon as it was gone, there lay before Faustus two great sacks, one full of gold, another of silver.

Lastly, was heard by Faustus all manner of instruments of music, as organs, clarigolds, lutes, viols, citterns, waits, hornpipes, flutes, anomes, harps, and all manner of other instruments which so ravished his mind, that he thought he had been in another world, forgot both body and soul, insomuch, that he was minded never to change his opinion concerning that which he had done. Hereat came Mephistopheles into the hall to Faustus, in apparel like unto a friar, to whom Faustus spake, "Thou hast done me a wonderful pleasure in shewing me this pastime; if thou continue as thou hast begun, thou shalt win my heart and soul, yea, and have it." Mephistopheles answered, "This is nothing, I will please thee better; yea, that thou may'st know my power on all, ask what request thou wilt of me, that shalt thou have, conditionally hold thy promise, and give me thy hand-writing." At which words the wretch thrust forth his hand, saying, "Hold thee, there hast thou my promise." Mephistopheles took the writing and willed Faustus to take a copy of it; with that the perverse Faustus being resolute in his damnation, wrote a copy thereof, and gave the devil the one, and kept in store the other. Thus the spirit and Faustus were agreed, and dwelt together: no doubt there was a virtuous housekeeping.

Dr. Faustus having given his soul to the devil, renouncing all the powers of heaven, confirming all his lamentable action with his own blood, and having already delivered his writing now into the devil's hand, the which so puffed up his heart, that he forgot the mind of a man, and thought himself to be a spirit. Thus Faustus dwelt at his uncle's house at Wittenberg, who died, and bequeathed it in his testament to his cousin Faustus. Faustus kept a boy with him, that was his scholar, an unhappy wag, called Christopher Wagner, to whom this sport and life that he saw his master followed, seemed pleasant. Faustus loved the boy well, hoping to make him as good or better seen in his hellish exercises than himself, and he was fellow with Mephistopheles: otherwise Faustus had no company in his house but himself and boy, and the spirit that ever was diligent at Faustus' command, going about the house, clothed like a friar, with a little bell in his hand, seen of none but Faustus. For victuals and other necessaries, Mephistopheles brought him at his pleasure, from the Duke of Saxony, the Duke of Bavaria, and the Bishop of Salzburg: and they had many times their best wine stolen out of their cellars by Mephistopheles, likewise their provisions for their own table: such meat as Faustus wished for, his spirit brought him in. Besides that, Faustus himself was become so cunning, that when he opened his window, what fowl soever he wished for, it came presently flying into the house, were it never so dainty. Moreover, Faustus and his boy went in sumptuous apparel, the which Mephistopheles stole from the mercers at Nuremberg, Asperg, Frankfurt, and Leipzig; for it was hard for them to find a lock to keep out such a thief; all their maintenance was but stolen and borrowed ware: and thus they lived an odious life in the sight of God, though as yet the world were unacquainted with their wickedness; it must be so, for their fruits be none other, as Christ saith in John, where he calls the devil a thief and murderer; and that found Faustus, for he stole him away both body and soul.

Dr. Faustus continued thus in this epicurish life day and night, believed not that there was a God, hell, or devil; he thought that soul and body died together, and had quite forgot Divinity, or the immortality of the soul, but stood in that damnable heresy day and night, and bethinking himself of a wife, called Mephistopheles to council: which would in no case agree, demanding of him if he would break the covenant made with him, or if he had forgot it.

"Hast thou (quoth Mephistopheles) sworn thy self an enemy to God and to all creatures? To this I answer thee, Thou canst not marry, thou canst not serve two masters, God and my prince: for wedlock is a chief institution ordained of God, and that thou hast promised to defy as we do all, and that hast thou not only done: but moreover, thou hast confirmed it with thy blood, persuade thyself that what thou dost in contempt of wedlock, it is all to thy own delight. Therefore, Faustus, look well about thee, and bethink thyself better, and I wish thee to change thy mind; for if thou keep not what thou has promised in thy writing, we will tear thee in pieces like the dust under thy feet. Therefore, sweet Faustus, think with what unquiet life, anger, strife, and debate thou shalt live in, when thou takest a wife, therefore change thy mind."

Dr. Faustus was with these speeches in despair: and as all that have forsaken the Lord can build upon no good foundation, so this wretched Doctor having forsook the rock, fell into despair with himself; fearing, if he should motion matrimony any more, that the devil should tear him in pieces. "For this time (quoth he to Mephistopheles) I am not minded to marry." "Then dost thou well," answered his spirit. But within two hours after, Faustus called again to his spirit, who came in his old manner like a friar. Then Faustus said unto him, "I am not able to resist or bridle my fancy, I must and will have a wife, and I pray thee give thy consent to it." Suddenly upon these words came such a whirl-wind about the place, that Faustus thought the whole house would have come down, all the doors of the house flew off the hooks: after all this his house was full of smoke, and the floor covered with ashes; which when Dr. Faustus perceived, he would have gone up stairs, and flying up he was taken and thrown down into the hall, that he was not able to stir hand nor foot, then round about him ran a monstrous circle of fire, never standing still, that Faustus cried as he lay, and thought there to have been burned. Then cried he out to his spirit Mephistopheles for help, promising him he would live, for all this, as he had vowed by his hand-writing. Hereupon appeared unto him an ugly devil, so dreadful and monstrous to behold, that Faustus durst not look on him. The devil said, "What wouldst thou have, Faustus? How likest thou thy wedding? What mind art thou in now?" Faustus an-swered, he had forgot his promise, desiring of him pardon, and he would talk no more of such things. "Thou art best so to do," and so he vanished from him. After appeared unto him his friar Mephistopheles, with a bell in his hand, and spake to Faustus, "It is no jesting with us, hold thou that which thou hast vowed, and we will perform that which we have promised, and more than that, thou shalt have thy heart's desire of what woman soever thou wilt, be she alive or dead, and so long as thou wilt thou shalt keep her by thee." These words pleased Faustus wonderful well, and repented himself that he was so foolish to wish himself mar-ried, that might have any woman in the whole city brought him at his command, the which he practised and persevered in a long time.

[Faustus is carried through the air to see the world and the planets, and hell; he visits the great cities, has a sight of Paradise, learns the secrets of the stars. He performs his magic tricks before the Emperor and plays many merry jests with the students. He conjures up the fair Helena of Troy and makes her his paramour. But his appointed end draws near.]

The full time of Dr. Faustus, his four and twenty years being come, his spirit appeared unto him, giving him his writing again, and commanding him to make preparation, for that the devil would fetch him against a certain time appointed. Dr. Faustus mourned and sighed wonderfully, and never went to bed, nor slept a wink for sorrow. Wherefore his spirit appeared again, comforting him, and saying, "My Faustus, be not thou so cowardly-minded; for although thou lovest thy body, it is long unto the day of judgment, and thou must die at the last, although thou live many thousand years: the Turks, the Jews, and many an unchristian emperor are in the same condemnation; therefore, my Faustus, be of good courage, and be not discomforted, for the devil hath promised that thou shalt not be in pains, as the rest of the damned are." This and such like comfort he gave him, for he told him false, and against the saying of the Holy Scriptures: yet Dr. Faustus that had no other expectation but to pay his debt, with his own skin, went (on the same day that his spirit said the devil would fetch him) unto his trusty and dearly beloved brethren and companions, as masters and bachelors of art, and other students more, the which did often visit him at his house in merriment; these he entreated, that they would walk into the village called Rimlich, half a mile from Wittenberg, and that they would there take with him for their repast, a small banquet, the which they agreed unto; so they went together, and there held their dinner in a most sumptuous manner. Dr. Faustus with them, dissemblingly was merry, but not from the heart; wherefore he requested them, that they would also take part of his rude supper, the which they agreed unto: for (quoth he) "I must tell you what is the victualler's due." And when they slept (for drink was in their heads) then Dr. Faustus paid the shot, and bound the students and masters to go with him into another room, for he had many wonderful matters to tell them; and when they were entered the room, as he requested, Dr. Faustus said unto them as followeth:

"My trusty and well-beloved friends, the cause why I have invited you in this place is this: forasmuch as you have known me these many years, what manner of life I have lived; practising all manner of conjurations, and wicked exercises, the which I obtained through the help of the devil, into whose devilish fellowship they have brought me; the which use, the art, and practice, urged by the detestable provocation of my flesh, and my stiffnecked and rebellious will, with my filthy infernal thoughts, the which were ever before me, pricking me forward so earnestly that I must perforce have the consent of the devil to aid me in my devices. And to the end I might the better bring my purpose to pass, to have the devil's aid and furtherance, which I never have wanted in my actions, I have promised unto him at the end and accomplishment of twenty-four years, both body and soul, to do therewith at his pleasure; this dismal day, these twenty-four years are fully expired; for night beginning, my hour-glass is at an end, the direful finishing whereof I carefully expect; for out of all doubt, this night he will fetch me to whom I have given myself in recompense of his service, body and soul, and twice confirmed writings with my proper blood.

"Now have I called you, my well-beloved lords, friends and brethren, before that fatal hour, to take my friendly farewell, to the end that my departure may not hereafter be hidden from you, beseeching you herewith (courteous loving lords and brethren) not to take in evil part, anything done by me, but with friendly commendations to salute all my friends and companions wheresoever, desiring both you and them, if ever I have trespassed against your minds in any thing, that you would heartily forgive me; and as for those lewd practices, the which these full twenty-four years I have followed, you shall hereafter find them in writing: and I beseech you let this my lamentable end, to the residue of your lives, be a sufficient warning, that you have God always before your eyes, praying unto him, that he will defend you from the temptation of the devil, and all his false deceits, not falling altogether from God, as I, wretched and ungodly damned creature, have done; having denied and defied baptism, the sacrament of Christ's body, God himself, and heavenly powers, and earthly men: yea, I have denied such a God, that desireth not to have one lost. Neither let the evil fellowship of wicked companions mislead you, as it hath done me: visit earnestly and often the church; war and strive continually against the devil, with a good and steadfast belief in God and Jesus Christ, and use your vocation and holiness. Lastly, to knit my troubled oration, this is my friendly request, that you would go to rest, and let nothing trouble you: also if you chance to hear any noise or rumbling about the house, be not therewith afraid, for there shall no evil happen unto you; also I pray you rise not out of your beds: but above all things, I entreat you, if hereafter you find my dead carcass, convey it unto the earth, for I die both a good and bad Christian, though I know the devil will have my body, and that would I willingly give him, so that he would leave my soul to quiet; wherefore I pray you, that you would depart to bed, and so I wish you a quiet night, which unto me, notwithstanding, shall be horrible and fearful."

This oration was made by Dr. Faustus, and that with a hearty and resolute mind, to the end he might not discomfort them; but the students wondered greatly thereat, that he was so blinded, for knavery, conjuration, and such foolish things, to give his body and soul unto the devil, for they loved him entirely, and never suspected any such thing, before he had opened his mind unto them; wherefore one of them said unto him, "Ah! friend Faustus, what have you done to conceal this matter so long from us? We would by the help of good divines, and the grace of God, have brought you out of this net, and have torn you out of the bondage and chains of Satan, whereas we fear now it is too late, to the utter ruin both of body and soul."

Dr. Faustus answered, "I durst never do it, although often minded to settle myself to godly people, to desire counsel and help; and once my old neighbour counselled me that I should follow his learning, and leave all my conjurations: yet when I was minded to amend, and to follow that good counsel, then came the devil, and would have had me away, as this night he is like to do: and said, so soon as I turned again to God, he would dispatch me altogether. Thus, even thus (good gentlemen, and dear friends) was I enthralled in that fanatical bond, all good desires drowned, all piety vanished, all purposes of amendment truly exiled, by the tyrannous oppression of my deadly enemy."

But when the students heard his words, they gave him counsel to do nothing else but call upon God, desiring him, for the love of his sweet son Jesus Christ his sake, to have mercy upon him: teaching him this form of prayer: "O God! Be merciful unto me, poor and miserable sinner; and enter not into judgment with me, for no flesh is able to stand before thee; although, O Lord! I must leave my sinful body unto the devil, being by him deluded, yet thou in mercy, may preserve my soul."

This they repeated to him, yet he could take no hold: but even as Cain, he also said that his sins were greater than God was able to forgive: for all his thought was on the writing. (He meant he had made it too filthy in writing with his own blood.) The students and the others that were there, when they had prayed for him, they wept, and so went forth; but Faustus tarried in the hall, and when the gentlemen were laid in bed, none of them could sleep, for that they attended to hear if they might be privy of his end.

It happened that between twelve and one o'clock at midnight, there blew a mighty storm of wind against the house, as though it would have blown the foundation thereof out of its place. Hereupon the students began to fear, and go out of their beds, but they would not stir out of the chamber, and the host of the house ran out of doors, thinking the house would fall. The students lay near unto the hall, wherein Dr. Faustus lay, and they heard a mighty noise and hissing, as if the hall had been full of snakes and adders. With that the hall-door flew open, wherein Dr. Faustus was. Then he began to cry for help, saying, "Murder, murder!" But it was with a half voice, and very hollow; shortly after they heard him no more.

But when it was day, the students, that had taken no rest that night, arose and went into the hall, in the which they left Dr. Faustus, where notwithstanding they found not Faustus, but all the hall sprinkled with blood, the brains cleaving to the wall, for the devil had beaten him from one wall, against another. In one corner lay his eyes, in another his teeth; a fearful and pitiful sight to behold. Then began the students to wail and weep for him, and sought for his body in many places. Lastly they came into the yard, where they found his body lying on the horse-dung, most monstrously torn, and fearful to behold, for his head, and all his joints were dashed to pieces: the forenamed students and masters that were at his death, obtained so much that they buried him in the village, where he was so grievously tormented.

After the which they turned to Wittenberg, and coming into the house of Faustus, they found the servant of Faustus very sad, unto whom they opened all the matter, who took it exceedingly heavy. There they found this history of Dr. Faustus noted, and of him written, as is before declared, all save only his end, the which was after, by the students, thereunto annexed: farther, what his servant noted thereof, was made in another book. And you have heard he held by him in his life, the spirit of fair Helena, who had by him one son, the which he named Justus Faustus. Even the same day of this death they vanished away, both mother and son. The house before was so dark, that scarce any body could abide therein: the same night Dr. Faustus appeared unto his servant lively, and shewed unto him many secret things which he had done and hidden in his life-time. Likewise there were certain which saw Dr. Faustus look out of the window by night, as they passed by the house.

And thus ended the whole history of Dr. Faustus his conjuration, and other acts that he did in his life; out of which example every Christian may learn, but chiefly the stiff-necked, and high-minded, may thereby learn to fear God, and to be careful of their vocation, and to be at defiance with all devilish works, as God hath most precisely forbidden; to the end we should not invite the devil as a guest, nor give him place, as that wicked Faustus hath done: for here we have a wicked example of his writing, promise, and end, that we may remember him, that we go not astray, but take God always before our eyes, to call alone upon him, and to honour him all the days of our life, with heart, and hearty prayer, and with all our strength and soul, to glorify his holy name, defying the devil and all his works; to the end we may remain with Christ in all endless joy, amen, amen: that wish I to every Christian heart, and God's name be glorified. Amen.

V

ENGLAND

*The Miseries of Mavillia*

# ❧ Jack of Newbury and the Widow

## by THOMAS DELONEY

Thomas Deloney's birth-date is unknown; he died apparently
in 1600. He was trained as a silk-weaver, but early began
writing broadside ballads and popular penny chap-books. His
first recorded publication is dated 1583. He joined the group
of balladists and free-lance journalists with their headquarters
in London's Grub Street, and when Fortune frowned he fell
back on silk-weaving. He was then a "poet of the people," a
petty-bourgeois, rendering the life of merchants and craftsmen
with fidelity and humor.

*The Pleasant History of John Winchcombe, in His Younger
Years Called Jack of Newbury* was registered for publication
in 1597. The first chapter is given here, somewhat modernized
in spelling and punctuation. It has already appeared in Edward
J. O'Brien, *Elizabethan Tales* (London, 1937).

IN THE days of King Henry the Eighth, that most noble and
victorious prince, in the beginning of his reign, John Winchcombe, a broadcloth weaver, dwelt in Newbury, a town in Berk-
shire; who, for that he was a man of a merry disposition and
honest conversation, was wondrous well-beloved of rich and
poor, specially because, in every place where he came, he would
spend his money with the best and was not at any time found a
churl of his purse. Wherefore, being so good a companion, he was
called of old and young Jack of Newbury, a man so generally
well-known in all his country for his good fellowship that he
could go in no place but he found acquaintance, by means
whereof Jack could no sooner get a crown but straight he found
means to spend it. Yet had he ever this care, that he would always
keep himself in comely and decent apparel. Neither at any time
would he be overcome in drink, but so discreetly behave himself

with honest mirth and pleasant conceits that he was every gentleman's companion.

After that Jack had long led this pleasant life, being, though
he were but poor, in good estimation, it was his master's chance
to die and his dame to be a widow, who was a very comely ancient
woman and of reasonable wealth. Wherefore she, having a good
opinion of her man John, committed unto his government the
guiding of all her workfolks for the space of three years together,
in which time she found him so careful and diligent that all things
came forward and prospered wondrous well. No man could en-
tice him from his business all the week by all the entreaty they
could use, insomuch that in the end some of the wild youths of
the town began to deride and scoff at him.

"Doubtless," quoth one, "I think some female spirit hath en-
chanted Jack to his treadles and conjured him within the compass
of his loom that he can stir no further."

"You say true," quoth Jack, "and if you have the leisure to stay
till the charm be done, the space of six days and five nights, you
shall find me ready to put on my holiday apparel, and on Sunday
morning for your pains I will give you a pot of ale over against
the Maypole."

"Nay," quoth another, "I'll lay my life that, as the salamander
cannot live without the fire, so Jack cannot live without the smell
of his dame's smock."

"And I marvel," quoth Jack, "that you being of the nature of
a herring, which so soon as he is taken out of the sea presently
dies, can live so long with your nose out of the pot."

"Nay, Jack, leave thy jesting," quoth another, "and go along
with us. Thou shalt not stay a jot."

"And because I will not stay nor make you a liar," quoth Jack,
"I'll keep me here still, and so farewell!"

Thus then they departed, and after they had for half a score
times tried him to this intent, and saw he would not be led by
their lure, they left him to his own will. Nevertheless, every Sunday in the afternoon and every holiday Jack would keep them

company and be as merry as a pie,* and having still good store of money in his purse, one or other would ever be borrowing of him, but never could he get penny of it again. Which when Jack perceived, he would never after carry above twelvepence at once in his purse, and that being spent, he would straight return home merrily, taking his leave of the company in this sort:

My masters, I thank you, it's time to pack home,
For he that wants money is counted a mome: †
And twelvepence a Sunday being spent in good cheer,
To fifty-two shillings amounts in the year;
Enough for a craftsman that lives by his hands,
And he that exceeds it shall purchase no lands.
For that I spend this day I'll work hard tomorrow,
For woe is that party that seeketh to borrow.
My money doth make me full merry to be,
And without my money none careth for me.
Therefore wanting money, what should I do here,
But haste home and thank you for all my good cheer?

Thus was Jack's good government and discretion noted of the best and substantiallest men of the town, so that it wrought his great commendations and his dame thought herself not a little blessed to have such a servant that was so obedient unto her and so careful for her profit. For she had never a prentice that yielded her more obedience than he did, or was more dutiful, so that by his good example he did as much good as by his diligent labour and painful travail. Which his singular virtue being noted by the widow, she began to cast a very good countenance to her man John and to use very much talk with him in private. And first, by way of communication, she would tell unto him what suitors she had, as also the great offers they made her, what gifts they sent her, and the great affection they bare her, craving his opinion in the matter.

* Pie: magpie.—Ed.
† Mome: fool.—Ed.

When Jack found the favour to be his dame's secretary, he thought it an extraordinary kindness and, guessing by the yarn it would prove a good web, began to question with his dame in this sort. "Although it becometh not me, your servant, to pry into your secrets nor to be busy about matters of your love, yet for so much as it hath pleased you to use conference with me in those causes, I pray you let me entreat you to know their names that be your suitors and of what profession they be."

"Marry, John," saith she, "that you shall, and I pray thee take a cushion and sit down by me."

"Dame," quoth he, "I thank you, but there is no reason I should sit on a cushion till I have deserved it."

"If thou hast not, thou mightest have done," said she, "but some soldiers never find favour."

John replied: "That maketh me indeed to want favour, for I never durst try maidens because they seem coy, nor wives for fear of their husbands, nor widows, doubting their disdainfulness."

"Tush, John," quoth she, "he that fears and doubts womankind cannot be counted mankind, and take this for a principle: all things are not as they seem. But let us leave this and proceed to our former matter. My first suitor dwells at Wallingford, by trade a tanner, a man of good wealth, and his name is Crafts, of comely personage and good behaviour, a widower well thought of among his neighbours. He hath proper land, a fair house well furnished, and never a child in the world, and he loves me passing well."

"Why, then, dame," quoth John, "you were best to have him."

"Is that your opinion?" quoth she. "Now trust me so it is not mine, for I find two special reasons to the contrary. The one is that he being overworn in years makes me overloath to love him, and the other that I know one nearer hand."

"Believe me, dame," quoth Jack, "I perceive store is no sore,* and proffered ware is worse by ten in the hundred than that which is sought. But, I pray, who is your second suitor?"

"John," quoth she, "it may seem immodesty in me to betray

* Store is no sore: Abundance does no harm.—Ed.

my lovers' secrets, yet seeing thy discretion, and being persuaded of thy secrecy, I will show thee. The other is a man of middle years, and yet a bachelor, by occupation a tailor, and dwelling at Hungerford, by report a very good husband,* such a one as hath crowns good store, and to me he professes much good will. For his person, he may please any woman."

"Aye, dame," quoth John, "because he pleaseth you."

"Not so," said she, "for my eyes are impartial judges in that case, and albeit my opinion may be contrary to others, if his art deceive not my eyesight, he is worthy of a good wife both for his person and conditions."

"Then trust me, dame," quoth John, "for so much as you are without doubt of yourself that you will prove a good wife, and so well persuaded of him, I should think you could make no better a choice."

"Truly, John," quoth she, "there be also two reasons that move me not to like of him: the one, that being so large a ranger, he would at home be a stranger: and the other, that I like better of one nearer hand."

"Who is that?" quoth Jack.

Saith she: "The third suitor is the parson of Speen Homeland, who hath a proper living. He is of holy conversation and good estimation, whose affection to me is great."

"No doubt, dame," quoth John, "you may do wondrous well with him, where you shall have no care but to serve God and to make ready his meat."

"O John," quoth she, "the flesh and the spirit agrees not, for he will be so bent to his book that he will have little mind of his bed, for one month's studying for a sermon will make him forget his wife a whole year."

"Truly, dame," quoth John, "I must needs speak in his behalf, and the rather for that he is a man of the church and your near neighbour, to whom as I guess you bear the best affection. I do not think that he will be so much bound to his book or subject to

* Husband: a thrifty manager.—Ed.

the spirit but that he will remember a woman at home or abroad."

"Well, John," quoth she, "I wis my mind is not that way, for I like better of one nearer hand."

"No marvel," quoth Jack, "you are so peremptory, seeing you have so much choice. But I pray ye, dame," quoth he, "let me know this fortunate man that is so highly placed in your favour."

"John," quoth she, "they are worthy to know nothing that cannot keep something. That man, I tell thee, must go nameless, for he is lord of my love and king of my desires. There is neither tanner, tailor, nor parson may compare with him. His presence is a preservative to my health, his sweet smiles my heart's solace, and his words heavenly music to my ears."

"Why then, dame," quoth John, "for your body's health, your heart's joy, and your ears' delight, delay not the time, but entertain him with a kiss, make his bed next yours, and chop up the match in the morning."

"Well," quoth she, "I perceive thy consent is quickly got to any, having no care how I am matched so I be matched. I wis, I wis I could not let thee go so lightly, being loath that anyone should have thee, except I could love her as well as myself."

"I thank you for your kindness and good will, good dame," quoth he, "but it is not wisdom for a young man that can scantly keep himself to take a wife. Therefore I hold it the best way to lead a single life, for I have heard say that many sorrows follow marriage, especially where want remains, and beside it is a hard matter to find a constant woman. For as young maids are fickle, so are old women jealous: the one a grief too common, the other a torment intolerable."

"What, John," quoth she, "consider that maidens' fickleness proceeds of vain fancies, but old women's jealousy of superabounding love, and therefore the more to be borne withal."

"But, dame," quoth he, "many are jealous without cause. For is it sufficient for their mistrusting natures to take exceptions at a shadow, at a word, at a look, at a smile, nay, at the twinkle of an eye, which neither man nor woman is able to expel? I knew a woman that was ready to hang herself for seeing but her husband's shirt hang on a hedge with her maid's smock."

"I grant that this fury may haunt some," quoth she, "yet there be many other that complain not without great cause."

"Why, is there any cause that should move jealousy?" quoth John.

"Aye, by St. Mary, is there," quoth she: "for would it not grieve a woman, being one every way able to delight her husband, to see him forsake her, despise and contemn her, being never so merry as when he is in other company, sporting abroad from morning till noon, from noon till night, and when he comes to bed, if he turns to his wife, it is in such solemnness and wearisome drowsy lameness that it brings rather loathsomeness than any delight? Can you then blame a woman in this case to be angry and displeased? I'll tell you what, among brute beasts it is a grief intolerable, for I heard my granddam tell that the bell-wether of her flock, fancying one of the ewes above the rest and seeing Gratis the shepherd abusing her in abominable sort subverting the law of nature, could by no means bear that abuse but, watching opportunity for revenge, on a time found the said shepherd sleeping in the field and suddenly ran against him in such violent sort that by the force of his writhen horns he beat the brains out of the shepherd's head and slew him. If then a sheep could not endure that injury, think not that women are so sheepish to suffer it."

"Believe me," quoth John, "if every hornmaker should be so plagued by a horned beast, there should be less horns made in Newbury by many in a year. But, dame," quoth he, "to make an end of this prattle, because it is an argument too deep to be discussed between you and I, you shall hear me sing an old song, and so we will depart to supper.

> A maiden fair I dare not wed
> For fear to have Actæon's head.
> A maiden black is often proud,
> A maiden little will be loud.
> A maiden that is high of growth
> They say is subject unto sloth.
> Thus fair or foul, little or tall,
> Some faults remain among them all.
> But of all the faults that be,

None is so bad as jealousy,
For jealousy is fierce and fell,
And burns as hot as fire in hell.
It breeds suspicion without cause,
And breaks the bonds of reason's laws.
To none it is a greater foe
Than unto those where it doth grow,
And God keep me both day and night
From that fell, fond, and ugly sprite.
For why? Of all the plagues that be,
The secret plague is jealousy.
Therefore I wish all womenkind
Never to bear a jealous mind.

"Well said, John," quoth she. "Thy song is not so sure, but thy voice is as sweet. But seeing the time agrees with our stomachs, though loath, yet will we give over for this time and betake ourselves to our suppers."

Then calling the rest of her servants, they fell to their meat merrily, and after supper the goodwife went abroad for her recreation to walk awhile with one of her neighbours. And in the mean space John got up into his chamber and there began to meditate on this matter, bethinking with himself what he were best to do, for well he perceived that his dame's affection was great towards him. Knowing therefore the woman's disposition, and withal that her estate was reasonable good, and considering beside that he should find a house ready furnished, servants ready taught, and all other things for his trade necessary, he thought it best not to let slip that good occasion, lest he should never come to the like. But again, when he considered her years to be unfitting to his youth, and that she that sometime had been his dame would perhaps disdain to be governed by him that had been her poor servant, and that it would prove but a bad bargain, doubting many inconveniences that might grow thereby, he therefore resolved to be silent rather than to proceed further. Wherefore he got him straight to bed, and the next morning settled himself close to his business.

His dame, coming home and hearing that her man was gone to bed, took that night but small rest. And early in the morning, hearing him up at his work merrily singing, she by and by arose, and in seemly sort attiring herself, she came into the workshop and sat her down to make quills.

Quoth John: "Good morrow, dame, how do you today?"

"Godamercy, John," quoth she, "even as well as I may, for I was sore troubled in my dreams. Methought two doves walked together in a cornfield, the one as it were in communication with the other, without regard of picking up anything to sustain themselves, and after they had with many nods spent some time to their content, they both fell hard with their pretty bills to peck up the scattered corn left by the weary reaper's hand. At length, finding themselves satisfied, it chanced another pigeon to light in that place, with whom one of the first pigeons at length kept company, and after returning to the place where she left her first companion, perceived he was not there. She, kindly * searching up and down the high stubble to find him, lights at length on a hog fast asleep, wherewith methought the poor dove was so dismayed that presently she fell down in a trance. I, seeing her legs fail and her wings quiver, yielding herself to death, moved with pity, ran unto her, and thinking to take up the pigeon, methought I had in my hands my own heart, wherein methought an arrow stuck so deep that the blood trickled down the shaft and lay upon the feathers like the silver pearled dew on the green grass, which made me to weep most bitterly. But presently methought there came one to me crowned like a queen, who told me my heart would die in time, except I got some of that sleeping hog's grease to heal the wounds thereof. Whereupon I ran in all haste to the hog with my heart bleeding in my hand, who methought grunted at me in most churlish sort and vanished out of my sight. Whereupon, coming straight home, methought I found this hog rustling among the looms, wherewith I presently awaked suddenly after midnight, being all in a sweat and very ill; and I am sure you could not choose but hear me groan."

* Kindly: in the nature of its kind.—Ed.

"Trust me, dame, I heard you not," quoth John, "I was so sound asleep."

"And thus," quoth she, "a woman may die in the night before you will have the care to see what she ails or ask what she lacks. But truly, John," quoth she, "all is one, for if thou shouldst have come, thou couldst not have got in, because my chamber door was locked. But while I live this shall teach me wit, for henceforth I will have no other lock but a latch till I am married."

"Then, dame," quoth he, "I perceive, though you be curious in your choice, yet at length you will marry."

"Aye, truly," quoth she, "so thou wilt not hinder me."

"Who, I?" quoth John. "On my faith, dame, not for a hundred pounds, but rather will further you to the uttermost of my power."

"Indeed," quoth she, "thou hast no reason to show any discourtesy to me in that matter, although some of our neighbours do not stick to say that I am sure * to thee already."

"If it were so," quoth John, "there is no cause to deny it, or to be ashamed thereof, knowing myself far unworthy of so high a favour."

"Well, let this talk rest," quoth she, "and take there thy quills, for it is time for me to go to market."

Thus the matter rested for two or three days, in which space she daily devised which way she might obtain her desire, which was to marry her man. Many things came in her head and sundry sleights in her mind, but none of them did fit her fancy, so that she became wondrous sad and as civil as the nine sybils, and in this melancholy humour continued three weeks or a month, till at last it was her luck upon a Bartholomew Day, having a fair in the town, to spy her man John give a pair of gloves to a proper maid for a fairing, which the maiden with a bashful modesty kindly accepted and requited it with a kiss, which kindled in her an inward jealousy, but notwithstanding very discreetly she covered it and closely passed along unspied of her man or the maid.

She had not gone far but she met with one of her suitors,

* Sure: betrothed.—Ed.

namely the tailor, who was very fine and brisk in his apparel, and needs he would bestow the wine upon the widow. And after some faint denial meeting with a gossip of hers, to the tavern they went, which was more courtesy than the tailor could ever get of her before, showing herself very pleasant and merry. And finding her in such a pleasing humour, the tailor after a new quart of wine renewed his old suit. The widow with patience heard him and gently answered that, in respect of his great good will long time borne unto her, as also in regard of his gentleness, cost, and courtesy at that present bestowed, she would not flatly deny him. "Therefore," quoth she, "seeing this is not a place to conclude of such matters, if I may entreat you to come to my poor house on Thursday next, you shall be heartily welcome and be further satisfied of my mind," and thus preferred to * a touch of her lips, he paid the shot and departed.

The tailor was scant out of sight when she met with the tanner, who, albeit he was aged, yet lustily he saluted her and to the wine she must, there was no nay. The widow, seeing his importunacy, calls her gossip and along they walked together. The old man called for wine a plenty and the best cheer in the house and in an hearty manner he bids the widow welcome. They had not sitten long but in comes a noise † of musicians in tawny coats, who, putting off their caps, asked if they would have any music. The widow answered no, they were merry enough.

"Tut," quoth the old man, "let us hear, good fellows, what you can do, and play me *The Beginning of the World*."

"Alas," quoth the widow, "you had more need to hearken to the ending of the world!"

"Why, widow," quoth he, "I tell thee the beginning of the world was the begetting of children, and if you find me faulty in that occupation, turn me out of thy bed for a bungler and then send for the sexton."

He had no sooner spoken the words but the parson of Speen with his corner cap popped in at the door who, seeing the widow sitting at the table, craved pardon and came in.

* Preferred to: granted.—Ed.
† Noise: band.—Ed.

Quoth she: "For want of the sexton, here is the priest if you need him."

"Marry," quoth the tanner, "in good time, for by this means we need not go far to be married."

"Sir," quoth the parson, "I shall do my best in convenient place."

"Wherein?" quoth the tanner.

"To wed her myself," quoth the parson.

"Nay, soft," said the widow, "one swallow makes not a summer nor one meeting a marriage. As I lighted on you unlooked for, so came I hither unprovided for the purpose."

"I trust," quoth the tanner, "you came not without your eyes to see, your tongue to speak, your ears to hear, your hands to feel, nor your legs to go."

"I brought my eyes," quoth she, "to discern colours, my tongue to say no to questions I like not, my hands to thrust from me the things that I love not, my ears to judge 'twixt flattery and friendship, and my feet to run from such as would wrong me."

"Why, then," quoth the parson, "by your gentle abiding in this place, it is evident that here are none but those you like and love."

"God forbid I should hate my friends," quoth the widow, "whom I take all these in this place to be."

"But there be divers sorts of loves," quoth the parson.

"You say truth," quoth the widow. "I love yourself for your profession and my friend the tanner for his courtesy and kindness and the rest for their good company."

"Yet," quoth the parson, "for the explaining of your love, I pray you drink to them you love best in the company."

"Why," quoth the tanner, "have you any hope in her love?"

"Believe me," saith the parson, "as much as another."

"Why then, parson, sit down," said the tanner, "for you that are equal with me in desire shall surely be half with me in the shot, and so, widow, on God's name, fulfil the parson's request."

"Seeing," quoth the widow, "you are so pleasantly bent, if my courtesy might not breed contention between you, and that I may have your favour to show my fancy, I will fulfil your request."

Quoth the parson: "I am pleased howsoever it be."

"And I," quoth the tanner.

"Why, then," quoth she, "with this cup of claret wine and sugar I heartily drink to the minstrel's boy."

"Why, is it he you love best?" quoth the parson.

"I have reason," said she, "to like and love them best that will be least offended with my doings."

"Nay, widow," quoth they, "we meant you should drink to him whom you loved best in the way of marriage."

Quoth the widow: "You should have said so at first, but to tell you my opinion, it is small discretion for a woman to disclose her secret affection in an open assembly. Therefore, if to that purpose you spake, let me entreat you both to come home to my house on Thursday next, where you shall be heartily welcome and there be fully resolved of my mind. And so, with thanks at this time, I'll take my leave."

The shot being paid and the musicians pleased, they all departed, the tanner to Wallingford, the parson to Speen, and the widow to her own house, where in her wonted solemnness she settled herself to her business.

Against Thursday she dressed her house fine and brave and set herself in her best apparel. The tailor, nothing forgetting his promise, sent to the widow a good fat pig and a goose. The parson, being as mindful as he, sent to her house a couple of fat rabbits and a capon, and the tanner came himself and brought a good shoulder of mutton and half a dozen chickens; beside he brought a good gallon of sack and half a pound of the best sugar. The widow, receiving this good meat, set her maid to dress it incontinent, and when dinner time drew near the table was covered and every other thing provided in convenient and comely sort.

At length the guests being come, the widow bade them all heartily welcome. The priest and the tanner, seeing the tailor, mused what he made there. The tailor on the other side marvelled as much at their presence. Thus looking strangely one at another, at length the widow came out of the kitchen in a fair train gown stuck full of silver pins, a fine white cap on her head with cuts of curious needlework under the same, and an apron before her as white as the driven snow. Then, very modestly making curtsey to them all, she requested them to sit down. But they straining courtesy the one with the other, the widow with a smiling countenance took the parson by the hand, saying: "Sir, as you stand highest in the church, so it is meet you should sit highest at the table, and therefore I pray you sit down there on the bench side. And sir," said she to the tanner, "as age is to be honoured before youth for their experience, so are they to sit above bachelors for their gravity." And so she set him down on this side the table over against the parson. Then coming to the tailor, she said: "Bachelor, though your lot be the last, your welcome is equal with the first, and seeing your place points out itself, I pray you take a cushion and sit down. And now," quoth she, "to make the board equal, and because it hath been an old saying that three things are to small purpose if the fourth be away, if so it may stand with your favour, I will call in a gossip of mine to supply this void place."

"With a good will," quoth they.

With that she brought in an old woman with scant ever a good tooth in her head and placed her right against the bachelor. Then was the meat brought to the board in due order by the widow's servants, her man John being chiefest servitor. The widow sat down at the table's end between the parson and the tanner, who in very good sort carved meat for them all, her man John waiting on the table.

After they had sitten awhile and well refreshed themselves, the widow, taking a crystal glass filled with claret wine, drunk unto the whole company and bade them welcome. The parson pledged her, and so did all the rest in due order, but still in their drinking the cup passed over the poor old woman's nose, insomuch that at length the old woman, in a merry vein, spoke thus unto the company: "I have had much good meat among you, but as for the drink I can nothing commend it."

"Alas, good gossip," quoth the widow, "I perceive no man hath drunk to thee yet."

"No, truly," quoth the old woman, "for churchmen have so much mind of young rabbits, old men such joy in young chickens, and bachelors in pigs' flesh take such delight that an old sow, a tough hen, or a gray cony are not accepted, and so it is seen by me. Else I should have been better remembered."

"Well, old woman," quoth the parson, "take here the leg of a capon to stop thy mouth."

"Now, by St. Anne, I dare not," quoth she.

"No, wherefore?" said the parson.

"Marry, for fear lest you should go home with a crutch," quoth she.

The tailor said: "Then taste here a piece of a goose."

"Now God forbid," said the old woman. "Let goose go to his kind. You have a young stomach. Eat it yourself, and much good may it do your heart, sweet young man."

"The old woman lacks most of her teeth," quoth the tanner, "and therefore a piece of a tender chick is fittest for her."

"If I did lack as many of my teeth," quoth the old woman, "as you lack points of good husbandry, I doubt I should starve before it were long."

At this the widow laughed heartily and the men were stricken into such a dump that they had not a word to say.

Dinner being ended, the widow with the rest rose from the table, and after they had sitten a pretty while merrily talking, the widow called her man John to bring her a bowl of fresh ale, which he did. Then said the widow: "My masters, now for your courtesy and cost I heartily thank you all, and in requital of all your favour, love, and good will, I drink to you, giving you free liberty when you please to depart."

At these words her suitors looked so sourly one upon another as if they had been newly champing of crabs. Which when the tailor heard, shaking up himself in his new russet jerkin, and setting his hat on one side, he began to speak thus: "I trust, sweet widow," quoth he, "you remember to what end my coming was hither today. I have long time been a suitor unto you, and this day you promised to give me a direct answer."

" 'Tis true," quoth she, "and so I have. For your love I give you thanks, and when you please you may depart."

"Shall I not have you?" said the tailor.

"Alas!" quoth the widow, "you come too late."

"Good friend," quoth the tanner, "it is manners for young men to let their elders be served before them. To what end should I be here if the widow should have thee? A flat denial is meet for a saucy suitor. But what sayest thou to me, fair widow?" quoth the tanner.

"Sir," said she, "because you are so sharp set, I would wish you as soon as you can to wed."

"Appoint the time yourself," quoth the tanner.

"Even as soon," quoth she, "as you can get a wife, and hope not after me, for I am already promised."

"Now, tanner, you may take your place with the tailor," quoth the parson, "for indeed the widow is for no man but myself."

"Master parson," quoth she, "many have run near the goal and yet have lost the game, and I cannot help it though your hope be in vain. Besides, parsons are but newly suffered to have wives, and for my part I will have none of the first head."

"What?" quoth the tailor. "Is your merriment grown to this reckoning? I never spent a pig and a goose to so bad a purpose before. I promise you, when I came in I verily thought that you were invited by the widow to make her and I sure together, and that this jolly tanner was brought to be a witness to the contract, and the old woman fetched in for the same purpose. Else I would never have put up so many dry bobs * at her hands."

"And surely," quoth the tanner, "I knowing thee to be a tailor did assuredly think that thou wast appointed to come and take measure for our wearing apparel."

"But now we are all deceived," quoth the parson, "and therefore as we came fools, so we may depart hence like asses."

"That is as you interpret the matter," said the widow. "For I, ever doubting that a concluding answer would breed a jar in the end among you every one, I thought it better to be done at one instant and in mine own house than at sundry times and in common taverns. And as for the meat you sent, as it was unrequested of me, so had you your part thereof, and if you think good to

* Bobs: jokes.—Ed.

take home the remainder, prepare your wallets and you shall have it."

"Nay, widow," quoth they, "although we have lost our labours, we have not altogether lost our manners. That which you have, keep, and God send to us better luck and to you your heart's desire." And with that they departed.

The widow, being glad she was thus rid of her guests, when her man John with all the rest sat at supper, she sitting in a chair by, spake thus unto them. "Well, my masters, you saw that this day your poor dame had her choice of husbands, if she had listed to marry, and such as would have loved and maintained her like a woman."

" 'Tis true," quoth John, "and I pray God you have not withstood your best fortune."

"Trust me," quoth she. "I know not, but if I have I may thank mine own foolish fancy."

Thus it passed on from Bartholomew-tide till it was near Christmas, at what time the weather was so wonderful cold that all the running rivers round about the town were frozen very thick. The widow, being very loath any longer to lie without company, in a cold winter's night made a great fire and sent for her man John. Having also prepared a chair and a cushion, she made him sit down therein, and sending for a pint of good sack, they both went to supper.

In the end, bedtime coming on, she caused her maid in a merriment to pluck off his hose and shoes, and caused him to be laid in his master's best bed, standing in the best chamber, hung round about with very fair curtains. John, being thus preferred, thought himself a gentleman, and lying soft, after his hard labour and a good supper quickly fell asleep.

About midnight the widow, being cold on her feet, crept into her man's bed to warm them. John, feeling one lift of the clothes, asked who was there. "O, good John, it is I," quoth the widow. "The night is so extreme cold and my chamber walls so thin that I am like to be starved * in my bed, wherefore rather than I would

* Starved: frozen.—Ed.

any way hazard my health, I thought it much better to come hither and try your courtesy, to have a little room beside you."

John, being a kind young man, would not say her nay, and so they spent the rest of the night both together in one bed. In the morning betime she arose up and made herself ready, and willed her man John to run and fetch her a link * with all speed, "for," quoth she, "I have earnest business to do this morning." Her man did so. Which done, she made him to carry the link before her until she came to St. Bartholomew's chapel, where Sir John the priest with the clerk and sexton stood waiting for her.

"John," quoth she, "turn into the chapel, for before I go further I will make my prayers to St. Bartholomew. So shall I speed the better in my business."

When they were come in, the priest, according to his order, came to her and asked where the bridegroom was.

Quoth she: "I thought he had been here before me. Sir," quoth she, "I will sit down and say over my beads, and by that time he will come."

John mused at this matter to see that his dame should so suddenly be married, and he hearing nothing thereof before. The widow rising from her prayers, the priest told her that the bridegroom was not yet come.

"Is it true?" quoth the widow. "I promise you I will stay no longer for him, if he were as good as George-a-Green, and therefore dispatch," quoth she, "and marry me to my man John."

"Why, dame," quoth he, "you do but jest."

"I trow, John," quoth she, "I jest not, for so I mean it shall be, and stand not strangely, but remember that you did promise me on your faith not to hinder me when I came to the church to be married, but rather to set it forward. Therefore set your link aside and give me your hand, for none but you shall be my husband."

John, seeing no remedy, consented, because he saw the matter

* Link: torch.—Ed.

could not otherwise be amended, and married they were presently.

When they were come home, John entertained his dame with a kiss, which the other servants seeing, thought him somewhat saucy. The widow caused the best cheer in the house to be set on the table, and to breakfast they went, causing her new husband to be set in a chair at the table's end with a fair napkin laid on his trencher. Then she called out the rest of her servants, willing them to sit down and take part of their good cheer. They, wondering to see their fellow John sit at the table's end in their old master's chair, began heartily to smile and openly to laugh at the matter, especially because their dame so kindly sat by his side, which she perceiving, asked if that were all the manners they could show before their master. "I tell you," quoth she, "he is my husband, for this morning we were married, and therefore henceforward look you acknowledge your duty towards him."

The folks looked one upon another, marveling at this strange news. Which when John perceived, he said: "My masters, muse not at all, for although by God's providence and your dame's favour I am preferred from being your fellow to be your master, I am not thereby so much puffed up in pride that any way I will forget my former estate. Notwithstanding, seeing I am now to hold the place of a master, it shall be wisdom in you to forget who I was, and to take me as I am, and in doing your diligence, you shall have no cause to repent that God made me your master."

The servants, hearing this, as also knowing his good government before time, passed their years with him in dutiful manner.

The next day the report was over all the town that Jack of Newbury had married his dame, so that when the woman walked abroad, everyone bade God give her joy. Some said that she was matched to her sorrow, saying that so lusty a young man as he would never love her, being so ancient. Whereupon the woman made answer that she would take him down in his wedding shoes *

* Take him down in his wedding shoes: prove more than a match for him.—Ed.

and would try his patience in the prime of his lustiness, whereunto many of her gossips did likewise encourage her. Every day therefore for the space of a month after she was married it was her ordinary custom to go forth in the morning among her gossips and acquaintance to make merry, and not to return home till night without any regard of her household. Of which at her coming home her husband did very oftentimes admonish her in very gentle sort, showing what great inconvenience would grow thereby, the which sometimes she would take in gentle part and sometimes in disdain, saying:

"I am now in very good case, that he that was my servant but the other day will now be my master. This it is for a woman to make her foot her head. The day hath been when I might have gone forth when I would and come in again when it had pleased me without controlment, and now I must be subject to every Jack's check. I am sure," quoth she, "that by my gadding abroad and careless spending I waste no goods of thine. I, pitying thy poverty, made thee a man and master of the house, but not to the end I would become thy slave. I scorn, I tell thee true, that such a youngling as thyself should correct my conceit and give me instructions, as if I were not able to guide myself. But i' faith, i' faith, you shall not use me like a babe nor bridle me like an ass, and seeing my going abroad grieves thee, where I have gone forth one day, I will go abroad three, and for one hour I will stay five."

"Well," quoth her husband, "I trust you will be better advised," and with that he went from her about his business, leaving her sweating in her fustian furies.

Thus the time passed on till on a certain day she had been abroad in her wonted manner and, staying forth very late, he shut the doors and went to bed. About midnight she comes to the door and knocks to come in, to whom he looking out of the window answered in this sort: "What! Is it you that keeps such a knocking? I pray you get hence and request the constable to provide you a bed, for this night you shall have no lodging here."

"I hope," quoth she, "you will not shut me out of doors like a dog, or let me lie in the streets like a strumpet."

"Whether like a dog or drab," quoth he, "all is one to me, knowing no reason, but that as you have stayed out all day for your delight, so you may lie forth all night for my pleasure. Both birds and beasts at the night's approach repair to their rest and observe a convenient time to return to their habitation. Look but upon the poor spider, the frog, the fly, and every other silly worm, and you shall see all these observe time to return to their home, and if you, being a woman, will not do the like, content yourself to bear the brunt of your own folly, and so farewell!"

The woman hearing this made piteous moan and in very humble sort entreated him to let her in and to pardon this offence, and while she lived vowed never to do the like. Her husband, at length being moved with pity toward her, slipped on his shoes and came down in his shirt. The door being opened, in she went quaking, and as he was about to lock it again, in a very sorrowful manner she said: "Alack, husband, what hap have I? My wedding ring was even now in my hand, and I have let it fall about the door. Good sweet John, come forth with the candle and help me to seek it."

The man incontinent did so, and while he sought for that which was not there to be found, she whipped into the house and quickly clapping to the door, she locked her husband out. He stood calling with the candle in his hand to come in, but she made as if she heard not. Anon she went up into her chamber and carried the key with her. But when he saw she would not answer, he presently began to knock as loud as he could at the door. At last she thrust her head out at the window, saying: "Who is there?"

" 'Tis I," quoth John. "What mean you by this? I pray you come down and open the door that I may come in."

"What, sir," quoth she, "is it you? Have you nothing to do but dance about the streets at this time of night and like a sprite of the buttery * hunt after crickets? Are you so hot that the house cannot hold you?"

"Nay, I pray thee, sweetheart," quoth he, "do not gibe any longer, but let me in."

* Sprite of the buttery: a drunkard.—Ed.

"O sir, remember," quoth she, "how you stood even now at the window like a judge on the bench, and in taunting sort kept me out of mine own house. How now, Jack, am I even with you? What, John my man, were you so lusty to lock your dame out of doors? Sirrah, remember you bade me go to the constable to get lodgings. Now you have leisure to try if his wife will prefer you to a bed. You, Sir Sauce, that made me stand in the cold till my feet did freeze and my teeth chatter, while you stood preaching of birds and beasts, telling me a tale of spiders, flies, and frogs, go try now if any of them will be so friendly to let thee have lodging? Why go you not, man? Fear not to speak with them. For I am sure you shall find them at home. Think not they are such ill husbands as you, to be abroad at this time of night."

With this John's patience was greatly moved, insomuch that he deeply swore that if she would not let him in he would break down the door.

"Why, John," quoth she, "you need not be so hot. Your clothing is not so warm, and because I think this will be a warning for you against another time how you shut me out of my house, catch, there is the key. Come in at thy pleasure, and look thou go to bed to thy fellows, for with me thou shalt not lie to-night."

With that she clapped to the casement and got her to bed, locking the chamber door fast. Her husband, that knew it was in vain to seek to come into her chamber, and being no longer able to endure the cold, got him a place among his prentices and there slept soundly. In the morning his wife rose betime, and merrily made him a caudle * and bringing it up to his bedside, asked him how he did.

Quoth John: "Troubled with a shrew, who the longer she lives, the worse she is, and as the people of Illyris kill men with their looks, so she kills her husband's heart with untoward conditions. But trust me, wife," quoth he, "seeing I find you of such crooked qualities, that like the spider ye turn the sweet flowers of good counsel into venomous poison, from henceforth I will leave you to your own wilfulness, and neither vex my mind nor trouble

* Caudle: warm potion, of wine, eggs, etc.—Ed.

myself to restrain you, the which if I had wisely done last night, I had kept the house in quiet and myself from cold."

"Husband," quoth she, "think that women are like starlings, that will burst their gall before they will yield to the fowler, or like the fish scolopendra that cannot be touched without danger. Notwithstanding, as the hard steel doth yield to the hammer's stroke, being used to his kind, so will women to their husbands where they are not too much crossed. And seeing ye have sworn to give me my will, I vow likewise that my wilfulness shall not offend you. I tell you, husband, the noble nature of a woman is such that for their loving friends they will not stick, like the pelican, to pierce their own hearts to do them good. And therefore forgiving each other all injuries past, having also tried one another's patience, let us quench these burning coals of contention with the sweet juice of a faithful kiss, and shaking hands, bequeath all our anger to the eating up of this caudle."

Her husband courteously consented, and after this time they lived long together in most godly, loving and kind sort, till in the end she died, leaving her husband wondrous wealthy.

# ❧ The Miseries of Mavillia

## by NICHOLAS BRETON

Nicholas Breton was a Londoner, born probably between 1545 and 1548. His father was a well-to-do merchant and property owner. He attended Oriel College, Oxford, traveled abroad, and returned to lead the literary life in London. He certainly knew Ben Jonson, probably Shakespeare. He died about 1626.

His *Miseries of Mavillia* is one of the earliest examples of the English realistic novel. It may have appeared as early as 1580, but the first extant copy dates from 1596. Our excerpt, somewhat modernized, is from Ursula Kentish-Wright's edition of *A Mad World My Masters and Other Prose Works by Nicholas Breton* (London, 1929).

IN THE troublesome time of a king unnamed, in a country too well known, in a certain town sacked by such soldiers as had little mercy upon the harmless enemies, it was my unhappy parents' hap (among many other) to fall into the hands of those bloody fellows, who, imbruing their blades in the aged breasts of my poor father and mother, caring no whit to hear me cry at this cruel act nor pitying the tears that bitterly fell from an infant's eyes, spurned me at their feet, spat in my face, flung me out of doors to go seek my fortune. Whereas I lay weeping, hearing some say: "Knock the elf on the head!" "Peace, squall!" quoth another. "Let her bawl!" says a vile boy. "Be still, you were best, baggage!" quoth a hard-hearted man with a drawn sword in his hand. Not one would say: "Alas, poor girl, take her up!" but still must lie upon the bare earth till some good mind would look upon me or merciless mind would make an end of me, or else God of His mercy would some way comfort me.

And being then betwixt four and five years of age, well able to bring out a word, I cried: "O Jesu, Jesu!" and said: "Sweet

God!" Though He had many to help besides me, yet, as in the Scripture you may read, Christ ever loved the little ones; so surely, being little and unable to help myself, He showed his great merciful might in helping me to the hands of a poor laundress that followed the camp; who taking me into a cabin where she kept her victualing, so entreated with her friend, a soldier of the camp, that he gave her leave to keep me (though hardly), yet better than to lie in the streets.

But Lord, what misery did I then abide! When my hours of breakfast, dinner, or supper came, then, as I was wont, I called "Mother!" But I heard no sound of "Daughter!" I was wont to be set in a lap and dandled and danced and colled * about the neck with many a sweet kiss. My father would take me by the chin, teach me to hold up my head like a pretty maid, and then call me good girl, sweet mouse, own wench, and Dad's bird, and in the end with a pretty smile please me with an apple or pear or some such children's joy or other. When I came out of the parlor, happy are they in the hall, could first catch me in their arms, with "God bless my sweet mistress! Love me? Yea, oh it is a fair gentlewoman; who could find in their heart to hurt such a sweet soul?" The maidens would sing me, the neighbors would give me pretty things, and strangers that I never saw would make much of me. In sum, the world went well with me.

But now this something kind but greatly cursed woman, with whom I must now make an ill change to take her for my mother, when I would cry: "A little drink! Some bread and butter! I would go to bed!"—"Peace, you little whore," she would say. "Learn to lie in the straw you are like! Tarry and be hanged; is meat so good-cheap? I will make you grate on a crust. Ha, you monkey, you shall have butter with a birchen rod!" Then if I cried: "Take me up!"—clap, clap, clap, clap! "Set me down again!" "Cry till thy heart burst; I think it longs to be knocked on the head. You were not best to keep such a wrawling.† Here is a trouble with a monkey!"

* Colled: embraced.—Ed.
† Wrawling: fit of anger.—Ed.

Oh, here was a miserable metamorphosis! Then got she me a book and a fescue; * now began a new misery. When I would be at play, either with the cat or a little dog, or making of a baby of an old ragged clout, then would she come with a rod. "Come on, you urchin, you will never come to good!" [She would] pull the clout out of my hand, slapped it in my face, toss me by the shoulders, and squat me down so mischievously that I had more mind to cry than to make my Christ's-cross row.† But yet at last, with much ado, it pleased God to make me somewhat apt to my book, that within a while I had learned to read any place in the Bible, so that then she took some delight in me, and then she would use me somewhat more kindly.

Then did she set me to my needle; there was another misery. I must learn to make a water flower in an old rag, good enough for a sampler for me. But many a time did she make me prick my fingers, with sudden shoving my hands together, before she would learn me to hold my needle. Many a whirret ‡ on the ear had I, before I could learn to take two stitches and leave two, with "Thou untoward ape's face, wilt thou never be handsome?"

But see how good was God unto me, yet in these my miseries He made me so cunning at my work that within a while I could make a pretty hem, gather a plain ruff, and make plain work prettily, so that then she began indeed to make very much of me, with "That's a good girl!" But oh what a misery of mind it was to me to hear that word! Alas, then I remembered my good father, who commonly was wont to say so when I held up my head at his bidding.

But with that misery see another; now was I set to my work, and if I wrought well and apace, so that I got her any money, then I had a piece of the better bread and a cup of indifferent drink—or else bread and water—and many an unhappy bang had I, poor wretch.

* Book and fescue: evidently a horn-book or alphabet, with a wire or pin to point out the letters.—Ed.

† Christ's-cross row, or criss-cross row: an alphabet commonly introduced by a cross.—Ed.

‡ Whirret: slap.—Ed.

And thus continued I, seely * wench, in this misery, till it pleased God to grant me deliverance by this blessed mean.

The town was besieged, the walls were scaled; the soldiers entered, slew a number; some they ransomed. This poor laundress I saved the life of by my humble suit to the captains, which being my countrymen and knowing my parentage, hearing my tale of her kindness (not as I tell it now, but otherwise to their content), granted her life, and with a hundred crowns sent her by water away with a poor fisherman, with commandment upon pain of death to see her safely conducted to the chief city, that she desired to go to. Thus was I now rid of my first miseries in my time of infancy, which continued with me for the space of three years and upward.

Now when I had sent away this old victualer with more crowns than she was mistress of many a day before, I now fell to work to mend the captain's ruffs, to draw up a break or a broken stitch. Which done, I would to my book, which both pleased God, and the captain liked very well of; and so well, as seeing me oftentimes sit sighing by myself, to think upon my parents' death, my loss of wealth, my hard life with the laundress, and my present unhappy estate, nothing to my heart's content, one day in the morning, walking about a garden, he called me to him, and there used this speech unto me. "Mistress, etc., I am sorry to see your sad and heavy countenance. I perceive though you be young of years, God hath blessed you with a good wit. Crave His grace to use it well; take thankfully the cross that He hath laid upon you, and give Him thanks for His great mercy in delivering you out of the hands of your enemies. No man is sure of life; the world is variable; you see today a man, tomorrow none. This scourge of war is a plague for our sins and a warning to penitency. We now have won the town, but God knows how long we shall keep it. Wherefore, seeing that I see you grow in years, likely in short time to prove a proper woman, and that now having escaped the hands of enemies I would be loath you should rest near them, I will send you to such a place with my page and

* Seely: simple.—Ed.

such gentlemen, my friends, that I know will for my sake conduct you thither."

What I said to him I have now forgot, save I remember this, that, yielding him thanks, I beseeched his speedy dispatch from thence, where being but a foolish girl I should be either attempted to vanity or fall in some too good liking, with, perhaps, one unworthy; or else in the captain's absence (the soldiers somewhat overseen *), I might be offered some villainy. Therefore I had no mind to stay, but thinking every day a year till I was gone, I remember within two or three days after I was sent away, with two or three gallant gentlemen and the little page, by whom the captain had sent a letter unto a brother of my father's there in the country, to whom he wrote for me in earnest and friendly sort, as you shall see hereafter.

But first I will tell you of a new misery that by great mishap befell me. As we were traveling toward the town that we were determined to go to, about fourscore miles from the place whence the captain sent me, suddenly, at unawares, there issued out of a wood a horseman or two, very well appointed, who, drawing somewhat near us, began to charge upon us, and, to be short, set upon us. And for the time (O Lord!) methought it was the sorest fight that ever was. The spears flew in pieces, then went the swords clish-clash. Anon they were unarmed; down were their horses; and the men on foot fell to it so fiercely that now one and then another were cut and mangled so sore that I was even half dead to behold them.

What shall I say? Long lasted the combat; but at last none had the better bargain, for first the horses and then their masters were forced to give the world a farewell.

Oh Lord, that ever seely wench should be born to see such a day! Judge now what miseries I was fallen into! My parents dead, their goods gone, I in enemies' hands—yet once escaped and safe in the captain's guard. Now looking for more liberty, am fallen into further danger; in the enemies' country deprived of

* Overseen: overlooked.—Ed.

my company, manned but with a poor boy and in peril of my
life, far from any town, my horse run from me, and I on foot.
How shall I do? A hungry stomach will call for meat, meat will
not be had without money, money is none here, except with the
dead soldiers; and alas, my heart will not serve me to rifle a carcass. But see what is use! The page is in their pockets, he is filch-
ing for crowns. But come away, boy; alas, what good will money
do, where there is no meat to get?

"Yes, mistress," quoth he, "you shall see, God will send us
some odd peasant or other this way with a bag of bread and
cheese, who will gladly sell his dinner for crowns. If not, I hope
to kill some odd pigeon in the field, or one thing or other, that we
will roast finely and quickly, and away."

"Why, alas, boy, what shall we do for fire?"

"Oh, mistress, the fire-lock of my pistol, my match and a little
powder in my flask, and light my match; and then a few rotten
sticks out of the hedge, and a few of these dry sedges, oh they will
burn roundly."

Thus did the poor boy awhile comfort me. But having wandered all that day, that night, and the next morning without either
meeting any man or seeing anything to shoot at for our relief,
sighing with sorrow, I prayed God to provide us some poor repast or other. Who heard our prayer, and graciously granted our
requests; for having passed a little further, we espied coming toward us a cow, which had a goodly udder. To whom we came
nearer and nearer, praying God that she would stand still, till we
had gotten of her milk to comfort ourselves withal. And, as God
would, the poor beast made no haste away, but seemed glad to be
milked, her udder was so full. Well, thanked be God, here we
sped well. For instead of a pail I took my hat, and though she was
the first cow that ever I milked, yet I fell to it so handsomely that
I got my hat full; out of which first myself and then my page
drunk so heartily that it sufficed us for that day, and that we left
in the hat served us till the next day at night.

When the poor page laying him down upon a bankside to take
a little rest, being heavy with great weariness, forgot to look to

his little dagge * that he had under his girdle, the spring whereof being started up and he leaning on it, made it of itself discharge a bullet into his right hip, so that he was not able to rise alone, but lay in such torments as that I was ready to swoon with sudden grief to behold him. But the little wretch, bearing a better heart than his poor mistress, made little bones at it. "Mistress," quoth he, "the hurt grieves me not so much as to think how I am hindered from my hearty desire to show my humble duty in conducting you to your uncle's house. But since God hath laid His punishments upon me, I beseech Him to grant me His grace to take it patiently. Alas, I think I am the most unhappy villain in the world. But mistress, this is the world. A man that hath traveled many countries and passed great perils, being tossed in many tempests among the boiling billows of sore seas, in the end comes home, and perhaps, walking but through his own ground, his foot slips off a bridge, and is drowned in a ditch. Though I be but a boy I have been among men, I have carried my master's piece and target † in hot skirmishes, when the bullets have flown about mine ears, yet always, I thank God, escaped hurt. And see, I am half spoiled, and no enemy near me. But alas, good sweet mistress, weep not so; then you will kill me outright; for the grief of your sorrow will go nearer my heart than the hurt, by a great deal. You shall see it will do well."

Was not this a wise boy? Yes, surely, and such a kindhearted wretch as it would have made a heart of stone to have bewailed his misery. But now in this extremity what was to be done? Alas, how did I devise to help this poor maimed page? First, the blood must be stinched; but how was that done? I remembered that in time that I lived with the laundress I saw a soldier come in one day with a wipe over the shins, that lay by ten days ere he could go on it. Now a surgeon of the camp, to stinch his bleeding, took certain drops of his blood that fell upon a hot brick, which being dried, he pared off the brick and strewed it into the wound; which dust did quickly stinch the bleeding. So took I the drops of

* Dagge: pistol.—Ed.
† Piece and target: gun and shield.—Ed.

blood, which being dried against the sun, fell to powder; which I used in like manner, and so helped the poor boy.

His bleeding stenched, the lad began to look somewhat cheerily, and with water in his eyes, for kind dutiful love, with humble thanks, thus spake unto me. "Oh dear mistress, how shall I ever live to deserve this sweet favor? Surely, if I may live to do you good, I shall think myself a happy man. Surely, mistress, the world is near at an end, when things fall out so contrary, the mistress to serve her servant. Well, God reward you; I will pray for you, and if I live I will somewhat deserve this your singular goodness. Alas, mistress, I remember my master was wont to use a kind of leaf that grows near the ground, there be great strings in it; I think they call it a plantain. Will you see if there grow any hereabouts? I will make shift to put it into the wound; it will draw it and keep it clean till we come to some town, where we may meet with some surgeon."

"No, boy," quoth I. "Look, here grows wild hyssop, and that is good indeed, for the old woman that I was withal, I see once heal her hand with it, which she thrust through with a knife, as she was opening of oysters."

"Even as you think, good mistress," quoth the boy. So now we have got some help for the hurt, our meat was far to seek. But God is a good God, and ever will be.

In this misery, as we sat sighing to think how we should do for meat, comes a fox with a little lamb on his back; whom first the boy espied, and cried: "Mistress, mistress! Look yonder is a fox with a lamb on his back! For God's sake run to him, and cry: 'Now! Now!' And the fox will be afraid, and leave the lamb behind him." And as the boy said it fell out. The weight of the lamb being too much for him to run withal, I overtook him; and fraying * him with a loud cry, he let fall the lamb, and away he went. Think how glad I was of this lamb! Which bringing to the boy, "Good mistress," quoth he, "let me help to flay him." And so kindly together we sat, plucking off the skin and cutting the

* Fraying: frightening.—Ed.

quarters one from another; which with the boy's device of powder and match and the fire-lock of his dagge we made fire and
roasted finely. And I remember oftentimes as I went for sticks to
make the fire, the poor boy would somewhat yet show his kind
honest duty. He would entreat me yet to let him turn the spit,
that we made of an old stick; and as he was turning, to make me
laugh (which was hard to do in this miserable case), he would
say: "Mistress, you are cook and I am scullion. If I burn the meat,
beat me for my labor. Who would think that such a young
gentlewoman could play the cook so prettily? Alas, do not burn
yourself in the fire. God deliver us quickly of this misery, and
defend us from all other." "Amen," quoth I. Anon he would sing
one merry song or other; now he would whistle in his fist, and by
and by tell me a tale of a roasted horse, only to make me merry
withal. But when he saw nothing could make me leave my heavy
thoughts, then fell he to sighing with me for company. And I
might perceive by little and little how his sorrow of heart more
and more increased, by the tears that did ever distil down his
cheeks. I was forced to force a smile. "Why, weep not for me,
boy," quoth I; "I am well enough, and I hope shall do better ere
long. I am sorry to see thee in this case."

"Alas, mistress," quoth the boy, "it were better I were hanged
than you should be so sad for me. For God's sake let me see you
merry, and I shall be even whole withal. Will ye have an old
song?" Then would he have up a piece of stuff that would make a
dog half dead to laugh at it.

Thus with a little pleasure we lived in this great misery a long
time. But oh good God, that sent us the good lamb to do us so
much good, the flesh served us many a day and the skin served to
lap about the boy's lame leg to keep it warm. Which being dressed
orderly, evening and morning every day, within a few days grew
so well that he was able to set his foot on the ground. And then,
leaning on my shoulder with one hand and resting on a staff with
the other, we went onward through a great forest, where when
we had traveled many a weary step at last we came to a great hill;
which when he had gone over, at the foot thereof lay a wild boar;

who when he had espied us came running with open mouth; and at the poor page he strook, who with the pistol that he had charged shot him full in the head, but not before he was sore wounded in the leg. I, poor soul, was in such a case as that heart I had not to fight with the boar, nor power to leave the lame boy. But abiding still the end of the combat, I stinched the blood, bound up the hurts, and took of the grease of the boar to anoint the old hurt withal.

Which done, we wandered on, till anon we came to a poor cottage where dwelt a poor shepherd; to whose house when we came, and finding none about the house, and not remembering common country speech: "God be here!" We heard none ask: "Who is there?" a great while. At last comes out a crabbed old woman with her daughter. "How now, what would you have? Here is not for you." The daughter, being of somewhat younger sight than the mother, pulled her by the arm. "Mother, mother!" quoth she. "It is a gentlewoman; she is in silk, and fine, she is as brave as our young landlady." "Is she? Then let us go see what she is; I will go talk with her." And so with a country courtesy, "Mistress," quoth she, "whence come you? And whither will you? What do you lack? And what young boy is that you lead so?"

"Good mother," quoth I, "a poor mistress as it falls out. I came from the camp, and am going I know not whither. This poor boy was a page unto a captain, a friend of my father's, who with two other gentlemen was sent with me to mine uncle's house, a gentleman here in the country. But my friends are both slain by the enemies, who likewise at one instant took all their leaves of the world together. This little lad only escaped away with me alive, who by misfortune caught a hurt first in the thigh with a bullet, and, scarce able to go alone, hath here been hurt again by a wild boar, at the foot of the hill, yonder by the wood-side. But he hath slain him; for witness, behold, here is some of his grease. But because the poor boy is somewhat stiff with the hurt of his leg, I beseech you let me have a chamber and a bed for him, and not of the worst. I will content you well for it."

"Yes, mistress," quoth she, "with all my heart. Come near; God be thanked that the wild beast is dead. Oh, it was a vengeable thief! He did much hurt here in the country. Many a time hath he made me leave my burthen of sticks behind me. He once frayed my child here almost out of her wits."

"Well, mother," quoth the page, "I warrant you now he shall do no more hurt. I am the last, I warrant you, that is or will be slain by the wild boar hereabouts. Wherefore, good mother, let us go in quickly. I find myself somewhat faint with bleeding."

"Marry, come," quoth she, "mine own sweet boy." And therewith she kissed his cheek. "Oh, mother," quoth I, "I thank you; believe me, it is the best natured boy on earth."

Thus in we went with him, had him to bed, opened his wounds, washed them with milk, for lack of white wine, and then asked counsel of the old woman what was best to lay to the hurt. "Tar, mistress," quoth she," we commonly use when the wound is not deep. But by 'r lady, for this I can tell you what we will do—a little flagre * and the white of a new-laid egg, mingled with a little honey. You shall see, I will make a medicine for him. But let him take a sleep first; oh, it will do him good; and against he awake, we will have some warm thing made for him."

"Content, good mother," quoth I, "with twenty thanks. Hold, here is five crowns; take them to you, lay out what you will for God's sake. If any good town be near, send for some white wine and sugar and a bottle of good ale."

"Yes, mistress," quoth she, "and God his blessing on you. While this holds you shall not want any good thing; and when this is gone I'll sell all the sheep I have before I'll see you miscarry."

"Gramercy, good mother," quoth I. "God reward you, and if I live and ever be able I will make you amends."

"I thank you, sweet mistress," quoth she. "But see, the boy is fast asleep. Let him alone; my daughter shall sit here at the door to watch when he wakes; and if he need anything, she shall see

* Flagre: candle.—Ed.

him have it. Will you go a little into the garden and gather a flower? Or cock's my bones, I have not bid you drink yet! Come, shall we have a mess of milk and a piece of cheese? I have a cup of good ale in my house; my good man loves it and he will have it, and he is worthy. For why? He gets it."

Thus went this old woman and I to our victuals, which I fell to full savorly. But as we were sitting (being in summertime, the window open against us) the old woman espied her husband coming home, through his field afore the door. Now under his arm he held a burden, which the old woman marveling at, "Mistress," quoth she, "look yonder comes my good man with somewhat under his arm. I muse what it is. Shall we go see?"

"Yea, mother," quoth I. And so we went to meet the old man, whom when we came near, we perceived it was a hog's head. "Nails, mistress!" quoth she. "What have my man brought home on God's name, a hog's head? Hath he come by it trome?" * Thus at last as we were talking, the old man put off his cap and made a leg or two. "What, landlady," quoth he, "how do your mustriship? † I have good news for you, to carry to mine old mistress. The wild boar is dead, and here is the head of him!"

"Gramercy, father," quoth I, "for thy good news. But I pray thee be covered; thou art deceived."

"No faith, man," quoth she, "but it is a good gentlewoman. Look here, man, what gold she hath given me. She knows of the wild boar's death; here is a little lad within that killed him; he is asleep. Oh, he is sore hurt. When he wakes, we will give him some warm drink."

"Is it true, woman?" quoth he.

"Yea, man," quoth she. "I pray you bid this gentlewoman welcome, and tomorrow go to my landlady's and tell her of her. I know she will send for her and make much of her, and for the boy too. There he shall be well tended and have better things made him than we can devise for him."

* Trome: honestly.—Ed.
† Mustriship: mistress-ship, ladyship.—Ed.

"Yes," quoth he, "I care not if I go tomorrow morning. Welcome, mistress," quoth he. "I pray you if you lack anything here, call for it."

Thus, as we were talking together, in comes the little girl. "Mother," quoth she, "the gentlewoman's boy would have his mistress." "Oh, Lord!" quoth I, "let me go to him." So to him we went all, asked him how he did. "Mistress," quoth he, "well; and better," quoth he, "I shall be shortly, for I feel myself at a good point. I am content to go whither God doth call me."

With that word I sunk presently down to the ground. And living in a trance a pretty while, at last I came to myself again; when looking on the poor boy, I was ready to fall dead again. "Good mistress," quoth he, "be contented. Doth it grieve you to think I should go to heaven? Believe me, but for you, I would not wish to live any longer. Mother," quoth he to the old woman, "here hold this purse full of gold. I took it out of the dead captain's pockets. Take it, spend it; but let not my mistress want. And here is another for my mistress. Lay it up for her till she demand it, but do not keep it from her for God's sake. Father, look well to my good mistress; it is the best gentlewoman that ever was born. Oh, what pains she hath taken with me, in dressing my wounds, in leading me up and down, not able to help myself. Alas, her parents are dead and she far from her friends, her years but young, her sorrows great, her comfort small, and she alone. If you should not use her well you will soon kill her, and God will plague you! Good father, remember my words. And good mistress, since I must needs bid you farewell, let me kiss your hand, for the honor I bear unto that most noble and virtuous heart of yours, which I know will pray unto God for me. Here, my sweet mistress, take this pearl joy,* set it in the ring that hangeth at mine ear. Wear it for my sake, and God send you great joy withal.

"Here is the letter that my master sent unto your uncle. The wax is so dried that it is almost open. I beseech you read it. Though my capacity be but gross, yet sure I had great delight

* Joy: jewel.—Ed.

in hearing of my master's talk, or to hear divers of his letters read. Therefore since this is the last that ever I look to hear, good mistress, leave your tears' weeping and do me this favor."

With much sobbing and sighing, at last, as I could, I read him these lines: "To the right worshipful his very good friend, Master H. F., Governor of such a town. (This with all speed possible.) Commendations considered, with thanks not forgotten for continual courtesies, present good will doth send you this news of our late good hap. So it is that we have had a sore conflict with the enemy, lost many of our men, and put to hard pushes. But in the end we drove them to retire, followed them to their fort, drove them out of their sconce,* home to their doors, laid battery to the walls, made breaches in many places, entered the town, and by God's help got the victory. To God be given the glory.

"Now in the town we found none of our countrymen nor women, but this little soul, your near niece, whose hazards and hard unhappy life I refer it to her own report. God hath done His part in her, and the wench is well minded. I am glad to have found her. I loved her parents well; for whose and for my sake, I pray you use her well. She is worthy to be made much of. Let this page attend on her, and send these gentlemen back again to me with all speed, that I may hear of her safety, which I greatly desire. No more; but God keep you. From the camp, this present and always, Your friend to command, F. W."

Oh Lord, what a world of miseries brought this letter to my mind! First, the remembrance of my parents' death, then my hard life with the laundress, my liberty got by the captain, his favor so greatly extended, so little to my good, the death of the gallant gentlemen, my hard escape with the boy, our perplexity for lack of meat, the boy's unhappy hurt, and last of all this deadly wound by the wild boar! Which of these was the most grievous thought? And then what grief was it to think of them all together? Well, to set me in further extremity of sorrow.

When I had read the letter, "Mistress," quoth the poor boy,

* Sconce: stronghold.—Ed.

"now I thank you. I see I was sent purposely to attend upon you. Now I trust I have performed my duty; I can but end my life with you. Farewell, good mistress; once again let me kiss your hand." Which when I gave him, he clapped it earnestly to his lips and kissed it twenty times together; and fetching a deep sigh, held up his eyes and called to God for mercy. And with these last words: "Farewell, good mistress!" the good poor wretch let go my hand and gave up the ghost. But Lord, how I cried; Jesus, how the old folks wept, and with tears entreated me to take it patiently. Good God, how the little girl cried: "Mother, mother! Father, father!" And oh sweet Christ, how then my heart throbbed and was ready to burst, with grief to think I had no father, no mother, no companion, no page, no friend, nobody to have comfort in. Well, this was such an hour of sorrow as never poor soul endured. And thus I continued, till what with entreaty of the old folks, that had me out of the room where the boy lay, with pity to see the old folks lament with me, and with crying so much, I could cry no longer. And with God's gracious persuasion I took it as quietly as I could. And for that night I got me to bed, where how little I slept I leave to indifferent judgments. . . .

[The shepherd's family, corrupted by greed, maltreat Mavillia; and she proceeds from misery to misery.]

A RENAISSANCE STORYBOOK

Designed by R. E. Rosenbaum.
Composed by Kingsport Press, Inc.,
in 10 point linotype Janson, 3 points leaded,
with display lines in Palatino.
Printed from letterpress plates by Kingsport Press,
on Warren's Olde Style India, 60 pound basis,
with the Cornell University Press watermark.
Bound by Kingsport Press,
in Interlaken Arco 3 Linen-smooth
and stamped in imitation gold foil.